The UNCOLLECTED

Henry James

Newly Discovered Stories

The UNCOLLECTED

Henry James

Newly Discovered Stories

Edited by

FLOYD R. HOROWITZ

CARROLL & GRAF PUBLISHERS
NEW YORK

THE UNCOLLECTED STORIES OF HENRY JAMES

Carroll & Graf Publishers
An Imprint of Avalon Publishing Group Inc.
245 West 17th St., 11th Floor
New York, NY 10011

Collection copyright © 2004 by Floyd R. Horowitz

First Carroll & Graf edition 2004

Library of Congress Cataloging-in-Publication Data is available.

ISBN: 0-7867-1272-4

Interior design by Kathleen Lake, Neuwirth and Associates, Inc.

Printed in the United States of America
Distributed by Publishers Group West

Contents

Acknowledgments

BECAUSE SEVERAL DECADES have elapsed since I began the journey to discover the early writings of Henry James, there have been literally hundreds of librarians across America and Europe that I wish to gratefully acknowledge for their most generous and professional help in locating important documents and in aiding access to the original magazines and papers in which I found the early James stories. I am indebted to these professionals at the libraries of Johns Hopkins University, Stanford University, Hebrew University in Jerusalem, Yale University, the Newport Library, the Bibliothèque Nationale, the Library of Congress, Princeton University, the Worcester, Massachusetts Historical Society, the New York Historical Society, Drew University, the University of Illinois, the Boston Athenaeum, the Boston Public Library, the New York Public Library, the University of Kansas, the British Museum, and the Houghton Library at Harvard. Steve Dykes, Melvin Landsberg, and Benjamin Horowitz Levi helped me search for some of the material in these great institutions. Susannah Druver and Molly Vaux gave invaluable service in editing and proofreading.

I also thank those who encouraged the ideas for my work from the start, for imaginatively foreseeing the importance of uncovering Henry James's early fiction. I would note several individuals who gave me their time and shared with me their insights: The late John MacGalliard of the University of Iowa, the late Charles S. Singleton of Johns Hopkins University, the late Professor Quentin Anderson of Columbia University, and Professor John Gerber at the University of Iowa.

Warmly introduced by Monty Hyde, a cousin of Henry James, I had the opportunity to meet cooperative members of the James family who let me examine pertinent family materials that enabled me to better understand the nature of the sources that informed Henry James's early writing efforts, which in turn contributed to the critical discriminators that I used to identify stories written by him.

For their careful and critical reading of the close scholarship that informed the identification of all the stories I am crediting to Henry James, I owe a personal debt of gratitude to Joseph Wittreich, William Kelly, David Katzman, Andrew Debicki, Rabbi Arthur Herzberg, my sons, Jason Horowitz and Benjamin H. Levi, and my wife, Frances Degen Horowitz. I am pleased to also acknowledge my agent, Sandy Choron, for her help.

Above and throughout all, Frances Degen Horowitz deserves my foremost thanks for her years of attentive and well-humored criticism.

Foreword

꙰

IN THE COURSE of studying and analyzing "The Story of a Year," the earliest signed short story by Henry James, published in the *Atlantic Monthly* in 1865, I became increasingly convinced that, woven into that text, beyond the literal level, was a highly ordered symbolic structure, involving a sophisticated set of allusions and philosophical themes. Was it possible, I wondered, that this young author, then twenty-two years of age, had practiced his craft in earlier, unknown writings? It was known, of course, that James had published one short story anonymously and secretively the year before. "A Tragedy of Error" had appeared, without author identification, in 1864 in the *Continental Monthly*. Based upon the reported claim of a family neighbor, James scholar Leon Edel and others had accepted it as a James story and Edel had included it in his complete edition of Henry James's short stories.

Reading "A Tragedy of Error" carefully, I felt it revealed itself as more structurally, symbolically, and thematically sophisticated than one might expect of a novice writer. Was it possible, I wondered, that Henry James had had a prior anonymous existence as writer in small magazines, journals, and newspapers that were known to have published the writings of very young aspiring authors? This simple question led me into almost three decades of exploration. I began to read in the many literary magazines, weekly newspapers, and other journals published in the mid-1800s that included short stories, some with author names, many anonymous.

Slowly, among these hundreds and then thousands of stories, using a set of critical discriminators, I began to indentify what I thought might be stories written by Henry James. Among the critical discriminators were the use of particular words, the employment of what I came to recognize as distinctive syntactical and word patterns, the use of puns and other wordplay, as well as the repetition of symbolic allusions, themes, and ideas. Many of these discriminators mapped on to characteristics of James's later signed work. I found intriguing linguistic patterns in these stories that related to what was known and what I discovered about Henry James's youthful reading and school texts—particularly his use of *Anthon's Latin Dictionary* and his acquaintance with *Liddell and Scott's Greek-English Lexicon*.

Supplementing the textual analyses, looking for sources, I reviewed what was known and searched out new information about the James family home library, Henry James's own reading records in the Newport, Rhode Island, Library, at Harvard University, and in the Boston Athenæum, the intellectual life of the James family, their comings and goings and their experiences.

I found corroborating ideational evidence in the texts, beyond the literal level, which appeared to reflect Henry James Sr.'s concerns with respect to the right nature of social issues and natural law. Some stories involved obviously borrowed details, and exactly the same structures Henry James had found in the articles of his father's books related to the logics of tragedy, comedy, and legal issues. Some involved playing out elaborate Christian themes conditioned by the philosophical ideas championed by Emanuel Swedenborg, the Swedish theologian and philosopher who had so influenced James's father.

Eventually, I subjected the anonymously authored stories and some with noms de plume, which I had identified as written by Henry James, to a computer analysis (described in appendix A of this volume) and compared the results of those analyses to analyses of a control group of stories written by other authors who had lived at that time. In all, using the results of the computer analyses as well as the set of discriminators described above, I identified a total of seventy-two stories as written by Henry James, with an additional twelve stories that I classified as probably written by James. The earliest of the definite stories, "The Pair of Slippers," appeared in the *National Magazine* in August 1852. Henry James was then ten years old. The last, "How Belle Million Found Her Husband," written under the nom de plume Leslie Walter, appeared in *Peterson's Magazine* in 1870, five years after the publication of James's first signed story in the *Atlantic Montly*.

Though sometimes what was found were writings involving childish interpretations in stories that were more like practice pieces, I realized that in its totality I was identifying a coherent linguistic and philosophical framework that was consistent with the structures and themes of James's later, signed work. The full scholarly treatment of all of the discovered short stories and the story of Henry James as secret author is beyond the purpose of this volume and will be published subsequently. Suffice it to say here that, in discovering and studying heretofore unknown James short stories, I came to the conclusion that these early pieces provided a clear window into the grand "figure in the carpet" of James's known fiction. It is the window that James had deliberately obscured by keeping secret his youthful endeavors, many of them sketch pieces, by burning his papers, and by employing in his signed work an elaborate and already practiced layering of symbolic literary levels upon symbolic literary levels.

* * *

AS NOTED, WHEN "The Pair of Slippers" was published, Henry James was then going on ten. It was, actually, not unusual in those days, unlike more modern times, for children as young as eight to be regularly published to supply the anonymous grist for the great magazine mill. The editor of the *National Magazine*, Abel Stevens, was known to have encouraged youthful writers when he was the editor of *Zion's Herald* in Boston, his home before he relocated a few streets from the James's New York City residence on Fourteenth Street in Manhattan. Both Stevens and Henry James Sr. were prominent clergymen; they traveled in the same social circles, enjoyed each other's company, and exchanged favorite ideas.

As it happened, several of the senior James's closest friends had published anonymously before they were ten. One in particular, George William Curtis—then the up and coming author of the popular New East travel books, *The Howadji* and *The Howadji in Syria*—became young Henry's mentor. Indeed, it was Curtis who introduced this young boy to the Near Eastern culture that imbues "The Pair of Slippers." The story more than alludes to Curtis's Howadji volumes. Henry Sr., a devoted friend, had in fact proofread the Howadji books for Curtis; and young Henry, a devoted follower, unquestionably had made them his model. Quite definitely, by the time he was ten, the junior James had acquired great skills of imitation.

And by the time he was ten, Henry had been writing a fair amount. He would later report in his autobiography, *A Small Boy and Others,* how he had begun at age five. Young Henry was taken to the theater with some frequency, and, when he returned home, he would fold a blank quarto page in four, compose a résumé of the drama on three of the quarters, and place a related picture on the fourth. Several years of this particular exercise in composition quite prepared James for the kind of story he would, at the age of ten, write and publish with Curtis's generous assistance and the cooperation of Abel Stevens as the *National Magazine's* editor.

In the months following publication of "The Pair of Slippers" I found other same-minded childlike stories, five in all, in the *National*

Magazine's pages. My reading and re-reading revealed that they, too, consistently and similarly included allusions to the sources that had been used in writing them. These first allusions became the clues upon which I began to fashion the small assumption that, for his youthful fiction, James drew upon the books that crossed his intellectual path, many of which, initially, were to be found in his father's quite extensive home library. Thus it was, here in these books, that Henry James Jr. truly began his writing career. And it was here as well that I found my first important keys to the authorship of the long-undiscovered stories of Henry James.

The twenty-five stories I have selected for this volume, beginning with the 1852 "The Pair of Slippers" and concluding with an 1869 story, "A Hasty Marriage," appeared in a diversity of venues: In addition to the *National Magazine,* they were published in *Putnam's Magazine,* the *Newport Mercury,* the *Knickerbocker,* the *Continental Monthly,* and *Arthur's Home Magazine.* More than half were published anonymously, the rest with noms de plume. They were chosen as a sampling of James's unacknowledged publications for their use of Swedenborgian ideas related to stages of maturing in a spiritually framed person, obviously borrowed details found in the books of Henry James Sr., topics involving the social issues about which James Sr. wrote, as well as the Christian themes involving charity, excess pride and resurrection that suffuse Henry James's published fiction. Presented chronologically, I invite the reader to take the journey that Henry James traveled from young lad/writer, to an increasingly confident and mature author, master of fiction.

Floyd R. Horowitz
New York City, September 2003

Note

T HE STORIES INCLUDED in this volume are presented with the exact text from their original-source magazines. The only alterations have involved modernizing some punctuation practices and spelling conventions of James's time. For example, the original hyphenation of such words as "New-York"and "to-day" has been changed to eliminate the hyphen. Also, compound adjectives, such as "half open," appeared in the original stories without any hyphen, but today's convention uses the hyphen and so it has been inserted. In addition, some of the inconsistent placement of commas has been made uniform. In a few instances, unreadable words from faded newspaper copy had to be omitted; a pair of empty brackets indicates when that has occurred. Lastly, obvious typographical errors in the original materials have been corrected for this edition.

· August, 1852 ·

The Pair of Slippers

From "Palm Leaves: Select Oriental Tales,"
in the *National Magazine*

In his early stories, the young Henry James drew upon the sources at hand and alluded to them liberally. If "The Pair of Slippers" owes much of its color to George William Curtis's Howadji travel books, it owes much of its language to *Anthon's Latin Primer and Reader* and *Anthon's Grammar,* which the nine- and ten-year-old Henry was studying in 1852–1853. In very diverting allusionary ways, the stories James wrote for the *National Magazine* reflect his Latin lessons. Sometimes an example provided by *Anthon's* in Latin is translated by James and incorporated whole into the story's text, so that he momentarily sounds remarkably like Virgil. More imaginative, though, is the game James plays with his Latin vocabulary. Beginning with a target word—*Crepida,* for instance; the Latin for "a slipper a sandal"—he would then move a page or two backward or forward from that target in the vocabulary and not only systematically learn the Latin words but also, as best he could, work into the text of his fiction the English translations of those words. The tight rules of this little inventive game challenged James to be flexible in his storytelling. Closely preceding

1

Crepida in the *Anthon's* vocabulary is the Latin verb *cremo, cremare,* for "burn," and following it is *culmen,* for "roof": So it is that Casem, the main character in this story, decides to burn his offending pair of slippers after first drying them on the roof. (For a look at just how elaborately young Henry played his vocabulary games in "The Pair of Slippers," see appendix B of this volume.)

T HERE ONCE LIVED in Bagdad a merchant named Abu-Casem, who was quite notorious for his covetousness. Notwithstanding his great wealth, his clothes were all in rags and tatters. His turban was composed of a large cloth whose colors were no longer distinguishable; but, above all the other articles of his dress, his slippers attracted everybody's attention. The soles of them were armed with huge nails; the upper leather was composed of as many pieces as a beggar's cloak; for, during the ten years they had been slippers, the cleverest cobblers of Bagdad had used all their skill in fastening the shreds together. Of necessity, therefore, they had become so weighty, that when people wanted to describe anything very heavy, they compared it to Casem's slippers.

As this merchant was one day walking through the great bazaar of the city, a considerable stock of glass was offered to him a great bargain, and he very gladly agreed to purchase it. Some days afterward, he heard that an unfortunate dealer in precious balms was reduced to selling only rosewater, as a last resource. He turned this poor man's misery to account, bought all his rosewater for half its value, and was consequently in the best of humors.

It is the custom of Oriental merchants, when they have made a successful bargain, to give a feast of rejoicing; but this our niggard would not do. He thought it more profitable to bestow a little extra indulgence upon himself; and therefore he went to the bath—a luxury to which he had not for a long time treated himself. Whilst he was taking off his clothes, one of his friends (so, at least he called him;

but such niggards seldom have a friend) said to him, that it was quite time for him to leave off his slippers, which had made him quite a byword in the city, and buy a new pair. "I have been thinking of it for some time," answered Casem; "but, when I look well at them, they are not so very bad, but that they may do a little more service." Speaking thus, he undressed, and went into the bath.

Whilst he was there, the Cadi of Bagdad entered; and because Casem was ready before the Judge, he went out first. He dressed; but sought in vain for his slippers. Another pair stood where his own ought to have been, and our careful man soon persuaded himself that the friend who had given him such good advice while he was undressing had made him a present of these new ones. He put them on with much satisfaction, and left the baths with the intention of thanking his friend for them.

But, unhappily, the slippers belonged to the Cadi; and when he had finished bathing, his slaves sought in vain for them; they could only find in their stead a miserable pair, which were immediately recognized as Casem's. The porter soon ran after him, and brought him back to the Cadi, as detected in a theft. The Judge, provoked at the unblushing avarice of the old miser, immediately sent him to prison; and, in order to avoid the open shame due to a thief, he had to pay richly: the law condemned him to give the worth of a hundred pair of slippers if he would escape with a whole skin.

As soon as he was safe out of gaol, he revenged himself upon the cause of his trouble. In his rage, he threw the slippers into the Tigris, which flowed beneath his window, so that he might never set eyes upon them again; but it was to be otherwise. A few days afterward, some fishermen, on drawing up their net, found it unusually heavy: they thought they had gained a treasure; but, alas! Nothing was there but Casem's slippers, the nails of which had torn the net so much that it would take whole days to mend it.

Full of indignation against Casem and his slippers, they threw them in at his window, which was just then open; and as, unluckily, all the flasks of beautiful rosewater which he had bought were neatly ranged beneath the window, those heavy iron foes fell upon them, the bottles were broken, and all the rosewater spilt upon the floor.

Casem's horror, when he entered his apartment, may be better imagined than described. "Detestable slippers!" he exclaimed, tearing his beard, "you shall not do me any further mischief." He took a spade, and ran with them into his garden, where he hastily dug a hole to bury his slippers; when, unhappily, one of his neighbors, who had long meditated some mischief against him, happened to look through his window, and saw him hard at work, digging this hole. Without delay, he ran to the Governor of the city, and told him as a secret, that Casem had found a great treasure in his garden. This was quite enough to rouse the Governor's cupidity; and it was all in vain that our miser declared he had not found anything, but had only buried his old slippers. In vain he dug them up again, and brought them forth in presence of the Judge; the Governor had made up his mind to have money, and Casem was obliged to purchase his release with a large sum.

In utter despair, he left the Governor's, carrying his expensive slippers in his hand, while in his heart he wished them far away. "Why," said he, "should I thus carry them in my hand to my own disgrace?" So he threw them into an aqueduct not far from the Governor's palace. "Now," said he, "I shall hear no more of you; you have cost me money enough—away with you from my sight!" But, alas! the slippers stuck fast in the mud of the aqueduct. This was enough; in a few hours the stream was stopped, the water overflowed; the watermen ran together, for the Governor's cellars were inundated, and for all this trouble and misfortune Casem's slippers were answerable! The watermen soon discovered the unlucky cause of the mischief, and as quickly made it known. The owner of the slippers was taken into custody, and as this appeared to be a vicious revenge upon the Governor, he was sentenced to atone for it by paying a larger fine than either of the foregoing ones. But the Governor gave the slippers carefully back to him.

"What now shall I do with you, ye accursed slippers?" said poor Casem. "I have given you over to the elements, and they have returned you, to cause me each time a greater loss; there remains but one means—now I will burn you."

"But," continued he, shaking them, "you are so soaked with mud and water, that I must first lay you to dry in the sun; but I will take good care you do not come into my house again." With these words he went up to the flat roof of the house, and laid them under the vertical rays of the sun. Yet had not misfortune tried all of her powers against him; indeed, her latest stroke was to be the hardest of all. A neighbor's pet monkey saw the slippers, jumped from his master's roof on to Casem's, seized upon and dragged them about. While he thus played with them, the unlucky slippers fell down and alighted on the head of a woman who was standing in the street below. Her husband brought his grievance before the Judge, and Casem had to atone for this more heavily than for aught before, for his innocent slippers had nearly killed one of his fellow creatures. "Just Judge," said Casem, with an earnestness which made even the Cadi smile, "I will endure and pay all and everything to which you have condemned me, only I ask your protection against those implacable enemies, which have been the agents of all my trouble and distress to this hour—I mean these miserable slippers. They have brought me to poverty, disgrace, ay, even to peril of my life; and who knows what else may follow? Be just, O noble Cadi, and make a determination that all misfortunes which can be clearly ascribed to the evil spirit which haunts these slippers, may be visited upon them, and not upon me."

The Judge could not deny Casem's request: he kept those disturbers of public and private peace in his own possession, thinking he could give no better lesson to the miser than this which he had now learned at so much expense, namely, that it is better to buy a new pair of slippers when the old ones are worn out.

Woman's Influence;
or, Incidents of a Courtship

From the *Newport Mercury,* signed "Isole"

Henry James Sr. was a thoroughgoing Swedenborgian and early on he introduced his son to the Swedish theologian's Christian works and words, among them his perspectives on the stages of man's progress from the innocence of infancy through indiscriminate love of the opposite sex to the virtuous love that is realized with the one right woman, and ultimately to a divinely joyful, angelic state of being in Swedenborg's seventh terminus of peace, which he called the Sabbath. In 1870 James's father wrote *The Secret of Swedenborg,* a book its modernistic critics found wanting lucidity in its attempt to illuminate the densely allusive biblical symbolism in that progress. Twelve years earlier, in 1858, much more simply but also more clearly, the young James, then fifteen, explored the Swedish master's key religious doctrine in this story, which was published in two Saturday installments of the *Newport Mercury.* In it, James's attractive hero, Lawrence Bayford, endures harsh worldly problems that in time cleanse him for his peace-filled Swedenborgian destiny. His is a progress from the flirtatious ballroom miss Cora, the prototype of the Jamesian coquette whom we meet again and again throughout his work, to the aptly and divinely named Celeste. James, after all, had been reading, in his father's collection of Swedenborg's works, the *Coelestia Arcana*.

❦

THE HAPPIEST PERIODS in a young man's existence are those during which he is permitted to bask beneath the bright smiles and enjoy the soft caresses of the being he loves. Golden spots are they on the dark and gloomy scene of the life before him. Visions of the overhanging shadows, or dreams of a more substantial bliss, do not enter his brain, for every thought seems absorbed in that overwhelming passion; that unconquerable desire, to be in the presence of his adorable. To the neglect of all studies, or business duties, his mind is only occupied by the thought, What can I do to fix her affections more firmly on me?

As regular as the sun in his daily course does he bend his steps to the beloved abode, bearing, perhaps, some little gift in the hope it may please, and wondering in his mind what kind of a reception he will meet with.

It is thus the sweet moments of youthful days are passed. The most verdant and delightful oases in the desert of life.

When, however, emerging into manhood, the youth leaves his parental roof, and the loved cottage of his adored, to seek a fortune in some distant land, away from those he loves, then come the trials and difficulties with which the life of man abounds.

Often those vows of constancy, so friendly and lovingly promised, are neglected, the days of happy joy are forgotten, and, all that is thought of is the enjoyment of the present. Who, but he who has suffered it, can tell the anguish of mind: the throbbings of the heart which ensue to the young man abroad, when he hears of the inconstancy of her he loved; that she, in thoughtlessness, had forgotten those thrice-told endearing promises, which were to bind [this couple] in constancy to each other? with which the young thus content rushes into the ranks of dissipation, or, into the whirlpool of an exciting life, to drown that bitter anguish, which seems to craze every energy and absorb every idea of peace?

It is, indeed, painful to recite a tale of such a character to the world, but regardless of the bitter feelings it may incur, we trust that the story now to be related may, perchance, warn many young men not too far gone in the ways of courtship, to be careful how they tread too confidingly on the serpent that sleeps beneath the garb of vain promises and bewitching smiles.

If we let our minds rest for a moment on the map of New England, that land of moral excellence and social worth, we will notice in one of the most beautiful portions of that section of our country, the small town of W——, nestling, as it were, between cities of larger growth, and among social prosperity. Here, amid the comforts and quietness only to be found in such a place, lived the hero and heroine of our story. Their parents were among the most respectable and influential of the citizens, bringing their children up in the nurture and admonition of Gospel truth, and with educations not to be excelled.

Lawrence Bayford, with his sparkling wit and gay repartee, shone among his fellows as true excellence always does. A friend to all, he made all friends to him.—The sweet, winning manners and bewitching beauty of Miss Cora Delvine left no hearts unconquered when once she bent her bright smiles in approving manner on them. Aware of her power to charm, and conscious of the homage paid her, she took pleasure in drawing within her circle the flower of that manly corps of youths who lived in W——.

Our friend Lawrence but seldom entered into the society of the ladies, preferring rather when business was over, to join in with the cordial mirth and social enjoyment to be found among his fellow associates. Chance, however, threw him into the society of Miss Delvine, and when once her beaming eye sparkled in his presence, and her gay laughing voice broke upon his ear, he was changed. He sought her society, joined in her merry laugh, and for the first time felt there was a charm in female society. Then it was that Cora felt the power of Cupid's shaft, and directing her energies to that one point, she strove hard to gain the friendship if not the love of Lawrence Bayford. In that she was successful, we need not say, for who could resist such combined forces of beauty and wit, or such endearing incidents as marked the first few weeks of his acquaintance with this charming being.—Bewitching as she was when only trying to please, how much more so must she have been, when awakened by a peace [ ] tiring love. For "The richest gift of earth is Love, The purest emblem of the bliss above."

How often do such cases occur, though, not seen or known to the world; when young persons struck either with the beauty or pleasing manners of a friend, cherish within their breast a mouldering spark of love, which needs only a breath to fan it to a flame. The spark that was fired in Cora's breast, still burned brighter, and brighter, though often did she wonder within herself if Lawrence felt the same towards her; whether he appreciated the kind attentions and many pleasant moments he had passed in her society.

While such emotions as these moved her breast to thoughts of love, Lawrence was pondering similar questions with himself. Could he but woo and win the fair Cora, he would be perfectly happy. He wanted to show more regard for her; to press his suit more earnestly, but he was afraid of the result; and was retarded no little from extending his attentions by the various gossips that had sprung up among the circle of unmarried ladies of the town. A lady friend had heard through friendship, some tender remarks, and construing it into something stronger, had in confidence told her friend, and so it went on like the breeze changing and increasing from mouth to mouth, till it came out as a stated fact that an engagement was formed. Heedless of consequences, this class of persons, either jealous of a more fortunate acquaintance, or from a love of such things, start and exaggerate such stories with little or no foundation, to the great injury of the social world. Few people like to be talked about, especially if the stories are false or greatly exaggerated, and more particularly those persons just sprouting into love.

But to return to our story, Lawrence was not to be impeded by such gossiping rumors, and feeling that Cora was a person worthy of his love, he took pains to be in her society; escorting her to places of amusement, and accompanying her in long walks or rides about the home of their youth. And now let us mark the change that came over our young friend. Interested as he now was in the existence of another being, he, through her influence, forsook in a great measure the haunts of his former associates. From jovial, free and unrestrained, his manners became affable, soft and refined. He felt that a new life was open before him, and looked forward to pleasures unrevealed. When relieved from business duties he would seek the society of his friend whose smiles and tender words filled his heart with joy, and drove all weariness or fatigue from his mind. Thus did they live in constant communication with each other while the mutual feelings of love were winding firmer and firmer around their hearts.

The town of W—— was not large and therefore offered but few inducements for her young men to remain at home. Thus many of them ambitious of gaining more worldly goods than could be obtained there left their parental roofs for larger cities, and the more active wants of trade. It was not long that such talent as Lawrence Bayford possessed could lie dormant in such a place as W——, and [when arrived] an opportunity offering for him to go the Australia, or the land of gold, he thought best, with the advice of his friends, to accept of it. One thing caused him to hesitate, that was the parting with all he held dear on earth—His intercourse and acquaintance with Cora Delvine had been now so long continued that she seemed almost a part of his existence; but the circumstances were pressing, and determining to ask her to remain constant to him during the few years he would be absent, he resolved to go.

A short time before his departure, a number of kind friends had arranged for a social party at a small but beautifully romantic grove some miles distant from the town. It was a magnificent day and the air seemed redolent with fragrance from the neighboring fields.

The song of birds, the music of the dashing waterfall, and the gay, joyous company around drove for a time the painful thought of leaving from his mind. The request he had to make of Cora was still uppermost, however, and rested like a dead weight upon his spirits. After spending the day most happily among the trees and flowers, and having partook of a delicious supper, such as can only be obtained in the country, they started for home.

Lawrence and Cora rode together, and as the soft rays of the moon stole in majestic splendor under the cover of the buggy, Lawrence thought that then or never must he tell her the subject of his untiring thought. With a faltering heart and a trembling voice, he spoke of the many happy hours they had known together, and of the parting which must soon come, then referred but briefly, to the prospects of his future life, and the desires he had in view on his return. It was a solemn moment to them both. The thoughts of so long a separation were hard, but when, after a short though painful silence, she sobbed forth the promise to remain constant to him alone, and the hope that on his return she might be his wife . . . [it] soothed every nerve and calmed every fear. He placed boundless confidence in her promises, and joy seemed mantling on his brows. With a fond and lingering embrace as they parted for the night were those words sealed.

It is thus in the moment of excitement, when worked up by the associations of the past and with no thoughts on the temptations of the future, that young persons bind themselves to promises that they always find hard to perform. While they could be in each other's company every day, and continually renew the wonted pledge, it might hold true, but the absent ones are soon forgotten. Not even the tender epistles of love which so often pass between them can restrain the desire of a man for change. Though the true nobleness of female character is a source of great happiness to man, yet when such cases of heartless abuse of the influence they do possess, do occur, we are forced to corroborate the lines of the poet Byron, who says: "Woman, experience might have told me, that all must love thee that behold thee, surely experience might have taught, thy firmest are naught."

But let us see how Cora Delvine fulfilled her promises. Lawrence

Bayford left his native place at the time agreed upon, leaving behind many friends and heartfelt regrets for his absence. For many days he was unable to shake off the lonely feelings that would steal upon him. Soon, however, new scenes and new friends directed his attention, and when absorbed in the new duties which fell upon him, he again felt happy. There was something that cheered him in his far-off home. The thought of the fair being who was living only for him, and of the prospects of happiness on his return.

Several years have now rolled by and still our hero was toiling on in that distant clime. The bright prospects of success kept him at his post, and the date of his return was as yet indefinitely postponed.—During this time constant communication by letter had been kept up between him and Cora Delvine. At first they were long, loving and full of tender regards for his success, then they became shorter, sometimes filled with nothing but the idle gossip or news about town, till at last they diminished down to mere apologies. He wondered not a little at the strange freak that seemed to have affected his [ ] have forgotten him. Oh, no! What, after such vows and so long a friendship. Impossible!— He thought perhaps she was trying to prove his love, and by neglecting him for a time to see if he would falter in the race. But he was ever firm. He still kept the vision. Did it affect her? Let us see.

There lived in the same town a young man of gay and dashing demeanor, but without those truly ennobling qualities that characterized Lawrence Bayford. The parents of Leslie Arnold were wealthy, and influential, so that he was not compelled to labor in the more confining duties of mercantile life. Being engaged but a few hours in the day, he had time to himself that other young men were unable to obtain. A great deal of his spare time was passed in the company of ladies, consequently he became very gallant and was recognized as an accomplished beau. Since the departure of our friend Lawrence, he had frequently been in the company of Miss Delvine; though considering her as the affianced of another, he kept aloof from too intimate an acquaintance.

It was not long, however, before the light and frivolous heart of

Cora was distracted by the gay, jovial manner of Arnold, and her love of excitement, that taste for something besides the monotony of written affection, caused her to show attractions to him that could not be mistaken. He was not the person to refuse or disregard any such demonstration of esteem as these, and therefore with the gallantry so natural to him, he entered into all her schemes for pleasure and remained as if spellbound under the influence of her vivacity. In her he had found a temperament so like his own that a continued stream of pleasure flowed around them.—No wonder that amid such influences as these, her heart had relaxed in a great measure from the hold when the love for Lawrence had held it. Careless and unheeding, she thought but little of the sad youth in that far-off land, whose heartstrings still vibrated with a firm love for her. Almost ashamed of her own frailty, she did not dare to write him of her pleasure, but still her letters grew colder and colder causing him to wonder at the change. Was this to go on and he remain in ignorance? No. Disinterested friends marked every movement and were grieved at the manner in which she acted. They hesitated from writing him, wishing rather to save him the anguish they knew it would cause him, and hoping that she would soon reform and act more as the affianced of an absent lover.

Thus things went on for a time. She had not intended to have caused so wide a separation, but had merely thought of present enjoyment, and trusted that all would be right in the end. Alas! Her fickle heart was too easily severed from its true course, the demon of temptation had too strong a hold upon her. And as it continued, so it became stronger and stronger, till at last she felt that to give up all idea of being the wife of Lawrence Bayford was easy enough.

Then it was that the report reached him. The, to him, overwhelming news of the frailty of her whose love was his very life. The magnetic influence that was drawing him on to fortune; the only true incentive he had to press on in the struggle for fame was gone. Broken as the reed, he felt that all the interest had fled. The thoughts of home and her he loved, which were formerly pleasant and agreeable, now came like instruments of torture to his already bursting heart.

Oft did he wander on the Ocean shore, that ocean which had borne him on its bosom so far from his friends, and recalling the past years of pleasure he had enjoyed, would, in the bitterness of his heart exclaim, "Why did I leave thee my native land, and the beings I loved?" Is the gold of Australia or riches of the world to repay me for the love I have lost? Oh, no! Had I but have stayed with thee, my Cora, all would have been well. In a lonely cottage together, I could have lived happier on frugal means than in the palace of Kings without thee. Then again at times the thought would come to him, "Why did I put confidence in the vows of woman!" Foolish male that I was to trust my heart's best affections to the word of woman so long. Ah, Cora, if you did not love me, why did you promise to be mine! I might have known that your gay and sprightly nature could not resist the temptations of the life around you, and yet I must blame you, for on the moment that your heart was changed towards me you should have told me. If for your own interest, I could have given you up. But after such a cold disregard as you have showed my love for you, my heart still reverberates the thoughts that are stirring me.

Love's hopes were fled thou didst awaken. Often do young men who are thus treated rush into all the vices and excitements of a degraded life, and many, very many, seek in the intoxicating howl, to drown the mortification and remorse of feeling consequent upon such a sequel to their earliest and best love. And yet how wrong a method is this; revenge or retaliation is not one half so sweet, as if with calm and sober earnestness, they determined to smother the fire that burns in their breast, and to rise above so heartless an infamy. Lawrence Bayford was of too noble and honorable a character to think of driving the gloomy thoughts from his mind by a life of dissipation. His better judgment told him that if Cora Delvine had no love for him; he could never have lived happy with her, and as the matter now stood, they were better apart. The regret that still lingered on his mind were counteracted by the thought of how fortunate it was the cloven foot had been shown before it was too late to mend it.

With such thoughts as these, he bent his energies with renewed vigor to the task before him. All he had to work for now was fame and wealth, and surely, Dame Fortune had smiled upon him, and poured her lavish favors in his lap. His rare business talents, and intellectual powers, had aided him to rise to a high position in the business he followed and his affable and polite manners had won him many friends in the land of his adoption. Among his most ardent admirers and best friends, was Signor Juan de Caracola, a rich old Spanish gentleman, who owned an immense estate near the place where our hero resided. Many and urgent were the requests of Signor de C, for Lawrence to visit him at his residence, never mentioning that the principal attraction there was an only daughter on whom his whole existence was bound up.

It was during a season of unusual prosperity, that he accepted the kind invitation of the Signor to make him a visit at his mansion. He was weariest and worn down by the constant attendance upon business, and tho still lingering thoughts of the once loved one he had lost. In such a state of mind and body, he thought that a short term of relaxation was necessary for his health, and surely where could he enjoy that time so much as beneath the hospitable roof of his best friend. At the close of a hot, sultry day in summer, he rode behind a splendid span of horses up the broad avenue leading to the Caracola mansion. The majestic shade trees spread their ample branches so closely around as to almost exclude the scorching rays of the setting sun, and the cool breeze upon his brow revived his drooping spirits. But who is that standing on the spacious porch, which forms the principal feature of the front of the house? The Signor had never mentioned so young, and lovely a creature as a member of his family, and Lawrence had never dreamed of such a flower, blooming outside of his own dear New England. He arrives at the door, and ascends the broad steps. With extended hand and smiling face, the fair and lovely Celeste steps forward to greet the handsome stranger, and to offer the hospitalities of her father's house. Is the Signor at home? he inquires, while the rich blood mantles his cheeks, and his dilated eye surveys the rich scene laid out before him, on the wide extending lawn, and contemplates the beauty of the lovely creature by his side.

The Signor had gone on business to a neighboring villa and would not be back in several hours; meanwhile with queenly grace, Celeste ordered refreshments for her weary guest. With pleasant chats and a short walk on the magnificent lawn did they pass the time till the arrival of the Signor, who was overjoyed at meeting his young friend. "Ah! Ah! making love to my darling Celeste are you already, Lawrence, *Bien hecho.* I see it will not do for me to be running off in this way," said he in a joking, laughing tone. "Come, let us seek something more substantial; and then to rest, that we may recall the [ ] that once characterized our friend's features."

Many happy days did our friend have at this noble mansion. But the relaxation from business, that he lost that excitement which had so long borne him up, and the troubles that harrassed him obliged him to give in and acknowledge himself ill. For many weeks did he lie unconscious of those around him. Often his wandering senses caused him to talk of his former love—of her cruel devotion, and of the many loved ones yet behind. Innumerable servants were in waiting to perform his slightest wish; but through all, the gentle though high-born lady, watching every movement, catching every word, and soothing his aching brow with her own delicate hand.

After a long struggle with the King of terrors, he rallied from the disease. With the kind care of his friend, and the balmy air of the villa, he was soon able to leave his room. Celeste, who had watched his weak form through his illness, now looked with joy upon his resuscitated and handsome person, wondering if life was as much a source of happiness to him as it was to her. She had heard the incoherent words he had uttered during the delirium of his illness and [ ].

The time had now arrived when he must leave the kind hospitality of the Signor, and return to the duties of his business—Celeste could scarcely believe that he was to leave them, and spoke of how lonesome it would be without him. The tender manner in which she expressed her regret at his leaving threw a new light into his mind. Could it be possible, the rich and beautiful Celeste de C, was in love with him? Would not the love of so divine a creature compensate him for the love he had lost, and perchance heal the still bleeding wounds in his heart. To think was with him to act. Delaying not the precious moments, he touched with delicate and tender words the chord of her affection, which he trusted would vibrate with the true note of love. It did, and the melody of those murmurs, which united so harmoniously with the beatings of his own heart, melted not till Heaven had sealed the union. The old Signor was overjoyed.—He had watched the tender care which his darling daughter had shown for his friend and prayed that an affection might spring up between them.

A life of happiness now dawned upon the stage of our hero's existence. He closed up his business and assisted the old Signor in taking charge of his immense estate. Shortly after the consummation of his highest joy, he wrote his parents of his success and marriage. He spoke briefly of the days gone by, and of the many heart achings he had experienced, but of the goodness of God in bearing him safely through the trying period, in granting him success in worldly gains, and above all, in giving a fond and loving wife graced with beauty and wealth,—he could not write enough.

Let us now return to the town of W——, and see how the news was received there. His parents and friends were pleased that success should have so crowned his efforts. His former friend, Miss Cora Delvine, heard it with a calm, unflinching brow, but the pangs that shot through her heart told how much she was hurt. The flirtation which had caused such a rupture between them, had lost its charms and was now forgotten. The many pleasant times she had enjoyed since served only to occupy the passing moment. She longed to hear from her former friend and lover, and hoped that he would soon return that she might beg him to forgive her, and once more receive her love. Now, however, the question was closed. He had married another. He was happy, rich, and prosperous. The heartbroken and forsaken, could she blame him! Oh no! It was her own fault, and, how bitterly did she now regret it. It was too late. Life indeed had no charms for her now. Gradually she pined away. Her friends tried to revive her drooping spirits, but to no purpose. Death received with gracious arms its lovely victim, and the grave eased that heart which had caused its own destruction by giving way to that fickleness so prone to humane nature.

Several years have passed away during which many changes took place in the little town of W——. Lawrence Bayford continued to enjoy the pleasures of his new home, and the gentle influence and pleasing society of his lovely wife. The old Signor had died and been placed by the side of his ancestors, his immense property descending to his daughter as the only relative. Celeste had often heard of the former home of her husband, and having nothing now to bind her to their present residence, she expressed a desire to visit it. Lawrence, who before, had not cared to return, had still a desire to see his aged parents, and now that his wife wished to go, willingly consented. It was with emotions hard to be expressed that he approached the home of his youth. The [thoughts] of former days came forcibly to his mind, and the thought of soon meeting his friends overcame him.

The inhabitants of W—— were surprised to see so handsome an equipage drive into their town, and many were the conjectures that passed from mouth to mouth as to whose it was. When, however, they learned that the rich and talented young Lawrence Bayford had returned with his wife and children, their joy was unconceivable. Cordial indeed was the greeting he received among his friends, and pleasant did the old spot seem to him where in his boyhood days he had enjoyed so much happiness. Of his former love he had as yet heard nothing.—His friends had hesitated to write him about her, and did not like to speak of her death now, so that he remained in ignorance of her demise.

A few days after his arrival he was walking with his wife and a friend through the cemetery, remarking on the persons he had once known, but were now beneath the sod. Coming to a tombstone of much finer carving than the others, his wife stopped to read the inscription. Husband, who is this? Did you know her? she inquired. All of his strength seemed to leave him at the sight of that name. What, she dead, and lying beneath that could stone. It was too much for his nature to withstand, and leaning upon the iron rail which surrounded the ground, he covered his face with his hands and wept. All his old love for her seemed to return in a moment. He could hardly have borne meeting her alive and well without losing his command, but to find that she was dead, broke upon his heart like a thunderbolt. For a long time he remained silent, when the tender expressions of regard uttered by his wife, recalled him to his senses. Nerving himself to the task he approaches the stone and reads aloud. ["]To the memory of Cora Delvine, who parted this life, Dec. 20, 18— aged 24 years. She was beloved and respected by all. The loveliest flowers of the field do fade, The fairest of earth's creatures die.["] Truly said he, she must have been beloved, for she was as amiable as she was fair and lovely. Yes, Cora "True thou did'st force me from thy breast, yet, in my heart thou keep'st thy seat, there, there thine image still must rest, until this heart shall cease to beat."

Celeste, my dear wife, continued he, you will forgive this outburst of my feelings over the grave of this lovely woman, when I tell you her story, and how intimate I once was with her. Come, let us retire from this place, my feelings have had a severe shock today; but believe me, the happiness that surrounds me now, resulting as it does, from your influence and tender care, will soon rest o'er me, and I know you will not begrudge that small corner of my heart which serves as a monument to the love I once bore for her.

It is now time to draw our story to a close, and we trust that all who read it may see the moral it contains. Under the influence of his lovely wife, the happiness of Lawrence Bayford continued unalloyed for many years. After going once more to the scene of his business career and settling his affairs there, he returned to his native town, where building a splendid residence he continued to reside. Leslie Arnold was married in high life to a lady of an entirely different temperament from his own, consequently lived an unhappy life. Many, yes too many, similar if not parallel cases to this occur, arising as they generally do from a too hasty desire to form engagements among young people, even when the day of its consummation is far distant or unknown.

Perhaps some may think that in the recital of our story, we have been too harsh upon the ladies, laying too much blame to their influence. This we must leave for everyone to form their own opinions upon. A woman does indeed have a great influence over the man who loves her.

Her smiles can make him obey her slightest wish. Her frowns drive him to destruction and despair. Yet how careless oftentimes are they of that influence. When, from a willful knowledge of her power, or from a careless use of it, woman drives man to desert—or to act unmanfully, the fault should not all be laid on him as heartless and devoid of principle; for that influence used aright would charm the strongest or worst of men to do her will.

Therefore would the wife live happily with her husband, or the young maiden obtain and secure a love, she must study to use her influence aright, and try her utmost powers to please him.

The Rainy Day

From the *Newport Mercury*, signed "Helen Forest Graves"

Among the materials that captured the imagination of the young James were the articles he found in William Smith's *Dictionary of Greek and Roman Antiquities*, especially one called "Tragoedia," in which Cambridge scholar Robert Whiston elaborates on the nature of tragicomedy. In the progress of a plot along a tragically bleak course of action to a sudden reversal that brings the drama to a happy, normal end, James found a model that he would employ in his fiction again and again. The pattern is already apparent in "A Pair of Slippers," and in "The Rainy Day" it builds to a solidly dramatic punch when, in a daringly short scene at the story's end, the coquettish Georgianna finds forgiveness in the arms of her charitable beau who, significantly, comes from Philadelphia, the city of brotherly love. Georgianna may find herself on the path to Swedenborgian redemption as well, not only in her pledge to marry the upright and virtuous Mr. Harry Carter but also in "a solemn compact never again to neglect the suffering of the poor." One should note that the Jameses were practicing socialists. James's clergyman father was listed on a socialist meeting poster in

1850, and his sister, Alice, openly sympathized with the dockworkers on strike in London in the 1890s. The social inequities that so unfortunately divided workers—who suffered in poverty from the rich who employed them unfairly—are clearly highlighted in this story as it takes a poor seamstress to her death for the sake of a lady's dress. That James signed this story with the nom de plume Helen Forest Graves underscores its darker social themes.

⁂

T HE BRIGHT OCTOBER rain!—oh how merrily it pattered down on the open fields and copses in the broad country domains—what a jocund tune it played on the quiet forest stream where showers of golden and scarlet leaves were drifting down at every breeze. How it danced on the slopes of the hoar-green moss where the banner fern kept watch and the purple asters clustered, spangling the woods with feathery groups of pale, clear amethyst. And in perfumed glens, where glossy brown hazel nuts shone through the half-open caskets of prickly burs, and the still wood paths were lighted up by drooping torches of goldenrod and the orange flower of the marigold—there it came pattering down on the tesselated carpet of fallen leaves, as if it loved to call out every breath of incense that lurked below. Ah, it is a merry roundelay that the October rain wakens among the solitude of the autumn woods.

But in the city the rain god came in a far different guise. On the wide pavements of stately avenues, to be sure, it was a cheerful sight, as it poured down in strait, sweeping columns of glittering crystal, born hither and thither by sudden gusts of wind, until it seemed as if the upspringing spray were instinct with life, and whole battalions of Lilliputian soldiers bearing tiny spears of silver, were flying in wild disorder before the enemy blast.

Not so, however, was it in the narrow streets and foul muddy lanes where the wan and wasted shapes of poverty are hidden in mouldering tenements and ruinous where it penetrated shattered roofs and shaking walls, and dripped down the mildewed sides—where the homeless poor shrank from its torrents, under pawning arches and gloomy doorways. Alas, the lot of these poor sufferers was hard enough in the noontide glow of the bright summer day, and their hearts ached as they looked on the last descending sheets of glimmering rain and the dull, gray expanse of clouds above!

"A rainy day, how provoking!" exclaimed Georgianna Middleton, as she put aside the heavy folds of pale green satin that draped the plate glass windows of her room, "and there is no prospect of its ceasing at present. O, dear me, why must it rain on this particular day of all others—the very morning I had appointed to ride out with Harry Carter, and he goes back to Philadelphia tomorrow? And then in the afternoon Lilly Champion and I were going to select her bridal dress. Isn't it enough to aggravate a saint, Lizzy?"

Mrs. Littleton, the sister in law of the pretty Georgianna, with whom she was spending the Autumn and Winter, looked up from the engaging pages of her novel with a languid smile. She was a regular woman of the world—soft and ladylike and innocent of the least pretense to originality.

"Dear me, Georgy, how you startle one," she lisped. "Yes, it is very provoking, but you'll have to submit to it," and she once more returned to her novel. Georgianna, however, was not so easily consoled. She paced up and down the luxurious room with an angry flush on her peerless forehead, and her rosy lips twisted into a curl of vexation. Perhaps if Harry Carter—her devoted chevalier, and the son of the Philadelphia millionaire—had seen her just then, he mightn't have thought her quite so lovely in mind and person as he fondly imagined her to be. Her pettish footfalls were drowned in the velvet pile of the rich Wilton carpet, whose tracery of golden lilies on an emerald ground covered the floor, and the only sounds were the cracking of the ruddy coal fire that glowed through the polished grate, the silver ticking of the jeweled clock, cased in ormolu and gold, and the clear warbling of a crimson plumed tropical bird, whose cage was suspended by a gilded chain from the frescoed ceiling. Yet surrounded by all these accessories of wealth and station, youth and loveliness, Georgy was unhappy because it had the presumption to rain when she wanted a clear day.

"Well, I don't care," she said pausing suddenly, and jerking the bell rope, very much to the discomposure of her sister-in-law's nerves; "I won't lose the day if it does happen to rain. I'll have that dress of rose-colored tissues fitted; this is the very time when I can't go out, and no one will call. Stephen," she said to the footman who answered her summons, "send for Amy Moore, and tell her I want her to come immediately and do some work for me.—Be as quick as possible."

The man bowed and withdrew. Mrs. Middleton, heartless as she was, was somewhat rattled at Georgy's summary proceedings.

"You surely are not going to call that sickly creature out in such weather as this," she said. "See how it rains—a perfect deluge."

"I surely am," said Georgy, pettishly.—"If you are at all distressed on the subject, you can send the carriage."

Mrs. Middleton arched her eyebrows with a superb expression of scorn.

"Send my carriage, on such a day, for a common seamstress—a girl who goes out sewing by the day!" she exclaimed.

"Well, don't find fault with my orders," returned Georgianna. "Such people are used to all kinds of weather, a little shower won't hurt them. Besides, Amy can wrap up well."

And thus the pampered heiress dismissed the subject. For was not her mind full of more important reflections? had she not to decide whether the new fabric was to be made flounced or plain—trimmed with puffings of rose-colored ribbon or ruches of pink tissue.

Amy Moore dwelt in a small room on the third floor of a narrow tenant house in one of the closest and foulest of the New York streets. It was a very neat though scantily furnished apartment—indeed there were some indications of taste in the arrangement of the darned muslin curtains, and one or two pots of blossoming mignonette on the wooden sill. Closely in the narrow window sat Amy, in a faded calico dress, sewing with unremitting industry. Poor girl—every moment was precious to her—she could not spare even a moment to gaze on her pots of mignonette, or to take a long breath to ease her wearied frame—for by constant effort she could barely earn enough for her scanty support and the rent of her wretched room.

She might have been called pretty if fate had seen fit to surround her with the trappings of wealth, for her closely braided bands of brown hair were veiled with threads of glittering gold and her large blue eyes were full of melancholy expression.—But the ill health and languor superintroduced by constant confinement and ceaseless toil, were too discernible in the unhealthy pallor of her face, and the dry, irritating cough that ever and anon shook her slender frame.

She was soon interrupted by the rough Irish girl whom Stephen, ever tenderly watchful of his own health and comfort, had charged with the message of his young mistress.

"And you're to come immediate, Miss Georgy says," was the peremptory intimation with which she closed her recital.

"But it is impossible," said poor Amy, much disturbed, "she surely cannot expect me to come such a distance in this terrible weather. See how violently it rains, and my cough is very bad today. Will not tomorrow do as well?"

"Sure, and that's the very reason the Miss wanted ye to come to day, 'cause she wouldn't be after going out or seeing company. An' she's dreadful set about it, ye see. 'Tell her to come immediate,' them was her very words, and you know she's one of the kind it won't do to contradict. Sure, it would be as much as one's place is worth to go against Miss Georgy's wishes."

Amy knew this imperative disposition of Miss Middleton perfectly well beforehand. She was fully aware that if she ventured to oppose the spoiled child's wishes, her most important customer was gone forever.—She could not afford to lose Miss Middleton's patronage. It was a starvation question with her—so, after a moment's reflection she replied with a sigh so deep that it was almost a wail,

"Tell her that I will come soon."

The Irish damsel trudged away well satisfied, and Amy prepared with a heavy heart, for her long and gloomy walk.—The then well mended shawl—not sufficient for a shelter against the pouring torrent of rain, yet the only one that she had—the plaid straw bonnet with its band of narrow mourning ribbon were soon assumed and the slender girl passed forth into the pelting storm with a shudder convulsing her whole frame.

Poor child! ere she had gone two blocks her worn shoes were saturated through and through, and her threadbare cotton umbrella was rent in several places, while the wind twisted its frame into so many wild fantastic shapes that she was fain to close it, or she would never have been able to face the blast. It was full an hour's walk and ere she reached the marble steps of Middleton's house there was scarcely a dry thread on her shivering body.

"So you have come at last," said Georgy as the drenched creature crept pale and weary into the boudoir, "I thought you never would be here! but good gracious, how wet you are! Do sit down and dry yourself."

Thank you," said Amy, as she cowered before the fire; but ere she had sat there five minutes, the impatient girl interposed.

"Make haste, Amy, for I've made up my mind to wear this dress to Madame Begnia's tomorrow night, and there is no time to lose. I am sure you must be dry by this time."

Amy rose silently and commenced the progress of fitting and adjusting, with native skill and taste; and, for some time, nothing but tissue and silk, braid and bias folds, filled Georgy's brain. At length, she said pettishly:

"I wish you wouldn't cough so constantly, Amy—it makes me so nervous! Mercy! how hot your hand is."

"I cannot help it Miss Georgy," said the girl, "I think the long, wet walk has made it worse. How do you like the fit?"

Georgy stood before the glass, with a delighted smile.

"Look, Lizzie," she cried, "is it not exquisitely fitted? Amy, I'll pay you five dollars if you finish it in this style."

"Five dollars!" it was like a fortune to poor Amy, and she smiled in spite of her pain and weariness, as she replied, "I'll do my very best, Miss Georgy, you may be sure."

And still Amy Moore worked tirelessly on, even though sharp pains were darting through her limbs, and her head ached with quick, fierce throbs. When Georgianna saw that the girl had no appetite, even for the luxurious viands of that home of wealth, she brought her a glass of ruby wine with her own hands, for though thoughtless and imperious, she was far from unkind. And Amy drank it with a smile, and said she felt better. But it was not the wine—it was the kind look of Georgy that gave her pain a momentary lull. Yet the heiress never once thought that she had done wrong towards the sickly seamstress!—Even so callous do we grow by custom!

At nightfall she folded up the delicate fabric to take home and finish by herself, promising Miss Middleton that she would bring it by eight o'clock on the following evening.

"It rains dreadful!" said Georgy, looking from the window with a tardy pang of conscience, after the girl had gone. "She will get very wet and the streets are dark and lonely. I wish I had thought to send Stephen with her."

"Oh, it does not matter," said her sister-in-law, "As you said this morning, such people get used to such things."

But Georgy made no reply, and only sighed.

Home again plodded the poor seamstress, home through the blinding rain and gloomy night—while Georgy sat in the velvet chair beside the glowing grate thinking of the triumphs awaiting her on the morrow's night.

But Miss Middleton was compelled to wear another dress on the eventful occasion, for the usually punctual Amy did not appear with the pink tissue, and day after day passed, and still she came not, until a week after, the dilatory Georgy was just making up her mind to send some one to inquire what had become of her, when Mr. Harry Carter (who had postponed his return to Philadelphia for reasons best known to himself, perhaps the lovely Georgianna might have had some hand in it) was announced.

"I'm on a very important errand," said Harry solemnly, "I want some linen made up in tip-top style, and as we poor scamps who have neither mother, sister, nor wife can't be expected to know much about such affairs, I come to you, Miss Georgy, for your advice. Where shall I go, and what shall I do?"

"Oh, I can recommend you to an excellent seamstress," said Georgy, for she was naturally kind-hearted, and the pale face of Amy Moore instantly recurred to her mind's eye. She gave the address and Mr. Carter immediately set forth in quest of the place.

"Don't forget to inquire after a certain pink dress of mine, which she is making," said Georgy, as he went downstairs.

"Pink, eh?" said Harry, "I never can remember dresses and their tints. I shall be sure to inquire after an orange-colored apron. Will that do as well?"

Georgy laughed, and her gay young lover walked away with hurried step.

In about an hour he returned, looking very grave and pale.

"Georgy," he said as he entered the parlor. "I have this day learned an awful lesson!"

"What do you mean!" said the heiress, terrified by his manner. Did you not see her!"

"I saw her corpse—she is dead!"

"Dead!" every drop of blood left Georgianna's face.

"She died last night, they told me, after several days of illness and delirium, and Oh Georgy! they said that her illness was immediately occasioned by the dreadful rain storm of last Tuesday in which her frail and consumptive frame was exposed by the heartless orders of a rich lady for whom she was working. I asked the name and they told me it was you! Georgy, is this so?"

Georgianna made no reply—she was too much shocked to speak.

"Dear Georgy, tell me it is false! I cannot bear to think it of you!" he paused.

She burst into a passionate flood of tears, and sinking at his feet, told him the whole story of her inexcusable injustice and her thoughtlessness—of the remorse that would ever sting her heart—of her sincere grief and distress—and beseeching his forgiveness, implored him to allow her to take the whole charge of funeral expenses, as some slight atonement to the memory of poor Amy.

Her ingenuousness and sincerity conquered him. He felt that her heart was true, even though surrounded by worldly wails, and folding her to his breast, he told her that she was forgiven; and together they breathed a solemn compact never again to neglect the sufferings of the poor.

Thus, even from the grave of Amy Moore sprang sweet blossoms of good deeds and gentle benefactions, for never after did Georgianna Middleton forget the sorrow fraught occurrence of the Rainy Day.

The Village Belle

From the *Newport Mercury*

"The Village Belle," a story of only 1,152 words, offers little more than a sketch that swiftly—and slimly—limns the destiny of a coquette named Annette. She both recalls Cora in "Woman's Influence" and prefigures Belle Savage in James's far more interesting 1862 tale "Breach of Promise of Marriage." All three women fall in with faithless courtiers whose conduct plainly violates the constraint Swedenborg places upon men who would love all of the opposite sex; and both Cora and Annette fail to find the virtue of a Swedenborgian marriage. Still, "The Village Belle," as a commentary on the pitfalls of coquetry, might have been written by anyone other than James, if it had no dimension beyond its literality. But it does.

Always allusive, James enriched the texture of his prose with threads of symbolism. In many of his stories, unsigned and signed, card games, especially whist and poker, are central to the dramatic and symbolic action. Throughout "The Village Belle," the imagery of a card game vitalizes an otherwise slight story and gives it a distinctly Jamesian touch. So it is that we are told in the end: "Fortune had finished the game, and Annette was left to pay the forfeit." And at the outset Annette is said to possess "the tact of winning hearts" and "at all points she played a most masterly game." As it turns out, she might well have been playing Old Maid.

DOUBTLESS MANY A pretty Miss expects in this story to read of a career of glorious conquests, and her blue eyes brighten and her little heart beats quicker at the thought of being, one day, the heroine herself of some legendary proser, and of having her own victories recorded. Well, the desire to be loved may reign in an amiable bosom—may possess a kind and benevolent heart—but power is dangerous, there are so many temptations to its abuse. These things I would have my fair readers to remember as they go along with me—and it may be we shall all be wiser, and therefore better, before we part.

If you should ever go to Alesbury, you will see a sweet little cottage in the meadows towards the river valley, half hid away amid a cluster of black alders with its white chimney and snowy palings, peeping through the foilage—and they will tell you that Annette Merton once lived there, for all the villagers remember her. It was one of those terrestrial paradises which the sick heart, weary with the wrongs of men, so often pictures to itself, so often longs for—and she, oh she was a beautiful creature—my heart even now beats quicker as her image rises before me.

She was a gay, lively girl—with the polish of a summer in the city, and a fine education—and whatever her talents might have been, she at least possessed the power, the tact of winning hearts in a most copious measure. I never could divine exactly how she did it—but there was a free, frank, friendly air about her that inspired confidence;—and gifted thus at all points she played a most masterly game among the village beaux. Every body was glad to gallant her— was emulous which should pay her the most attention—and every young gentleman in the village, who could afford to spruce himself up a little once in twenty four hours, paid her an afternoon or an evening visit.

It would have been amusing to one who went as a spectator to have attended a Saturday evening levee at the Alber Cottage—amusing to see the address practiced by the competitors for her smiles in eliciting some distinguished mark of her favour—they gathered around her in the little parlour, and if she spoke, there was a strife as to who should most approve what she said; if she dropped her handkerchief, two or three heads were thumped together in the effort to restore it to her—and if she walked, they were happy who got at her side, and all the rest were miserable. There were to be seen all kinds of faces and every description of temper—and such a spectator might have been edified, but the principal impression on his mind would probably have been, that courting under such circumstances was a most particularly foolish kind of a business.

But Annette sang—"The moon had climbed the highest hill,"—and told boarding school stories—and talked eloquently about love, and poetry—was witty, sentimental, and good natured—was invincible, always, absolutely always the conqueror. The young ladies of the village saw themselves undeservedly deserted; looked month after month on the success of their general rival; and prayed probably, if young ladies ever pray about such matters, that Annette might speedily make a choice among her worshippers, and leave them the remainder. It was a forlorn hope, she intended to do no such thing: she was the village belle, and the village belle she meant to be.

It so happens, however, that great beauties, like all other great folks, who have to take the common chances in the fortunes of humanity sometimes, in the end, outwit themselves. In process of time, one and another, and again another wedding took place in the village; the girls whose names were seldom spoken, whose modest pretentious and retiring habits were perfectly eclipsed by the brilliancy of the reigning star, secured their favourites, were wooed and won, and married; and still Annette coquetted with all, and was still admired by all. How many good offers she refused or slighted were only recorded in her own memory. "Hope deferred," saith the proverb, "makes the heart sick." Those who were sincere in their addresses, gradually, one after another, offered themselves, were rejected, or put off, and fell into some easier road to matrimony. She was at last left with courtiers, as heartless in love matters as herself, who sought her company because she was agreeable, flirted with her because she was "the belle,"—and romped with and kissed her, whenever they had an opportunity, because it is always worth some pains to win such a favour from a beautiful girl. We never, never get to be too much of the bachelor for this—well might Byron ask—

Who can curiously behold
The smoothness and the sheen of beauty's cheek,
Nor feel the heart can *never* all grow cold?

But time rolled on, and the grass at length began to grow in the path that led over the meadows to the cottage—Annette became alarmed at the symptoms, and seizing the only chance that was left, engaged herself to her only remaining beau. He was at the time about, going to spend a season in the city; they were to be married on his return.—She accepted him, not because she thought him the best of all her suitors, but because he was the only one left, and had always held himself at her service. Her part of the play was ended; she became domestic, sedate, and studied housewifery.

The time finally arrived; her old beau came back to the village, and a day or two after, strolled over to the cottage with his pipe, in appearance quite an antiquated man. But he said nothing about the subject of matrimony.—Annette at last took the liberty of reminding him of his engagement. He started, "indeed madam you surprise me"—"Surprise you why sir?"—"Because," said he, "I never dreamed that you could be serious in such a thing as a matrimonial engagement—and meeting with a good opportunity, I got married before I left the city."

Fortune had finished the game, and Annette was left to pay the forfeit; she never married, because she never had another chance. And hers is but the history common to hundreds of those fair creatures, who trifling with the power that beauty gives them over the minds of men, sacrifice every thing at the shrine of ambition, and only to enjoy the title and the triumph, that lights for a little while the sphere of the Village Belle.

· June 25, 1859 ·

The Sacrifice

From the *Newport Mercury*

In charity lies the thematic key to both "The Rainy Day" and "The Sacrifice," but whereas it is denied the poor, doomed Amy in the former story, it enables Janet, the beleaguered seamstress in this latter story, to save the life of her dying brother. (The remarkable recovery of a dying victim under the care of a loved one figures significantly in James's first signed novel, *Watch and Ward*, 1871, as well as in several unsigned stories of the 1860s, among them "In a Circus" and the Civil War story "Ray Amyott.") Unlike the slow-witted, worldly Georgianna in "The Rainy Day," Janet's employer, Mrs. Clark, immediately recognizes that her seamstress is in dire need and responds with unstinting generosity. In Swedenborgian terms, she responds to God's silent voice of divine instruction. For she is, after all, a "fair young wife" who has "made a little earthly paradise of [her husband's] cottage home. . . . And here dwelt, also, the peace which God giveth to those who love Him." The Clarks, it would appear, have reached that seventh terminus of Swedenborgian peace to which Lawrence

Bayford, at the end of "Woman's Influence," aspired with his wife Celeste.

⚜

"**T**HERE, MARY—NOW don't you think I deserve to be called a pretty good husband?" laughed the young man, as he dropped down in the lady's palm half a dozen gold pieces.

"Yes, you are, Edward, the very best husband in the world," and she lifted up her sweet face, beaming with smiles, as a June day with sunshine.

"Thank you, thank you, for the very flattering words. And now, dear, I want you to have the cloak by next Christmas.—I'm anxious to see how you will look in it."

"But, Edward," gazing seriously into the shining pieces in her rosy palm, "you know we are not rich people, and it really seems a piece of extravagance for me to give thirty dollars for a velvet cloak."

"No, it is not, either. You deserve the cloak, Mary, and I have set my mind upon your having it. Then it will last you so many years, that it will be more economical in the end than a less expensive article."

It was evident the lady was predisposed to conviction. She made no further attempt to refute her husband's arguments, and her small fingers closed over the gold pieces, as she rose up saying, "Well, dear, the supper has been waiting half an hour, and I know you must be hungry,"

Edward and Mary Clark were the husband and wife of a year. He was a bookkeeper in a large house with a salary of fifteen hundred dollars. His fair young wife made a little earthly paradise of his cottage home in the suburbs of the city, for within its walls dwelt two lives that were set like music to poetry, keeping time to each other. And here dwelt, also, the peace which God giveth to those who love Him.

* * *

MRS. CLARK CAME into the sitting room suddenly, and the girl lifted her head, and then turned it away quickly, but not until the first glance told the lady that the fair face was swollen and stained with tears.

Janet Hill was a young seamstress whom Mrs. Clark had occasionally employed for the last six months. She was always attracted by her young bright face, her modest yet dignified manners, and now the lady saw at once that some great sorrow had smitten the girl.

Obeying the promptings of a warm, impulsive heart, she went to her and laid her hand on her arm, saying softly, "Won't you tell me what is troubling you, Janet?"

"Nothing that anybody can help," answered the girl, trying still to avert her face, while the tears swelled in her eyes from the effort which she made to speak.

"But perhaps I can. At any rate, you know, it does us good sometimes to confide our sorrows to a friend, and I need not assure you that I sincerely grieve, because of your distress."

And so with kind words, and half caressing movements of the little hand laid on the seamstress' arm, Mrs. Clark drew from her lips her sad story.

She was an orphan, supporting herself by her daily labors, and she had one brother, just sixteen, three years her junior. He had been for some time a kind of under-clerk in a large wholesale establishment where there was every prospect of his promotion; but he had seriously injured himself in the summer by lifting some heavy bales of goods, and, at last, a dangerous fever set in, which had finally left him in so exhausted a state that the doctor had no hope of his recovery.

"And to think I shall never see him again, Mrs. Clark," cried the poor girl, with a fresh burst of tears. "To think he must die away there, among strangers in the hospital, with no loving face to bend over him in his last hours, or brush away the damp curls from the forehead which mama used to be so proud of. Oh, George—my darling, bright faced little brother George," and here, the poor girl broke down in a storm of sobs and tears.

"Poor child, poor child," murmured Mrs. Clark, her sweet eyes swimming in tears—How much would it cost for you to go to your brother, and return?" she asked at last.

"About thirty dollars. I have not so much money in the world. You see it is nearly four hundred miles off, but I could manage to support myself after I got there."

A thought passed quickly through Mrs. Clark's mind. She stood still a few moments, her blue eyes fixed in deep meditation. At last she said kindly, "Well, my child, try and bear up bravely, and we will see what can be done for you," and the warm, cheerful tones comforted the sad heart of the seamstress.

The lady went up stairs, and took the pieces out of her ivory porte-monnaie.—There was a brief sharp struggle in her mind, "Somehow I've set my heart on this velvet cloak," she thought, "and Edward will be disappointed. I was going out to select the velvet this very afternoon. But then, there's that dying boy lying there with strange faces all about him, and longing as the slow hours go by, for a sight of the sister who loves him, and would not this thought haunt me every time I put on my new cloak? After all, my old broadcloth is not so bad if it's only turned and, I am sure, I can bring Edward over to my way of thinking. No, you must go without the cloak this time, and have the pleasure of knowing you've smoothed the path going down to the shadow of the valley of death, Mary Clark." And she closed the port-monnaie resolutely, and went downstairs.

"Janet, put up your work this moment—there is no time to be lost. Here is the money. Take it, and go to your brother."

The girl lifted her eyes a moment, almost in bewilderment, to the lady, and then, as she comprehended the truth, a cry of such joy broke from her lips, that its memory never faded from the heart of Mrs. Clark's life.

"George! George!" The words leaped from her lips, as the sister sprang forward to the low bed where the youth lay, his white, sharpened face gleaming deathlike from amidst his thick yellow curls.

He opened his large eyes, suddenly, a flush passed over his pallid face. He stretched out his thin arms and exclaimed, "O Janet! Janet! I have prayed God for the sight of you once more, before I die."

"His pulse is stronger than it has been for two weeks, and his face has a better hue," said the doctor, a few hours later, as he made his morning visit through the wards of the hospital.

"His sister came yesterday and watched with him," answered an attendant, glancing at the young girl, who hung breathless over the sleeping invalid.

"Ah, that explains it. I'm not certain but that young man has recuperative power enough left to recover, if he could have the care and tenderness for the next two months, which love alone can furnish."

How Janet's heart leaped at the blessed words! That very morning she had an interview with her brother's employers. They had been careless, but not intentionally unkind, and the girl's story enlisted their sympathy.

In a day or two, George was removed to a quiet, comfortable private home, and his sister installed herself by his couch his nurse and comforter.

Three years have passed. The shadows of the night were drooping already around, Mrs. Clark sat in her chamber, humming a nursery tune, to which the cradle kept a sort of rhythmic movement. Sometimes she would pause suddenly and adjust the snowy blankets around the cheeks of the little slumberer, shining out from their brown curls as red apples shine amid fading leaves in October orchards. Suddenly the door opened, "Sh—sh," said the young mother, as she lifted her finger with a smiling warning as her husband entered.

"There's something for you, Mary. It came by express this afternoon;" he said the words in an undertone, placing a small packet in her lap.

The lady removed the covers with her eyes filled with wonder, while her husband leaned over her shoulder and watched her movements.

A white box disclosed itself and removing the cover, Mrs. Clarke descried a small, elegantly chased hunting watch. She lifted it with a cry of delighted surprise, and touching the spring, the case flew open and on the inside was engraved the words:

"To Mrs. Mary Clark. In token of the life she saved."

"O, Edward, it must have come from George and Janet Hill." exclaimed the lady and the quick tears leaped into her eyes. "You know she has been with him ever since that time, and she wrote me last spring, that he had obtained an excellent situation as head clerk in the firm. What an exquisite gift, and how I shall value it. Not simply for itself either."

"Well, Mary, you were in the right then, though I am sorry to say. I was half vexed with you for giving up your velvet cloak, and you have not had one yet."

"No, I've not had one but I never regretted it."

She said the words with her eye fastened on the beautiful gift.

"Nor I, Mary, for I cannot doubt that your sacrifice bought the young man's life."

"O, say those words again, Edward,—Blessed be God for them," added the lady, fervently.

The husband drew his arm around his wife and murmured reverently, "Blessed be God, Mary, who put it into your head to do this good deed."

The Rose-Colored Silk

From the *Newport Mercury*

A beautiful young heiress, an overworked seamstress in deplorable circumstances, a stylish new ball gown to be finished in little more than twenty-four hours—the narrative details are strikingly similar to those of "Woman's Influence," but the unspoiled, near saintly Ellen in this story is no Georgianna. Another Swedenborgian model of womanhood, Ellen experiences profound remorse, which leads to her selfless act of charity, as she advances in the Swedish master's ascending states of consciousness of Deity (Swedenborg concordance notes A6400 and A9118e). Divinely charitable, Ellen "takes up" the orphaned seamstress when she faints from exhaustion both literally, by taking her up in her arms, and symbolically, as a deific surrogate for the Lord: Central to the story is the allusion to Psalm 27:10, "When my father and my mother forsake me, then the Lord will take me up."

In this story, too, James for the first time devotes several paragraphs to an exploration of his heroine's background and a profile of her inner person. He might, however, have been writing of himself as an artist at this stage in his youthful career, when he says of Ellen that her

"Christian nurture was bringing forth its fruits, tender yet, and immature, yet capable of ripening under the sun and dews of Divine Grace,
with a rich and abundant harvest." For in "The Rose-Colored Silk"—
in James's growing grasp of allusive and imaginative storytelling, in the
wedding of Swedenborgian thought to Dickensian sentiment, in the
attention to psychology—emerges the recognizable aesthetic promise
of the future literary artist.

"YOU WILL SEND it without failure at six o'clock tomorrow?" said the clear, soft voice of a young girl who was
standing before a splendid mirror in Madame Beaujue's fashionable
dressmaking establishment. "Our invitations are for eight o'clock,"
she continued, "and the dress ought to be tried on as early as that, to
see that no alterations are needed."

"Certainly, mademoiselle, you may rely upon me. I have never yet
disappointed a customer, and I will not begin with you."

"Can you always be so very prompt?" rejoined Ellen, now gliding
into a tone of girlish curiosity. "Does not some one have to suffer for
it when you have such a pressure of work?"

"Oh, as to that, mademoiselle," replied Madame, with a shrug and
a slight, well-bred laugh, "that is not the question—'Never disappoint a patron' is my motto, and one way or another it can always be
obeyed."

"Send it then precisely at six, with some one to try it on and see
that it is right."

And Ellen turned for one more glance at the lustrous silk that so
well set off the light, graceful form and radiant face in the mirror. She
knew that she was beautiful, and yet it was rather a childlike gladness
in all beautiful things than a vain love or desire for admiration that
added the faint flush to her dimpled cheek, and the gleam of brightness to her eyes. Though the only child of a wealthy and indulgent
father, Ellen was not spoiled by fashionable life.—The teaching and

companionship of a saintly and now sainted mother, amid the safe
seclusion of home, had kept the young heart as yet unspotted from
the world—that world on whose glittering portal she now stood, half
trembling, half-expectant. Her school education was now completed,
and, at her father's request, Ellen was now preparing for her first
large party, the brilliant anticipations of which had set her thoughts
in an unusual flutter of excitement.

Ellen was called 'quite a little saint,' among her young associates.
Her ideas of fashionable life were so unsophisticated, so original,
they said, she was so appallingly unacquainted with beaux and billet-
doux, subjects which most of her schoolmates knew at least as well as
their grammars and algebras; she seemed to care so little, in choosing
her associates, for wealth or station, and so much for real worth of
character, that the shallow, little souls knew not what to make of her.
And yet they liked Ellen W——. Oh, yes! She was a dear simple little thing that no one could find fault with, and her sincere affection-
ateness of nature weighed more with even her shallow critics, than
the more brilliant qualities of her more selfish associates. Or else it
was the share in her continual generosity, and in the hospitalities of
her father's elegant mansion or the name of being the intimate friend
and constant companion of a millionaire's heiress that they liked.
Older and wiser heads than theirs have been puzzled to define the
difference in similar cases.

The truth was, Ellen's Christian nurture was bringing forth its
fruits, tender yet, and immature, yet capable of ripening, under the
sun and dews of Divine Grace, with a rich and abundant harvest. She
cherished sacredly the instructions of her mother, and the exercises
of prayer and meditation which she taught; but she turned, with
more than a passive acquiescence to the social gaieties which her
father was planning for her—not suspecting any evil in them, not
dreaming that they would deaden her spiritual sense, or infringe
upon her hours of devotion. Indeed, unless some providential event
should interpose, Ellen may fall into the case of those semi-Jewish
pagans of old, and fashionable Christlars of modern times, who 'fear

the Lord and worship idols.' Her piety had taken, as yet, chiefly the passive and imaginative form. It inspires beautiful visions of heaven, but not practical efforts to relieve the sufferings of earth. This is not strange, for, surrounded by the illusions of wealth, Ellen has seen nothing of the hard suffering world as it really is. It may be that the germ of active benevolence is planted in her heart, ready to spring forth when emergencies shall call.

Rehabited in her usual dress, Ellen turned from the room to leave the establishment of Madame B——. In doing so she passed through long rows of workwomen, and for the first time the care worn expression of every face attracted her notice. Every attitude was constrained, and the hollow chests, the sunken cheeks and heavy eyes, told of exhausted labor, which infringed upon the natural hours of food and rest. Suddenly her eyes were drawn to one pale face half-hidden behind the lustrous folds of her own rose-colored silk. The work had just been resumed, and there was an expression almost of despair upon the girl's features, as she thought, doubtless of the long hours far into the night, which must be superadded to the already excessive toils of the day. There was a convulsive twitching of the muscles of the mouth, as if the will was making one desperate effort to subdue rebellious nerves and compel them to renewed exertion. Then the effort was manifestly ineffectual, for the pale cheeks grew paler, the heavy eyes more sunken, and she sank forward into the midst of the fluttering flounces, which shone in glittering contrast to the faded hands that unconsciously clutched them.

Ellen sprang forward to raise the fainting girl in her arms.

"Ah! Mademoiselle, your beautiful robe!" exclaimed Madame, in an apologetic tone.

"Take it away! I did not think of that," replied Ellen, indignantly.

"Mademoiselle need not be alarmed. This happens quite frequently. The girl shall be well attended to."

"It was my work. I have killed her," said Ellen, with unfeigned remorse. The truth became most painfully real to her then

That evil is wrought by *want of thought,*
As well as by want of heart.

"Can you go with me to her home?" she asked of the young girl who was supporting the fainting form of her companion.

"Yes, miss," replied the girl with some hesitation, "but it isn't a place you would like to go to."

"Why not? Are her parents living?"

"No, miss, or at least her mother is dead, and her father is worse, they say."

At this moment a handkerchief being drawn from the patient's pocket, a small clasped Testament fell out. Ellen stooped to pick it up, and read upon the title page its owner's name. 'Margaret L——' Beneath were written in trembling characters, 'When my father and my mother forsake me, then the Lord will take me up.' 'Casting all your care upon him, for He careth for you.'

If a shadow of distrust had crossed Ellen's mind, it was quite gone now. The first verse had been written in her own little Bible, with almost the last movement of a hand now cold in death. But what a contrast between her own condition and that of the motherless girl before her! The one favored, indulged almost to the risk of forgetting her heavenly Father, amid the manifold gifts of the earthly one. The other alone, destitute, and working away the slender remnant of life in the desperate struggle for the means of subsistence. It was a phase of human experience which Ellen had never before witnessed. Tears were in her eyes, and an unwonted tremor in her voice as she said, "Do you think you could take her down to my carriage? I will take her home with me."

Madame B—— now came up with millions of apologies.

'She was sorry, she was infinitely grieved that Mademoiselle had been so *gênée*, so annoyed. She would do her utmost to restore the beautiful silk to its original lustre, but if this could not be done, it should be replaced—whatever the city had of most elegant.'

Ellen cut short her apologies.

"The silk is not of the slightest consequence. This will pay you for your work. You will please send it to the carriage—if I ever want the dress, Margaret may finish it for me at home."

The dress was never completed, though for many years it hung in Ellen's wardrobe, and often met her eye. It always called to mind the fainting, deathlike face which she had seen crouching amid its rosy folds, and the page of human experience that had then opened to her view never became obscured. From it Ellen learned the work which the Father of all had assigned her to do, and if life was no longer the light and beautiful dream which it had been to her, it was now rich with the only real joy, that of soothing the sorrows, lightening the burdens, and aiding the advancement of her fellow beings. One special lesson was sympathy for slaves of the needle. Her visits to Madame B—— were less frequent than before, but when they occurred, that eminent priestess of fashion was often surprised to hear orders followed by a caution like this: "And please be sure that no one is overworked on my account. I have given you ample time, and it is no matter if you exceed it."

But this was only one application of the lesson of love. The orphan Margaret from a transient guest became a valued inmate of Ellen's home. Her meek and patent spirit revealed new traits of Christian attainment, which Ellen's bright and peaceful life had given her no opportunity even to conceive; and her deep experience of poverty and loneliness, and acquaintance with other sufferers from similar causes, furnished a wide field for exertion. And still, as their circle of beneficiaries enlarged, the love of doing good burned brighter in Ellen's breast, and threw its light and warmth through the whole circle. She had found the rest and prize of life. She had verified her own narrow measures of those wonderful words which our Divine Master had dropped to us, as it were, from the heights of His own infinite experience: 'It is more blessed to give than to receive.'

A Winter Story

From the *Newport Mercury*

Charity is again the theme, and the situation again intimately domestic, in "A Winter Story." Add to the sentimentality that imbues the story, the fact that it is set during the Christmas season, and you have a perfect tale for the readers of Newport's *Mercury* magazine. Whether young George, the narrator, who is reading the mystical Sir Thomas Browne (a favorite in the James household) but who fails to see truly what he sees when he answers the knock at the outside door, represents Henry himself or his brother William matters less than that he experiences remorse for his lack of charity. And altered by that remorse, like the heroes in several of James's youthful fictions, he advances to a higher state of consciousness in the progress of a Swedenborgian destiny.

A COLD NIGHT! The wind, sharp as a Damascus scimitar, cut through the fine chink in the windows, causing my mother to continuously change her seat, to avoid what she calls the draught; but as the draught comes everywhere, she is at length fain to come to a settlement close to the mantlepiece, where she keeps cutting out mysterious hexagons and rhomboids from some linen stuff, hereafter to be united by cunning fingers into some wonderful article of female apparel. My two sisters are playing chess. Fanny, triumphantly over a checkmate, leans back on her chair, and watches with an air of proud pity, the cogitative countenance of Lizzie, whose little brain is throbbing with a thousand stratagems by which to extricate her unhappy queen from the pending disaster. I, wrapped in all the dignity of nineteen years, am absolutely smoking a cigar in the sacred chamber, (a privilege awarded to me on rare occasions by my mother, who would generally dismiss me to my room the moment I displayed an Havana) and reading Sir Thomas Browne's poetic essay on Urn Burial. There is a solemn quiet reigning through the room.—The pine logs on the hearth fling out spasmodic jets of fire and hiss like wounded snakes, as the bubbling, resinous juice oozes out from each gaping split. The click of my mother's scissors snaps monotonously, and at regular intervals. The winds scream wildly outside, and clatters at the windowpane, as if it was cold and wanted to come in. Through the dusty panes themselves, half-revealed by the partially drawn curtains, glimmer whitely the snowy uplands, and on the crest of the ghastly hill a bare old oak lifts up its naked arms, like an aged Niobe frozen in an attitude of sorrow. The smoke of my cigar goes curling ceilingward in concentric rings of evanescent valor, and I am whispering to myself one of those sonorous and solemn sentences with which the old knight of Norwich terminates his chapters and which, after one has read them, reverberate and echo in the brain, when— tat—tat—there comes a faint irresolute knock at the door. My mother shuts her scissors and looks up inquiringly, as much to say, "Who in Heaven's name is out on a night like this?" The chess players are immovable, and it seems as if an earthquake would be a matter of indifference to them. I lay down my book and go to the door. I open it with a shiver, and a resolution to be cross and uncivil; the

wind rushes triumphantly in with a great sigh of relief, the moment
the first chink appears, and I look out into the bitter ghastly night.

What a strange group stand on the piazza! Winter seems to have
become incarnate in human form, and with the four winds as his
companions come to pay us a visit.

There is a tall, old man, with a long gray moustache, which, as it
hangs down his jaws, the rude breeze snatches up, and swings about
and pulls insolently, as if it knew he was poor and could be insulted
with impunity. He looks bitterly cold! His long, arched nose is as
blue as the blue sky above him, in which the stars twinkle so clearly,
and he has on a scanty little coat, on which a few remnants of braid
fluttered sadly, like the shreds of vine that hang on walls in winter
time, which they, in the golden summer had wreathed with glossy
leaves so splendidly. He holds a little child in his arm—a little shivering child that trembles most incessantly, and tries, poor thing, to put
its head in the scanty threadbare folds of that insufficient coat.—By
the side of this pair is another effigy of poverty and winter. A small,
pale, delicate woman, with great blue eyes—profuse hair, which, mat-
ted in frozen intricacies, burst out from a most remarkably shapeless
bonnet, a shawl so thin that it must have been woven by spiders;
another little shivering child clasped in her arms, and carefully
enveloped in the poor old shawl, though one can see by her blue neck
and thin dress, that she is sacrificing herself to keep the little one
warm. A huge umbrella dangling from one of her hands, and which
she leans on occasionally with great dignity, and the ice picture is
complete.—But the main picture is not yet finished. A girl about ten
years old, standing a little back, clings to her mother's skirts with one
of her hands, while with the other she tries to keep something that
looks like a pair of trousers wrapped round her neck. She is shadowy
and pale, and seems like a northern mirage ready to dissolve into cold
air at a moment's notice.

"Who are you, and what do you all want?" I said, in a gruff tone;
for the wind blew bitterly on my cheek, and I made up my mind to
be cross.

The old man inclined his head slightly, and spoke,

"We are Poles," said he in excellent English, with a slight foreign accent; "we are going to Boston, which we hear is but one day's journey from this, but we do not know where to lodge the night. We are here to ask you for a night's shelter."

"Pooh!" said I, swinging the door almost to; "we know nothing about you, and never admit beggars. We cannot do it."

The man fell back a pace or two, and then looked at the little woman with the great eyes. Heavens! Heavens! how full of despair those great eyes seemed just at that moment. I saw his arm tighten convulsively round the little shivering child in his arms. A sluggish, half-frozen tear rolled down that frozen blue nose of his. He brushed it away with his cold, shriveled hand, and nodded mournfully to the little woman, who clutched her umbrella firmly, and then turned to depart without a word. As the door was being slowly closed, he shook his head once or twice, and said in a very low tone, "God help me."

These words had scarcely been spoken, when I felt a slight touch on my shoulder.

"George," said my mother, "call those people back."

I never felt so relieved in all my life.— When that old man turned away in silence at my sudden refusal to his prayer, disdaining to address himself to me, but whispering for mercy to God, a pang of remorse shot through my heart; I would have given worlds to have him called back, but the hideous, sullen pride, which has through life chained up my nature until it has become like a cooped bear, put a padlock on my lips. How glad I was when my mother came and dissolved the bonds with a touch.

"Come back," I said, "my friends, we wish to speak with you."

I am sure my voice must have been very gentle, for as the old Pole turned his rugged cheek seemed to soften, and the great eyes of his pale wife actually flashed through the dim night, with the fire of hope. They had landed from an emigrant ship in New York, with only a few dollars in their possession, which was dwindled away to a few shillings. They could get no employment. The old man was a modeler of medallions, and said bitterly—"They don't care about art in New York." So they made up their minds to go to Boston; there they heard that such things find encouragement. With a few remaining shillings, and what money they could obtain by pawning their little wardrobe, they struggled this far on their journey. They were now penniless, and scarce knew what to do, but the old man said proudly, "if we could only get through to Boston tomorrow, we have nothing to fear."

My mother shut the door; by this time the old man, the pale little woman and three shivering children, were on the inside, and Fanny and Lizzie left their game of chess, with their poor queen still in prison, and were passing round the pale little woman, whose eyes were now larger than ever, and shining with tears of joy; and they somehow got hold of the two youngest children; and they were petting them and talking to them in the wonderful language, supposed to be the tongue commonly spoken by infants, the foundation of which is substituting the letter d for the letter t, and soothing all the l's and h's in a remorseless manner.

The little foreigners were therefore informed, confidently, by the young ladies, that 'dey was deed little tings, and musn't gry zo, far zey would ave nize vorm supper.' And whether they understood it or not, the 'little tings' ceased to shiver or cry, and looked wonderingly about with small editions of their mother's great eyes, and the old man twirled his moustache as it thawed in the heat of the pine fire, and made many bows and looked the wordless gratitude which cannot be interpreted.

But the little wife said nothing; only she leaned on her umbrella, and gazed at my mother as she gave orders to the servants for the preparation of a sleeping room and a liberal meal for the wayfarers; and she gazed at me, as I stirred up the fire with immense energy, (between ourselves, I tried to battle off the recollection of that cruel speech with which I first met their appeal,) and made her husband sit down so close to it, that his legs were nearly scorched through his threadbare trousers; and so continually gazing at every one, until she could stand it no longer, and flinging away for the first time that ponderous umbrella of hers, she cast herself on my astonished mother's neck, and sobbed out a heap of Polish blessings, that if there is any virtue in benedictions, will certainly canonize her when she dies.

I declare to you, that when all was over, and they were sleeping soundly, I went into a remote corner and wept bitterly for the wrong I had so nearly done.

Well, they staid with us that night, and the next; and my mother got up a little subscription among the neighbors. And we rigged them all out in good warm clothing, bought them tickets on the cars to Boston, and one fine, frosty morning, we all sallied down to the depot, and saw them on their journey, and I tell you there was a waving of hands, and Polish gesticulations, and far, far away in the distance, we could catch a glimpse of that great umbrella, with the little woman flourishing it by way of farewell.

We heard nothing of our Polish friends for a whole year. Often over the fireside, we would talk about them, and our neighbors sneered at us and wondered if our spoons were safe, and moralized upon foreign imposture and ingratitude. My mother got much for her charity; but none of us minded, for there was something so true in the ways and manners of those poor wanderers, that it would be impossible to distrust them.

Well, Christmas came. Winter again, snow, yule logs glowing fiercely on the hearth, and mistletoe and ivy swinging merrily in the hall. Again the uplands were sheeted in white; again the old oak was naked and sorrowing; again we were seated around the fire, listening to the roaring of the wind as it tore over the hills like a mad steed. In the midst of a deep silence that fell upon us all, there came a rat-tat-tat. It was strong, determined, and eager. I went to the door. I had scarcely unbarred it or took a new peep at the new comer, when it seemed as if a whirlwind with a bonnet on his head scoured past me and swept into the parlor. The next moment I heard a great commotion. Sobbing and laughing, and broken English, all swept along, as it were, in a cataract of Polish. It was the little pale woman with the great eyes. No longer pale though, but with ruddy cheeks; and the eyes, this time, looked larger and brighter than ever thro' the tears. They had been ever since in Boston, she breathlessly told us, and had been doing well, thanks to the blessed lady who helped them get there. The husband modeled medallions, she composed polkas, and their only daughter taught music, and they had saved three hundred dollars, and bought a piano with it. And she had said to herself that on Christmas she would come and speak her gratitude to the blessed lady who had sheltered her and her little ones; So she set off in the cars, and here she was. And then she commenced pulling things out of her pockets. Christmas presents for us all!—There was a scarlet fortune teller for Lizzie, and a curious card case for Fanny; and a wonderfully embroidered needle case for my mother; and there was a beautiful umbrella for Mr. George, she intimated, producing an enormous parachute. She knew he would like it, because when she was here last year thanks to the blessed lady who had sheltered her— she had seen him look very much at her umbrella, and she would have offered it to him then, but she was ashamed, it was so old. But this was a new one, and very large!

And then she kissed us all round, and produced an elaborate letter from her husband to my mother, in which she was compared to Penelope, and one or two classical personages, and told us everything that had happened to them since they had left us, until, having talked herself into a state of utter exhaustion, she went off to her bedroom, where she was heard praying in indifferent English, that we might ascend into Heaven without any of the usual difficulties.

She and her family are still in Boston, where they make quite a respectable income. And every Christmas sees her arrival with presents for the blessed lady, and her eyes and her gratitude are as large as ever.

It is, you see, a simple Winter Story.

· April 6, 1861 ·

Sober Second Thought

From the *Newport Mercury*

Henry James Sr., on at least one occasion, found reason to complain that his wife's expenditures on clothes were doing him in financially—to the tune of three hundred dollars a year. Therein may lie the germ for James's "Sober Second Thought."

Forty dollars for a new silk dress prompts the crisis in this story of the sober-faced Charles Whitman and his young wife, Ada, whose name means "happy"—doubly so, as at the outset she is misguidedly happy in her spendthrift pleasures and finally, truly happy, as she averts marital tragedy. She thus brings the potentially tragic tale to a comic end and changes the face of her husband to a more cheerful mien: evidence, perhaps, of more of James's reading in *Smith's Dictionary of Greek and Roman Antiquities*, particularly of the article titled "Persona." With Charles, as with most of the characters in another 1861 story, "The Death of Colonel Thoureau," we must read the mask, and beyond the mask, the man. So, too, must Ada, as with Swedenborgian intuition—and a few receipts—she resolves the problem in her marriage and restores her husband's quietude. "Receipts,"

by the way, is the English translation of the Hebrew word *kabala*—
and may be a clue to some other of James's reading in his father's
library.

✹

"I MUST HAVE it, Charles," said the handsome little wife of Mr.
Whitman. "So don't put on that sober face."

"Did I put on a sober face?" asked the husband, with an attempt to
smile that was anything but a success.

"Yes, as sober as a man on trial for his life. Why, it's as long as the
moral law. There, dear, cheer up, and look as if you had at least one
friend in the world. What money-lovers you men are!"

"How much will it cost?" inquired Mr. Whitman. There was
another unsuccessful effort to look cheerful and acquiescent.

"About forty dollars," was the answer, with just a little faltering in
the lady's voice, but she knew the sum would sound extravagant.

"Forty dollars? Why, Ada, do you think I'm made of money?" Mr.
Whitman's countenance underwent a remarkable change of expression.

"I declare, Charles," said his wife, a little impatiently, "you look
at me as if I were an object of fear instead of affection. I don't think
this is kind of you. I've only had three silk dresses since we were
married, while Amy Bright has had six or seven during the same
period, and every one of hers cost more than mine. I know you
think me extravagant, but I wish you had a wife like some women
I could name. I rather think you would find out the difference
before long."

"There, there, pet, don't talk to me after that fashion. I'll bring you
the money at dinner time, that is if—"

"No ifs or buts, if you please. The sentence is complete without
them. Thank you, dear! I'll go this afternoon and buy the silk. So
don't fail to bring the money. I was at Sithskin's yesterday, and saw
some of the sweetest patterns I ever laid my eyes on. Just suits my

style and complexion. I shall be inconsolable if it is gone. You won't disappoint me?"

And Mrs. Whitman laid her soft, white hand on the arm of her husband, and smiled with sweet persuasion in her face.

"Oh, no, you shall have the money," said Mr. Whitman, turning off from the wife, as she thought, a little abruptly, and hurrying from her presence. In his precipitation, he had forgotten the usual parting kiss.

"That's the way it is always," said Mrs. Whitman, her whole manner changing, as the sound of the closing street door came jarring upon her ears. "Just say money to Charles, and at once there is a cloud to the sky."

She sat down, pouting and half angry.

"Forty dollars for a new dress," said Mr. Whitman mentally, "pretty thoughtless, Mrs. Whitman," as he shut the door after him. "I promised to settle Thompson's coal bill to day, thirty-three dollars—but don't know where the money is to come from. The coal is burned up, and some more must be ordered. O, dear! I'm discouraged. Every year I fall behind-hand. This winter I did hope to get a little in advance, but if forty-dollar dresses are the order of the day, there is an end for that devoutly wished for circumstance.—Debt! Debt! how I have always shrunk from it; but steadily, how it is closing its Brirarian arms round me, and my constricting chest labors in respiration. Oh, if I could disentangle myself now—while I have the strength of early manhood, and the bonds that hold me are weak. If Ada could see as I see—if I could only make her understand rightly my position. Alas! that is hopeless I fear."

And Mr. Whitman hurried his steps because his heart beat quicker, and his thought was unduly excited.

Not long after Mr. Whitman left home, the city postman delivered a letter at his address. His wife examined the writing on the envelope, which was in a bold masculine hand, and said to herself as she did so:

"I wonder who this can be from?"

Something more than curiosity moved her. There intruded on her mind a vague feeling of disquiet, as if the missive bore unpleasant news for her husband. The stamp showed it to be a city letter. A few times, such letters had come to his address, and she had noticed that he read them hurriedly, thrust them without remark into his pocket, and became sober and silent-faced.

Mrs. Whitman turned the letter over and over again in her hand, in a thoughtful way, and as she did so, the image of her husband, sober-faced and silent as he had become, for the most of the time of late, presented itself with unusual vividness.—Sympathy stole into her heart.

"Poor Charles," she said, as the feeling increased; "I am afraid something is going wrong with him."

Placing the letter on the mantlepiece where he could see it when he came in, Mrs. Whitman entered upon some household duties, but a strange impression, as of a weight, lay upon her heart—a sense of impending evil—a vague, troubled disturbance of her usual inward self satisfaction.

If the thought of Mrs. Whitman recurred, as was natural, to the elegant silk dress of which she was to become the owner that day, she did not feel the proud satisfaction her vain heart experienced a little while before. Something of its beauty had faded.

"If I only knew what that letter contained," she said, half an hour after it had come in, her mind still feeling the pressure which had come down upon it so strangely, as it seemed to her.

She went to the mantlepiece, took up the letter and subscription. It gave her no light. Steadily it kept growing upon her that its contents were of a nature to trouble her husband.

"He's been very mysterious of late," she said to herself. This idea affected her very, very unpleasantly. "He grows more silent and reserved," she added, as thought, under a kind of feverish excitement, became activity in a new direction. "More indrawn, as it were, and less interested in what goes on around him. His coldness chills me at times, and his irritation hurts me."

She drew a long deep sigh. Then, with an almost startling vividness came before her mind in contrast, her tender, loving, cheerful husband of three years before, and her quiet sober-faced husband of today.

"Something must have gone wrong with him," she said aloud, as feeling grew stronger. "What can it be?"

The letter was in her hand.

"This may give me light," said she, and with careful fingers, she opened the envelope, not breaking the paper, so that she could seal it again if she desired to do so. There was a bill for sixty-five dollars, and a communication from the person charging it. It was a jeweller.

"If not settled at once," he wrote, "I shall put the account in suit. It has been standing for over a year; and I am tired of getting excuses instead of my money."

The bill was for a lady's watch Mrs. Whitman had almost compelled her husband to purchase.

"Not paid for? Is it possible?" exclaimed the little woman in blank astonishment, the blood mounting to her forehead.

Then she sat down to think. Light began to come into her mind. As she sat down thus thinking, a second letter came in from the penny postman. She opened it without hesitation. Another bill and another dunning letter.

"Not paid! Is it possible?" she repeated the ejaculation. It was a bill of twenty-five dollars for gaiters and slippers, which had been standing three of four months.

"This will never do," said the awakened wife—"Never, no, never!" And she thrust the two letters into her pocket in a resolute way. From that hour until the return of her husband at dinnertime, Mrs. Whitman did an unusual amount of thinking for her little brain. She saw the moment he entered the morning cloud had not passed away from his brow.

"Here is the money for that new dress," he said, taking a small roll of bills from his vest pocket, and handing them to Ada, as he came in. He did not kiss her, not smile in the old bright way. But his voice was calm if not cheerful. A kiss and a smile just then would have been more precious to the young wife, than a hundred silk dresses. She took the money, saying—

"Thank you, dear! It is kind of you to regard my wishes."

Something in Ada's voice and manner caused Mr. Whitman to lift his eyes with a look of inquiry, to her face. But she turned aside, so that he could not read its expression.

He was grave and more silent than usual, and ate with scarcely any appearance of an appetite.

"Come home early, dear," said Mrs. Whitman, as she walked to the door with her husband after dinner.

"Are you impatient to have me admire your new dress?" he replied with a faint effort to smile.

"Yes, it will be something splendid," she answered.

He turned off from her quickly, and left the house. A few moments she stood, with a thoughtful face, her mind indrawn, and her whole manner completely changed. Then she went to her room and commenced dressing to go out.

Two hours later and we find her in jeweller's store on Broadway.

"Can I say a word to you?" she addressed the owner of the store who knew her very well.

"Certainly," he replied, and they moved to the lower end of one of the long showcases.

Mrs. Whitman drew from her pocket a lady's watch and chain, and laying them on the showcase, said, at the same time taking out the bill she had taken from the envelope addressed to her husband—

"I cannot afford to wear this watch; my husband's circumstances are too limited. I tell you so frankly. It should never have been purchased, but a too indulgent husband yielded to the importunities of a foolish young wife. I say this to take the blame from him. Now, sir, meet the case if you can do justice to yourself. Take back the watch, and say how much I shall pay besides."

The jeweller dropped his eyes to think. The case took him a little by surprise,—He stood for nearly a minute; then taking the bill and watch, he said: "Wait a moment," and went to a desk nearby.

"Will that do?" He had come forward again, and now presented her with the bill receipted. His face wore a pleased expression.

"How much shall I pay you?" asked Mrs. Whitman, drawing out her pocket purse.

"Nothing. The watch is not defaced."

"You have done a kind act, sir," said Mrs. Whitman, with feeling trembling along her voice. "I hope you will not think unfavorably of my husband. It is no fault of his that the bill has not been paid. Good morning, sir."

Mrs. Whitman drew her veil over her face, and went with light steps, and a light heart from the store. The pleasure she had experienced on receiving her watch was not to be compare with that felt in parting with it. From the jeweller's she went to the boot-maker's and paid the bill of twenty-five dollars, and from thence to the milliner's and settled for her last bonnet.

"I know you are dying to see my dress," said Mrs. Whitman gaily, as she drew her arm within that of her husband, on his appearance that evening. "Come over to our bedroom, and let me show it. Come along! Don't hang back, Charles, as if you were afraid."

Charles Whitman went with his wife passively, looking more like a man on his way to receive sentence, than in expectation of a pleasant sight. His thoughts were bitter.

"Shall my Ada become lost to me?" he said in his heart—"lost to me in the world of folly, fashion and extravagance?"

"Sit down, Charles." She led him to a large cushioned chair. Her manners had undergone a change. The brightness of her countenance had departed. She took something in a hurried way from a drawer, and catching up a footstool, placed it on the floor near him, and sitting down, leaned upon him, and looked tenderly and lovingly into his face. She then handed him the jeweller's bill.

"It is receipted, you see," Her voice fluttered a little.

"Ada! how is this? What does it mean?" He flushed and grew eager.

"I returned the watch, and Mr. R—— receipted the bill. I would have paid for damage, but he said it was uninjured, and asked nothing."

"Oh, Ada!"

"And this is receipted, also, and this," handing the other bills which she had paid, "and now, dearest," she added quickly, "how do you like my dress? Isn't it beautiful?"

We leave the explanation and scene that followed, to the reader's imagination. If any fair lady, however, who, like Ada, has been drawing too heavily on her husband's slender purse, for silk and jewels, is at a loss to realize the scene, let her try Ada's experiment. Our word for it, she will find a new and glad experience in life. Costly silks and jewels may be very pleasant things, but they are too dearly bought when they come as the price of a husband's embarrassments, mental quiet and alienation. Too often the gay young wife wears them as the signs of those unhappy conditions. Tranquil hearts and sunny homes are precious things; too precious to be burdened or clouded by weak vanity and love of show. Keep this in mind, oh ye fair ones, who have husband's in moderate circumstances. Do not let your pride and pleasure oppress them. Rich clothing, costly laces and gems, are poor substitutes for smiling peace and hearts unshadowed by care. Take the lesson and live by it, rather than offer another illustration, in your own experience, of the folly we have been trying to rebuke.

Alone

From the *Newport Mercury*

A Swedenborgian inevitability drives the narrative in this story of Jennie Dell, another in James's line of socially disadvantaged seamstresses living in penury, and her good-hearted employer, Mr. Brewer. In the emotionally turbulent course of the story, Jennie, whose name means "grace of the Lord" in Hebrew, fulfills her destiny as she is elevated to the status of a Swedenborgian angel through the marriage of her spirit, her inner beauty, to Mr. Brewer's truth. Mr. Brewer, likewise, proves himself to be the Swedenborgian model of a most modest admirer of but one desired lady. Allusively, too, he is Jennie's biblical savior as well as her romantic knightly protector and wealthy Prince Charming. Before all, however, he is her "kind, disinterested . . . considerate and appreciative . . . good friend"; and as such, he stands as the first of a common Jamesian type: the potent yet sacred epitome of manhood who can safely, without sexual threat, tend to a woman's deepest needs. Like many Jamesian women, Jennie finds strength and solace as much in friendship as in love with a genial, kind-spirited man. But in "Alone" the mutuality of mind she and Mr. Brewer discover raises friendship, as Swedenborg would have it in his *Conjugial Love,* to the full dimensionality of love. Exploring the dramatic possibilities of tragicomedy while gracefully blending allusions to Swedenborgian models with socialist sentiments, romance conventions, and Dickensian circumstances, Henry James, still in his teens in 1861, proves himself to be well apprenticed in a promising literary career.

A RESTLESS, SAD, longing little heart was beating under a worn calico dress, in a little room in Fourth Street. Tears as warm and grief swollen as any that gush from woman's eyes crept down the cheek a little farther, waited, trembled, and then swelling as the bosom swells with sighs, ran down the maiden's cheek, and fell upon the faded chintz. Through and through, and through again, slipped the nimble needle, shining with the never-ending attrition of muslin, and linen and silk. The Argus-eyed thimble—nothing better than steel, though worn to the polish of silver—clicked against the needle, pressing it through the close fabric into the calloused finger-tip, fretted and notched and blackened by many another needle-point, during many a weary day and many a weary night.

A cooking stove, one chair, two beds, a few dishes on a shelf in the corner, a broom, a large stone pitcher, a bonnet and shawl, a few pieces of stove furniture, half a dozen plants in rough wooden boxes on the windowsill, four or five books on the one table—these comprised the furniture.

The room was elevated far above the noise and dust of the dirty street—above the usual flight of city pigeons even; in the fifth story; and the roof in sloping had cut off a corner of the ceiling. The little low windows—a pair of stunted ones—did the best they could with the sunlight, but were too much crowded by the falling roof to accomplish much.

Had you slipped noiselessly in—which you could not have done, in fact, for the sagging of the door and its heavy scraping upon the threshold—you would have been struck first by the bareness, and then by the singular neatness of the attic room.

A little black and white kitten would have glanced up at you from a soft bed of cotton in its own corner, or skipped, frightened, upon the smaller bed of the two; and a still figure in the window would have presented not only a bowed head, but busy fingers, and a worn and faded print.

But if your tread had been heard on the stairs and mistaken for that of an old man, just before you reached the threshold, you would have heard a springing step upon the attic floor, the door would have scraped open with a good-natured growl, a pair of black eyes would have shone at you from a face wreathed in smiles, and possibly, in the shadow and haste, you might have got a pair of arms about your neck. At any rate, you would have followed a tall, little figure into the room, and on taking your seat would have found yourself vis-à-vis with as expressive and proud a face as ever shone from voluptuous plush, airy laces, rustling silk, and sparkling diamonds.

Indeed, while the teardrops were falling under the pressure of thoughts which the heart could not possibly hide under its lifting lid, a step was heard upon the stairs, the staircase did creak like the stage driver's horn, with the news of a coming, the door did open, and a pair of white arms were flung passionately around the neck of a white-haired old man.

Jennie had been crying of thoughts aroused by a brief walk in a populous street that afternoon.

She avoided these better thoroughfares when she could, hurrying along where the streets are narrow and dingy—where the glistening of silk and the tremble of plumes is seldom seen—where bright eyes and fair faces radiate only from faded and worn surroundings. But this afternoon her errand to the store had taken her through one of the comely streets. Indeed, it stood on the very corner of Main Street around which human tides swept, eddying, every hour. She had seen poverty, comfort and wealth—plainness, comeliness, beauty—stupidity, sense, intellect.

Sitting at her window in the dull, unseemly room, worn, tired, discouraged with the labors and forebodings of life, Jennie's thoughts could do no less than bring tears. She was thinking of the happiness which floated about her in the crowded street; of the laughing eyes; of the haughty tread; of faces brimming with careless merriment and conscious beauty. She had seen hundreds in that one street—hundreds of maidens to whom she was consciously superior. And this was not egotism in the weeping girl. Does the doe imagine itself a snail, or the eagle fancy itself a blue jay? Was it wrong that all this beauty, all this innate refinement, all this spirit, and taste, and mentality, should pine and sorrow for that appreciation for which we all long and strive? And if Jennie wept that her scant and faded calico had drawn forth sneers, as though it were herself and not the accident of covering; and if she wept that simple-minded and narrow-thoughted girls carried themselves proudly, and won attention, while she slipped meanly into byways, and shrunk from the observation which was only cold and contemptuous, can we blame her? She was a woman, with a woman's beauty and a woman's power. But, alas! Jennie was caged by circumstances, her jewels covered with the dust of labor, her young life hidden, and dull, and sad.

Besides, an incident at the store had wounded her severely, and reawakened her consciousness of weakness and semi-degradation. It was this: She had taken a bundle of work to the inspecting clerk, and thence had been directed to the cashier with a ticket for her pay. On former occasions she had suffered from curious and wicked glances while passing the clerks of several departments, as well as from a peculiar tone in which the cashier addressed her. Today she was either more painfully sensitive or the glances of admiration were more disgustingly prominent; and the cashier, after fumbling as long as possible, handed her the silver she had earned with a careless but insulting remark. Jennie flashed with indignation, threw the money upon the counter, and curling her lip with scorn left the desk. A hand touched her arm, and a kind voice said, "Wait a moment, Miss Dell," in so assured and commanding a way, that she involuntarily paused. The gentleman stepped up to the cashier, struck him a smart blow on the side of his face with the palm of his hand, tipping him over, took the vacated stool at his desk, and by the time the fellow had picked himself up, had balanced his account, and was ready for him with the residue of his wages. Then leading the fellow to the door by the arm, he kicked him into the street. All this was done so coolly, with so much ease and gentlemanly decision, that Jennie could take no exception to even the last act of drama.

"My store will be safe to you in future, Miss Dell, but I will not put you to the inconvenience of bringing your work. I will send a boy for it," and directing a lad to take the lady's bundle, Mr. Brewer bowed Jennie out of the store before she had time to cry or do anything more than thank him with a glance, which, breaking from her late indignation, was a curious intermingling of pride and gratitude.

The incident had recalled for the hundredth time a terrible consciousness of her unprotected situation, and she felt more keenly than ever the utter helplessness of poverty. Sometimes the blood of a proud ancestry dashed to her cheeks and throbbed at her temples; but the next instant womanly tears chased each other down her cheeks.

"I am so glad you have come, father.—I have been so very lonely, and then I was fearful something had happened."

The old man bent a little to kiss the eyes of his daughter—kissing her eyes was the emphasis of his affection—and his lips were moistened by a tear that Jennie had unwittingly left there in the haste of brushing them away to meet his coming step.

"What is this, daughter? Crying, my child? You are not sick, dear? Why, I thought my brave girl never cried, however dark the day might be"; and, with a hand on each shoulder, the white-haired man held the bright-faced daughter at arm's length before him, gazing loving inquiries into her eyes.

Not a trace of sadness was in the beaming face of the daughter now; so after meeting his gaze laughingly for a moment, Jennie slipped to his side, leaned close to his shoulder, clasping his arms into her hands, and said,

"Oh, nothing of any moment, father.—We women have little foolish thoughts and troubles of our own when we are left alone all day. But when father comes back again, Jennie is happy enough, isn't she?" and the girl looked into his face with so much of beauty, and love, and joy, that the old man forgot the dewdrop which had dried on his lips, and went to wondering what made his daughter so happy, alone and hard at work in that sober room all day.

The father forgot the sadness sooner, for a jewel of good tidings which he was holding tight in his heart, longing to give it to his daughter, but wondering what was the most perfect way to show it. Whether to raise the lid with a spring and permit the Koh-i-noor to flash with its diamond lightning full in her face at once, or to lift the lid gently so that the loved one's eyes might catch its brilliance, ray by ray, and beam by beam. While the daughter was making the tea kettle cover dance, and then pouring sputtering water into the little black teapot, in the bottom of which very few but very nice little leaves lay curled in fragrant exclusiveness and concentration, the glad father thought the matter over. While the torpid little leaves warmed into inevitable expansion by the heated flood, the glad father continued to think it over.

"You look tired, father; have you worked hard today?"

"Not very, daughter."

"Why, you are pale, father; you are sick, I know."

It is well that the girl dropped the plate from her hand, though it went down with a crackle into fragments, for the old man was reeling out of his chair. She was just in time to save him. Without a word the daughter held him a moment, till she could glance into his face, and then with a strength which she could always command when aroused, bore him to the nearest bed and laid him there.

"Father! Father!"

Not a word nor a sigh of consciousness. Jennie bathed his temples with water, rubbed his arms, his hands, his chest, called on him, kissed him and wept. His lips moved.

"What is it, father?" and the daughter's ear is close by the trembling lips.

"I have heard"—faintly—"from—Robert"—fainter. "Robert is—he is"—the voice is too faint to be heard—the lips cease to move—the old man is dead.

No cries of "Father, dear father!" no chafing of hands, no bathing of that calm, snow-fringed brow will ever bring back the soul now freed at last from its cheerless imprisonment of eighty years.

Straighten the stiffening limbs, lone daughter; close tighter the eyelids; he is gone. And the secret hidden in that unfinished sentence—it, too, is gone, and vainly will you try to fathom its import. The blow was a terrible one. Not only that this was her stay and companion, but her only support and her only friend. Now she was alone. Alone!

When all hope of restoration was gone, Jennie stood erect a little way from the bed, her head buried in her hands, and let the tide of loss and loneliness sweep over her. In that instant of time she drank the full cup and tasted each and every ingredient. This made her calm.

Another nature might have sunk; she was lifted, strengthened. All the energies of her heart came into active life; and now, tearful or quiet, busy or still, she was the same strong, self conscious woman she had ever been. She was even stronger and more calm.

A quick step upon the stairs, and a careless rap at the door. It was the bright-faced lad with a bundle.

"Mr. Brewer says as how this is nicer work, and you may send back the other bundle," said the little fellow, boylike, as he came abruptly into the room, his face beaming with pleasure and exercise. "Oh, Miss Dell!" and the boy fell into awe-stricken quiet as he felt the presence of death.

The second day before the funeral, when, with the aid of an old woman below, the body had been carefully prepared, a careful knock at the door. Mr. Brewer entered without a word, gave his hand, and sat down. Then gently alluding to her loss, asking to look on the features of her father, noticing her plants in the window, he skillfully led the conversation into appropriate channels, and, without a single profession, made Jennie feel that here was a true and appreciative friend.

Gradually the talk receded from the sad topics of the chamber of death to more general subjects—to such thoughts as we find written in books and such conclusions as we read in long meditations and careful analyzing. In this, her visitor was struck with the clearness and stretch of thought of the humble girl at his side. And she found herself roused and quickened by the outdrawing influence of a superior but congenial mind.

Thence the conversation was brought gently to personal affairs, where at length a point was gained at which Mr. Brewer ventured to ask,

"Have you no other friends but this?"

"None in all the world, except, perhaps, a brother."

Mr. Brewer could scarcely ask a further question.

Breaking the silence, Jennie said:

"My younger brother, Robert, left us three years ago—he was only fifteen then—in the rush to California; thinking that though only a boy, he might bring back gold enough to make his father comfortable for life. We heard of his arrival and promising beginning, but nothing since. Two years ago we came to live in this part of the city, and possibly at that time he changed his location. At any rate his letters have never reached us, nor have ours reached him. The other day, when father came home he had received tidings from him, for he said so just as he was dying; but the news itself died on his lips, and I have no clew whatever to its nature.—Brother Robert was a noble boy, sir—the bravest and the best boy I ever knew."

Just here the tears would start, and a long silence followed.

Mr. Brewer had brought a purse with a little gold in it, thinking to slip it into the hand of the girl whose trials had so touched his sympathy; but when he rose to go the act seemed impossible; he did not dare to do it; he could only ask, with the deepest respect,

"Can I be of any service to you?"

"I thank you very much for your call, Mr. Brewer—very much. There is only one thing you can do for me—employ me, if my work pleases you."

No need to follow the plain board coffin—rough casket for such a father—to its place among the silent poor in the great cemetery. If the faded shawl clung close to the poor girl's form, chilled by the autumn wind, dropping tears upon the turf alone by the poor man's grave, under it beat as warm a daughter's heart, and lived as rich a woman's nature, as ever moved gay and proud in choicer and happier scenes.

Jennie could not and would not leave the dear old room, hallowed now by the memory of a sainted father. She lived there alone. There was no objection to it now, for only a young and elastic tread walked the creakings in the long flight of old stairs.

The bright-faced boy came and went every day with a bundle. The work was very nice, and the pay was so much better as to give a new chintz to a deep brown with a tiny white figure. Mr. Brewer came occasionally. He slid quietly into the place of a friend, brought books for Jennie to read, and then discussed their content with her.

There were many points upon which they differed. Both loved very well to differ; for Jennie found pleasure in arousing his deep, earnest strength of expression, and he was never weary of awakening that flash of her large brown eyes and easy dignity of talk which served to distinguish her from all other of his friends.

Mr. Brewer's calls were not frequent, but they never failed during the many months in which she sat and sewed in the humble attic room.

Alas for the struggling, tossed, brave and weary girl! These visits so comforting at first, were coming to be a source of pain—in fact, and especially in prospect.

He came and went as a kind, disinterested friend, always considerate and appreciative, but always self-poised. Knowing and trusting him as a true friend, she knew nothing of the man but what she saw of him in her own home. He never talked of himself. The lad who came and went with the bundles had once or twice spoken of 'father' in a manner which convinced her that Mr. Brewer was a husband, and this his son. That was all! but it was decisive. And yet, though settled on this from the first, as time wore on, the companionship and sympathy of her one visitor grew into a need, and then a necessity.—No reasonings, no willful checkings, no self-condemnation even, could stay the growth of that giant presence by which at last she was covered and overpowered. In vain Jennie flashed indignation on herself, that she should love the loved of another woman's heart—a husband and father. In vain she wept, and struggled, and prayed. The chains grew tighter, holding her to a misery to which all the sadness of her life bore no comparison.

THE AFTERNOON SUN of a September Sabbath wrapped in a cheery light the dark and sea washed hull of an ocean steamer coming up the bay to the crowded pier.

At the same moment, Jennie's friend turned down a dull, dark street, entered a doorway, and ascended the cracking stairs. It was one of the pleasures of Jennie's room that, far away over the brick houses, with their smoked and smoking chimneys, lay the always changing picture of the bay. Today, after a long discussion of the beauties and blemishes, first of The Old Curiosity Shop, and then of De Quincey's Confessions, with other and minor talk, Jennie touched upon the scenery of the bay, with its white-winged butterflies and the black beetle that, an hour or two before, had been crawling up the harbor.

"I always think," she said, "when I look out upon the harbor, that perhaps some day it will bring my brave brother home to me; and then I shall not be alone, or unhappy, nor tired any more. Oh! If I could only know whether he is living or dead—whether I shall ever have him again!"

The tears would come, and her eyes were all glistening as she looked into the face of her friend.

Mr. Brewer seemed absent, yet present; tender, yet ill at ease. The thought darted into her mind, "perhaps he knows more of my brother than I,"— it was so new a thing to see him perturbed.

"Have I ever told you anything of myself?" he asked, at length.

"Never."

Upon this he moved a chair close beside her, but so as not to meet her glance, and told the story of his life down to the present hour. It was told concisely, but all the prominent facts were there. Then changing his place, taking her cold hand, and looking into her eyes, he brought tears to them again, and blushes to her face, by the question,

"Will you trust me and love me?"

Jennie whispered—she couldn't find her voice.

"Will I? I always have."

When they had both found words for other sentences, and Jennie has been talking, Mr. Brewer exclaimed,

"Married! I never even loved before."

A slow step was heard on the staircase, a gentle rap at the door, and a pale young man entered.

"Jennie!" "Robert!"

And the maiden had another joy added to the sweetest bliss of life.

But Robert had come home to die—to die as the day dies, slowly receding to the other side of life.

He had brought the gold which he had spent his young life in earning for the two at home. One had no need of gold now; the other had no wish for it, but the dust was hers; and when the weeks had gone in which they had sweetened his receding with the breath of love, leaving him at last where flowers grown upon live stalks, and chains and clusters cut in snow marble, made his last home beautiful, it flowed from her own and her husband's hands in channels which gladdened many a poor girl's life, and made the sister and her other noble self happier for the joy of thus making his lost life bloom in many a relighted eye and rekindled cheek.

The Death of Colonel Thoureau

From the *Knickerbocker*

With the publication of "Dr. Brown: And How He Drowned His Cares" in the August 1861 issue of that venerable if financially foundering mainstay of urban style and sophisticated wit, New York's *Knickerbocker Magazine,* the eighteen-year-old Henry James made his first big literary splash. In September, again seizing the opportunity to reach a larger, more urbane audience than that which read the *Newport Mercury* (and again for no pay), he published a second story, unsigned, in the pages of the *"Knick"*: a story demonstrating more of the lively authorial imagination and cosmopolitan wit the magazine's editor, James Gilmore, demanded. It was titled "The Death of Colonel Thoureau."

While the treatment of the relationship between Colonel Thoureau and his wife, Emily, at the heart of the story again owes much to Swedenborg, particularly his *Conjugial Love* and its dicta regarding deceit in marriage, in narrative form and execution it smacks strongly of Edgar Allan Poe's "The Murders in the Rue Morgue," what with a bloody death by a razor slit across the throat, the question throughout as to who did it (and as to who knew what when it got done), clues that include a locked door and open window, virtually mystic analysis requiring skills in chess and mathematics, and the jailing of an innocent man before the case is purportedly truly solved. James's story also scrambles time, so that (melo)dramatically a significant, shocking revelatory detail remains hidden unto the last. So it is that what Poe, in his opening comment on "The Murders in the Rue Morgue," called "enigmas, conundrums, and hieroglyphics" accumulates to become the base for an apparently "preternatural" analysis and solution of the mystery. Indeed, the raw intuition brought to the District Attorney's analysis at the end effects a revelation so shocking that Emily Thoureau falls to the courtroom floor as she suffers a paralytic stroke. She thus fulfills the prophecy in her name, which has three meanings: "black," "spotted," and "stroke." Likewise, the villain Randall, who blackmails Emily with the shame of her blemished history, fulfills his. Randall means "wolf."

I AM A Northern man by birth; a lawyer by profession; and reside and have a tolerable practice in a Southern city, which must be nameless here, but which is not more than a thousand miles from Charleston, S.C.

So much of myself I have thought it proper to state, by way of introduction to the singular story I am about to relate.

Three years ago the present month of August, I found time to make a visit to the home of my childhood in Massachusetts. Sojourning some days in Boston, I was one day in the office of an old schoolmate and fellow graduate—Mr. Richards let us call him—a lawyer already of some note as a counsellor, and occupying the responsible position of confidential adviser to the most solid Life Insurance Company in New England's capital.

'You are just here in time,' said R. to me; 'I have a matter submitted to me, in which you can, perhaps, give me some information.'

Thereupon he proceeded to tell me that the Volcano Life Insurance Company had but that morning received a proposal for effecting an insurance upon the life of a Colonel Thoureau resident in the city of which I also was an inhabitant. The proposition had come directly to the Company in Boston, not, as usual, through their local agent. It was accompanied with the necessary medical and other certificates as to health, habits, etc.; and so far, was perfectly regular. The amount desired to be insured alone caused hesitation on the part of the Directors. Colonel T., who was already forty years of age, desired to secure to his legal heirs the sum of $25,000.

The Company, R. informed me in confidence, had recently sustained some severe losses by the unexpected demise of persons insured to considerable amounts. At least one of these deaths had excited suspicion of foul play on the part of claimants; and it was determined, while investigating the causes of past losses, to be extremely guarded in the future.

'Now, our correspondent is a townsman of yours: can you not give me some information concerning him?'

I knew Colonel T. by sight. He boarded at a hotel where I lived; and I had noticed him there chiefly on account of his partiality for a game of chess, and his generally quiet and unobtrusive manners. He was a moderately stout, hale-looking man, with slightly gray hair, erect carriage, and good complexion. This was all I could say of him; and this—so far as it went—looked quite favorable.

'When you return, I wish you would ascertain something of this gentleman for me. We shall hold his proposal under consideration for some weeks. The risk is too large to act precipitately.'

Two weeks thereafter I was back in my office. I lost no time in making such quiet inquiries among my friends concerning Colonel T. as I thought would elicit the information desired by R. I could learn, however, but very little. In fact, there seemed but little to be known. The Colonel—so I was told—was a Louisianian, of French descent. He had been a planter, but some years before, for what reason no one knew, sold out his plantation and negroes, and removed to New York, where he spent a winter, and then removed to his present place of residence. He had brought his wife with him; but during the first year of their residence here, they had disagreed, and separated in a very quiet way. For the last three and a half years the Colonel had lived alone in a quiet but pleasant part of the city, occupying the first floor of a small house, having but one hired servant, an old negro woman, who was lodged in the attic; and taking his meals, as I before mentioned, at an hotel in the neighborhood. In his habits he was reputed simple and regular. He made much use of cold and shower baths; played at chess more or less every day, and was somewhat curiously given to mathematical studies. He had no regular employment, but was a gentleman of leisure. As for his means of subsistence, no one could give me any information. Only, that his income was sure and sufficient, seemed certain from the fact that his wife lived handsomely, at the other extreme of the town, and there appeared to be no debts. I ought to have mentioned before that they had no children.

All this seemed satisfactory, and I lost no time in communicating these details to my friend R. in Boston.

To my surprise, the Directory did not find them so full as I had thought. Their local agent, a young legal friend of mine, received directions to communicate with me on the subject, with the request that I lend my aid to its farther elucidation. It was thought especially desirable to ascertain something about the actual pecuniary circumstances, and the family affairs of the Colonel.

I counselled Millard, the agent, to put these remaining questions frankly at once to Colonel T. himself. He did so, and received for reply that his wife was his only heir, that though unfortunately separated from her, he desired to provide for her in case of his sudden death; that his property was so tied up, that though it would keep him and her while he lived, it might not serve her after death. All this was communicated to Willard with such an air of frankness and honesty, that he was induced to counsel the Directory to close with the proposal; and when the resident physician of the Company, Dr. Evarts, had again instituted a most careful examination of the Colonel's physical condition, and pronounced also a favorable opinion, the Directory in Boston no longer hesitated, but sent on the necessary documents; and on presentation of the insurance policy, Colonel T. at once handed over the amount of the premium and other charges.

It was quite natural that, having had so much to do with this affair, Colonel T., the chief party in it, should have henceforth more interest in my eyes than hitherto. In fact, my curiosity had been excited—as much by what had not been ascertained concerning the man, as by what had—and when we met, as we did daily, either after dinner in the reading room of our hotel, or in the evening on the promenade, I looked curiously at the somewhat inscrutable face, and sought—but vainly—to cast some momentary glance into the soul which I was soon convinced used these features to conceal rather than to display the emotions by which it was stirred. I am a man of regular habits myself—a bachelor—and Colonel T. soon became, so to speak, a part of my daily life. I looked for him in his usual haunts each day, and was at rest if he were there—or felt uneasy if, perchance, my eye did not rest upon his manly figure during my evening walk; or if his quiet corner on the hotel verandah was without him.

As for the Colonel himself, he exchanged but few words with any one. Every body knew him—by sight, that is—and so he passed current in our society. He seemed essentially a solitary man. Not misanthropic, but simply solitary. And this, at least, was so plainly written upon his face, that he was not troubled by social appeals on the part of those among whom he moved, but was left to pursue his pleasures unmolested.

To be sure, once in a while some newcomer among us would ask, 'Who is Colonel T.?' and we, shrugging our shoulders, would repeat the question, by way of answer, and ourselves wonder who he was. But then, he dressed well, was civil to every body, and was evidently a man of the world; and one soon loses curiosity about people who have no striking peculiarity to distinguish them from the mass.

Yet I could not help watching the Colonel. And so much did my interest in him increase, by reason of his taciturnity, I suppose, that I finally determined at all hazards to approach him and seek his acquaintance. It was already late in autumn, when I proceeded one afternoon, as usual, on my daily promenade, thinking that when I meet the object of my speculations, I would make some occasion for addressing him. But he was not there.

In vain I walked and looked. I walked on, and had already contin-ued my promenade much farther along the seashore than I had intended, when I was suddenly made aware, by a few big premoni-tory drops, that a rain cloud was about to burst overhead. I had on light summer clothing, and, fearful of taking cold, looked hastily about for a shelter. At a little distance, I saw an unfinished house, and within its walls I found shelter from the rain, which soon began to pour down in right earnest. The clouds had shortened the twilight, and it was now quite dark.

Presently I became aware that I was not the only occupant of the shelter. I heard voices, seemingly at but a little distance. I was enabled to distinguish two; both bass, but one evidently belonging to a young man, the other, the deeper and energetic tones of an older man.

The rain ceased as suddenly as it had begun. As I was preparing to step forth from my place of shelter, the owners of the voices approached. I stepped back involuntarily, when the tones of the elder struck my ear familiarly.

'You have all, now?' asked he.

'Yes, all,' was the answer of the younger, in a somewhat excited tone.

'And you recollect your oath?'

'Yes, Sir; you may depend upon me.'

'Neither sooner nor later; let nothing prevent you. You know the house. You will surely go.'

'Punctually, Sir.'

'Well, you may remain now, and let me pass on in advance. Remember your reward. Good-bye till tonight.'

'Till tonight; I will not forget, Sir.'

The steps approached the doorway near which I had taken shelter. I stepped back silently, and peered out at the speaker, who walked swiftly by. As he passed, the sky brightened a little and I beheld—certainly, and beyond the shadow of a doubt—my mysterious friend, the Colonel. He walked at speed; and ere I had recovered from my surprise, was lost to sight in the gloom.

Singular, thought I, as I walked along homeward. It was certainly the Colonel. But what was he doing here? And who was the young person whom he adjured to 'remember his oath'? And what about tonight?

The next morning I was sitting in my private office, busily studying up an important case, for which I had to prepare the papers, when I heard my copyist denying admittance to some one who evidently desired to see me. I recognized the voice of my friend W., the insurance agent, and willing to be excused even from him, listened to hear him go downstairs again.

'I *must* see him,' said he. 'It is important to me. Just announce my name; and say I will not stay more than five minutes.'

I flung open my door, and greeted W., saying that business of pressing importance forced me to deny myself to every body for some hours.

'But what is the matter? You look agitated.'

'Why, yes,' said he; 'it is a misfortune, so to speak. You remember Colonel T.?'

'Certainly; what of him,' said I quickly—remembering also the incident of the previous evening.

'He is dead. He was found dead in bed this morning—his throat cut. I have just seen the corpse.'

He continued, after a pause: 'You can see how unpleasant this is for me, when you bear in mind the large risk taken on his life, and that it was at my advice it was taken.'

I still stared him in the face in vacant surprise. The news was so unexpected.

'Tell me,' said I, 'how it was.'

'The negro woman who took care of the Colonel's rooms, had gone as usual about nine o'clock to clear them up for the day. She had found the outer door fastened; had knocked repeatedly, and, not receiving any answer, had informed her master, who lived near by. A locksmith was called to open the door, and behold a tragedy! In the inner room they had found the Colonel lying upon the bed, dead, and in a pool of blood.'

'In what condition were the rooms?'

'The inner communicating doors were wide open. The windows of the sleeping apartment were open, they opened upon the street. The furniture was in perfect order. The Colonel's gold watch and purse lay upon a toilet stand near the head of the bed. There was some disarrangement of the bedclothes, but not much—apparently the result of the struggles of the death agony. Aside from this, no article of apparel or furniture in the room seemed in the slightest degree disarranged. Life had evidently fled some hours ago. The corpse of the unhappy man was stiff and cold. A razor lay on the floor, at the bedside, as though it had fallen out of his hands.'

'And no sign of outside violence?' I asked.

'Not the least. Clearly a case of suicide; and I am not going to let our Company suffer for such a rascally proceeding,' said the irate Willard, who evidently regarded the deceased Colonel as one who had designs upon the coffers of the Volcano Life Insurance Company.

'Of course the coroner has the matter in hand?'

'Yes.'

'Well, telegraph immediately to Boston,' said I, after momentary consideration. 'In two hours I will meet you at Colonel T.'s rooms.'

When I arrived upon the scene of the tragedy, Dr. Davis, the coroner, had already impannelled a jury, and examined the other residents of the house. My head full of the strange colloquy to which I had been an unwilling listener the previous evening, and mystified by this far more than any of the others, I listened eagerly to the evidence.

The ground floor of the house was occupied as a dry goods store. Its owner slept elsewhere. The floor above the Colonel's apartments was rented by an invalid with her servant. The attic was occupied by the negro woman who attended the Colonel's rooms, and by a negro laundress.

The lock of the outer door of the Colonel's apartments had not been tampered with. The key was found under the pillow, in the bed. The window, as before mentioned, was found open; but a close scrutiny of the wall, outside and in, and of the windowsill, revealed no marks of unlawful entrance.

On the floor lay the mystery! From the bed-side, where a little pool of blood had gathered on the floor, to the door, *and one step beyond, on the outside of the room,* there were the tracks of a human foot! *tracked in blood!* Only once was the impression of the whole foot given; the other tracks were as of one walking on his toes. All were of a bare foot.

The dead man's feet were bare, but they were bloodless. Moreover, on comparing, his foot was not quite so large as that which had made the track. So said one of the persons who measured. But the doctor, who examined all very carefully, was of opinion that the Colonel's bare and living foot would have left just such a track.

So far, those present were about equally divided between the two suppositions: *murder* and *suicide.*

'Why should he be murdered? He was not robbed,' said one jury-man to another.

'Why should he commit suicide; and why go out of the door after he had cut his throat; and how get back?' was asked in answer.

Several persons were now examined. A night watchman deposed to seeing a light in the Colonel's room till about ten o'clock the previous night.

The lady who resided above, had heard, between two and three o'clock in the morning, a noise as of one hastily throwing open a door, in the Colonel's room.

The woman servant of the invalid lady had seen the Colonel going upstairs to his room about nine the previous evening. She noticed no change from his usual appearance, but thought he walked slower than in general.

The laundress, being interrogated, stated that she was awakened about three o'clock, by a noise as of a door or window being opened. That, having to go early to work, she presently arose, dressed, and sallied out into the street. That she found the street-door simply latched—not locked—though the key hung up upon its usual hook upon the back of the door. Finally, that as she emerged into the street, she saw a man stooping down, on the other side of the street. Hearing her step, he got up hurriedly, but slowly walked away. Owing to the darkness, she could not distinguish his features; but he was short, stout, and dressed loosely, somewhat like a sailor.

Just at this stage of the proceedings, a carriage stopped before the house. 'Here is Mrs. T.,' said Doctor Davis.

She had been sent for. As she was ushered into the sitting room, the Doctor advanced to meet her; the rest of us remained in the adjoining room. I looked through the door crack, and beheld a slender form, a face showing traces of suffering, but also traces of a beauty now in its decline.

After some words of respectful condolence upon the sad occasion which drew her hither, the coroner proceeded to ask her some questions as to the deceased.

'How long is it, Madam, since you last saw your husband?'

Her tears fell fast, and a heavy sob interrupted her as she essayed to answer—at last:

'I have not spoken to him for nearly four years,' said she in a voice still broken with emotion.

'Would you like to see him?'

She was led into the next room, and there left alone with the corpse. She sank upon her knees at the bedside, yet without touching the corpse, and wept silently, her whole body heaving convulsively with the violence of her grief.

When she returned, the coroner again interrogated her.

'Was your husband given to fits of melancholy, Madam?'

'No, Sir.'

'Were his circumstances embarrassed?'

'So far as I know they were not, Sir.'

'Did he ever speak of committing suicide, in your hearing?'

She buried her face in her hands, and trembled in silent agony, for a while, ere she could answer, with much hesitation: 'He did, Sir; but only once.'

'I told you so,' whispered the suicidal juryman, to his murderous fellow.

'Will you explain the occasion of that, Madam?'

After consideration, the lady looked up with a somewhat stern, composed face, and said calmly: 'No, Sir, I would rather not. It has nothing—' and then stopped abruptly.

There was a little consultation among the lawyers and the coroner and the latter asked again:

'I am sorry to put the question, but it is necessary, Madam: do you know any circumstance which would elucidate the mystery of your husband's death?'

Again she covered her face with her hands, and wept and trembled in that dreadful agony of spirit which seemed to seize her, but when she could speak, answered with a tolerably clear voice, and certainly a truthful look: 'No, Sir, I know nothing.'

'We shall not need you more for the present, Madam,' said the coroner presently.

The lady retired, casting a last and seemingly almost despairing look of sorrow toward the corpse, and even making a step toward the bed, as though she would catch the hand of the deceased in hers. But she refrained.

The waitress was recalled, and asked if she missed any accustomed object about the room. She said no. The fireplace, which was protected by a tight-fitting screen, was exposed. There was no mark of an extraordinary advent or exit in this direction. Finally, I related what had occurred to me the preceding evening. My statement, as may be readily conceived, excited the liveliest attention. But it had no real bearing upon the mystery of the Colonel's death. I could not even depose certainly that it was the Colonel I saw. And if it was he, the circumstances by no means cleared up the case. It rather complicated it. The more we heard the deeper the mystery became. The jury agreed to suspend their verdict; indeed, they were so divided between suicide and murder, and there were so many floating theories and suppositions, that a verdict was an impossibility. The coroner thought it a case of suicide. Willard, the agent, thought it a complicated case of conspiracy to defraud his company, and desired to have Mrs. T. arrested as a leader of the plot. The jurymen were wise, as all jurymen are. But whatever they guessed, they knew so little that, as I have said, they finally agreed to suspend the verdict and await the possible developments of the day. Meantime, the papers of the deceased were being looked over. Every thing was in apple-pie order, as a fruitseller on the jury observed. But they shed no light upon the mystery. There was no will found; of silver, ready money and jewelry, there was absolutely scarce a trace. This was astonishing in one of the Colonel's habits and means. Willard remarked that it strengthened him in the belief that the man had committed suicide with felonious intents upon the Volcano; while a keen-scented juryman thought he smelled a robbery, perhaps a murder.

We were about to retire, when entered a gentleman who claimed to be a friend of the deceased, and whom I recognized immediately as a person with whom he sometimes played chess. Captain Snyder, so he gave his name, appeared astonished and grieved at the sudden death, but could give no information. He had just received a note from Mrs. T., asking him to attend on her part to the obsequies, etc., and now offered to take charge of any thing not in the hands of the authorities.

'By the way, Doctor,' he remarked to the coroner, as were going out, I would like very much to have a remembrance of my deceased friend. If the effects are sold, I desire to purchase for myself a set of silver chessmen, with the help of which he and I have passed so many pleasant hours, and also I would like to have a St. George's sovereign, which my friend used to carry in his pocket as a pocket piece.'

'You say there was a set of silver chessmen?'

'Yes, you will probably find them in this little table. You see the top is thrown over in this way'—performing the action—'and you have then a chessboard. But the chessmen are not here!'

Nor were they to be found. Nor was the St. George's sovereign any where to be discovered.

Here was evidence of a robbery!

The Captain assured us that he had played at chess with his deceased friend on Tuesday morning, that is, two days preceding the night in which he died.

This discovery gave a new turn to the affair. If robbed, why, then, there was either murder or a most strange coincidence between an accident and a crime. At any rate, there was now something to be traced up, and a prospect of arriving, by the discovery of the lost property, at some clue to the singular complication. A description of the missing articles was at once made out and sent to the police, who were requested to make earnest search in pawnbrokers' shops and other localities for them. The room of the Colonel's waitress was searched, but ineffectually, and the honest negress shed tears at thought that she was suspected of having robbed a master who had always treated her with kindness.

The police gained no clue to the lost articles. It became highly probable that the thief had melted up the valuable silver chess set. As for the sovereign, it might circulate unsuspected, and might possibly have gone through many hands without being remarked. For in so considerable a seaport, foreign coins excite but little attention; and the only peculiarity of this sovereign was one so far common that a dozen like it might be in circulation in the city at the same time. It was, namely, a coin of the last century, having upon one of its sides a device of St. George and the Dragon, whereas sovereigns of a later date bear a bust of the reigning sovereign instead. The old sovereigns are worth some cents more than the newer ones, and have consequently been nearly all called in or melted up. Yet are they not so scarce that the possession of one of these old coins could be called remarkable.

More than two weeks passed without a clue to the mystery; the matter was already dropped from the papers; and as neither Mrs. T. nor any one else had laid claim to the insurance, Willard was more than ever convinced that the deceased Colonel was a rascal, when one day a new development really promised, or half promised, a denouement. The wife of the chief of police, settling a grocery bill, received in change for a bill an English sovereign. On handing the change to her husband in the evening, he at once perceived that this sovereign was of the identical coinage with that which had so mysteriously disappeared from the Colonel's pocket. He immediately made inquiries of the owner of the grocery store, and succeeded in tracing the coin to the possession of a small dealer near the waterside. This man stated that he received it some days ago, perhaps ten, perhaps more, of a man whom he did not know, but who was dressed as a common seaman. He had purchased an article of clothing from the general assortment, had received his purchase and the required small change, and was gone—whither no one knew. The dealer described his person, but the description was little worth as a clue.

A few days thereafter, however, happening into this small dealer's shop, an individual was pointed out to the chief, quietly, as the one who had paid out the sovereign.

'You are sure?' asked he of the dealer.

'Yes, Sir, I remember him very well.'

The man was about going out. The official approached him, and placing his hand upon his shoulder, said: 'Where did you stow the silver chess-men and the money you stole at Colonel T.'s house?'

The man turned pale, trembled violently, and finally when he had partially recovered his self-possession, vehemently protested entire ignorance of that with which he was charged. He even denied all knowledge of the sovereign he was said to have paid out; but afterward admitted that part of the charge against him, alleging that in his fear at so unexpected an accusation he had been led to deny every thing; and that his embarrassment was the result only of utter innocence of the evil with which he was charged. He gave himself out to be a ship's carpenter, out of employment; had been in the city but a few weeks, having travelled overland from New Orleans, where he found it difficult to procure employment; had lived at eating-houses, and slept in different places while in the city, having no regular stopping place; had no friends to vouch for his character, which he violently maintained to be irreproachable, and begged with tears that he might be let go. Though the suspicions were slight, he was locked up;

and it was determined to examine him thoroughly the next day. Pending which, I was curious enough to call and see him, in company with Willard, who wanted to talk to him. The prisoner's voice seemed strangely familiar to me, but I could not remember having ever seen him before. But being informed that I was a lawyer, he insisted upon my 'taking care of him to-morrow,' as he termed it, and begged this so piteously, that, not believing him to have any concern with the Colonel's death, I consented. He assured me of his innocence of the slightest wrong, and repeated the story told already to the Chief.

The examination came on. The lodging-house keeper where George Gordon (this was the name of the prisoner) had slept deposed that he saw him to his room at about eleven o'clock on the night in question, and that he came down from his room to breakfast about seven the next morning. The prisoner maintained that he had not quitted the room in the intervening period. The testimony of the laundress pointed to the hour of two as that when the robbery most likely took place. The District Attorney being called upon, was unable to prove even that the suspicious coin which had caused the prisoner's arrest, was the identical one owned by the Colonel. Strangely enough Captain S., the witness whose testimony was most necessary to identify this coin, was missing. When inquiry was made for him, it appeared that he had suddenly left town, for New Orleans apparently, but even of this no reliable information could be obtained. When the District Attorney mentioned the unaccountable absence of Captain S., the prisoner's face brightened up, and he leaned over the dock and whispered to me: 'They will have to clear me now. They can bring no proof against my alibi.'

The lodging-house keeper was recalled. He was sure that it was eleven o'clock, perhaps a little later, when the prisoner came up. He (the prisoner) had originally maintained that he was in bed by ten.

'Where were you before eleven?' the District Attorney asked. 'It was quite possible that this robbery should be committed at an early hour of the evening.'

'You need not answer this question if it will criminate you,' said I to him, by way of caution.

'Will I certainly be discharged if I can give a satisfactory account of myself for the earlier hours of the evening?' he asked me eagerly.

I said, as matters looked then, it was almost certain.

'Then,' said he, with a sudden resolve, 'I will tell you. I was at Mrs. Thoureau's house!'

'At Mrs. Thoureau's, the widow of the deceased?' said I, looking aghast. The whole court was electrified at the announcement.

'If you will send for the lady she will doubtless bear witness to the fact.'

Mrs. T. was immediately sent for. Meantime, my client, in answer to interrogations from the Court, stated that he had been employed in the house of Mrs. T. to repair and polish some pieces of furniture; that the lady had learned something of his poverty, and had kindly given him good advice and means to supply his most pressing necessities, and that on that evening he had called there to get some money due him, and had remained until his return to his lodgings.

Mrs. T. was announced. She corroborated the story of the prisoner in every particular.

'One more question, Mrs. T.,' said the District Attorney. 'Have you never, perchance, in the prisoner's presence, made any allusion to the circumstances and mode of life of your deceased husband?'

'Never, Sir.'

'Do you know if the prisoner was acquainted with Col. T., and familiar with his location and habits?'

'On the contrary, I know that he did not know Col. T., and I don't think he ever saw him.'

There was a silence of a minute's duration. The prisoner looked hopeful. The District Attorney, who had for some minutes been studying first the face of Mrs. T., and then that of the prisoner, turned suddenly upon the former, and asked, 'What relation does George Gordon, the prisoner, bear to you, Madam?'

The face of the witness flushed up for a moment, then grew ashy pale. She essayed to speak, but her lips moved without producing any sound. She grasped the table for support, then sank lifeless to the floor. The fainting woman was quickly borne into the fresh air. A physician was called. He ordered her to be conveyed to her home, and pronounced her to be attacked with paralysis. Her presence in court was therefore impossible.

'It was not certain, even, that the poor lady would survive the night through,' said the physician, hastening away after his patient.

'My mother! My poor mother! I killed you!' cried out the prisoner, wringing his hands with anguish, and losing at last all self-control.

His mother? Here was a new complication.

The session of court was adjourned; the prisoner was remanded to his cell. We who had become interested in the case were more puzzled than ever. Was Mrs. Col. T. concerned in the crime which seemed to have been committed? She looked too honest to be aught else than an honest woman. Beside, had she not denied all claim to the estate of the deceased? And yet—

The first news I heard when I arose the following morning, was that my client, the prisoner, had made his escape the previous night, disguised in the garments of one of the jailer's assistants, whom he had overpowered when he was locking him in for the night. The escape was not known until some hours after, and I may as well mention here that the poor fellow concealed himself on board a vessel just sailing for Curaçoa, and successfully evaded pursuit. He left a note for me, which was slipped under my office door during the night. In this he promised a full account of his share in the mysterious transaction as soon as possible, making at the same time most solemn asseverations of his entire innocence of the supposed murder, and stating that he never knew Col. T. as such, or by any other name, having only on two occasions accidentally met him, one of those being on the evening of the rain. Hence I recollected his voice.

Two days thereafter we were agreeably surprised at the reappearance of the missing Captain Snyder. From him was now obtained finally an explanation of the mystery which had so long excited the attention of the few who knew of it. I will give the Captain's account in as few words as possible:

Mrs. Thoureau was the daughter of a Louisiana planter. She was educated at a Northern boarding school. Being of a romantic temperament, at the age of seventeen, she fell in love with an individual who occupied in the institution in which she found a home, the post of instructor in rhetoric. This man was possessed of a showy figure and considerable personal grace, but was at the same time entirely devoid of principle. Seeing the artless young girl's infatuation, he pretended to return her affection. The result of the amour was a child, born but a month before its mother was to leave her school for home. Her shame was known to but three persons—the seducer, who fled when the fruits of his crime became apparent, and the two maiden ladies who owned and carried on the school. Alarmed at the consequences to their establishment should Emily's misfortune become known, they aided her in concealing her shame, and when she was safely delivered of a male child, provided a home for that in a distant farmhouse, where its origin would not be inquired into so long as the means for its support were forthcoming. The poor mother asked vainly for her infant. It was only upon her solemn promise never to seek for it any manner, that the two maiden principals of the academy consented to preserve inviolate the secret of her shame.

When fully recovered, she returned to her Southern home. Here, after five years spent in quiet repentance and the exemplary performance of the real duties of life—for the young girl had sinned through weakness, not for love of sin—she met Col. Thoureau. There was a mutual attraction. He saw in her quiet, grave but kindly demeanor and the conscientious rectitude of all her actions the embodied ideal of his soul. She found in the frank, noble gentleman all those real qualities whose sham semblance had deceived her young heart to so fatal an error. Fancy her anguish when the Colonel spoke his love, and asked her to return it. Her eyes brightened for a moment, but in the next appeared before her mind's eye her sin and shame, and with tears and sobs she hurried unanswering from the presence of her lover.

Could she tell him all? Him who had loved her as a being all purity and innocence. And yet dared she wed herself to any one, keeping to herself that dread secret which drove happiness away from her? What bitter struggles, what vain resolves, what tears and prayers were hers it were vain to attempt to tell. Suffice it that, submitting to her lover's persistent entreaties, she became his—but without that frank confession of her single error, which might have made her a happy woman, and would certainly have made her an honest one.

The marriage was a happy one. Emily—now Mrs. Col. T.—had been informed that the fruit of her error had disappeared—was probably dead. Her seducer was a wandering profligate, living in a distant part of the country. Was she not safe? She thought so; and ventured to enjoy a few years of truest bliss. Her father died. Her mother was long since dead. Of brothers or sisters, she had none. Her husband was all to her, and she devoted herself to his happiness.

Who knows the abyss upon whose brink he stands? Emily's seducer, ever going downhill on the broad road of vice, was mastered by necessities which must be supplied at all hazards. He applied by letter to his former victim, coolly stating his needs, and desiring relief at her hands. The wretched lady was forced to parley with the villain, and from her own means satisfy his demands, vainly hoping and entreating that she might be left in peace.

Vain hope it was! So good an opportunity for spoils was not to be given up. Again and again she submitted to his demands, enforced by threats of exposure. And when at last, rendered desperate by the growing audacity of the villain, she refused to hold farther communication with him, there came one day, directed to her husband, a package of old letters and tokens, which proved but too clearly the guilt which the sender alleged.

At this time the happy pair were residing in our city, whither Mrs. T. had induced her husband to move, in the vain hope of eluding the clutches of the villain who was torturing her. The Colonel, who tenderly loved his wife, compromised with the quondam Professor on such terms as were likely to insure his future silence, then made separate provision for his wife, and thus they parted, both unhappy.

Anxious to secure from want the woman whom he still loved, the Colonel had finally hit upon the expedient of insuring his life, determined while he lived to have her comfort looked after, and by securing her a sum after his death, to place her beyond necessities of any kind. He effected the insurance in good faith. But a month thereafter he was once more made unhappy by a threatening letter from the brute who had destroyed his peace. This affected him much. He wrote to the wretch—who shall be nameless here—and by dint of a considerable sum of money, gained from him a written obligation to leave America, never to return. But to complete the Colonel's distress, the sum he had payed his persecutor was spent at the gambling-table, and the miscreant now refused to depart without an additional subsidy.

Meantime, Emily's son had grown up to be a stout young man. He was apprenticed to a steamboat builder, on one of the Western rivers. His foster mother died, and on her deathbed revealed to him the secret of his birth, and the place of residence of his mother. Animated by a desire to see her to whom he owed his life, he raked together his little means and at once proceeded to C——. He called upon Mrs. T., and upon telling the poor lady his story, was received by her with a joy and love which he little expected. Both felt the necessity of preserving the secret bond existing between them; and the poor mother never, even to her son, revealed those particulars of her life, which we have but just glanced at. He thought her a widow; and little suspected that her husband lived in the same city with her.

Now, on his first coming to the city, (he had actually come around by ship from New Orleans, instead of overland, as he asserted on his trial,) he had fallen among thieves, and was robbed and nearly murdered by a part of his former shipmates. Col. T. coming up just as he was about to be overcome by his assailants, had dispersed these and taken the poor lad home to dress his bruises, little suspecting the tragic connection of their fates.

'A few days thereafter,' continued Captain Snyder, who, I must admit, proved himself an acute and courageous man on this occasion, and who had brought all parts of this strange story together, 'Jeremiah Randall, the Professor before mentioned, made another demand upon Colonel Thoureau. He was desperate. So was the poor Colonel. He had seen a considerable part of his fortune slip into this miscreant's hands, to be wasted in all manner of low dissipation. He lived in abject terror of this fellow's indiscretions. Many a time must the poor hunted Colonel have thought longingly of the gallows which was waiting for this 'Professor,' and through all it seems certain that the good gentleman loved with his whole heart his unfortunate wife. If only he had had the wisdom to own this love, to take her to his bosom, and to fly with her out of reach of this defamer! But it was not to be so.

'What I am now about to relate,' continued Captain Snyder, 'I have literally choked out of the infernal rascal whom I caught so snugly in Poydras Street, New Orleans, and who is now lodged in the tightest cell in our prison. Blast him! I did not want to forestall the hangman, or my hands would have held him till his wind was gone!' And the Captain showed a hand which I should not like to feel at my throat. 'You must know, then, that my poor friend appointed a meeting for that fatal Thursday night, when he and the 'Professor' were to have a final settlement. As the hour was a late one, he sent to the 'Professor' the key of the house and a duplicate night-key, and at eleven Randall came up silently and found the Colonel waiting for him. He says the Colonel cursed him, which I can believe; and threatened his life, which is a cowardly lie; and that while they talked, suddenly there was a scuffle, in which he got Thoureau down. That then he (Randall) felt that blood was about to be spilled. He looked for a pistol and did not see one. He had only a piece of stout packing-twine in his pocket, and he owned to me, the infernal scoundrel!' hissed Snyder in our horrified ear, 'that he tied the Colonel's feet as he held him down, then his arms, gagged him, and then laying him upon the bed, deliberately cut his throat with his own razor! After which he took three hours of moonlight to arrange the room, whose general disposition he knew well, for he had received money there frequently, and then he went out barefooted. But taking a last look at his victim, now lying upon the bed, his feet got inadvertently into the pool of blood, and hence the tracks, which ceased at the outside of the door, where he first discovered them. And the coward did not dare to return to the room after the door was once closed behind him to erase these fatal tracks.'

'And the negro laundress saw him putting on his shoes on the other side of the street, as she came out of the street-door?' I queried.

'Exactly,' said Snyder. 'Poor Mrs. Thoureau, whom I have known and respected for a long time, called for me after the Colonel's burial, and with many tears, told me not only her own sad story, but also her suspicions as to the author of her husband's death. She put me upon the track to find him, and I scarce slept till I had him before a revolver, with part of a confession upon his cowardly lips. Thank the Devil! they hang people for murder in this State. If they didn't, I should have killed this brute myself.'

And that was the solution of a mystery which had puzzled us all a good deal.

Professor Jeremiah Randall was hanged. I saw him swing. I shall never go to see another man hanged. It is too horrid.

Poor Mrs. Thoureau lingered on for a few weeks, but her system, enfeebled by much mental distress, finally succumbed to paralysis, and she died before Randall was hung. Her ill-fated son I have never seen since. Three days ago I received a note inclosing a hundred dollars, and a few words, saying: 'Once you defended me when I had no friends. Many thanks.' This brought the story to my mind which is told above. Names and dates are somewhat altered, but for the rest, any lawyer of ten years' standing, in our district, will tell you of the remarkable murder of Colonel Thoureau.

The Story of a Ribbon Bow

From *Arthur's Home Magazine,* signed "Mademoiselle Caprice"

Arthur's Home Journal, a popular no-frills publication, catered to an audience that pretty much valued straight talk and plain points. With its high-mannered characters both in word and deed making a virtue of temperance, "The Story of a Ribbon Bow" more than apparently fit the *Arthur's* bill. Yet Mademoiselle Caprice, under whose signature Leslie Walter, or Henry James, published this story, is up to more than that in this amazingly sophisticated piece of writing. Indeed, the plain point as to the deleterious effects of wine-drinking is mostly incidental to the author's real imaginative concern.

Mademoiselle Caprice's neatly measured tale hinges, notably, on a caprice—that of the belle Agnes Clair, who has chosen to wear a blue gown to a ball honoring the dashing Captain Frank Wilton and his volunteer corps. In lively dialogue charged with verbal wit and subtleties, that blue gown is first seen as a complement to Frank's military blue, then compared to the colors medieval ladies wore to honor their knights, and finally, furthering the allusion to knightly romance, viewed as a cause for tokens and missions—and pledges of abstention that prove to be declarations of love.

※

THE MEXICAN WAR was the absorbing theme of every tongue; its conquests or failures, the first thought of every mind; its ultimate success the first hope of every heart, at the time of which I write. The crisis was rapidly approaching, and all over the Union the excitement had enlisted, in their country's cause, troops of eager volunteers, who hurried to reach the scene of action before the glory of the national arms was forever tarnished by some disastrous defeat.

Of these volunteer corps, none was more strong in numbers or courage than that which was about to depart from the little city of H——, in one of the central States. Its commander, Lieutenant Wilton, was a fine young officer from the regular army, who had been sent home disabled soon after the commencement of the war; but being once more restored to tolerable health by the tender care of his friends, had obtained leave to raise and equip a company, and return again to battle. Still pale and thin, from recent illness, he was untiring in energy and action till his command was completed, and better drilled than could have been expected in so short a time. They were mostly picked men, sons of good families, gentlemen by birth and education, who had caught the "war fever," and hastened to gratify it, by enlisting as privates, in an army where all could not be officers, as in the present one, and regardless of the loss that would be so deeply felt by the hearts they left at home.

The evening before their departure, the gallant volunteers were complimented by the citizens with a ball, which everything contributed to make a most brilliant affair. The sighing belles, so soon to lose their lovers, saw at least an opportunity of bidding them a tender farewell; and the brave wives, mothers and sisters of the band lent their presence to reanimate and strengthen each other for the trying scenes of the morrow; while the devoted volunteers, divided between admiration of their own courage and uniforms, and the sorrow of parting, were glad of an occasion to display the one, and stifle the other. Thus, with heavy hearts and smiling faces, the brilliant company assembled in the splendid rooms.

Perhaps the handsomest, certainly the most admired couple present, were Lieutenant Wilton and his partner in the first dance, Agnes Clair, who in right of her acknowledged belleship, and his constant preference, attracted universal attention. She was beautiful in a rich blue silk, evidently worn in complement to the blue uniforms of the soldiers, and trimmed with costly lace about the white arms and shoulders, with floating ribbons elsewhere; while from her shining brown hair dropped sprays of delicate flowers of the same hue, but not half so lovely as were her eyes. Perhaps some such whispered hint as this from her partner colored her clear cheeks and made her long lashes droop as she listened; or perhaps it was the more than admiration she read in the dark eyes of Frank Wilton—called "handsome Frank," by his regiment—whose tall, fine figure, black curls, Spanish complexion, and good gifts in the way of whiskers and moustache, to say nothing of his fascinating qualities, made him the despair of his rivals and the envy of his friends. Withal, his nature was too frank and free for vanity or self-love, and his fine social powers made him as attractive to gentlemen, as his elegant personage to ladies.

He was apparently, as yet, unspoiled by this position, save in one respect, unnoticed by any but the clear eyes of Agnes. It was she only, who observed how his society was sought by the most reckless and convivialof his acquaintances, how at all wine parties he was sure to be present, how his sinking energies and overtaxed strength were sustained by stimulants, how with a blush of shame he had once checked an associate for speaking in her presence of some revel, which he said was not a story fit for her ears; and how, after a ball supper, she dreaded to see his dark eyes brighten, and his pale cheeks glow with the inspiration and warmth of wine. All these things Agnes kept and pondered in her heart, for he had grown very dear to her, and she mourned in secret, not only for the danger of death to which he would be exposed in returning, but for the temptation sure to assail him there, which might bring what was worse—disgrace. In this sad parting hour, therefore, her heart was very heavy, and she was glad when the changes in the quadrille allowed them to remain idle and interchange a few words.

"I am glad to see that you wear our color, Agnes," he said; "was it in imitation of the ladies of olden time, who wore their knights' colors, when they sent them forth to battle?"

She could almost have fancied it, as she noted the chivalrous grace and noble bearing of her partner; but replied—

"Oh no, nothing so romantic; it was only a caprice of mine."

"A very charming caprice," he answered, "and a prettily paid compliment; you will see that it is gratefully received by us all."

"Oh pray, don't say so," she hastily interrupted, "indeed I hope no one but you will notice it. I thought only you—" she stopped and blushed, embarrassed at the unguarded half-admission.

The soldier smiled, well pleased; but a graver shade came upon his face as he marked her painful confusion, and he hastened to relieve her by saying,

"I am sorry you will not allow me to fancy that we are indeed true knights, taking leave of our liege ladies, whose beauty and interest shall secure victory to our banners, in battle. Really, this scene and occasion almost make me realize it, and I don't like to lose the idea in spite of your disclaimer."

"Believe it then," said Agnes, laughing at his earnestness, "and I will not attempt any further to prevent you.

"There needs only one thing to complete the illusion."

"And what is that?"

"The knight received a token from his ladylove, which he wore like a charm against the perils of battle; and also she laid upon him some behest which he devoted his life to fulfil. I have neither token nor mission, shall I receive them from you?"

She blushed slightly, for his gravity and the expression of his eyes as they sought hers gave his words far more importance than the trifling request warranted; but she skillfully concealed her agitation by bending to detach from her corsage one of the bows of blue ribbon with which it was ornamented. He kissed it, as he took it from her hand, and hid it in his breast.

"And now for the command?" he said, in a low voice.

Agnes grew grave with the remembrance of her solicitude for him, and its cause, and her oft-repeated wish for opportunity and courage to say what she ought. But now that the moment was come she faltered and wavered, fearful of losing what his eyes so sweetly told her she had won; hesitating before the risk of offending him, now, when he might thereby bear a bitter memory of her to his death. She flushed and paled alternately, under his searching, earnest look.

"If I might ask anything of you," she said, at last, "it would be, I am afraid, what would put to a heavy trial, not your courage and endurance, for those, I do not doubt, but your patience with me, and your friendship for me."

"Oh, Agnes, do you fear that anything you could say would lose them? Do not speak of requests, but believe that your lightest word is my law; and command me to do what you may, I will perform it; if only my life could be spent in serving you, how gladly would I lay it down!"

"Preserve it for my sake, then," she could have answered, and her beautiful eyes were bright with tears; but glancing about the circle to see if their romance of the ballroom was unheard, she perceived that a temporary pause in the music had been improved by others besides herself, and that the call to resume their places had broken up many an eager tête-à-tête like her own. Much relieved, she returned to the business of the quadrille, and when her partner relinquished her to his successor, could reply to him with tolerable self-possession as he murmured in her ear,

"Remember that I vow to obey you in everything you ask."

"No, no," she returned, interrupting him, "wait till you hear it, and don't pledge yourself to grant my first request."

He promised, looking anxiously into her face, and wondering that she dared not ask anything from him; then her hand being claimed by some one else, she left him, again the brilliant belle, whose soft eyes drooped, and whose sweet voice trembled only for *him*. Yet she could see that though her actual presence was removed he seemed still under the influence of her words, and moved dreamily through his part in the pageant of the evening, while his looks wandered constantly to that place in the room which was lighted by her presence; and where, surrounded by attentive admirers, or lightly dancing, she was equally the cynosure of all eyes as of his. They did not meet again till he came to claim the privilege of taking her in to supper, and a murmur of admiration followed the handsome pair as they passed.

Their place was near that of the most important citizens, the grave and reverent seignors who had given the compliment of the ball, and who, when their elderly appetite was somewhat appeased, began to call for wine, and settled themselves for a giving of toasts and other formulas. And now for Agnes the time of trial drew near, for the glasses blushed ruby-red, and the Mayor cleared his throat for that speech, in which, as all of H—— knew, he would propose success to the gallant young officer of the tenth volunteers, Lieutenant, now Captain Frank Wilton, and thereby inaugurate a series of toasts and glasses, to follow *ad infinitum.*

A negro waiter quietly filled the empty glass at Wilton's elbow, like a black, tempting demon, and Agnes, his white angel on the other side, laid her detaining hand lightly on his arm and made him bend his proud head to listen—

"Frank," she whispered, in a trembling voice, "would you obey me, if I asked you not to touch that wine?"

There was no answer, and she remained overwhelmed at her own audacity, silent and with downcast eyes, while the Mayor made his speech, which was shorter than could have been expected, and ended with the anticipated flourish. But if she could have looked up, she would have seen that Frank Wilton's regards were bent on her, instead of on his eulogizer, while his right hand was thrust in his breast where the ribbon lay.

The Mayor's speech met with great applause, and Captain Wilton's health was drunk with all the honors; it behoved him next to return thanks, which he did in a few well-chosen words, while Agnes dared not look up to read anger or aversion towards herself in that face, which had always been turned to her with an expression so different. "In conclusion," he said, "allow me to propose the health of the Mayor, whom I shall pledge, if he will permit me, in a glass of water, that being the beverage with which I intend to supply the place of wine in this campaign, as the best mode of securing the success he so kindly wishes me."

The company stared, and many young men, his boon companions, smiled, but the young Captain remained unmoved even when the jolly Mayor addressed him—

"What, no more wine, Frank?" said he.

"No more for me, sir" answered the young man, with a smile. "It is quite clear that if wine is too much for me, Mexicans will be, and I propose to do the country better service this time than before. I made my last disastrous campaign upon Madeira, and intend to try now what my success will be without it."

"Three cheers for Frank Wilton *without* the wine!" called out an enthusiastic youth in the back-ground, and the walls soon echoed to the "three-times-three" of the volunteers.

The long list of prepared toasts was quickly despatched, for the wine drinking was broken up for the evening; the soldiers followed the new example of their commander, and the old men were ashamed to be behind the young in temperance and sobriety. A few more moments of speech-making, mingled with sincere good wishes and touching farewells, and the company dispersed to return to the ball-room. One couple lingered last in the dark corridors on the way back, as the gentleman reverently lifted the little hand that lay on his arm to his lips, and said,

"Agnes, my life is likely to be a short one, but I wish it were long, that I might show you a long gratitude for this, the first token of a woman's interest in my course for good or evil, that I have had since my mother died."

His voice trembled and faltered as if tears were very near it, and there was an agitated pause, which she first broke.

"I thought you would be angry," she whispered.

"Angry with *you*? I hardly know how to thank you for your kindness; your words have opened my eyes; they showed me all at once, the dangerous path I was pursuing, which with heaven's help and yours, I will tread no more. For you will remember me in your prayers sometimes, Agnes?"

"Always, always," she answered, weeping.

"Tears for *me*, sweet guardian angel? I am not worthy them; but every drop, to my fancy, washes a stain away, so weep my memory clear! You can never know—heaven forbid that you should—the dangers, the temptations, the difficulties that beset a man in my place, for which there is no safeguard save the love of some pure woman, and how dare I ask for that? How dare I propose to a mind unstained with evil and a heart unconscious of guile, the task of guiding and guarding mine, so far different, so erring and so wrong? I dare not do so, Agnes, and I dare not peril your friendship by another word unless you give me leave."

There was a moment's silence, in which both hearts beat almost audibly.

"My follies have forfeited your esteem, I feel," he continued, after a brief struggle with the emotion that his voice betrayed, "but it shall be my future care to win it back, and then if I live I will strive for something dearer still; if I die I will bless you for your kindness till my death; I am a poor fellow, I know, to need such a reproof, yet from you I receive it gladly, since you could inflict no wound my love could not heal; and your words had but one pang for me, that they came in the name of friendship, and only that sweet womanly instinct of pity prompted you to save me."

"It was not friendship," she murmured.

"Not even friendship, but a common philanthropy," he muttered, in a sad and bitter tone; "you are right, and I deserve no such blessing; but it is the last drop in my cup of humiliation, and I never felt humility till I knew you, Agnes—to hear that just distinction drawn. Yet I beseech you by the love of my whole heart, and the devotion of my whole life, which are yours forever, valueless as they are, to recall the word, and let me carry that name of comfort with me when I go. Do not at least deny me your friendship!"

"Listen!" she said, looking up with wet eyes, but with a lovely smile that made her face brilliant through its tears, "listen, oh self-deceiver, and blind! it was not friendship, for I love you!"

He caught her in his arms and kissed the mouth that uttered those sweet words; then kneeling down, he vowed, "by that kiss whose touch upon my lips has made them sacred, I swear no wine shall ever pass them more! Now Agnes I may dare to love you!" and then they were happy.

They returned to the ball-room together in that sweet dream of happiness, to the music of which, not less than the Strauss waltzes, they slowly moved, and parted in the gray light of morning beneath the elms which shaded her father's house. That was an hour of anguish indeed, when they sundered so quickly their newly found ties, and at the command of fate, separated till years or death should reunite them. Yet that hour passed, as even the bitterest hours will, and the young officer marched away; the seal upon his lips, the token in his breast, to the battle grounds where his gallantry and courage won him so high a name in many a bloody action, while Agnes was left at home, like so many others, to wait, and watch, and weep, to tremble, fear, and rejoice alternately as the chances of war exposed or favored her beloved; but not like many others whose hearts and homes were desolate, alas! When the war was over—received him back into her arms one summer day, not unwounded or unchanged, but truer than steel to her and to his vow. And when, not long after, and as soon as the wounded bridegroom was able to go to church, a splendid wedding was celebrated there—the bride, in strange contrast to her rich and costly dress, her silvery silk and frostwork veil, and gleaming jewels, wore on her breast, all stained with the brave blood which made it now dearer to her than ever to her noble husband, in token of the love that had won him to virtue and to her, a faded ribbon bow!

A Summer Adventure

From the *Knickerbocker*, signed "O. Chickweed"

In a lightly humorous, almost breezy style, this nicely constructed and bittersweet tale of a summer romance revisits familiar Jamesian themes as it relates the infatuation of Orestes Chickweed, a none-too-sophisticated young city fellow, with the slender, elegant, socially adept Nannie H——, whose coquetry and fondness for all the opposite sex assign her to a certain lower order of Swedenborgian womanhood. Nor can the love of Orestes, the story's poor, pained narrator, redeem her, especially as it goes undeclared. Needless to say, for the story, according to *Knickerbocker* editor Gilmore's game rules, O. Chickweed and Henry James went unpaid.

O F COURSE I have a story to tell, else I should not be here. And yet I feel so unacquainted, and am so particularly bashful before you, gentle reader, I must say, that very large doubts rest on my mind, as to the most appropriate method of introducing myself. Shall I go back to that immensely early period of history, when my excellent ancestor, Timothy de Chikwede, attended the primary school, as a playmate and favorite of William the Conqueror? I say commencing there, shall I trace the line down to myself, telling you who were famous for good or evil in the Chickweed family, who were hanged, and who ought to have been, but by some hocus-pocus were not? And shall I honestly confess that, like many another 'old family,' owing to some one's carelessness in the matter of records, we are compelled to supply a few links from our imagination? Or shall I simply hand you my card, 'Mr. Orestes Chickweed,' 'Good Public,' and requesting said public to imagine me, hat in hand, very gracefully making my bow?

I think I'll try the latter. There is so little that is really reliable occurring nowadays, that if I tell you a long story on the first plan, I entertain serious doubts whether you would believe it. I judge you a good deal by myself. In fact, as you may have noticed, that mode of forming an opinion is quite prevalent in the world. So, as a general thing, when I hear people boasting of their 'ancient family,' I quietly close my lips, and execute an inward whistle.

But now you see by the second plan, being in possession of my card, you have only to send down to the Mercantile Agency of Messrs. Know 'em and Black 'em, and you will be supplied with an accurate (more or less) description of my financial standing, personal character, my age, whether I am married or not, and whether at the last Presidential election, I cast my vote for the excellent gentleman who now dwells in the White House, or threw it away on the late Mr. Bell, (politically late, I mean,) at least very possibly. I have noticed the agency clerks are very minute in their descriptions sometimes.

I can save you a great deal of trouble, I suppose, by saying—but hold, I'll go on with my story, and you can satisfy your curiosity, if you choose to go with me.

I may say this much, however. I am a junior partner in a hardware concern, downtown. If you wish to find us, I will say, our store is between Broadway and the East River; at the same time, below Canal Street. In fact, considerably so. Quite a walk, I may add. Last summer, quite early in June, I rose from a sickbed, where by reason of overexertion and exposure, while travelling westward, I had been a prisoner for rather more than a month, and thought I would go home to New England, recruit, and visit what few relations I could find.

Of course I stopped a day or two in Newport, but 't was too early to find any one there, and I was soon off for the North.

A few miles out of one of New England's best cities, I had several aunts, who lived together in a fine old place, in the village of Ashland. Thither I went, received a hearty greeting, after an absence of five years, and was soon sufficiently at home to see what changes had occurred since my previous visit. The village had increased greatly; and when I went to meeting of Sunday, I was surprised to find how very few people comparatively I could recognize, though I could not but feel gratified at the amount of attention bestowed upon myself.

Of course a vast amount of calling and tea-drinking followed. I evaded what I could, for I found myself entirely too weak for the incessant talking that was required of me; and a walk in the woods, with old Towser only to talk with, was undoubtedly much more for my physical benefit.

As I came home, just at dusk, one night, I found sitting on the doorstep, talking with my aunt Keziah, a young lady and gentleman, whom I found, by an introduction, to be Miss Nannie H——, and her brother Ned. I knew by the name that the family were rather newcomers, who occupied a fine house, about half a mile distant, and were reputedly wealthy. Only that very morning my aunt Keziah had said I should certainly like Miss Nannie. As for the young lady, it was hardly light enough for me to particularize, but I concluded she was pretty. Her figure was slender, and her features apparently good. Her voice was gentle and clear, her language elegant, and she seemed familiar with society. A very pleasant conversation was kept up, mostly by Miss H—— and myself, until my aunt Elizabeth, who had assumed my physical care, issued the most positive orders that we must come in out of the dampness.

It is 'a good thing' to have a careful aunt, especially in the country, where the night air is so chilly and damp. But still I hardly appreciated her kindness, I am afraid, that night, because it reminded our visitors that it was getting late, and I was consequently deprived of further intercourse with my fair friend that evening. But they left an invitation to tea, of course, which was duly honored, and our acquaintance and friendship progressed rapidly. My physical condition speedily improved under her gentle nursing, and my inventive mind was sorely taxed to keep my partners under the impression that my health still required a few weeks' delay.

Sweet Nannie! How well tonight thy bright face comes up before me! Thy clear blue eye I seem to see, looking affectionately up to mine. Thy gentle head is leaning on my shoulder, and I feel thy warm breath on my sunburnt cheek.

But I am getting ahead of my story. Day after day our friendship strengthened. Idler as I was, I learned that the H—— mansion was a pleasant place, and I was cordially welcomed there. I took interest in the old man's beautiful trees and flowers, the brother's youthful plans, and Nannie's kind mother I loved as my own. Nannie brought out her sketchbook, and taught me what she knew; and piece by piece, I believe we copied almost every thing on the estate. In turn I taught her the soft language of Italia, and told her all I could recall of that beautiful land; for a year of my life was passed there, and Rome was as familiar as the village where I was born.

I had not asked her to love me yet; I can hardly say why, for I felt almost certain of success.

I got back to my aunts' residence one night, from a day's sporting, and found a letter from old V——, (our senior partner,) which said that 'ma' (Mrs. V——) was tugging away at him to go to Newport; and he would be gratified, if I felt able, to have me return the next week. As I bestowed an inward malediction on the fashionable lady, the doorbell rang, and two young gentlemen of the village were ushered in, who announced themselves a committee from a party going down the harbor on a sailing and fishing excursion, on the second succeeding day, and would be very happy if Mr. Chickweed and Miss

H—— would accompany them. I am sure I blushed a little, as I heard this message, and I think my thanks and conditional acceptance must have been expressed in a rather stammering tone. How should they know I was interested in Nannie? But they find out things rapidly in the country. I expect Nannie's greyhound must have spread the news. No one else had seen me kiss her.

It was a beautiful summer morning, half an hour before sunrise, as our party, about fifty in number, and nearly equally divided, climbed into several large wagons, which were to take us the half-dozen miles that intervened between the village and the city. I am sure I tried to be generally agreeable; but without any special effort on my part, a seat was saved for me by the side of my dear little Nannie. Still we were all wide awake and very happy; and the ride was much too short that brought us to the pier, where our beautiful yacht, 'Gypsey,' was taking in provisions, ice, fishlines, and darkies, for our voyage.

After considerable delay, the 'Gypsey' cast off, and with a moderate breeze we went gently down the harbor, with the mainsail and jib set, the foresail being arranged to form an awning from the sun, under which tables were placed, and we ate a hearty breakfast. Meanwhile, the wind freshened, and breakfast done, we set the foresail, and our little bark dashed gallantly on.

The fishing ground was reached in good season, and a number of lines were dropped to the finny tribe below, inviting them on board to dinner. I fear some deception was practised, for in a brief season about thirty cod, haddock, and sculpins were on board, and exhibiting by their activity, that they hadn't quite seen the 'point of the thing,' in their hasty acceptance, and in fact rather regretted the same. But it was too late, and our sable cook listened to them with the most heartless indifference.

Finding ourselves drifting badly, and several of our party seasick, our vessel was headed for the shore of a small island, on the sheltered side of which a landing was effected, and we were allowed to run onshore while dinner was preparing.

A jolly lot we were around that table. Toasts and speeches and presentations were the order of the day, and all went 'merry as a marriage bell.' One young collegian, I remember, had two speeches to make: one in accepting a prize for his fayre lady, and one in presenting a prize to another. By one of those queer accidents that will sometimes occur, he ruined his whole reputation, by making the wrong speech first. And our commander, whose engagement to a young damsel was but of recent date, was, by 'a curious combination of circumstances,' as he said, compelled, by virtue of his office, to present a prize to his ladylove; and then, by virtue of his near relationship, to thank himself for it.

Once more aboard of our beautiful 'Gypsey,' the fresh breeze and long afternoon invited a sail a few miles further out. Our skipper reluctantly consented; and I confessed with my little experience in boating, that I feared we should find it too rough for our gentle passengers. Still, apprehending no real danger, and they urging so hard for a sail, I had not the heart to raise further objections. So on we went, toward the broad Atlantic.

A half hour brought us to rough water, with a vengeance—the wind increasing, and fully one third of the party were dreadfully sick. I kept Nannie on deck, and as many others as I could influence, and we got along bravely.

We were now within a mile, or a little less, perhaps, of the lighthouse, which had been our destination, and the vessel's head had been turned homeward. As we wore ship, the yacht careened a great deal, which, added to the confusion of the moment, fairly frightened our passengers, who were not very nautical, into the belief that we were all going to the bottom; and several who were standing near me lost their balance, and rolled down the deck. I sprang after, and helped them on their feet, but before I could return to my place a piercing scream told me some one was over-board. It was my darling Nannie. She had been talking with a gentleman near the stern of the vessel, and an unnoticed rope, rapidly tightened, had thrown them both overboard. Our little boat had been in tow, to which the gentleman caught in passing, and after being dragged nearly a mile, was picked up comparatively uninjured. The moment I heard the scream, feeling instinctively what had happened, I sprang over the taffrail, and by the merest good fortune, as

I now consider it, in a moment reached the object of my search. She would fain have clasped me instantly, to the destruction of both, but I managed to hold her at arm's length, and devoted my attention to keeping afloat, trusting shortly to be picked by our boat. But though the 'Gypsey' again wore and passed us twice, we drifted so rapidly as to be completely lost to them. My first thought was to try to swim toward the vessel, but finding the tide against me, I changed my course for the lighthouse, which I judged to be three quarters of a mile distant.

I am not a particularly strong swimmer. But the immense stake that depended upon my exertions seemed to give me superhuman strength. The wind and the tide helped a great deal, and my dear Nannie, after the first few moments of terrible fright, was able by my directions to assist us materially in keeping afloat. But the waves ran high over our heads, and in spite of my best efforts, one would occasionally completely submerge us. Still we made steady progress, I was rejoiced to see, as we frequently rose on a wave.

It may not have been a long journey, but it seemed terribly so. Little was said, for we felt that no breath could possibly be spared; and I could plainly see Nannie was becoming exhausted. I begged her to hold out a few moments longer, and she succeeded in doing so, until within a dozen yards of the shore. I supported her as well as I could, and in a moment we were thrown by the surf violently on the beach; but as I struck first, she escaped this disaster.

As the wave receded, I dragged my burden farther up, out of harm's way, and we were saved—at least from the watery grave that had threatened us. The lighthouse was on a small island, and I was soon pounding on the keeper's door for assistance, which was cordially and promptly rendered by the good man and his wife.

It seemed an age, that we worked over Nannie, but success crowned our efforts, and I retired to take some care of myself. On my way to another room, I passed a small mirror, and stopped a second to take a look at myself. I was very pale, and the blood was oozing from my head and shoulder, where I had been bruised in landing. My head began to swim, and I sank exhausted and senseless upon the floor.

When I became restored, I found the good people working hard over me; and I learned that Nannie had, under the influence of a gentle draught, fallen asleep, and was doing well. So, yielding to the motherly hands of the keeper's wife, I was soon asleep. Not soundly, for the storm raged fearfully that night, as three shipwrecks within sight told terribly in the morning. They were neither very near, and we could learn nothing about them.

To return to the 'Gypsey.' After cruising about longer than there was any hope of finding their lost passengers, (for indeed we were not seen at all after the first few moments,) the vessel was reluctantly turned homeward, where the sad tale of our drowning was rapidly-circulated—a touching account in the next evening paper reaching New York the next day, and old V—— came immediately on.

Meanwhile, we were prisoners at the lighthouse, for it stormed all the next day, which was Saturday, and we were both weak as children. Nor could any communication be had with the shore. Sabbath morning was bright and beautiful, though the waves ran high yet, and our passage was delayed until afternoon, as a matter of prudence.

I shall never forget that forenoon, as we sat there gazing upon the ocean, from whose perils we had so providentially escaped. My heart was full of gratitude. I had never yet told Nannie I loved her; nor could I bring myself to do it now. It seemed too much like taking advantage of an accident; and that under a moment of gratitude to me, she might be led to make a decision afterward to be regretted. Beside, we were not yet ashore, so I concluded I would say nothing until she was once more beneath her father's roof.

In the afternoon, the sea became tolerably calm, and bidding an affectionate good-bye to our kind hostess, we were carried ashore to a small village, by the keeper, where I succeeded in procuring a carriage, and we were soon on the way to Ashland. Little was said, but I felt very happy, as with one arm thrown around my darling, I held 'a soft white hand in mine.'

It was nearly nine o'clock when we drove up to my aunts' door. Didn't we create a sensation! Two aunts fainted on the spot; and the third hugged me first, and then Nannie, almost to strangulation. Nor was Towser wanting in his extravagant attentions.

A messenger was immediately dispatched to the H—— mansion, with a note telling of our safe arrival. The family carriage was immediately prepared, and I dispatched Nannie, in care of my aunt Elizabeth.

About midnight the household was aroused by the arrival of old V——, who learning of my safety, insisted on waking me up, to see if I was still alive. Dear old boy, rough but kindhearted, how much I owe to you, who for so many years have been to me a second father! He sat on the bed, and I told him my story.

'You shall stay here, and marry her at once,' said he.

'But I haven't asked her to have me yet.'

'Oh! well, she will of course.'

'But,' said I, 'Mrs V—— wants to go to Newport.'

'Mrs. V—— be hanged! She shan't interfere with this business,' said the excitable old man.

The next day we were all invited to tea at the H—— mansion. After which we wandered into the garden. I, of course, with Nannie on my arm. I was a good deal her senior, and I think she loved me as she would an elder brother. I told her I must leave immediately for home, but would come back before winter; and begged she would write me occasionally, in answer to my notes, which it was agreed would be written in Italian. I need scarcely say that this arrangement was with the consent of her father; only being loath to lose her yet, he begged there might be no engagement for the present. But as we parted that night, I could not help taking the sweetest kiss I can ever remember.

Three days more found me at work in the dingy old counting room, and such a parcel of work as I found accumulated! Still, before I touched it, I sent off my first note to Nannie. In good time it was answered very sweetly, and several dispatches were interchanged within a month, when, as the result of my ocean exposure, and incessant labor since, I was thrown into a high fever, and for six weeks was scarcely conscious.

The first thing almost I can recollect was my aunt Keziah, sitting at my bedside, with her everlasting knitting. What became of the immense number of stockings she must have finished in the course of her long and valuable life is a question which had often puzzled me. But there she sat, until I aroused her by an abrupt inquiry for Nannie. Simply saying Nannie was well, and I mustn't talk, she immediately left the room; nor on her return could I extract further information. The next morning, however, she brought me three letters from my darling. The first was sweet and good as ever. The second shorter, and mentioned a handsome young Alabamian, Captain Warren, a friend of her brother's, who was stopping with them. The third was very brief, written in English, regretting my sickness, and trusting I should soon be restored. The last letter was a fortnight old; so had she taken any pains to ascertain, she must have known I was too unwell to read letters.

But, as I afterward learned, that between not hearing from me, (from some queer delay, my aunts did not know I was sick for a fortnight after the attack,) and the assiduous attentions of the elegant and wealthy young Southerner, I was to all appearance forgotten. Nor had I had been out a week before I had positive news of their engagement, with the probability of an early marriage. My young friend, nothing but experience can make you realize the crushing pain of centring all your love on one object, and getting nothing in return. I felt discouraged, weary, sick. I spent my time devotedly in the store, and tried to work it off. But with poor—in fact, no—success. I was pale and emaciated. A foreign tour was urged, and I was half-inclined to go to Florence. I did not care to hear from Ashland now, and a letter from my aunt I carried unopened in my pocket for several days.

One morning, by invitation of my old friend Dr. Thornton, I met him at Taylor's, for a lunch, after which we took a cab for the British steamer, for my friend was outward bound.

As I came out of the Doctor' s stateroom, I heard a familiar voice, and in a moment Nannie and her husband were before me.

She started back instantly, and nearly fainted. But recovering herself, she extended her hand, and asked if I was to be a fellow passenger.

Angry as I was, I touched her hand with mine, and wishing her a pleasant voyage, hastily sprang ashore, a colder, sterner, sadder, and I trust wiser man.

And so we parted. A letter from Dr. Thornton yesterday, tells me the Warrens are at Florence, that the Captain is too fond of wine, and his sweet wife is losing the roses from her cheeks. The Doctor doesn't know how much I am interested, though he learned from Nannie on the voyage I am an old acquaintance.

As for myself, I am better; have gained appetite and strength, am devoted to the hardware line, and talk no longer of travelling. But I notice my face is pale yet, my lips set, as I look in the mirror. In my pocketbook are a couple of verses I cut from a daily journal, wrapped up with a bit of paper, on which is my name in Nannie' s handwriting:

'FIRST love will with the heart remain,
When its hopes are long gone by,
As frail rose-blossoms still retain
Their fragrance when they die;
And joy's first dream will haunt the mind,
With the scenes 'mid which they sprung,
As summer leaves the stems behind
On which spring's blossoms hung.

'I do not dare to call thee dear,
I've lost that right too long,
Yet once again I vex thine ear
With memory's idle song.
I felt a pride to speak they name,
But now that pride is gone,
And burning blushes speak my shame,
That thus I love thee on.'

My Guardian and I

From the *Knickerbocker,* signed "Anonymous"

It was a busy year, 1862. The declining *Knickerbocker* needed fiction, lots of it, and James obliged, ever without a fee. *Knickerbocker* editor James Gilmore had already published at no authorial fee a number of stories by the ambitious young James, like his surprisingly fine "Dr. Brown: And How He Drowned His Cares" and "The Death of Colonel Thoureau," which would have made even Mr. Poe sit up and take notice. Under the same terms, Gilmore continued to accept whatever tales—and they were largely undistinguished and slight, if sweet enough—the always-productive sometime storywriter and full-time Harvard Law School student submitted.There were any number of these, many of them unsigned, most of them hackneyed and slim both on character development and plot complications. "My Guardian and I," published in May 1862, is typical.

L IFE APPEARED VERY pleasant to me, Eleanor Warrenne, as I sat considering its different possibilities the morning after my return from school. It is apt to seem so to girls of eighteen, with a sufficiently pretty face, a sufficiently pretty fortune, and not a known care.

Left an orphan at eight years old, I had been ever since under the care of a maiden aunt, who came at my father's death to take care of little me, and the guardian he had appointed. This was a man a good deal younger than my father, but whose true and noble qualities outweighed the objection of youth some would have raised against Mark Anderson. Under my Aunt Lucy's immediate care and his occasional direction, I had quietly passed my childhood, and for the last two years had been at a large boarding school. I had as much education as girls with such experience usually acquire, a natural taste for drawing and music, and an 'inquiring mind.'

Reaching home at last, I found my aunt unchanged. She was of the kind whose soft brown hair never grows gray, whose mild blue eyes are undimmed by age, whose plump hands are always smooth and white, do what they may. I gave her an abbreviated account of my educational doings, delighted her heart with the beauties of the worsted and crochet-work I had brought her, gave a small sample of my musical skill, showed her the last shawl stitch—she had that weakness for fancywork that mild natures are given to—and asked for my guardian.

'He will be here tonight. He would not come last night, thinking you would be tired. A very worthy young man, my dear.'

'But I don't like worthy young men, as a general thing. They are generally stupid: as if nature couldn't make people good and smart at the same time.'

'Only wait until tonight. We should never allow ourselves to form rash opinions.'

Dear soul! She thought me a little girl still. That evening, neither late nor early, Mr. Anderson came. I had not seen him for a long time, and we had both of us changed. A tall, grand figure, such as gives the idea of strength and protection too. I was large myself, and appreciated size when I met it. And I had an idea of my own that great hearts were often found in corresponding bodies; that big souls were *not* always crowded into little forms.

Strong, clear cut features, dark hair, kind eyes; refined hands and feet. A man of thirty, looking his age.

'And is this the little girl I saw last? Have two years done all this?'

'And is this the grave guardian I remember with such awe? If I have grown old, you have grown young to meet me.'

'I have not retrograded much; it is you who have grown up to me. Eleanor, you are fine! If you are as honest as the little girl was, it will not hurt you to hear it.'

'I hope I have kept the good qualities of little Eleanor, and added innumerable ones in the grace that comes with growth.'

Before we had talked much longer, I decided that this guardian of mine was splendidly unlike most people. Not in the small way which affects eccentricity, mistaking it for strength, but in such ways as a strong mind might indulge in. Without seeming to question me, he yet drew from me all about my school life; and whatever his thoughts on its superficial history, he kept them to himself. Had he assumed the office of mentor, I would have hated him at once.

I have dwelt upon this evening because it was the commencement of an acquaintance which brought an influence upon my whole life.

Gradually I fell into the routine of the quiet home life whose domestic nature was so new to me. I had few young acquaintances, but my guardian brought his own to me, and I found he knew the best people. But I had more acquaintances than friends, knew many and loved few. For my guardian spoiled the rest to me by contrast. I read what he told me, I did as he wished: I was growing a truer and better woman. And I thought I liked him only as a wise friend.

It was some six months after my return home that the tranquil course of my days had an interruption most unexpected to me. Among the gentlemen of my acquaintance was one of whom, when I thought at all, it was that he was honest and good. Willard Harvey had scarcely shown me more attention than had others, but that little was delicate and respectful. Still I was greatly surprised when, escorting me from a party one night, he offered himself. I tried to tell him of my surprise, how I had never thought of him in that way, and all the rest that women say when they mean to refuse a man kindly.

'I know you have not thought of me so, but I have of you since I first knew you. It is long since you became so much to me that no one else was any thing. I never showed you before, but you are all the world to me, Eleanor Warrenne. I shall never care for any other woman as I have for you. I shall never marry, if I cannot marry you.'

His simple earnestness touched me. I believed every word the man said, and asked for time to answer him. I asked my guardian the next time I saw him, what to do. I was not prepared for the effect on him.

'Eleanor! Eleanor! You do not love him or you would not have asked me that. If you had, you would have felt at his first word that you must be his wife and no other's. And if, not loving him like that, you marry him, it will be sin. But you do not love him; do you, Eleanor?'

There was passion in his voice, there was a strange light in his eyes as he leaned forward; there was a quiver of repressed strength in his hands that grasped mine. And I—I was blind!

'No, I think I do not love him. I have for him only respect and esteem that might ripen into love. I know him to be worthy in every respect.'

'That is not enough, be sure of it. Never trust to mere regard for happiness. It is starving. But I am not giving you the calm advice you asked for. I am forgetting myself.'

'Guardian, I shall not marry him.'

'Do not let me go away thinking that my selfish influence has kept you from what might have made you happy. I said what I did, believing you did not love him, and knowing that then you would be miserable.'

But I had resolved what to do. So Willard Harvey had his answer. It is long ago that all this happened. He never married, and I think all he said that night was true. But his trouble made him gentle, instead of hardening him, and he was always tender and chivalrous to women, perhaps for the sake of one of them.

After a time, it seemed to me my guardian changed. He was never less true and gentle, but he was often grave unto sadness; and one night, looking up suddenly at him in one of these moods, I caught his eyes full of a tender sadness.

'Oh! what is it?'I cried.'Tell me if you can, or if it is something I may not know, then be sure of my sympathy, the same as if I knew what I gave it for.'

'I cannot tell you now; but you must know it all too soon. You must have known there was something that was changing me so?'

'Ah! yes, I have seen it all the while. It has troubled me in troubling you. It is not any thing I have done?'

'You! GOD bless you, no. It is because you are so true and good to me, that this is the harder to bear. No wonder you do not understand me; how should you? Eleanor, don't look at me so, or I shall forget myself and what I have to do. When you recall this night afterward, think of me at my best, not as of late.'

I felt he was going from me, that great trouble was hanging over me.

'Stay with me! Only stay with me! Be indeed my guardian, as you always have been.'

'Guardian! What a guardian I have been to you! I know you will not soon forget me; but think of me as leniently as you can. And— GOD in heaven bless you, dearest Eleanor.'

One moment I was drawn to him, one kiss was on my mouth; then he put me down very tenderly and was gone. Gone! The thought was so bitter that I could not at first accept it. I said over and over in dreary repetition: 'He has gone! He has gone!'

Early next morning came a letter from him. It was dated at midnight of the night before, and it said:

> 'Since I left you, Eleanor, I have been trying to frame the words
> that will tell you what you must know. I could not have greater
> punishment than to write you now these lines. I have ruined

you! speculated away all your father left you in my care, in the vain hope of increasing it. Yet I meant it for the best; try to believe that. It is weak to leave you now, but I cannot stay and see you whom I have so wronged. I shall never come back unless I can make you full reparation. In happier days I had hoped for the blessing of telling you how dearly I loved you, and perhaps hearing a return from you. But when this trouble came, I said you should never know it from my lips. Pity me, who might have been so happy.

'I have directed a friend to help you settle your affairs. He is an honest man, and will do all he can for you.

Farewell, Eleanor.'

And was this the end of it all? Was I only to know his love with his loss? I never knew how much suffering I could endure till then. But I was young and strong, and the first shock over, I began to think of what to do. My aunt bore the announcement of our losses better than I had expected. With the help of Mr. Raymond—the friend my guardian had appointed—we obtained a clear statement of our affairs. There was nothing to expect from the lost property. We sold our dear old house, took quiet lodgings, and I commenced giving lessons in music and drawing.

I write now of a time three years after my guardian left us. In those years we had done well. My scholars had increased so as to support us comfortably; many people had been kind to us, foremost among them Mr. Raymond. If often and often my heart sank as I thought of him who was away, I tried to be as brave as he would have wished to have me.

One quiet afternoon Mr. Raymond came in. I saw by his face there was something for me to hear.

'I have news of your friend Mr. Anderson, Miss Warrenne.'

'Tell me at once, please!'

'He has come back. Do not be alarmed, but he is ill. He sent that word to me on his first arrival.When I went, I found him in a brain-fever. He is dangerously ill, but there is hope. Indeed, I would not deceive you, even to quiet you.'

And then—for I thought every moment lost that we were not near him—he took Aunt Lucy and me to his own house, whither he had had him carried at first. All the care that we could take of him we did. I pass over the detail of dreadful days, in which we could not tell if he would see the morning's sun. But GOD was very good to us, and spared him to our prayers. The first time he was conscious, I was sitting by him—and Aunt Lucy had left the room a moment.

'Eleanor! Is it really you?'

I leaned toward him.

'It is all like a dream. I can realize nothing but the happiness of seeing you again, myEleanor, my darling!'

'I have been with you in all your sickness, though you could not know me. I will never leave you again.'

'You forgive me? You love me then?'

'How dearly, my whole life shall show'.

After that, his recovery was rapid. It was springtime when this came to pass. We were married the next summer, and my life has been summer ever since.

Breach of Promise of Marriage

From *Peterson's Magazine,* signed "Mademoiselle Caprice"
(later listed as Leslie Walter)

The title of this story sounds at if it was—and it may well have been—
the topic of a class at Harvard Law School, where James had recently
matriculated. More notable than the legalities introduced into the
story, though, are the psychological nuances in the portraits of the
playful coquette Belle Savage and her smart but quite smitten beau,
Ned Vernon, and the marked fluidity of James's prose style—or
Fanny Caprice's, or Leslie Walter's. Published in *Peterson's Magazine*
in November 1862 under the name of Mademoiselle Caprice (a nom
de plume James used in *Arthur's Home Magazine* and the *Continental
Monthly* as well), this story also appeared in the list of author credits
for the February 1863 *Knickerbocker* publication, unsigned, of "The
Sprite Transformed," a story that would later be attributed to Leslie
Walter. Over a period of approximately ten years, forty stories would
appear, under Leslie Walter's signature in all of the aforementioned
periodicals as well as in *Lady's Friend* and *Frank Leslie's Lady's
Magazine.* Some are fairly long and evidence a Jamesian flair; some
are nondescript. Others repeat James's favorite themes and point

toward the accomplishment of his first novel, *Watch and Ward*, published under his own name in 1871.

꙲

"THERE WAS NOT a single young man in church today," said Miss Belle Savage to my wife.

She spoke complainingly, as if her just dues had been withheld; and, indeed, I never see a beautiful creature of her kind, a graceful, agile, polished, perfect, dangerous, young coquette, without paying it that hasty deference the East Indians pay to the spotted sovereigns of the jungle, and casting about immediately among my friends and neighbors for a desirable offering that shall leave my own household gods unharmed. The pretty, sprightly feline, whom we pet and pamper at our firesides, unsheaths her velvet-covered claws and seizes her unwitting prey; her sleek and splendid sister of the woods softly steals upon the traveler and bears him away to her distant den, to be munched at her leisure; and a certain type of the adorable sex, graceful, subtle, brilliant, caressing, soothes and steals her way to the guarded avenues of your heart, and, once getting that fragile organ into her velvet hands, mangles and tears it with the barbs of steel, and leaves the bleeding remnants to go in search of a fresh victim.

So with all due deference, and not intending any personal or pointed application of the above irrelevant remarks, (my wife, Caroline, says my remarks are always irrelevant,) it seemed to me very natural that Miss Belle Savage—I think it should be written Sauvage—should feel aggrieved at the deficiencies of our locality in material for her favorite amusement, and complain of the dearth of young men, her natural victims; and I immediately began turning over in my mind the names of all the families in the neighborhood, with whom we had exchanged cards, to see if among them there could be found any desirable young person of my own sex, who would be likely to accept an invitation to come to Birdsnest Cottage and be devoured.

I was proceeding rather awkwardly to remind our fair guest, that, among the inducements held out to her to visit Birdsnest, young men were not specified; and in default of any more suitable subject, to recommend myself, when my Caroline interrupted me, as she usually has the good sense to do, when I am about to say anything particularly silly, by observing,

"Well, certainly, Belle, I should have thought your memory would have been a little longer, and the recollection of the agreeable flirtation you began this morning might have lasted till you got home." My wife's tones were rather sharp, and her manner was slightly acid; the two young ladies had been school friends in youth, and occasionally renewed the remembrance of those early days by playful "spats" and skirmishes. "Would you believe it, John," she added, dragging me into the conversation to my great discomfort, "that ungrateful darling had the nicest little adventure in church this morning? I would have given my eyes for it—before I was married, of course—and she takes no more account of it, I suppose, than the fact that she dropped her handkerchief."

"And did a fairy prince in disguise pick it up?" said I.

"Something very like it. Your friend, Ned Vernon, blushing like a rose."

I winced. The arrow had struck near home. My dear Vernon, my kind, brave, chivalrous young friend, the truest heart, the noblest mind, the purest soul—why, in the name of Queen Hecate, and all sorceresses and witches, must he have gone to church on this particular morning, to hear old Bishop Slocum, whom I know he detests, and to meet his fate in this superb creature, losing his heart in the meshes of her glistening lashes and the maze of her glossy hair? Why didn't he stick to the Litany and refuse to look up, as he read, "From all crafts and assaults of the devil, Good Lord deliver us!"

"Perhaps he thought it was *your* handkerchief," I suggested, feebly, addressing Caroline.

"Then he must have thought I married under a false name," retorted my wife, inexorably, "for it was written plainly enough in the corner; and I am sure he never took his eyes off the lettering, except to look at Belle's face to see if she corresponded to the title."

"And yet she didn't see him?" I said, satirically.

"How could I when he was behind me?" retorted the saucy beauty. She sat before us, swaying from side to side on the piano stool, her gorgeous painted muslin dress, a parterre of glowing tulips and roses on a black ground, fluttering like a gay butterfly in the breeze, and falling away, with stiff flutings of rich black lace, from the perfect arms and neck. I don't know that I use the technical terms properly in describing her dress, Mrs. Smith always assures me that I know nothing about ladies' fashions; but I am sure I can describe her, as she sat there, fair, calm, and roseate, her clear eyes brightening, and her scarlet lips smiling with the pleasing excitement of the subject. One little careless hand (there was witchery in every tapered nail and every dimpled knuckle) lay indolently pendant from the black keys, and her musing glance, beneath the drooping eyelash, followed the motion of the fairy finger, from which had lately flashed a splendid jewel, young Midas's diamond engagement ring, now a brilliant trophy from a heart as hard. For the ring had been returned, and the lover rejected, and my prescient heart told me who next was to ascend its sacrificial steps.

My wife had gone to "fix" her hair, and we were alone. Should I stand idly by while another, and, oh! how much worthier victim, was offered up to the Moloch of her vanity on the altar of her pride? I resolved to speak.

"Miss Belle," said I, with a sickly attempt at jesting, "do you remember the old fable of the boys and the frogs, and 'What is fun to you is death to us?' May I hope you will lay aside your usual pastimes at Birdsnest?"

She looked at me steadily from under her long eyelashes, and a raven tint of color rose in her ivory cheeks; but I was not prepared for the clear, haughty tone in which at last she spoke.

"Will you please explain your meaning?"

"Simply this," I answered, with the energy of desperation. "My friend's heart is too noble to be idly won, too true to be lightly cast away, like those I have seen you trifle with—forgive me, my dear Miss Belle—in the city. There I own your triumphs deserved, your warfare just; but this is not a foe worthy of your steel, an ardent, generous, enthusiastic boy, with a soul *sans peur* and *sans reproche*, like that of the Chevalier Bayard, and a heart that provokes because it knows not evil."

"And what is this to me? What do you ask of me?" she demanded, in low, uneven tones.

"Not to break this noble heart; not to embitter this generous temper; not to blight his fresh, young life, and darken his brilliant future; not to destroy his grand ideal of womanhood, and use the power of beauty and fascination God gives you, to torture one of the noblest creatures he has formed!"

Hearing Mrs. Smith's footsteps approaching, I retreated, without waiting for an answer, sure that, with my usual discrimination, I had said exactly the wrong thing: and deriving little comfort from the reflection, so dear to well-meaning persons, that I had been "trying to do my duty," and was suffering in its cause.

Of course this ill-judged interference only precipitated matters, as such attempts are always sure to do; for when, on that very evening, Ned Vernon, looking even more handsome and elegant than usual, walked up "to consult me," as he said, on some trifling point of law that his clear brain could have settled, unaided, in five minutes, and I reluctantly presented our beautiful visitor, who had made her toilet on purpose, entering our secluded "smoking piazza" in triumph with my wife, just as I had made their excuses; Miss Savage, shining clear and fair from the mist of her snowy draperies, as the moon from veiling clouds, dawned on his sight a goddess, and reigned in his heart a queen, to fill and bless its waiting throne at once.

Poor boy! how he loved her! Sometimes railing at me, for my impertinent interference, sometimes at himself, for his preposterous folly, again at her inaccessible beauty and bewitching reserve. For Belle, in revenge for my advice, had entrenched herself in that factitious armor of coldness and indifference which appealed most surely to his pride and love, to his strong will and gallant courage, and dealt out shafts of icy hauteur that pierced his heart more surely than the most tender acts of kindness could have done, wounding and winning it every day. He laid aside the claims of his profession, to which, for years, he had been so devoted, and spent day after day of that sunny summer in the not less engrossing pursuit of winning a woman's heart. Wholly unskilled in this new science, his past experience of life and study availed him little now; and he entered on the laborious task Belle had set him, ignorant of its difficulties, but with a patience, sweetness, and humility that would have won any other woman at once. His strong, manly intellect was brought within the petty scope of hers; his brilliant talents were displayed for her pleasure as jewels are laid within the grasp of a spoiled child, unconscious of the treasures it toils and trifles with and idly flings away; his dominant, firm will, which I had never before seen subdued by fate, or fortune, or mortal power, bent like a duetile reed in her hands, and all the passion and pride of his nature were subject to her despotic sway. It was his first experience of the *grande passion*, and, like a ship without compass or pilot, he floated serenely on the smooth, treacherous sea of her favor, or tossed helplessly at the mercy of every tempest that rose in the sky. Carrie pitied him, and thought it hard that he should be sacrificed to the vanity of her coldhearted friend; but she dared not interfere, and I had found my counsel and advice but cavalierly received, and stood aloof, contenting myself with such occasional sarcasms and severities upon Miss Belle and her prey as I could not avoid, and gaining little favor from both. Time, wearing on, made my representations the more improbable, as her wounded self-love and vanity were comforted by the earnestness and ardor of his pursuit; and her innocence, in this affair, at least, completely vindicated to heretical eyes like mine. It was evident that Mr. Vernon's delusion was no fault of hers, and, this fact once fairly established, the chilling reserve of her manner disappeared like a dream, and a softer and sweeter sentiment took its place, greatly to the comfort of all. Our spirits rose to "concert pitch" again, and gayety and good humor ruled in the family councils. Pleasure-parties were projected and carried out; little schemes of amusement occupied our vacant minds; we went sailing, rowing, riding, driving, and walking; we had strolls by moonlight, music on the river, picnics in the woods; and, but for the haunting anxiety, continually postponed to an uncertain future, that sometimes oppressed three, at least, of the merry quartette, never was a gayer summer spent by four happier people.

I am bound to say that Miss Belle's conduct was perfect, and that, after the memorable change noted above, nothing but our previous knowledge of her character proved her a coquette. No schoolgirl, just from Corrine and Mrs. Hemans, could have seemed more artlessly tender and impassioned, more innocent and sincere. Ever varying but ever true, by turns a goddess and a child, a thoughtful woman and a happy girl, she was always beautiful, lovable, and loved. At times I almost shared in Vernon's infatuation and believed her in earnest, finding thereby a charm in the sunny days we were spending, when-the happiness of the two lovers recalled our own courtship, and restored us to the land of romance and enchantment in which they seemed to wander. Careless and gay as the birds and butterflies that loved and lived in the same sweet atmosphere, the two friends basked in the blissful sunshine, and floated through the idle happiness of the day; and we, admiring and unresisting, followed where they led. Whether we rode, and Belle, brilliant and majestic in her black habit and plumed hat, kept her graceful seat like a princess and emulated Vernon's perfect horsemanship; or whether we walked, she loitering on his arm through bloomy fields and fragrant lanes, talking in the sweetest, lowest cadence, romance suited to the place, and to the time; or whether we rowed out on the river, dipping white hands in the wake of the little boat, and shading dazzled eyes that spoke too plainly by the light of stars, joining with trembling voices in the refrain of the serenade; or whether we fished and flirted in the bright sunny morning, gay, saucy, and indifferent, the sunbeams glittering in the netted gold of her hair, lighting up her brilliant eyes, and flushing to deeper hue the coral of her lips and cheeks, while she held the quivering prey in her gentle grasp, and watched its unavailing struggle to escape from the tender mercies of her soft, white hands; whatever we did, Belle seemed natural, sincere, and loving.

Matters were in this pleasing state when old Mr. Mills from the city, who had been Vernon's faithful friend, and was adopted by us as uncle and general guardian, having helped us all many times in many ways, came out to pass a day with us, and find what had become of his young *protégé*, whose letters had almost ceased since his acquaintance with Belle began. Mr. Mills was a Friend and an old bachelor; in both capacities he disapproved of the gay coquette; and moreover, carried a life long wound in the kind heart that beat under his drab waistcoat, received from just such a fair and careless hand, thirty years before. He knew her well by sight and reputation, and his keen eyes lighted upon her from under his gray eyebrows, as he sat opposite her at our little dinnertable, and saw how her eyes drew Vernon as a lodestone draws steel.

"Thee finds it very pleasant here, I believe?" he said to Belle, in his harsh voice.

She started and colored guiltily, more at the look he gave her, than at the words accompanying it; but instantly recovering composure, responded with graceful indifference.

"Very pleasant, sir; my friends are most kind. I have passed the time delightfully."

"They have given thee their prettiest plaything to amuse thee?" he continued, glancing at the ardent boy.

"I do not understand you, sir."

"Thee will soon return to the city, perhaps?"

"Very soon, sir. I have many engagements to fulfill there."

"Thee has left many unfulfilled. Young Amory is expecting thee, his house is nearly ready for his bride; he believes that thee will abide in it."

Belle flushed and paled, but was speechless in her anger. The relentless old man went on quite coolly.

"John Midas is buying magnificent jewels; report says they are for thy wearing. Two of thy lovers have sailed away to Europe last week to forget thee; the rest await thy return. Thee had better go!"

"What does this mean?" cried Vernon, starting up as Belle began to sob and tremble in her chair, and I stood aghast at the scene at my quiet dinner table.

"It means," said Carrie, interposing with cool presence of mind, "that uncle will say disagreeable things; but he mustn't do it at my friend's expense, or before me. Mr. Vernon, don't notice it!" she continued, in a private whisper. "Belle, dear, it isn't your fault that you are pretty; and we all know that the old bachelors try to avenge the wrongs of the young ones."

Silence and tranquility being thus restored, the irate Friend remained quiet while he devoured his dessert, and then led the attack again.

"What does thee do to amuse theeself?" he demanded.

"We walk," said Carrie, laconically speaking for her friend, "and fish."

"With diamond baits, and pretty arts, and silken nets, eh! my dear?" said the irrepressible old gentleman. "I've seen such things before, and felt them, too. There's no wickeder or more cruel amusement in God's world, than that which inflicts suffering and pain on the creatures he has made."

Nobody answered this protest, and, when the ladies had left us, Mr. Mills turned suddenly about, on his young friend, and made his application.

"Does thee not see that she is playing with thee, eh! boy?"

The young man turned very pale, then his handsome face flushed deeply. He rose up, and went and leaned against the mantle, looking moodily down.

"I heard what she was doing," his mentor continued. "I knew what she could do. I came to try and save thee, if I can."

"From what, sir?"

"From misery thee knows nothing about," said the old gentleman, with tears on his frosty eyelashes. "From having thy heart torn and trampled by a heartless woman. From beginning the world broken in spirit and in hope as I did, by some fair Delilah of a girl, who forgets thee as soon as she has won away thy happiness and peace. I tell thee I have felt it all before."

"You mistake her, sir," returned Edward, in a low, earnest voice; "you do her great injustic in your opinion of her."

"I know her well," the Friend retorted, "better than thee can do. I know her ways and her class. I advise thee to leave this at once, unless she goes very soon. John, canst thee not make her quit thy house and return to her friends? She is too gay and wealthy for thy small means at best."

"I cannot send away a guest," said I. "And whatever may be my opinion of Belle's character for coquetry or insincerity, I will not prefer those charges against her under the shelter of my own house, or again allow any one else to insult her by doing so."

"Thee has a fine spirit, nephew John, and thee is right. I will not again become the girl's accuser. But, for my boy here, I want to save him from her arts, if I can. What does thee say, Edward?"

"I believe her to be sincere," said the young man, low and tenderly. "I believe that she loves me, and is true,"

"Foolish and blind! A score in yonder city believe as much, only they will suffer less from the pretty cheat, because they have less to lose. But thee, who hast heart, and mind, and soul, and sense, far, far beyond this butterfly's desert, will throw them all down idly at her feet, and despise the guardian who loved thee before she ever came in thy way!"

"I do love you, sir," said Edward, with tears in his beautiful eyes, "I do respect your advice; you have been my best friend in this world to this hour. But if you knew how deeply my heart was involved in this—"

"I *do* know," said the old man, with a groan.

"You would not ask me to throw away my only hope of happiness in life till I had proved it false. Leave me alone to ask her if she cares for me; let me be free to find if I am beloved or deceived, and I promise you then to do everything you wish, except to give her up if she is in earnest. If not, and you are right in your estimate of her character, nothing can wound or pain me further, and I will go or stay, live or die, as it please heaven and you; but I must know this first."

So after long argument and confused noise of battle, ending as it began, with Vernon's immovable decision, from the pain of which his old friend would have spared him if he could, Friend Ira Mills took the late train for the city, Vernon went silently and slowly home, and I returned to my Carrie, to inform her that a new and thrilling drama, which we hoped might be a version of "All's Well That Ends Well," or, at least, "Much Ado About Nothing," was to be enacted at Birdsnest Cottage, and that she and I, though not principal characters, were to play a part by no means subordinate, and be eaves-droppers like Benedick and Beatrice, but with less stake in the result. Carrie was less willing to play her part than I had expected, (are women more honorable than we have been used to think them, I wonder?) even though the happiness of both her friends was the reward of success, and the plot and plan mine, whom she was vowed to obey and believe infallible. "It was such nonsense, and cruel besides," she said, remorsefully, going to look at the unconscious Belle, who lay on the sofa in her dressing room, where she had cried herself to sleep with tears on the curved points of her long eyelashes, and her sweet lips sighing even in dreams. In spite of my own belief in the ephemeral nature of her emotions, I felt some of Carrie's misgivings; and, during her slumber, profound and deep as that of the Enchanted Beauty, we went softly and guiltily about the house, and sat, conspirator-like, talking in whispers in the quiet parlor when Vernon joined us.

At twilight she descended, gay as a bird and brilliant as a star, dressed with even more than usual taste and skill in some floating, fleecy robe of lucent white, with ribbon bows and streamers of faint, rosy shades on waist, and breast, and rounded arms. She was evidently dressed actress-like for the "occasion," which we all knew was now impending, and I looked at my young hero to see how he bore it. He was very pale, and his beautiful eyes followed hers with an expression of admiring doubt, which all her skill could hardly read, though she did her best to dispel it. She sang and played for us, her fairy hands lightly lying on the keys, as her ravishing voice rose and sank in Italian arias, German romances, and Spanish madrigals, softly passing at last to the old-fashioned English ballads we all love best, thrilling, quaint, and sweet; and here she seemed to forget our presence entirely, and with her golden head bent, her confessing eyes drooped before her lover's steadfast, inquiring gaze, murmured the melodies of the dear old words that have set so many hearts at rest. Then came "Allan Percy,"and the "Long, Long Weary Day," and as she sung—

Alas! If land or sea
Had parted him from me,
I should not now sad tears be weeping.

Mrs. Smith and I rose softly and disappeared from the room, quite unnoticed; and soon afterward the enamored pair, crossing the sheet of moonlight that lay before the glass doors, followed us, sauntering up and down the chestnut avenue in front of the house, and pausing at last before a row of rustic pillars, whose bases were of turf, and whose capital were roses, to remark on the beauty of the night.

"I wonder what has become of Mr. and Mrs. Smith," said the vibrant voice of Belle, but with some soft and sweet change, as I fancied, in its silver tones.

"They are not far off, I imagine," was her companion's reply.

Nor were we; for close aginst the luxuriant screen of roses, like a snake in the grass, I lay *perdu*, a reluctant, but intentional listener; and behind two spreading lilac bushes stood my wife, her head bent down, her arch eyes lifted, her warning finger held up to me, like a very statue of eavesdropping, both eagerly waiting for the words that were to break the charmed stillness around us, the only words whose utterance would not desecrate the beauty of the hour and the scene. Before us nestled the little fanciful cottage, with its tiny minarets, and lattices, and balconies, its curving roofs and wide verandahs, built in a sort of barbaric style, that was as much Moorish as anything; and quite incongruously, but picturesquely surrounded by the chestnuts, pines, and hardy creepers of our colder climate; behind us lay the sloping velvet lawn, bathed in a flood of silvery splendor, that transformed my stiff little summer-house into a fairy temple, and my wife's prim flowerbeds to enchanted gardens, whereof the white blossoms reflected, and the red absorbed the luster in which they lay. Interested, however, in nearer issues, we turned from the exquisite landscape to the trembling lovers near us, and waited for the spell of silence to be broken, by the dear old story that some human lips have been telling and answering every hour since the world began.

It came at last, and since Adam first whispered it to Eve, in the lovely solitude and stillness of Paradise, I think no voice could ever have repeated it in words so simple and sweet, in tones so courageous and so sad, that yet never faltered in the telling. My wife privily put her handkerchief to her eyes, and I stood abashed and self convicted, unworthy of success in my own wooings before love so deep and unselfish, affection so tender and true. How dared I, or any man of my stamp, ask and receive the heart of any innocent and loving girl, while this godlike nature wasted love and trust on a shallow and superficial shrine? I saw his handsome face, stern and pale in the moonlight, turn anxiously toward his fair companion as he ceased, and I certainly expected that the answer she faltered forth would unbend its fixed rigidity, soften its sculpturesque beauty; but I should never have anticipated the new form which coquetry took in the shape of Belle, as all trembling, flushing,weeping, she clung to her lover, and, with her beautiful face hidden against his own, sobbed out broken confessions, and made sweet promises in a way than he must have been more than mortal to resist. The marble firmness of his face relaxed and glowed with happiness: he took the sweet deceiver to his heart and impressed the seal of forgiveness on her pretty, penitent lips. Mrs. Smith's surprised eyes met mine, as the rapt pair went slowly down the walk, and she watched their mutual—yes, mutual— tenderness at parting with new and eager curiosity. A few moments later, the triumphant lover, with the steps of a conqueror, strode away from the little gate, and Belle floated past us, soft and slow, on her way to her own room; while Mrs. Smith and myself, after an elabo- rate stroll around the garden, locked the outer doors of Birdsnest Cottage and retired for the night.

The next morning our fair guest appeared rather subdued and quiet, and watched all day restlessly for a visitor who never came. Toward evening, however, he presented himself, pale and grim, at an unconscionably early hour, while we were sitting down to tea in fact, and, meeting Belle in the hall, openly kissed her on the cheek, like a husband of several years standing, to the boundless astonishment of Biddy bringing in the tray. She received it quietly enough with a soft blush and a pretty air of submission; but the little phrases of proper indignation and rebuke, that she had begun, died unfinished on her lips, as she caught sight of his stern, determined face; and, half bewil- dered and wholly frightened, she tried to withdraw her hand from the strong grasp in which he held it and brought her to us.

"This lady is my promised wife," said he, loudly. "Tell them so, Belle."

"Last night—" began Belle, in faint explanation, as she tried to droop her blushing face.

"Say whether it is the truth or not," he repeated, in tones of stern command, "that you promised to marry me last night?"

"Yes, I did," said she, desperately; "but—"

"You hear this young lady, Biddy?"

"Sure, sir, I do."

"And you understand that she then consented of her own free will to marry me?"

"Yes, sir; but—"

"I heard her last night," said my wife, composedly.

"And I also," said I, feebly supporting Mrs. Smith.

Belle lifted her drooping head proudly, and shot glances of fire at us. What did all this mean?

"Three very good witnesses," said the poor boy, magisterially, "absolutely invincible in a court of justice. On this hand," he continued, holding out the soft, little member, with a grim smile, "she wears a ring which I placed there in token of the bond or covenant of marriage between us. Your coachman, John, saw and heard me buy it with that intention. Is it so, John?"

"Yes, sur [*sic*]," responded the gruff tones of the invisible John.

"Another good and credible attestation," resumed Vernon, "and a proof that this ring was given and received in token of said compact between us. I summon you all as my witnesses, when needed, to repeat what you have said. Miss Belle," he added, turning on her a severe and searching gaze, beneath which her angry glance fell, "I have heard of many suitors whom you have at first accepted and afterward jilted and rejected; of bonds and rings worn awhile, then cast away; of vows made to be broken, promises never meant to be kept; of hearts first bent, then broken. But mine you will find of less malleable stuff, and I will not submit without a struggle to the fate of my predecessors. I now hold you to your solemn promise made in the presence of lawful witnesses, which renders you *de facto* and *de jure* my betrothed wife, and demand of you present acknowledgment and immediate fullfilment of that promise and of all your obligations to me, or offer you as the alternative the public arbitrament of my claims in a court of justice and a suit for breach of promise of marriage!"

He bowed to us all round, carried Belle's captive hand to his lips, relinquished it, and walked out of the house, followed by my wife's admiring glances.

His *fiancee* (by compulsion) turned on us like a tigress as he disappeared.

"This is your friendship!" she cried, fiercely, to Carrie, and "this your revenge, sir," to me. "I thank you both, and will remember the humiliation you have been the means of procuring me, as long as I live. I will neither eat nor sleep again under your roof, and shall leave it by the earliest morning train. I would quit it this instant, but for the additional publicity and disgrace. Oh! Carrie, how could you strike me such a blow?"

Trembling, weeping, and unnerved, but proud still, the stately Belle swept out of the room; my sympathetic wife, sobbing remorsefully, followed her; Biddy, with her apron to her eyes, withdrew to the back kitchen; and I, left alone, proceeded to fulfill my harder task of comforting the author of all this woe.

I found him distractedly pacing up and down after the manner of excited lovers, in a remote part of the garden, and accusing himself of every crime known on the docket of a grandjury. When I had argued him out of these hallucinations in respect to himself, he fell fiercely upon me, and proceeded to charge me with enormities which never dawned upon the modest ambition of Mr. John Smith; and when I had with some difficulty cleared myself from the guilt of these allegations, I had to listen to a rhapsody in behalf of Belle, whose character was depicted in such angelic colors as would have astonished even her, whose vanity I know to be boundless, and whose appetite for flattery has been largely gratified. Having spent the short summer night in these agreeable diversions, he grew calmer toward dawn, and we returned to the house, where I ensconced my victim in the cheerful company of some bottled adders, in the inner sanctum of my study, which is, in fact, a cabinet of natural curiosities and specimens of entomology, anatomy, zoology, etc., whose horrors my wife conceals with a set of red curtains—and, with his last solemn charge, "Smith, you've ruined me," gloomily sounding in my ears, went to inquire after my visitor.

Miss Savage was savage indeed; she had spent the night in pacing up and down her room like a wounded tigress, and had just called her maid and set her to packing her trunks. She sent down word that she should like to bid me goodby in the library, but utterly refused all intercourse with the heartbroken Carrie, who, being the most innocent of the parties implicated in the plot, was held most responsible for it, as is the way of the world. Having essayed in vain to comfort her in her disgrace, I left her accusing me of it all, and returned to my library to await the injured Belle.

In the gray of the morning she came, pale, worn, dejected, and wretched; a single night of watching and grief, the first she had ever known, had worked a startling change in her brilliant face. I softly closed the door behind her, and mutely offered a chair, which she was obliged to accept, for she was shaking like a leaf and could hardly stand.

"Mr. Smith," she said, steadying her trembling voice, "was this well done?"

"Was it ill done?" said I.

"It was," she cried, passionately; "you know it was. You and Carrie were the friends of years. Even if I deserved such humiliation, was it for your hand to strike the blow?"

"Was it mine that did strike?" I persisted.

She colored all over, her pale face glowed crimson from chin to forehead, and she hid it instinctively in her hands. I was struck with a new idea and boldly seized upon it.

"After all, my dear Miss Belle," said I, lightly and argumentatively, in pursuance of my experiment, "you cannot assume to regard my wife's share and my own in this absurd affair as anything but a foolish, practical joke. As such I assure you we considered it when we engaged in it: and if you can forgive the annoyance caused you, it will always be a source of gratulation to us, as we thereby discovered and exposed the real character of my friend Vernon."

"How?" she asked, in muffled tones, for her face was still hidden.

"His mercenary attempt on your hand," I gravely declared, "by which, of course, he intended to secure a share of your fortune in either case. He is a poor lawyer, and money tempts such men, you know."

"It was not his temptation," she quickly rejoined, "for, except through you, he could have no knowledge of my antecedents. I do not do you the injustice to suppose that you would be, knowingly, engaged in such a plot, and, unless you betrayed the fact of my fortune, there could be none."

I truly averred that I had not done so.

"Mr. Smith," said she, raising her sweet, serious face with a look of evident relief, "won't you be my friend? If I forgive your share in the pain and mortification I have suffered, and which I confess is deserved, won't you advise me what to do? Remember, I am an orphan, I have no real friends—I never meant to do wrong, but vanity led me astray, and I was not taught any better."

"Well!" said I, much moved by this frank confession.

"What shall I do? Ought I—should I submit to such demands?"

"Certainly not," I rejoined, promptly. "Give the fellow five hundred dollars and let him go."

"But—" she stammered, blushing deepest pink again, "do you think that would compensate him?"

"Whatever you please then," said I, musingly. "Of course it must be compromised somehow."

"Yes," said she, eagerly.

"And no doubt you would rather give a thousand dollars than—"

"It's not the money!" she cried, springing up with a gesture of impatience. "He might have it all, and welcome: I have often wished he had; and should be glad of any way to help him, poor struggling fellow!" I saw the red curtains of the cabinet move, and shook my fist at them privately to be still. "But is there no other way, Mr. Smith?"

"Yes," said I, "one other."

"And would you—have you ever known people submit to it?"

"Plenty of times!"

Dead silence fell between us for awhile.

"What is it?" she at last whispered, under her breath.

"Why, you might give him your whole fortune."

She turned to me, half-crying, half-laughing, pretty and petulant, but with great earnestness and impatience, and said, "I told you once before that he should have it in any case."

"Commend me to the tender mercies of the wicked!" I cried then.

"You, my cruel coquette, who so torment and trifle with your lovers and friends, are the most placable of enemies, and the most Christian of foes. What! You would give your whole fortune to a man," raising my voice for the benefit of the red curtains, "who has humiliated, mortified, and deceived you?"

"I deserved it," she murmured. "I had done it before to others—"

—"And threatened you with public disgrace, and ruin, or an alternative—"

—"I am going to take it," she faintly declared—

—"Which, of course, you scorn and despise?"

"No, I don't despise him!"

"Not despise him? What! Not despise such a selfish, heartless, mercenary, unfeeling—"

"He is *not*!" she passionately cried; "and you should be ashamed, Mr. Smith, so to traduce your friend, while I, who have every reason to hate him, am obliged to defend him against your aspersions."

"Well, why don't you hate him then?"I proposed, maliciously.

A long silence followed, during which the red curtains of my museum quivered with great violence and seemed about to fly asunder.

"Ah! Why not?" I persisted.

"Because, Mr. Smith, ('stupid!' under her breath,) because I happen to love him!"

A rush and a smash in the inner room, and I hastened to the rescue of a large glass jar of green snakes, which lay scattered upon the carpet, regardless of our excited lover flying past me, and of everything but the alcoholic fumes assailing my nose, and the bits of broken glass that set my hands bleeding. When at length I emerged, injured and innocent, from my profaned sanctuary, Belle was leaning, rosy and happy, against the broad shoulder of her enemy, and looking up into his softened and agitated face, with eyes full of tears and pride.

"Well, what has become of my two litigants in the threatened breach of promise case?" inquired I, carefully setting my plate, full of recovered snakes, on the table. "Where's the implacable plaintiff, the

Shylock who wanted his bond, the brigand of a lover, who literally-demanded your money or your life?"

"Here!" said Vernon, whose handsome face was illuminated with the morning sunshine, and with a dearer glow. "If the devotion of a life can win your pardon, Belle!"

"And where's the ferocious defendant, the cruel coquette, the manslayer, the destroyer of your peace, Vernon?" I pursued.

"Here!" said Belle, softly laying her pretty left hand in her lover's; "and this is the only ring I'll ever wear, believe me!"

"The court ought to begin," said I. "*Oyes, oyes!* Where's the crier?"

"Here!" said poor Carrie, putting in her tearstained face at the door, and receiving ample satisfaction therefor.

"And as I am both judge and advocate," said her husband, "I report the case settled byamicable adjustment of a compromise between the contending parties, and adjourn the court for breakfast."

People in Belle's circle in the city, when they received cards and cake, and went about gossiping over it, wondered exceedingly how Belle Savage, with all her advantages, and all her conquests, could ever be content to settle in that horrid place, with no society but those two stupid Smiths, and a poor young lawyer for a husband; when she might have done, as all the world knows, so much better!

But that was long ago, and many things have since occurred to give the "sacrifice" quite a different aspect. Friend Ira Mills, who has long since been reconciled to Vernon's lovely and loving wife, has declared his intention of devising his whole fortune between them and my wife; and as the sum is sufficiently large to raise even the stupid Smiths to a high pitch of popularity, what will it not do for the handsome Vernons? Then the "poor young lawyer" is a judge now, and an honorable; for he took his seat in Congress during the brilliant session of the winter before last, and his beautiful and fascinating wife was greatly admired among the critics of the capital. The French ambassador termed her *la belle des belles*, and compared her to the imperial Eugenie. The Spanish envoy employed all the prettiest epithets of his musical mother-tongue in describing her charms; and the stolid nobleman, who represents England at our republican court, is said to have pronounced, with enthusiasm unbecoming a Briton, that she is the most perfect specimen of the American woman he has yet seen. But with such admiration Belle's vanity would not now be satisfied without the sweeter incense of her husband's love and praise. Her beauty, her talents, her fortune, and her life, are all devoted to his service; and, if so, they aid andhonor him. She is content; for thus she keeps his heart, and strives no more to win the hearts of others.

Mrs. Smith and myself are well.

A Sealed Tear

From the *Knickerbocker*

Henry James's Civil War stories—notably among them "The Mystic Telegraph" (1862, *Knickerbocker;* unsigned), "A Sealed Tear" (1863, *Knickerbocker;* unsigned), "My Lost Darling" (1863, *Continental Monthly;* unsigned), "Ray Amyott" (1864, *Peterson's;* signed "Leslie Walter"), and "The Story of a Year" (1865, *Atlantic Monthly;* the first story to appear under James's own name)—share more than a topic or category. They also develop similar themes and follow a common pattern of dramatic action. The hero receives serious war wounds, and the heroine, bound to him by true love, finds him out and strives selflessly to nurse him back to well being, usually successfully. By temperament, the heroes in James's war stories are not unlike himself at the time: alert to political issues and critical of failures in Union strategy but neither eager to enlist themselves nor ashamed of their hesitance. So it is in "A Sealed Tear" that Rick Randall, who had resisted soldiering, has now chosen the path of "patriotism" and joined the military, though not without some drastic complications in his relationship with Maud

Hillton, or hers with him. Yet he will be doubly saved by her—first, in fiercest battle, by her tear, and then, in a hospital bed, by her love.

M AUD HILLTON SAT by the window that afternoon, bowed and motionless, with a letter crushed in her white hand, and a look of compassionate yearning on her whiter face; sat there for hours, with a strange dream-light in her mournful eyes, conscious of nothing external; sat there statuelike, frozen, apathetic, apparently, while a dire conflict raged within her. At last, there stole over her face a pallor of terrible anguish, her head drooped slowly, until her forehead pressed the sharp edge of the marble table: the battle was at its height—on the one side, love, forgiveness, happiness; on the other, pride, doubt, and parental reproaches. For a few moments the heartbeats in the girl's bosom convulsed her whole slight form, then there came from some unsounded depth of her being a great, agonizing sob, and then she lay there so still, so nearly breathless, that she seemed as one dead. But the battle was over, and pride had won the victory! you could see that when she lifted her head once more, for the very movement was queenlike. With deliberate icy calmness, she rose, crossed the room, brought back a little ebony writing desk, and sat down before it; then she smoothed out the crumpled letter, and read it over carefully, slowly, critically; then she wrote:

'RICK: You do not love me today, more than you did a year ago, when you decided that we were not fitted for life companions. I have prayed GOD to enable me to crush and conquer my love for you, and I believe HE has done it. I cannot see you, and the ring you took from my finger then *must not* be placed thereon again. I am glad that you are going to fight—it is noble, it is honorable—and I can ask our FATHER, with a sincere heart to watch

over and protect you. I shall think of you, for I shall always try
to be a real friend to you.

MAUD.'

There was no trembling in the hand that wrote, no shadow of
relenting in that calm pale face, as the perfumed note was enclosed
and superscribed—only once, as the tiny seal was descending, a single tear dropped from the long curved lashes, and became a part—the
soul?—of that plain initial 'M.' Ah! Captain Rick, when, with nervous fingers, you tear open this letter tomorrow, be tender with that
seal; don't bruise it; don't break it—for the heart of the only women
you ever loved, ever will love, is imprisoned within it.

POOR CAPTAIN RICK! the night-hours are fleeting away, the soft
haze and purpling shadows of yesterday are gone; there are black
shreds of clouds painting the sky with long inky streaks, and the sad
autumn wind wails desolately; there is storm in the air, and storm in
the soldier's heart, as he paces with quick strides up and down the
narrow limits of his tent. No battle here, no opposing forces, only
fierce, hot, scathing storm; and the proud, strong man bends before
it like a broken reed. 'Here is a *billet-doux* for you, old fellow,' his
lieutenant had said, 'laden with all the spicy odors of 'Araby the
Blest.' Love and war always! you're a lucky dog, and then he left
him with a light laugh. Rick sprang up from his camp-lounge, threw
his meerschaum across the tent, and seized the little delicate note
with a flush of impatient joy on his manly face. Her writing! her
seal! he pressed his lips to it, opened, and read. Do you think men
have no feeling, no heart? you should have seen this proud young
officer then; you should have seen his face pale, his lip quiver, his
hand drop nerveless to his side: you should have seen those appeal-
ing eyes raised to heaven, while the broken voice cried, piteously:
'GOD, be merciful to me!'

Then the storm burst upon him, and the gray of the early morning was filling his tent with its melancholy light, when he wrapped his cloak around him, and sank wearily upon his narrow couch.

He had sinned, and this was his punishment! and yet when, one year before, he had said to Maud Hillton that they two were unfitted for life companions, he had been honest, he had believed that he was doing a sad duty to her and to himself. For months, a nature naturally noble and true, had resisted the stirring appeals that came with every breath, for more men to fight in a cause, than which there could not be a nobler or better. He shrank from the trials and hardships of a soldier's life, from the horror and uncertainty of battle, as every man, born and reared in luxurious peace, must shrink; but, at last, the true nobility of his soul had risen above all this, and he enrolled himself as one of his country's defenders.

It was the last evening he was to spend at home, before he led the company he had recruited to the camp; every thing was settled, no business affairs troubled him: if he was killed! why, that would be all—would it not? He sat before the fire dreaming idly; suddenly there came a little gust of wind; the gaslight flickered; he started, and rose to shut the creaking door. Then he saw glittering on his finger a plain gold band, and sitting down again he drew it off slowly, and read the graven life's history inside: 'Rick to Maud.'

Ah! was every thing settled? was there nothing more to be done before he went away from these familiar scenes, perhaps—never to come back again? Again he relapsed into his thoughtful mood, but it was no idle dreaming now; he reviewed the past year, he remembered that he had been gay and happy, that he had been flattered and petted by many fair women; and yet, through it all, a pale quiet face, with glossy dark hair waving back from the white forehead, had haunted him—through it all, he had known that only [one] woman in the wide world could fill the vacant place in his heart, and that one he had cast off! Now, he was certain that he still loved that pale-browed girl, that he had always loved her, and with him, to decide was to act. 'Yes, it shall be done,' he said aloud, and then he wrote, telling her all—

how he had been mistaken, rash, wrong—how he still loved her, begging her to see him, and let him plead his own cause, begging her to wear again the ring that had no right on his finger. When he had finished, he was proudly happy, for he felt sure of success, and was conscious that he had done his duty. How that letter was received, how it was answered, we have seen.

ONE DAY THERE was a sharp, fierce battle, The ———— Massachusetts Regiment was in it, and came out decimated; Company A was a mere fragment, and its captain, it was feared, had received a mortal wound. He had fought with a splendid, reckless bravery; where the fray was thickest and hottest, there he was always in the van; at last, with his clenched hand pressed convulsively to his heart, he fell, and was borne away senseless, tenderly and reverently, as men bear heroes. When he awoke from what seemed a long, troubled dream, he found himself in a rude hospital, with a surgeon by his side, holding in one hand a bullet, and in the other a little morocco letter-case, gazing at them alternately, with a quizzical smile. Captain Rick Randall looked at him with questioning eyes, and feebly reached out his hand. 'A pretty narrow escape for you, my brave fellow,' said the surgeon; 'here is a bullet which was evidently intent on exploring your heart—fortunately on its way, it met with an obstacle in the shape of this pocketbook, and lost so much of its energy in penetrating it, that it was turned aside a little, and stopped short of its destination; the result is, that your pocketbook has a clean-cut round hole through it, and that you have a continuation of said aperture uncomfortably near your heart. However, my dear fellow, jesting aside, although you are badly wounded, there is no danger, if you are properly attended: I must try and find a good nurse for you.'

Poor Captain Rick! and he had really hoped to die! He opened the letter-case, as the kind surgeon hurried away, and there, within it, lay a tiny perfumed note, pierced through its centre; he held it up before his eyes with a melancholy smile—the seal was cut completely out! He wondered if that talismanic initial was not graven for ever, where the ball had lodged close by his heart; then he sighed and closed his eyes; it was strange! that morocco letter-case would never have been in that left breast-pocket but for the letter, which was all it contained.

MAUD HILLTON DREAMED one night of battle—and, strangely enough, she dreamed of Rick Randall; she saw him at the head of his men, with his sword aloft, and his bared head proudly erect; she heard the familiar voice ringing, above the roar and din, like a clarion note, and then—he was gone! There was a quick, sharp pang through her heart, and she awoke, trembling and weeping.

Next morning the newsboys cried under her window: 'Another great battle! splendid victory of the Union army! the enemy routed and flying! list of the killed and wounded!' and somehow their shrill, cheery voices seemed full of foreboding, knell-like.

When she leaned over her father's shoulder, as he sat at the breakfast table, poring over the morning paper, one hour later, it was not without an inward shudder that her eyes searched the columns for the fatal list, with a sort of sceptical curiosity. She found it readily enough, and followed it down carefully with her finger; then, suddenly, she caught her father's arm with a sharp grasp, and over her face stole the ashy pallor we have seen once before; then she bent down until her cheek brushed his, and, hiding her face, wept silently, softly. He did not ask why, for his eye had followed her finger till it stopped at this: 'Company A, wounded, Captain Richard Randall, mortally!' That was all. Ah! Maud Hillton, did you think GOD had helped you to crush your love for him? Afterwards, with luminous eyes, Maud sat, pale but calm, idly balancing the spoon on the rim of her coffee cup—suddenly she had looked up to her father, and said quietly, 'I must go.' He did not ask where, for he knew, and the remonstrances that rose to his lips he did not utter, when he saw the light of a holy determination in her eyes.

POOR CAPTAIN RICK! he had suffered terribly with his wound, and, at last, a fever set in upon him, that wasted him to a mere skeleton in one little week; but the crisis was past, and he was safe, though if you had seen him lying there on his rude bed, with sunken cheeks, closed eyes, and folded hands, you would have thought him dead—he was so white and motionless.

Maud Hillton thought so, as she bent gently over him, in the gathering twilight of an autumn afternoon, and just touched his forehead with cool, caressing fingers; and her heart beat warningly. Captain Rick knew that touch in an instant; he opened his eyes, and met her tearful gaze; then he drew from his bosom a morocco letter-case, opened it nervously, while she looked at him wonderingly, took out a little note, and held it up before her—'I have loved you always, Maud,' he said. 'And I you, Rick,' she murmured, sinking on her knees by the humble bedside of the wounded hero, and throwing her arms around him.

'I'; or, Summer in the City

From the *Continental Monthly*

The epigraph to "'I'; or, Summer in the City" acknowledges James's debt to Charles Lamb for both the substance ("the sweet security of the streets") and the style of this fanciful literary essay. As does Lamb in his Elia essays, James here assumes the persona of a pleasantly witty observer of nature as he walks through Boston—the Public Garden, the Common, Beacon Hill—one luminous summer morning. Expansive and rhetorical, his fancy unrestrained, he brings to his playful, allusive banter Bible wisdom, off-the-cuff aphorisms, snippets from Shakespeare, and twists on school-level poetry. He also alludes to his habit of daily renting novels to abate his insatiable appetite for books, his fondness for bottled cologne water, his eclectic Sunday church-going—all predilections that the persona shares with James himself. The Jamesian persona also invests the scene that he surveys with symbolic significance, as he, like Swedenborg, reveals the divinity hidden in it, something gloriously like the sparkling New Jerusalem prophesied in the Revelation of St. John the Divine, as when he sees "angels ascending (not Beacon Street, as in the winter season) the charmed air around me." Similar imagery illuminating the same idea at the same location to the "enquiring mind" of a similar persona will reappear in James's 1905 book-length essay *The American Scene*. The imaginative gambol through Boston's greens in August 1863 takes James's persona by nine o'clock to Washington Street, there to join editor Charles Leland at the *Continental*'s office—and perhaps to see another of his pseudonymous prose pieces come into print.

'I love the sweet security of streets.'—Charles Lamb.

'**I**', MY CHARMING friend, do not fully sympathize with the late Mr. Lamb's statement, as quoted above; which statement I always have believed partially owed its origin to its very tempting alliterative robe.

For myself, I do *not* particularly like the 'sweet security of streets,' but vastly prefer 'a boundless contiguity of shade,' especially during the present month—August—or

'A life on the ocean wave.'

I do not mean a permanent residence there—that would be liable to be damp and unhealthy, and altogether too insecure to be 'sweet';— but when I say a 'life of the ocean wave,' it is merely my poetical license for a cottage at Newport. (I wish, indeed, that I had any *but* a poetical one for such a possession!)

But what folly for me to talk of a cottage there! when my limited income does not even admit of a cot in the cheapest of seaside inns.

Gentle reader! shrink not from me when, in addition to this melancholy confidence, I also announce to you that I live in town— in 'Boston town,' to be accurate—during August! I belong to the 'lower orders of society'; and my only Newport is the Public

Garden, or a walk to Longwood, and, when I am *very* affluent, a horsecar drive to Savin hill, where a teaspoonful of sea view is administered to the humble wayfarer.

Yes! I positively did exist in the city, not only through the month of August, but all the summer days of all the summer months. I mention *August* in the city, because I know that has a peculiarly God-forgotten and forsaken sound.

I should soon cease to exist anywhere, I fancy, if I did *not* stay in town, (for horror No. 2!) I work at a trade in order to earn my daily bread and coffee! What my particular trade is, I am not going to divulge—that shall remain a delicious mystery (the only delicious thing about it); only this much I will confide: I do not, *à la* Mr. Frederick Altamont, 'sweep the crossing.' Unhappy Altamont! he did not appreciate the sweet security of streets.

'Poor thing!' you exclaim, 'work at a trade?'

Rest tranquil, fair one; the phrase doubtless sounds harshly to your delicate, aristocratic ears. (Oh, what lovely earrings!) Be tranquil! I do not work *very* hard; my hands are perhaps so audacious as to be as small, as white, as soft as your own.

But I have to 'work reg'lar,' every weekday of all the months of every year; and when the time arrives for me to go into the country, I shall not return again to Boston; for I shall go to a land from whence no traveller returns. *Apropos* of this rather dismal topic: A queer cousin of mine, 'Sans Souci,' who has a taste for 'morbid anatomy,' was the other day enjoying himself with Mr. Smith, the cheerful sexton of the King's Chapel. These two were 'down among the dead men,' under the church, when Mr. Smith apologized for leaving my cousin, on the plea that he had a previous engagement to take a young gentleman into the country—a delicate way of stating that he was about to convey a body out to Mt. Auburn!

Some fine day, I too shall take a drive with some Mr. Smith—not, of course, *the* S. C. Smith, for as I have mentioned, 'I' belong to the 'lower orders.'

Now let me tell you of *my* Newport and of what mitigations there are for the poor wretches who pass their summer in the city, to whom the joys of Sharon, Saratoga, the Hudson, and of Lake George are as impossible as though these delightful resorts were in other planets. Perhaps, like Mr. T. A.'s 'good Americans,' they have a vague hope that when they die they can visit these famous places! For myself, I long ago made out my 'visiting list.'

Oh, bless you! as soon as I shall be 'out of the body,' I shall start on the most delightful tour (no bother about the luggage, checks, or couriers!); it will be years and years before I fairly 'settle down' in that

'bright particular star'

I have selected for my permanent residence. Yes! you horrible madame! oh, you horrible madame, who express your fears that I shall 'never be settled,' speaking of me as if I were the coffee in your coffeepot—(only, of course, such a well-regulated dame's coffee is never anything but *quite* clear and settled)—yes, to relieve your poor, narrow mind, I can bid you hope that in another and pleasanter world I fully expect to be—'settled.' I tell you this beforehand, for I am very sure that you won't go to the same planet, and therefore will never have the satisfaction of knowing the fact from personal observation.

But what am I about? Building castles in the skies! Mr. Editor Leland, as usual, protests against my sad lack of con-cen-tra-tion! Let us concentrate, therefore, my beloved hearers! With or without sugar? Oh, I was beginning you tell you about Newport—*my* Newport, the Public Garden of Boston, *alias* Hub-opolis—which you, poor things! belonging to the 'higher orders' and living on Arlington, Berkeley, Clarendon, and the Duke of Devonshire Streets, never have a chance to see in its Augustan pomp and glory. In fact, till this summer, its 'pomp and glory' were quite concealed by dust and ashes; but now, thanks to the 'City Fathers,' it is

'Ye land of flowers.'

Let me describe it to you; for though your dwellings are directly opposite, yet, custom compelling you to leave them before the flower season begins, you in reality know less of it than I do, living in a street whose name must not be mentioned to ears polite. 'Tis far from the Beacon 'haunts of men,' far from the Garden, and uncommonly far from the Common. I rise betimes on these summer mornings, and, before I go to my work, shaking off the dust of my obscure street, I enter your sacred precincts, oh F. F. B.'s! Bless you, it can do you no harm, for even your boudoirs do not look out at me; their eyes are shuttered to all such vulgar sights. It was impertinent, but this morning I pitied you (*you*!) that you could not see the wondrous beauty of the—*city in August*!

The morning was gloriously beautiful: it might have been the sister to that one born so long ago, on which its Creator looked, and said that it was 'good.' I actually forgot that I had no position; I imagined I had, for the very brightest beauty filled my soul—I saw angels ascending and descending (not Beacon Street, as in the winter season) the charmed air around me. 'Ye land of flowers,' indeed! All of them mine—mine, though I must not pluck the humblest one. In truth, I had no desire to do so. Why should I take the lovely creatures from their beautiful home, to the close, dull room where I must sit all the bright day? Let me rather think of them fresh, free, and happy there, as I often think of a golden-haired child in heaven; one so dear to my heart of hearts, I bless God that I *can* think of her there with the angels who stand nearest the Throne—and far, far away the weary paths that I must tread—to the end. But if heaven had not wanted another cherub, and she had been left to be the flower of my life, think you I could have seen her beauty wither in the dull room to which I must hasten in an hour? No! a thousand times no! I should leave her with her sisters in the garden here, with her cousins, the birds and butterflies, while I worked for both. Lilies must neither 'toil nor spin.' How idly I am dreaming! She is far away from this worky-day world; I shall never see her again, but in dreams, as now! Little sister! with starry eyes, and soft curls clustering around the sweet infant face; so many nights the same bright vision—with the same wreath which I myself placed on her head, of May's pale flowers, and she the palest. Only lilies of the valley, I remember, seemed fitting for my darling's brow, or to grow on

ANNIE'S GRAVE

Bright Roses, wither on the spray!
Your sweetness mocks the doom
Of her whose cheeks, so pale today,
Were rivals of your bloom.

Sweet Violets, I charge ye, fade!
Wear not those robes of blue,
For eyes are closed which Nature made
Of a more lovely hue.

Pale Lilies, sad and drooping low,
With perfume like her breathe,
On Annie's grave alone shall grow,
Fair flower, plucked by Death.

Call it an affectation, if you will, but I never take a flower from its home without a slight twinge of pain. I *know* it suffers! However, I have no scruples in accepting flowers after they are plucked by others. So pray do not hesitate about sending me that superb bouquet, which you intended to send me *tomorrow*! Have you never observed the brutal habit which 'some persons' have, of recklessly attacking shrubs and flowers, as though they were rank weeds (or secessionists), and, without in the least enjoying their spoils, tossing their quivering, trembling victims aside, before they are dead or even withered? Such are not worthy of flowers, excepting French flowers, which are not supposed to suffer. Oh, my countrywomen! would that they *did* suffer a little from our neglect.

Do you know who Lacoontolâ is? I have made her acquaintance this summer, and find it one of the compensations for passing the summer in town.

She is to be found at the City Library—'Lacoontolâ, or the Fatal Ring,' translated from the Sanskrit. Go there for her, I pray you, and you will admire with me the exquisite description of her tenderness to these 'flower people,' as Mrs. Mann calls them.

But, pardon! You who belong to the 'highest orders' must be already intimate with Mlle. Lacoontolâ, for she is highly connected: her papa was a king (quite equal in position to Mr. Abe Lincoln); her mamma, I regret to state, though a very charming person, was an actress or goddess, or something in that line. Lacoontolâ, however, in spite of her papa's indiscretion, married a prince, and was, in fact, perfectly genteel and quite religious. Before her marriage, she appears to have 'lived in the woods' the year round; her wardrobe being 'turu-lural.' She used to wear the 'dearest' little zouave of the 'tender bark' of the 'Aurora tree.'

'Rich and rare were the gems she wore,'

for her bracelets were the 'long perfumed stems of the waterlilies!' and in her hair the lotus flower, in place of a lace *barbe*!

There is a very beautiful description of Lacoontolâ's love and tender treatment of all the flowers and shrubs—her companions—and of all *dumb* animals. (*On dit* that the prince was henpecked by *Mrs. L.*!)

This wild girl had a human love for the forest flowers; she says to thee, Madhari Creeper: 'Oh, most radiant of twining plants, receive my embraces, and return them with thy flexible arms: from this day, though at a distance, I shall forever be thine.' How unconventional! I fancy Mlle. L. must have inherited this style of conversation from her mamma; all very well, when confined to flowers and 'creeping' things; but one day, as she was out walking, she met 'by chance—the usual way,' Prince Dushuranti, and our young lady said pretty much the same sort of thing to him as to the 'Creeper,' falling violently in love with him at first sight. It struck H. R. H. as a little peculiar—rather extraordinary in a well-bred miss; but as it was leap year, and learning that she was the only child, and would inherit all of papa's immense fortune, he married her 'offhand';—well, that very afternoon at four o'clock—by the sundial. You see it didn't take so long 'in those days,' to get the trousseau, and all 'the things' in readiness. Papa raised his sceptre-wand, and mumbled some infernal gibberish—and, lo! all the trees and shrubs blossomed instanter, with the 'sweetest loves' of things trimmed with 'real point';—well, with something just as delicious to the soul of a young (or middle-aged) maiden on the eve of matrimony. There was no necessity, either, for an order to Bigelow Bros., Boston—since, if Dushuranti wished to present her with a pair of bracelets on her wedding day, he had but to 'push out' on the pond, and get some waterlilies!

The 'gibberish' in which the old gentleman is said to have invoked the backwoods 'Chandlers' and 'Hoveys,' I will obligingly translate for you, as possibly you may not be able to read it in the original Sanskrit! Oh! don't tell *me* that you 'won't trouble me,' and all that. I *will* bore you, and nobody can save you!

'Hear, O ye trees of this hallowed forest, hear and proclaim that Lacoontolâ is going to the palace of her wedded lord. She who drank not, though thirsty, before you were watered; she who cropped not, through affection for you, one of your fresh leaves, though she would have been pleased with such an ornament for her locks; she whose chief delight was in the season when your branches are sprayed with flowers,' &c., &c. Should you like a photograph of this charming person, Lacoontolâ, taken by Black & Batchelder, at the time of her marriage, 'Williams & Everett' can oblige you. You will perceive, from her picture, that she is not too fond of dress, or a 'slave to fashion.'

'Rappaccini's daughter' (one of Hawthorne's Mosses) was a morbid 'Lacoontolâ.' She loved her flowers,—'not wisely, but too well!'

She became a sort of exterminatrix—a strychninus young person! From the poisonous *arsenic* embraces of her garden loves, she acquired, you remember, her fatal, glowing beauty—beauty altogether 'too rich for use, for earth too dear,' since it consigned the 'party' ensnared by it to the silent tomb!

'Rappaccini's daughter,' indeed! Lovely girl-woman, seated at yonder bay window (to be accurate, the 'Back Bay window'!), playing with your ten cherub children; your tropical 'midsummer-night's-dream' beauty recalls Beatrice (Hawthorne's Beatrice I mean). How many have *you* slain, my love? And Madame Grundy echoes: 'Their name is legion!' 'A quick brunette, well moulded, falcon-eyed'! As in the description of Beatrice, one is reminded 'of all rich and intense colors'—the purple-black hair, the crimson cheek, the scarlet lips. And the eyes? ah! gazing into those wonderful eyes, one forgets the color they wear, in trying to interpret their language! 'Cleopatra!' who would not be an Antony for thee? *I would not!*

I have unconsciously interrupted a lady in her morning bath!—the 'stone lady' of the fountain. She seems to be looking for her Turkish towel, judging from her anxious expression! Rather a good-looking person—quite pretty, if only she would go to Summer Street and purchase a black silk. Dress, I fancy, would improve 'her style of beauty.' Poor thing! it's rather a long walk to take, *à la* 'Lacoontolâ'! I must lend her my waterproof, only she appears already to be water-proved! How she *must* envy the coloring and the clothes of my beautiful dame of the window!

But my hour is passing away! '*Resurgam*'—as the sun incorrectly remarked this morning—and go on my way, rejoicing to say 'bon jour' to all my dear flower friends. And first, the 'Asters'—they always were rich, you know, from ''John Jacob' down; but this summer, *malgré* taxes and curtailment of incomes and go-comes, the family appear in unprecedented splendor. What gorgeous Organdies! all quilled in the fashion—but not by Madame Peinot: her cunning right hand, with all its cunning, ne'er quilled so exquisitely. Those graceful, fragile Petunias (what a family of sisters!), in their delicate *glaze* silks

(ratherish *décolleté!*), and the Superbia, Empress 'Gladiolus,' in bro-
cade of such daring hues, may call the Asters 'stiff and prudish' in
their quilled muslins; but, what say the Asters in return? Ah! what do
they *not* say?

The Verbenas seem fairly delirious this morning, as though the
consciousness of their own beauty made them run wildly from their
beds into the paths, to say to the passersby, with their bright little
faces:

'See! am I not charming?'

Well, you *are* pretty—*very* pretty; but I care not for you as for
your plainer stepsister, the 'sweet-scented Verbena.' She has a pale,
sad face; but she has a *soul,* which you have not, poor things! for perfume is the soul of 'flower people.'

But, who wants gold? Lives there a man with purse so full who
does not want it? Well, then, snatch that heap of sunshine, that dazzling Coreopsis, and be off before the policeman turns into this path.
Ah, ye Daylilies! You break my heart with your moonlight faces.
Standing apart from the world-flowers, like novices in their white
veils, who offer the incense of their beauty to Heaven—oh! give a little of your perfume to a poor un-otto-of-rosed mortal—breathe on
me, and I can laugh at the costly 'Wood Violet,' 'Eglantine,' and
'Rose,' with which Harris and Chapman scent their patronesses—to
be dollared in return!

Daylilies, your perfume is too subtle, too vague, to be coined or
'cabined, cribbed, confined' in scent bottles.

Ah! the flowering Mosses; they seem to be having one eternal picnic with the Myrtles and Verbenas, playing forever that dear-to-chil-
dren game of 'Tag'! Some are arrayed in Solferino velvets, rather
heavy for this warm day! Prettier these, in soft rose-colored robes,
and this in a

'Oh! call me fair, not pale'—

well, *almost* pale robe, the very climax of delicacy: the faintest thought of rose color alone prevents one from calling it lily-white. I am reminded of you, O flower-named friend! Vision of loveliness! which has in a few never-to-be forgotten days oasised my Sahara life. Now I have reached the pond—*my* Lake George! It is fresh and breezy this morning, after last night's thundershower, and the mimic waves are impatiently breaking over the thus-far-shalt-though-go stone. I cannot blame them for rushing over that green sward to give a morning kiss to the blushing 'Forget-me-nots,' and just to say to them, 'Remember *me!*'

Yes; I have a few crumbs of time left to sit in the rustic arbor and give one lingering look behind, that I may carry a picture with me when I go to my work.

How fortunate it is for one that these flowers are Londoners in their habits, and pass August in the city! I can go to their receptions daily, if I choose; they are always at home to the poorest, the most unfashionable; they keep no 'visiting book' in their hall.

Hark! the bell rings seven o'clock. There is a 'knocking at the gate' of my fairy land; it warns me that I must be on my Washington Street way, to earn my bread.

Bien! my first meal of today has been satisfactory. Heaven hath sent me all manner of manna for breakfast—and for lunch? a banana. Yes; on my way 'downtown' I shall pass the Studio Building, where the B.s live; I will buy one of them, but shall also steal—many glances at the Hamburg grapes, those peachiest of peaches, bombastic black-berries, and, O Pomona! *such* pears.

I escape! purse uninjured, only bananared. I reach Winter Street, where I must turn my back on the Common pleasures of Boston life—but yet, one glance at that seductive window of the corner store, which, indeed, is nearly all window. Flowers are there, of course,— flowers from January to January; any poor devil can have a tempo-rary conservatory at that window, 'all for nothing'; I ought to pay a yearly tax for the pleasure I steal in that way. The woman who carries my porte-monnaie, only permits me to open it for the 'necessaries' of life: the luxuries of hothouse grapes and flowers ever wear for me that fatal label: 'Touch not, taste not.' Bread and cologne are, of course, the first necessities of life; in rolls and religion I am a Parkerite; in cologne, I swear by 'Mrs. Taylor'! Beacon Street, I beg that you won't faint at this horrible disclosure!

Who *is* 'Mrs. Taylor'? and echo answers, 'We haven't the faintest odor of an idea!' None knew her but to praise, wherever she may be. With Sancho Panza we say, 'Blessings on the man who invented Mrs. Taylor at seventy-five cents *per*—the hock bottle. I catch a glimpse of her long neck, stretching up among the roses and Geraniums: my cologne nature can't resist that sight! I obey the siren's call, though it will leave me a beggar, but with Mrs. T. in my chaste embrace.

'The man I work for' treats me, for some reason, with 'distinguished consideration.' Though I may sometimes be a little after the required hour, it's all right; and though he's a Yankee, no questions are asked! I still have a precious quarter remaining—not of a dollar, but of time. I have in my purse one postage stamp; but that will warrant a visit to Loring's! One must have books as well as bread and cologne. O Loring! what an institution art thou! Name dear to all classes, from Madame ———, who steps from her carriage, to the pretty shopgirl, who always wants Mrs. Southworth's last—and worst—novel.

Who, indeed, 'so poor' as not 'to do *him* reverence,' and find two cents *per* day, when for that sublimely small sum one can get a companion for any and every mood,

'Grave to gay, from lively to severe?'

But will 'LORING'S' be open at this early dawn? 'Open,' indeed! one does not catch *him* napping; yes, open and so inviting! A literary public garden so fresh and clean, as

'Just washed in a shower.'

In the rear, behind the desk, one is always sure of finding at least *two roses,* and *on* the desk a vase of flowers is certainly to be seen—the offering of some one of the hundreds of admirers who go to Loring's, nominally for some entertaining book—and they always find one!

'What book did you say, miss?' asks Fleur de Marie. ('Where *does* she get those lilies and roses? I saw none like them in the garden this morning. Ah! many of the dames who enter here from their carriages would also like to ask my question—since they do not seem to find them even at Newport!) 'If you please, *what* book?' again inquire the Roses.

'Oh!' I answer, 'I was looking, and forgot what I came for; is 'Out of his Head' *in* yet?'

The fair librarian evidently thinks I am out of mine. Ah! would that I were, and out of my whole body; but no! ingrate that I am, today I should be content—simply to *be*: even a cabbage ought to be happy in such perfect summer weather. T. B. Aldrich is in—as much as he ever is supposed to be; but I recall now that I read his sketchy book the other night, while I was brushing my hair, giving it a sort of 'good time generally,' letting it run wild a little before going to sleep. I read 'Pierre Antoine's Date Tree' quite through, and liked—the *last part* very much indeed. There are some people whom I am always very glad to have visit me, because I feel so 'dreadful glad' when they go away. So, also, it compensates one to read certain books for the sake of the delicious sensation one experiences on finishing them! What a pile of '*Les Misérables*,' Fantine? *C'est assez misérable.* The 'Hunchback' is the least deformed of Hugo's offspring; but I read *that* last Sunday morn—no; I mean last Saturday evening; for I went to church on Tremont Street, last Sunday. What's this? it looks as tempting as a banana, and is not unlike one in color. 'Melibaeus in London,' in the summer, too: good! I'll take that, it shall 'assist' the banana at my lunch. I hurry out of this 'little heaven,' murmuring, as I depart: 'LORING, live forever!'

Lady Macbeth undoubtedly alluded to you when she says:

'We *fail*? there's no such word as fail!'

I believe the Macbeths, and, in fact, everybody but Loring, has failed during the war times. McClellan certainly has—not succeeded.

The police (those gentlemen of elegant leisure) do not even suspect how much I have stolen, and what treasures I am carrying off before nine o'clock A.M.! All the splendors of the early morning are mine; they will gild the dull grey of my working hours. What a stock of perfumes stolen from the garden! they will sweeten the 'business air' of Washington Street. The fountain's glistening spray will sprinkle the dusty walk to 'the shop.'

I have not yet told you of the kisses taken—not from Féra's, but from the cherry-ripe lips of two lovely children, with whom I formed an intimacy in the garden by the pond; they were 'sailing' their mimic boats there. I almost wished

'I were a boy again,'

and had a boat to sail! These children had such a brave and haughty beauty, and their dress being of purple and fine linen, I supposed their name must be Berkeley or Clarendon, but was grieved to learn from the artless darlings that it was Muggins! However, their kisses were unexceptionable, whatever their origin may have been.

But what a 'heap' of Beauty I stole in my return walk through Beacon Street mall! No wonder those magnificent elms are in love with each other, and embrace over the people's heads! When I come into my fortune, I intend, early the next morning, before breakfast, to make the first use of my 'funds' in purchasing Mr. George Ticknor's house. (Of course, he will not object.) I shall then laugh at the mill-dam principalities and powers when I look from my library windows down that long vista of noble trees. Come and see me when I am settled there! You shall have a warm welcome in winter, and a cool one in summer. And now, fare thee well, whoever thou art, who hast kindly walked with me to the door of—my 'place of business.' I will not ask you to enter there. I can worry through the day: unseen companions go with me to soothe and cheer; so do not pity me that I am what I am—'nobody,' living 'nowhere.' You have seen that the Angel of Beauty disdains not to appear in my humble path—and sometimes hovers so near, I can almost touch her wings!

And so God be w'ye! Little joys to you are great joys to me. There be those above you, 'kinges and princes and great emperours,' to whom your luxuries and badges would seem as little as mine are to you. When you are beautiful, you adorn my street; when you are unlovely, I—pass you by. *Bon jour la compagnie!*

· February 1863 ·

The Sprite Transformed

From the *Knickerbocker* (no author given but subsequently
identified as having been written by Leslie Walter)

Published in the *Knickerbocker* under no signature, "The Sprite
Transformed" was identified three stories later as the work of Leslie
Walter though, in the spirit of self-allusive fun, perhaps, it features
"Harry the frivolous collegian" among its cast. More prominent is the
character George Curtis, named after the longtime friend of the James
family who had mentored Henry. The story owes more to Curtis than
a name. In 1852 Curtis had published "All Baggage at the Risk of the
Owner: A Story of Watering Places," which draws comparisons
between a proper young lady pursuing socially acceptable pleasures at
a summer watering place and Undine, the beautiful water nymph of
Baron de la Motte-Fouqué's romantic myth, who without human soul
or conscience heartlessly follows her amatory inclinations. With
appreciably more literary imagination than either Curtis or Fouqué,
James not only transforms the sprite but also makes of romantic fantasy a brilliantly allusive, realistic tale of social and psychological substance.

An uninhibited coquette who cares little about the pains she inflicts upon her seamstress or her suitors (by now a familiar Jamesian type), the sixteen-year-old Luly embodies the spirit of Undine and unquestionably proves that water is her element when she saves the handsome, magnetic, worldly (as his name implies) Desmond from drowning. Ironically, it is when Luly begins to fancy herself Undine that she begins her spiritual progress and Swedenborgian transformation. For Luly has discovered the joy in loving another before oneself, and, advancing further, in forgoing coquetry and idle, meaningless flirtation with all the opposite sex; in doing so, she also abandons the false, shallow social values embraced by the privileged class. That the class-bound Desmond doesn't respond similarly impedes Luly's journey to Swedenborg's celestial heights and conjugal bliss; but it does not abnegate her glorious possibilities. For this sprite can more than woman be.

MY COUSIN, FRANCIS Desmond, was reading aloud by the centre table, and I with my work, in my favorite seat by the window, listened to the beautiful 'Undine,' of Fouqué, and enjoyed an interval of the rest that comes so rarely to busy house-keepers. The softness and silence of June were in the air, the vines and trees embowering our pretty home swayed gently in the sweetest breeze, and the canaries on the porches piped their shrill songs at a pleasant distance. Happily situated, where my eyes commanded the morning bustle of the kitchen, and my nose satisfactorily reported the successful processes of boiling and baking there proceeding, I could afford to sit at my ease, and entertain my unconscious guest, at full liberty to listen to the mellow fall of his voice, and admire, if I chose, a singularly handsome man.

Don't be frightened, dear reader, you are not about to be the confident of a tender confession, nor shall I write a love story, with myself for its heroine. My part in that kind of thing was over long ago, thank goodness! I have been Mr. Jones's faithful wife these dozen years; I keep his house, I superintend his wardrobe, I lecture his shortcomings, and never have changed or wished to change my place; but I have an eye for beauty, and sometimes wonder why Nature should have been so unkind to Mr. Jones, and so prodigal to his handsome cousins—

"A wonderful work of art, Sara," said Desmond, interrupting some such meditations.

"What?" cried I, starting guiltily. "This strange, impossible, beautiful 'Undine.' One wishes she were human, and could be found and won."

"Not so very impossible, after all," cried I, briskly, glad to find what he had been talking about. "I have seen just such soulless people."

"O indeed!" cried Desmond, leaning back, and eyeing me with cool superiority.

"Not your water witches and sprites, of course," I hastened to explain; "but creatures beautiful, fascinating, and intractable as she— as destitute of heart, soul, or principle; apparently born to be admired, obeyed, and endured; who seem to think the world and its tenants only made for their amusement and pleasure."

"Who become tender wives, and devoted mothers of families," interpolated Desmond.

"Some, but not all. There are women, I tell you—for I know my sex—brilliant, capricious, irresponsible, as the lightning that dazzles and slays; not wicked, but soulless, thoughtless, heartless, careless— *less* every thing almost that makes your ideal woman."

"I don't want to believe it," said Desmond, suddenly pale.

"I know of what you are thinking, but Augusta is a grown woman, her character is developed, and you should know it well by this time. But, fortunately, it is mostly very young girls who possess this nature, some of them grow wiser as they grow older; of others, I despair—little demons with angels' faces that they are. I know one— ah! *quand on parle du loup on en voit le queue*—here she comes!"

"Who is it?" inquired Desmond, as, with some curiosity to see so dreadful a personage, he approached the window.

A slight young girl, in a blue silk dress, and an incongruous gingham sunbonnet, had just parted from a tall, fair, gentlemanly young man, at the gate. The one walked slowly, reluctantly, soberly away; the other ran gayly up the gravelled walk, singing to herself.

"George Curtis and my niece Luly," I explained.

"Does she always have a lover *en attendance*?" he enquired.

"More commonly two. But, away with you, *fiancé* of Augusta that you are! I won't allow you to fall under the fascinations of this worst of witches; I'll have no heart-breaking in my house. Go!"

"Perhaps I have a counter-charm," he laughed.

"None that will avail, I warn you. Besides, she comes to see me— *avaunt!*"

He half-obeyed by entering the next room, separated from the other by an arched doorway, with a fall of heavy curtains, and Luly appeared before me, the next minute, swinging her discarded sun bonnet by the strings, from a little white hand, and laughing like a silver fountain.

I could not forbear kissing the little traitress, though I knew she had just been planting a daily dagger in George Curtis's faithful heart, though I knew her guilty of a thousand cruelties, and capable of not one good action; vain, selfish, exacting, fickle, unfeeling, and unprincipled as she was, all was forgotten at sight of her lovely face, and I could not help welcoming her presence, and rejoicing in her beauty. I have, as I said before, a taste for such things; and even the dullest perceptions could not but recognize and admire, what was so delightful to the eye, and irresistible to the heart, a charm better than the "Open Sesame" to the locked-up treasures of feeling, when she knocked at the door.

"And what brought you here so early, my dear?" said I.

"Just because there was such a fuss in the house, Aunty. Jane's sister is sick, and Biddy is gone to be married; so mother and Laura had to do every thing themselves, to-day, and such a scolding, and sweeping, and fixing, and frying! I came over here to get rid of it."

"But you should have staid to help them, Luly."

"Now, Aunt Sara, do you suppose I want to spoil my hands with hot water and brooms? I did do what I could; I went and practised, and, you know, mamma wants me to practise all I can; until they made such a noise I could not hear any thing; and then Laura put her head into the parlor, and asked me to dust it, and I ran away here."

"But Laura will have the more to do."

"Oh! well, what if she does? She won't mind it. She'll have to do it, if I don't; and she knew I wouldn't, for I told her so. Besides, she's sort of an old maid, any way, and expects to do more than I can do."

I looked at Luly with intent to scold, but she made such a pretty picture that I forgot my purpose, and admired instead. Her blue silk dress was exquisitely made, and trimmed with rich white lace, from which the round, childish arms fell, and the fair shoulders rose, pearly in tint and texture, just touched by the silken masses of half-uncurled amber hair that hung about her face. That little witching face, with its pale cheeks and vivid lips, and changeful, wonderful eyes, just now dark violet under their network of amber lashes, was too enchanting to be clouded, and I turned to something else.

"And what made you put on that handsome dress, so early in the morning?"

"Isn't it handsome? it's just finished, and I wanted you to see it. I was so afraid Miss Hennessy wouldn't get it done for Lizzy Marshall's party, that I told her it was this evening instead of to-morrow, and she kept one of her girls sitting up all last night to do it—that pale, hollow-eyed thing, Maria Bean. She looked as yellow as an orange this morning, when she brought it home."

"Oh Luly! how could you be so cruel?"

"Dear me, Aunt, it's her business, and I had to have it. I hadn't a thing to wear, though father wouldn't believe it when I told him. You've no idea how stingy he is growing; every time I buy any thing new, he says I shall ruin him with my extravagance; I had to tease for a month, I do believe, before I got this; he thought he couldn't afford it!"

"He has lost a great deal of money lately, and you ought to be careful."

"But he has plenty left, I know," she insisted, "and I mean to have what I want, anyway. I don't care now though, for I've got my dress, and George Curtis said I looked 'divine' in it; and I told him I had it blue, because Harry liked that color best."

"And that was why he went away so soberly? For shame, Luly, to set two brothers in rivalship against each other; and a man like George Curtis, too, with his age and attainments, against a frivolous collegian like Harry!"

"I like Harry much the best!" she retorted; "he keeps step so nicely. One, two, three; one, two, three!" whirling off in a waltz, "while George won't dance, or let anybody else, if he can help it. He belongs to the church; I told him he ought to be a missionary."

"I wish he would convert one heathen I know of," said I, no longer able to repress a smile; "but tell me one thing more, Luly, did you go in to see old Aunty Brown? Your mother said she should try to persuade you to do it; she was your nurse, you know, and used to love 'her baby,' as she called you, so much. Now she is sick, and wants to see you, you ought to go, and do every thing you can to please her."

"Yes; I know she is always sending for me to come and receive her dying blessing; I believe this is the twentieth time; but I can't go, so there, now! Suppose she should die while I was with her, I should be frightened to death. I don't see how people can expect me to go to such a place; down in that horrid old Wash Street, too, where nobody goes. I told mother I wouldn't, and I won't."

The voice that uttered these ungracious words was as sweet as a lark's; and she sat down to the piano, and began to dash off the "Sweet Sixteen Polka," with great spirit.

"I always play that before Laura," she remarked; "it teases her so, to say it was her piece, that she had when she was sixteen. Then people look at the music, and see it dated eighteen hundred and ever so many years back, and know just how old she is."

"Oh Luly!"

"Well, you don't know how tiresome it is. Every time I have a new dress, Laura has one just like it, as if there were no difference between twenty-seven and seventeen; she doesn't go out either, half as often as I do, to need so much dress. Then, the other evening, when Edward Beach and Harry, and that new Mr. Brace, all called to see me, she came in, just as cool as possible, in her black and brown silk, and sat down by Mr. Brace, and quite engrossed him."

"He is two years older than your sister, and Laura is very interesting."

"She was very provoking, for I especially wanted to talk to him myself; so I waited till there was a pause, and then asked her if she had been giving him any maternal advice. She colored up like fire, and moved away."

"Oh Luly! how heartless you are!"

"But I had my revenge afterwards," she resumed, quite unheeding. "That horrid little Doctor Bird, who comes to see Laura, was there one evening, and I sat in the room, all the time, though their talk made me dreadfully sleepy, for I was determined they shouldn't have it quite their own way. So he was telling about his travels—he always is—and about a race of monkeys somewhere in Asia or Africa, that you can hardly distinguish from men. Laura pretended to be very much interested."

"'Yes,' said I, 'and Laura said the other day, that she knew some men you could hardly distinguish from monkeys.'

"It wasn't much to say, but I *looked* the rest; she did say it once about Harry Curtis, and I meant to pay her for it; but Doctor Bird looks just like a monkey, and of course he took it to himself at once; so very soon it was 'Good evening, Miss Fay,' with a stiff bow, and the beau disappeared. Oh! how Laura lectured, and how I laughed when we went upstairs! It was good fun!"

"Go away, you malicious imp," said I, shaking her by the shoulders.

"Yes, Aunty; I am just going. I want to ask Katy for a piece of cake; we don't have it good at our house, and I can't get any at the confectioner's, for papa warned him not to trust me again, when he paid my last bill there. Only think! eighteen dollars for the few things I had to make my luncheons endurable while I went to school!"

She sprang away through the hall, and Desmond appeared from his hiding place.

"You are right; she is a second 'Undine,'" he said.

I was quite disconcerted, for I thought he might have heard enough of Luly's heartless frivolity and malice, to resent a comparison with the innocent mischief of the sprite; but the charm had already begun to work, and he sat silent and abstracted, looking at the beautiful illustration on the first page of his book.

"She looks like the 'Undine,'" he murmured.

"She doesn't act like it," said I.

"She is perfectly lovely."

"And perfectly unprincipled."

"How can you blame her?" he pleaded. "She has no more soul than the water spirit."

"Then it is time she had," I rejoined, determined to be didactic.

"Her nobler nature has never been developed; her powers of thinking and feeling lie dormant; I believe I could awaken them."

"Try, then," I proposed, laughing. "Try to Christianize a guileful leopard, to find the spiritual essence of a floating butterfly, and lose your senses doing it. Go and immolate yourself; you won't be the first, but remember I warned you that she was a witch."

What he would have answered I don't know, for just then Luly was heard coming back, and entering, with her hands full of cake, like a hungry schoolgirl, she was presented to him.

Desmond had receded into his usual manner, and bowed from his lofty height, like a prince of the genii; taking no further notice of the lovely visitor, who, angry and embarrassed, only looked shy and sweet. It was a sight to see her reception of him, though she was taken by surprise at first; the manner of timid, gentle grace; the silky splendors of her dropped lashes, lying long on the tinged cheek, usually waxen-pale as my white camelia buds, but now flushed with tender pink, like the heart of a seashell; her soft, hesitating speech, and the deprecatory curve of her red lips, all apparently thrown away on the stern stranger, who sat like a statue of bronze, and said no more than civility required. I left them alone until dinnertime, but they seemed to make small progress in acquaintance during the interval; and at the table, Luly's delicate little courtesies were received as apathetically as those of his subjects, by King Log, in the fable.

Dinner over, the guest disappeared with an apology and a segar; and Luly, awestruck more than piqued by this haughty neglect and indifference, returned to the parlor, and examined the books on the centre table, to see what the attraction among them had been for him; the picture of 'Undine' lay open, and she bent long over it, while the color slowly rose in her cheeks, and the tears gathered in her dilated eyes, as she read the story. She carried the book away with her when she went home at dusk; and Desmond, standing tall, dark, and silent by the gate, opened it for her with the same mechanical courtesy she had just seen him display to Betsy, the chambermaid, going out to fetch the milk.

Notwithstanding this unpromising beginning, the acquaintance afterwards progressed, though in a novel way, at which I could hardly wonder enough. It was Luly who sought Desmond's society, who courted his attentions, and hung upon his words, and watched his actions; even putting strong constraint upon herself, lest she should betray the jealous pangs—keen and new they were—that assailed her, as she saw him brilliant, courteous, fascinating to others; stern, cold, and austere to her; a master, not a lover. Her admirers resented this behavior to the worshipped sovereign of their little court; the sovereign herself capricious, imperious, exacting enough to them, was gentle, patient, almost humble here, and seemed indifferent to their homage, while this proud Mordecai sat unheeding in her gate; she looked impatiently beyond their smiling circle, for some token of fealty from the dark and haughty stranger who defied her power.

Not only were they puzzled, but I wondered much over the new means Luly had taken to attain a conquest. In George Curtis's case, as in a dozen others, she had behaved outrageously from the first; she tortured , harassed, afflicted him, in every way that malice could invent, or love endure; she only allured to repulse him, and never smiled but she stabbed him afterwards. If he had a vulnerable point, she assailed it; if she could find a tender place, she wounded it; and never wearied of the cruel game. That he loves her still, I count among the modern miracles, as unexplainable as those of old; for she had a thousand capricious moods, and he was the victim of them all. Laura has said with a sigh, that she was never so naughty (it should have been diabolical) as during the progress of these attentions; but in her acquaintance with Desmond, he was the tyrant, the despot, the aggressor, from the outset. He criticized her dress, her manners, her very face, which the poor bewildered fairy had always thought irresistible, and which he could hardly refrain from worshipping, I am sure, while he abused it; he openly exposed and rebuked her faults, he blamed, and ridiculed, and ordered, and interfered, unchecked; establishing a kind of tacit authority over her, which she implicitly obeyed; and domineered ruthlessly afterwards, by virtue of what right I don't know, except that the power he usurped she yielded, and he governed her by a look or word, where others failed to move her with prayers and tears.

"It will do her good," said I to Mr. Jones, and I fancied his gruff response meant acquiescence.

But the catastrophe (there is always a catastrophe) came sooner than in my ignorance I had dreamed; and, not content with legitimate victims, involved me, innocent and unfortunate, in its dire results.

We live a few miles from the seashore, where a delightful beach tempts adventurous swimmers; and 'bathing picnics' form a frequent amusement. One summer morning we set forth, gay and clamorous, on one of those excursions; and returned at nightfall, damp, wretched, and frightened, having had a 'hairbreadth escape,' a rescue, and a scene. Of course the heroine was my pretty niece, and the hero, my paladin of a cousin; nor would my ill fortune have been complete, without Mr. Jones among the party, to whisper a reminder in my ear, that he had always told me so, and it was all my fault; and to glance ominously at me, when Luly, wet and wilful, insisted on being carried to my house instead of her own, and being there brought back to life, in the light of Mr. Francis Desmond's fine eyes.

For there had been a 'scene,' as I said, though I am the last person in the world to describe it, and, in spite of Mr. Jones's assertion, could not have prevented it. Was it my fault that Desmond, silent and sullen, chose to enter the water alone, and, going out to a great distance, was seized with cramp, and sank? Was it my fault that Luly only of all the party, standing ready to plunge into the surf, graceful as a Naiad in her pretty bathing dress, her white feet twinkling on the sparking sands, her amber hair floating on her shoulders, should see him struggle and sink, and strike out like a mermaid to his relief? He was drowning, and knew it; he was pale, but resolute; he had less reason to fear death than many a poor fellow! and refused to endanger her by availing himself of her slender aid. But she bravely locked her arms about him, and, in spite of his resistance, managed somehow to uphold and save him, till the other swimmers came to the rescue, and brought them both, half-drowned and wholly insensible, to shore. I ask the candid reader how I was responsible for this exploit, that I should never have heard the last of it from Mr. Jones?

I never saw any one so changed as Desmond, when he recovered; he hung over Luly in an agony of remorse and self-reproach, and, to the indignation of her lovers, insisted on carrying her in his strong arms to the carriage, and there supporting her all the way home, where in my bewilderment I received her as my guest, and Desmond, as his special charge, during her remarkably protracted convalescence. His stern severity, his hauteur, and coldness were gone; he watched her with the care of a mother, the tenderness of a lover; while Luly, satisfied and happy, received the change with unquestioning gratitude, and even seemed to alter for the better, in the sweet atmosphere of love and protection, in which she lived. I was very busy at that time, but Mr. Jones was 'laid up,' as he phrases it, in the house, with a violent cold, from the effects of the water party, and to him I entrusted the preservation of the proprieties, while I was engaged with my housekeeping duties. As I afterwards learned, he left the responsibility entirely on my shoulders, and immersed himself in posting books. So they read, rode, walked and talked, and were daily together, even after the fair invalid had recovered, and returned home; while I could only comfort myself by remembering that Desmond had no hand to give, and Luly no heart, and leave them to fate, to chance, or to ALLAH!

I was very glad, however, to hear from Desmond, during this state of things, that he was soon to leave us; and, regardless of hospitality, encouraged the idea, and strengthened him in his determination. There was to be a large party in his honor, on the same evening in which I received this gratifying news, and it was with particular pleasure that I arrayed myself in my matronly lavender silk, and assisted Mr. Jones into his white waistcoat, to do honor to the occasion, resolved to exercise unusual vigilance in behalf of the pair now so soon to be separated.

Luly came in very late, and created a great sensation as usual, her face and dress making her the beauty of the night. I was accustomed to see her a belle, and tastefully attired, but something novel and peculiar in both her manner and appearance made me watch her earnestly till I knew what it was. Her dress was of misty white tulle, long, full, and floating; enveloping her graceful figure like a cloud of spray, and looped up here and there with clusters of water lilies, from which it fell again like transparent fountains. Her fair, round arms, and white shoulders, were without ornament; and her amber hair was bound with a coronal of waxen lily buds, and dark green, shining leaves. Her lips and cheeks were touched with living red; her eyes, like pansies, violet and velvet; something timid, pleading, hesitating, and all-enchanting in her manner, lent it a last charm and made it divinely lovely. It was Undine, as she appeared before her lover on their marriage day, the impersonation of the beautiful vignette in my volume at home; but I was sorry to see that the knight 'Hildebrand,' before whom she bent, was the dark Desmond, instead of the fair-haired George Curtis; and that even when she had left his side, her eyes and thoughts returned to their allegiance. Still she was kinder than ever before to that unfortunate slave of her whims, giving him an unusual and marked preference over his younger brother; while her dark cavalier, with olive cheeks deeply flushed, and eyes that stole long looks away from under their sheltering lashes, paid his stately devoir to the pretty, pleasing Laura—leaning over her chair to talk, in low, sweet, even tones, and insuring for her the torments of the early martyrs, when the jealous beauty had her safely at home.

I snatched an hour from my cares next morning to run down to my sister's—ostensibly to discuss the party with Laura, but really to have a little serious conversation with Luly. She was not at home, however; and resolving to speak to Desmond instead, I devoted the time to the worship of that household divinity, which Mr. Jones calls GOSSIP.

The doorbell rang while we were talking, and Maria Bean, Miss Hennessy's overworked apprentice, came in with a bundle in her hand: "Miss Luly's new dress, Ma'am," she said, delivering it.

"Why, I thought it was to have been done long ago?" remarked Mrs. Fay, looking over it. "Luly is so particular about her things, I'm afraid she will be very angry."

"I think not, Ma'am," said Maria; "we are very much pressed with work just now, and as the most of it comes on me, Miss Luly was good enough to say there was no hurry, and she would wait for her dress till we were less driven—and she gave me something extra for my trouble sitting up so late to finish the last one. I don't think she'll find fault this time, Miss Laura."

"I don't know what has come over Luly lately," said Laura musingly, looking after the girl with her finger on her lip; "she is more thoughtful of others than I ever knew her. Last week when a gentleman called whom she always annoys me about"—Laura was very pretty with her deep blush and her dropping eyelids—"she left us in peace; and last night when we came home from the party, she put away her own things herself; and when I said 'good night' she kissed me, and begged my pardon for something she had done. Papa was so surprised, too, that she did not worry him about a new dress for the party; she wore her white tulle."

"Well, I suppose she is growing more sensible as she grows older," said Mrs. Fay. "I wish you would go in and see Aunty Brown, as you go back, Sara; I'm afraid we have rather neglected her these two days."

Aunty Brown I found very comfortable, and in very good spirits for a dying woman: "Which I lay to the fact," she explained when she remarked upon it, "that my darlin' nuslin' was in to see me, and staid quite awhile yesterday."

"Not Luly, and the day before the party!" I exclaimed in amazement. "Who brought her?"

"Nobody but her would have done my old eyes so much good," the woman insisted proudly; "and she came all by herself, like a pretty angel as she is, and seemed quite sorry for her poor, old nuss. She read me a verse in the Bible when I asked her, and said she'd come again."

Luly reading the Bible by a sick woman's pillow! Luly mourning for any body else's misfortunes! I began to think the invalid's mind was wandering, when Jane, my sister's servant, who was busying herself about the room, came forward to corroborate it. "It's quite true, Ma'am," she said; Miss Luly was here yesterday, and very kind. To my thinking she's changed somehow, lately—I hope nothing ails her? We servants notice it, Ma'am, she is so different to us about the house."

I knew well the custom of the imperious beauty to the servants in her father's house, and went out without remark. George Curtis passed me with a smiling bow—the barometer of his hope was high, his honest brown eyes were bright with cheerful courage. His brother Harry lounged along the opposite sidewalk, by the side of Luly's intimate friend and rival, Emma Drake—sign sufficient of the change of his prospects. Much wondering I went home.

"SHE left the wheel, she left the loom,
She made three paces through the room,
She saw the water-lily bloom,
She saw the helmet and the plume,
          She looked down on Camelot."

Desmond and Luly were reading poetry together in the little parlor, as it was now quite their custom to do. I entered quietly and sat
down by the window, with my sewing, not altogether unobservant of
the pair.

"Let *me* read it," Luly interrupted in a breathless way, laying her
little hand on his arm in her eagerness to enforce the demand.

Desmond glanced down at it a moment, and shook his head in
reply; but just raising his eyes while the words went on, suffered their
light to rest a moment on her face, and with a smile hovering on his
music-making lips finished the poem. As he read the last lines—

"BUT Lancelot mused a little space,
He said, 'She hath a lovely face,
GOD in His mercy lend her grace,
The Lady of Shalott:'"

he threw down the book so suddenly that I was startled; and removing my eyes from him, saw that Luly had hidden her face in her
hands, and was weeping convulsively.

Desmond was bending over her in some agitation, but I pushed
him back.

"This is not your affair, Sir; go away."

He gave me a glance of defiance from his great, gloomy, black-
fringed eyes, and went; while I tried to soothe the suddenly sensitive
child, who sobbed and nestled in my arms.

"What is it, Luly?" I persisted, till at last I got an answer.

"Oh aunt! nothing to make me so disturbed. Only it struck me, as

I heard the story read, how true it was; how like all our lives are to hers—all we women, I mean."

"As how, my foolish little woman—sixteen years old, I believe?"

"We are kept so ignorant of the world; like her we think it such a gay and happy place, we don't know it is dark and sad; they ought to tell us—they ought to tell us! We live like the Lady, in a fairy isle full of illusions; we see only the shadows of the realities of life, till something comes to break the spell, and make us only mortal after all; and then it seems so sudden and so hard!"

She paused to wipe away the flowing tears, and look up into my grave face.

"Do all women feel it, Aunty?"

"What is it, my child?"

"I don't know what it is—such a sudden remorse and trouble as I feel here. All my life I have been selfish and careless, and unmindful of others' feelings; but I never knew it till now—it has come to me lately with everything else. Now I know what pain I gave, for I feel it myself. I feel like 'Undine,' when she came to possess her soul; like the 'Lady of Shalott,' when the doom came upon her. Oh! what is it—what is it that makes me suffer so?—that gives me this miserable heartache?"

She asked it with wide eyes, and hands locked over her heaving breast; and there was something so childish in her sorrow, so womanly in her suffering, that my eyes filled with tears of compassion. It reminded me of the fate of some beautiful, wild creature, caged and hurt, and bound, that struggled against pain and bonds, and defied them; helpless, hopeless, frightened, tortured, instinctively resisting but subdued. I could not bear to see her heart-broken and humbled, who had been so free, so bright, so wild; and I forgot all her faults and follies in dismay at this new change in her nature. Worst of all, it would not do to give a name to her feelings, or to express my sympathy in words; she must never guess the cause of the conflict in her mind, or understand the awakening of her heart. I soothed her, therefore, with tender caresses and commonplace endearments; and when she was a little recovered, and had gone upstairs to bathe her wet eyes, and brush her silky curls, I took my life in my hand and went, with desperate courage, to confront Desmond.

He met me like a duellist, with dogged defiance: "You have come to lecture me, I see, Sara. What is it? Come, give your wrath words."

"I won't have that child's feelings played with," I broke out; "I won't see her tortured, to please your passing whim."

"I forbear to ask you whether you yourself, told me she had no feeling, and was given to torturing others; you compared her to a pretty, soulless butterfly, a bright, spotted leopard. Did you not? I tell you, honestly, I did not believe there was danger."

"Be it so; you do right to reproach me. I should have been more careful than to expose her to your satanic experiments; it was like leaving the gay butterfly to the steely mercies of the entomologist; the wild leopard to the searing irons and keen whips of its keeper's mysterious *ménage*. I tell you I will not have it: you must go."

"I wish I were her keeper," he murmured with softening lips; "she should never fear me more or love me less."

"She shall never have the opportunity to do either," I retorted, impatient and warm—vexed to find him so callous; but he heeded neither me nor my remark, his arms were crossed upon his breast in calm repose, his eyes and thoughts fixed intently on a wide, arched window, through the bright plate glass, and half-closed blind of which, a fairy figure was clearly visible, flitting about in graceful restlessness like a fluttering bird.

"You are mad, I believe," said I at last, in short and sharp impatience. "Do you forget what you are, Mr. Desmond? Do you remember you are to marry Augusta Asten?"

"True," he answered, and his face settled into pale sternness again; "you are a harsh monitor, Cousin Sara, but you speak like an oracle. I must go."

"The sooner the better," I promptly rejoined.

"I was in a delicious dream"—he seemed quite unmoved—"I had forgotten every thing I most needed to remember—sacred vows, earlier promises, untarnished honor, and unblemished name."

"And Miss Asten is an heiress, I believe?" I sarcastically suggested.

"Sara, you wrong me," said he, flashing out at last, "by such impu-tations. Augusta's fortune is settled upon herself; I will never touch a penny of it—she will need it all, for her frivolities and charities. I have enough for my wife and myself."

"Then why will you not marry my Luly?" I asked abruptly; "she is the only child besides Laura. Her parents will never object to any fancy she may take."

"My honor is pledged," was all he could say—for I saw now how strong was the passion that mastered him, expressed in the very silence and strength of his struggle, and the grim quietude of his face. It changed and grew more mobile as I looked, moist drops gathered in his stern eyes, and an impassioned fervor softened the lines about his rigid mouth. I hastened to seize the melting mood.

"Poor child! poor baby! she has a hard lesson to learn," said I.

"Pity *me*, Sara; she is young and will forget"—I did not believe it; but I saw he did, and would not interrupt him; "but I, in thirty years, have never before known what it was to be loved. For one sweet, supreme moment I have felt it, and you dash the cup from my lips!"

"Nonsense; it was your own fault. I warned you. Besides, you have Augusta."

"Augusta is a woman of the world; her feelings will never run away with her discretion; but such as she has, I believe are enlisted. She was marble, and I warmed it into life—another cursed experiment. I deserve to be immolated on the shrine of my own vanity and folly."

"Why not break off now, before it is too late?"

"Within two weeks of my marriage day—for which preparations have been making two years? A regiment of seamstresses have equipped the bride; the robes are sewed; the feast is spread; the altar is prepared; the priest stands ready to give the blessings; the parents, the settlements, the relatives, the spoons. Shall I, at this last moment, repudiate a contract of such long standing? destroy the peace and humiliate the pride of a woman who does me so much honor? Against this, and my pledged word—the honor I hold dearer than life, love, or liberty—I place in the scale the delicious but evanescent sentiment of a child not yet out of school, who does not know her own mind, and might bitterly repent the impulse; and my own dear-bought happiness, purchased at a price that makes life intolerable. Now do you pity me, Sara? Do you see?"

"Yes, yes, I pity you, Desmond; but you must go at once, without attempting to see her again—this instant. Do you hear?"

I was the more anxious and hurried, because in his face, with its expectant quiver of feeling, its impassioned change, I saw as in a faithful mirror, that she was coming; and immediately her steps sounded softly down the garden path.

"Are you going? will you go?" I cried, quite shaking him in my enthusiasm; but I might as well have tried to sway a stone statue. He stood immovable, his eyes eagerly lifted, while I could hear his very heart beat in loud and strong pulsations. What was to be done? no explanation must take place, and the little feet were coming nearer; the air felt as close and oppressive, as before a thunder-storm. I stood perspiring and despairing, till Luly came through the trees.

"Aunt Katy wants you about the ice cream; she sent me for you, to come in."

Her pretty head was held down, and Desmond and I exchanged glances of defiance across it. Every impulse of the man's nature was in revolt against Reason, Fate, and Justice; and the sight of what he had just denied to himself inflamed him into a wild fever of contradiction, desperation and rebellion. I knew, that were I not present, he would throw himself at her feet and worship her as saint and angel—knowing she was neither; that he would offer love he had no right to bestow, and a hand that was pledged; that he would, in short, be guilty of every extravagance and folly that temporary insanity could dictate, and which he would have to repent for a lifetime afterwards. I was determined not to leave him with Luly for a moment, and I laid my hand with a tolerably tight hold upon the flying glories of her dress.

"Not without you," I said decidedly.

183

"Yes, Aunty," she assented, but lingering and looking back like Eve upon Paradise.

"Say good-bye to Mr. Desmond, my dear," I continued like an executioner, with one arm around her slight waist; "he is going away."

Poor Luly raised her paled and frightened face to his, and again I stood astonished at the womanly emotions it expressed. Love, sorrow, tenderness, and regret, darkened the clear spheres of her eyes, and disturbed the lovely curves of her flexile lips; she did not speak, but her look told all the trouble of her heart. His face was full of bitter, yearning anguish, of passionate pain, that moved me almost to tears, angry as I was, and with just cause, against him. He opened his arms mechanically, and I believe Luly would have fled into them, but for the hold I maintained upon her; her little hands trembled to go and clasp about him, but I held one of them in my policeman-like grasp, and she could only stretch out the other in mute farewell. He bowed over it, and clung to it, till I thrust my leave-takings between them; and we turned away and left him standing there, a handsome statue of despair under the oleander trees.

Luly looked up into my face as we hurried along, with quivering lips: "He is sorry to go, Aunty?"

"Yes, my dear. Because he will not be back—he is going to be married to a lady to whom he has been long engaged. She is a very beautiful and accomplished person, and will make him very happy. In a week or two we shall get wedding-cards."

She said no more, nor I, and a silence that has never been broken by Desmond's name, fell between us. What she suffered, therefore, of childish grief or womanly sorrow I cannot tell; I could only note with wonder the gradual change that stole upon her beauty, that made her eyes softer, her smile sweeter, and lighted her fairy face with the radiance of an awakened soul. Long since she married George Curtis: she is a true and faithful wife to him, a tender mother to his children, a kind mistress to his servants, a good guardian of his house, his honor, and his name—what wrought the miracle I dare not guess, and do not ask.

Desmond I see but seldom, in the brilliant establishment he maintains for his fashionable wife, and in which he bears as active a part as one of the bronze statues on the stairs. The metal that was once warmed to life, and fused in a glowing furnace, has hardened to a colder surface than before. One sentient point it has, or had—for in a little corner den he calls his study, where he murders time, and idles life away in aimless pursuits, smoking, reading, painting—he might be an artist, if he were not an amateur—his lady-wife showed me a picture hanging on the wall, which she called his tutelary divinity. It was a fanciful figure, half-fountain, half-fairy; a wreath of white and green bound the amber hair; the shoulders shone like alabaster, the eyes like sapphires; the lips were coral red, and I knew too well the enchanting smile they wore. I looked from the exquisite face of the sprite to the dark and sallow one of the painter; from the beautiful, bewitching eyes, in which the soul was visibly dawning, to the gloomy gaze fixed upon them; and I longed to say that the Naiad—half-nymph, half-angel there—was wholly angel now, and worthy indeed to be the saint of his visions. But Mrs. Desmond was blandly explaining that the picture was a fancy sketch by her husband—his idea of the water witch 'Undine,' in that very pretty story by the Baron de la Motte Fouqué.

The Blue Handkerchief

From the *Continental Monthly*

When James Gilmore retired the *Knickerbocker* and began publishing the *Continental Monthly*, which he advertised as a new politically liberal voice, he did not expect to be once again facing a financial impasse. Yet he was, and not only could he not afford to pay for new fiction, but even his stock of free fiction had dwindled. So had James's own stock of stories, which he had continued to contribute to Gilmore's publications without payment. In consideration of Gilmore's deplorable circumstances, James dug up a short short-story he had written ten years earlier for the *National Magazine* under the title "The Fatal Gift." The very same issue of the *National* had carried an account—written in French and translated by young Henry, then in his fourth year of studying the language—by a naval officer who had seen the execution of a poor, possibly innocent man in the Plaza-Major of Lima, Peru. With some revision and retitled "The Blue Handkerchief," the story appeared in the *Continental Monthly* in 1863. In 1864, with still further revisions, James yet again published the story in *Frank Leslie's Lady's Magazine*. No doubt, James felt that the "legalized injustice" illustrated in the tale of the innocent soldier—a social principle often decried by Henry's father in the James household—warranted the attention of his imagination.

The 1863 version of this poignant tale is reprinted below. The 1853 version did not include the lengthy first paragraph introducing the circumstances of the narrator. Instead, it began:

In the year ———, about the end of October, as I was returning on foot from Orleans to the Chateau of Bardy, I beheld before me, on the high road, a regiment of Swiss Guards. I hastened forward to hear the military music, of which I am extremely fond; but before I had overtaken the regiment, the band had ceased playing, and the drum alone continued to mark the measured footsteps of the soldiers.

After marching for about half an hour, the regiment entered a small plain, surrounded by a wood of fir trees. I asked one of the captains, if the regiment was going to perform evolutions? "No, sir," he replied, "we are going to try, and probably to shoot, a soldier belonging to my company, for having robbed the citizen upon whom he was billeted.

What! I exclaimed, is he to be tried and condemned, and executed all in an instant?

From the fifth paragraph on of the 1863 "The Blue Handkerchief," it and the earlier "The Fatal Gift" are essentially the same.

I HAD PASSED my last examinations, and had received my diploma authorizing me to practice medicine, and I still lingered in the vicinity of Edinburgh, partly because my money was nearly exhausted, and partly from the very natural aversion I felt from quitting a place where three very happy and useful years had been spent. After waiting many weeks—for the communication between the opposite shores of the Atlantic were not then so rapid as now—I received a large packet of letters from "home," all of them filled with congratulations on my success, and among them were letters from my dear father and a beloved uncle, at whose instance (he was himself a physician) my father had sent me abroad to complete my medical education. My father's letter was even more affectionate than usual, for he was highly gratified with my success, and he counseled me to take advantage of the peace secured by the battle of Waterloo to visit the continent, which for many years (with the exception of a brief period) had been closed to all persons from Great Britain; he enclosed me a draft on a London banker for a thousand pounds. My uncle's letter was scarcely less affectionate: my Latin thesis (I had sent my father and him a copy) had especially pleased him; and after urging me to take advantage of my father's kindness, he added that he had placed a thousand pounds at my disposition, with the same London banker on whom my draft was drawn. A letter of introduction to a French family was enclosed in the letter, and he engaged me to visit them, for they had been his guests for a long time when the first Revolution caused them to fly France, and they were under other obligations to him; which I afterward learned from themselves was a pecuniary favor more than once renewed during their residence with him.

It was toward the end of the month of October—the most delightful month of the seasons in France—as I was returning on foot from Orleans to the Chateau de Bardy, from a rather prolonged pedestrian exploration in that neighborhood, where I had accurately examined all of the curiosities, when I thought I caught a glimpse of some soldiers. I was not mistaken: on the road before me a Prussian regiment was marching. I quickened my pace to hear the military music, for I was extremely partial to it; but the band ceased playing, and no sound was heard except an occasional roll of the kettledrum at long intervals to mark the uniform step of the soldiers. After following them for a half hour, I saw the regiment enter a small plain, surrounded by a fir grove. I asked a captain, whose acquaintance I had made, if his men where about to be drilled.

"No," said he, "they are about to try, and perhaps to shoot, a soldier of my company for having stolen something from the house where he was billeted."

"What," said I, "are they going to try, condemn, and execute him, all in the same moment?" . . .

"Yes," the captain replied; "such are the terms of our capitulations." This to him was an unanswerable reason; as if all things had been in the capitulations; the fault and its penalty—justice, and even humanity.

"If you have any curiosity to witness the proceedings," said the captain politely, "I shall be happy to get you a place. They will soon be over."

I never avoid such scenes; for I imagine that I learn, from the countenance of a dying man, what death is. I therefore followed the captain.

The regiment formed into a square. Behind the second rank, and on the borders of the wood, some of the soldiers began to dig a grave, under the command of a subaltern; for regimental duty is always performed with regularity, and a certain discipline maintained, even in the digging of a grave.

In the center of the square, eight officers were seated on drums; on their right, and a little more in front, a ninth was writing upon his knees, but with apparent negligence, and simply to prevent a man from being put to death without some legal forms.

The accused was called forward. He was a fine, well-grown young fellow, with mild, yet noble features. By his side stood a woman, who was the only witness against him. The moment the colonel began to examine this woman, the prisoner interrupted him:—

"It is useless, colonel," he said; "I will confess everything: I stole this woman's handkerchief."

The COLONEL.—You, Piter! why you passed for an honorable man and a good soldier.

PITER.—It is true, colonel, that I have always endeavored to satisfy my officers. I did not steal for myself; it was for Marie.

The COLONEL.—And who is this Marie?

PITER.—Why, Marie who lives—there—in our own country—near Areneberg—where the great apple tree is—I shall then see her no more!

The COLONEL.—I do not understand you, Piter; explain yourself.

PITER.—Well, colonel, read this letter: and he handed to the colonel the following letter:—

"MY DEAR FRIEND PITER,—I seize the opportunity of sending you this letter by Arnold, a recruit who has enlisted in your regiment. I also send you a silk purse which I have made for you. I did not let my father see that I was making it, for he always scolds me for loving you so much, and says you will never return. But you surely will come back, won't you? But whether you come back or not, I shall always love you. I first consented to become yours on the day you picked up my blue handkerchief at the Areneberg dance, and brought it to me. When shall I see you again? What pleases me is—the information I have received, that the officers esteem you, and your comrades love you. But you have still two years to serve. *Get through them as fast as you can,* and then we will be married.

"Adieu, my good friend Piter! Your dear

"MARIE.

"P.S.—Try to send me something from France—*not* for fear I should forget you, but that I may always carry it about me. *Kiss what you send, and I am sure I shall soon find out the place of your kiss.*"

Thus the sympathetic affection which exists between two fond hearts, however distant, travels far more rapidly than the electric fluid. We see with the brain; we feel with the heart.

When the colonel had finished reading the letter, Piter resumed: "Arnold," he said, "delivered me this letter last night when I received my billet. I could not sleep all night for thinking of Marie. In her letter, she asks me for something from France. I had no money; I have mortgaged my pay for three months in order to help my brother and cousin, who set out on their return home, a few days since. This morning, on rising, I opened my window. A blue handkerchief was drying upon a line, and it resembled the one belonging to Marie. The color and the blue stripes were actually the same. I was base enough to take it and put it into my knapsack. I went out into the street; my conscience smote me, and I was returning to the house to restore it to its owner, when this woman came up to me, with the guard, and the handkerchief was found in my possession. This is the whole truth. The capitulations require that I should be shot; let me be shot instantly; but do not despise me."

The judges were unable to conceal their emotion; nevertheless they unanimously condemned Piter to death. He heard the sentence without emotion; then, advancing toward his captain, requested the loan of four francs. The captain gave him the money. He then approached the old woman from whom he had taken the handkerchief, and I heard him utter these words:—

"Madame, here are four francs; I know not whether your handkerchief be worth more; but if it be, it costs me dear enough, and you may excuse me from paying the difference."

Then, taking the handkerchief, *he kissed it*, and gave it to the captain. Captain, said he, in two years you will return to our mountains; if you go near Areneberg, do me the favor to ask for Marie, and give her this blue handkerchief; but do not tell her the price I paid for it. He then knelt, and after praying fervently for a few minutes, rose, and walked with a firm step to the place of execution.

I retired into the wood, that I might not witness the last scene of this tragedy. A few shots soon made known—that all was over.

Having returned to the little plain an hour after, I found the regiment gone, and all quiet; but as I followed the border of the wood, in order to reach the high road, I perceived traces of blood, and a mound of freshly moved earth. Cutting a branch of fir, I made a rude cross, which I placed upon the grave of one already forgotten—*by all save myself and Marie!*

A Cure for Coquettes

From *Arthur's Home Magazine,* signed "Leslie Walter"

A modest story but well designed and playfully symbolic, "A Cure for Coquettes" may have earned for its pseudonymous author, Leslie Walter, perhaps ten dollars—not a princely sum, but better than naught—as it was published by *Arthur's Home Magazine* rather than the now (in 1863) virtually dead *Knickerbocker* enterprise. The coquette referred to in the title is Letty Mayfield, who, out of her coquetry and petulance, courts danger at the cost of responsibility, not just for herself but for two innocent children. The titular cure is a wolf, literally, and its harmful intentions bring Letty to her Swedenborgian senses as she rises spiritually to a commitment to the love of but one good and truly insuperable man. More than literally, though, her perfect husband has "no need to war with wolves since his marriage."

I N THE SPRING of 18——, the inhabitants of a frontier settlement in one of the newer states began to suffer from the ravages of a more savage enemy than the treacherous Indians, by whom they were surrounded; the wolves, rendered perfectly fearless by starvation and cold, poured down from their hilly fastnesses, and completely invested the town, lurking in the thick forests around it, and as they grew more bold and fierce, venturing within its limits at night, and hardly retiring with the daylight. The townspeople, though few in number, were hardy backwoodsmen, who feared no living thing, but they did not consider the advent of a few wolves in their neighborhood as a matter of sufficient importance to justify alarm, till one day the news came of a traveller killed and devoured by the fierce brutes in the woods a few miles distant, and the angry hunters now regarding the danger as of some consequence, leagued themselves together to meet it.

In this they were reinforced by the soldiers of a government fort, recently established, who, having always been quartered nearer civilization, knew nothing of this savage war-fare, but being weary of the monotony and forced inaction of their position, were glad to join in anything for the sake of excitement. The commandant of the post, Major Sheldon, considered that as he and his force had been stationed there to fight Indians, they ought to remain always in their place, to guard against attacks and surprises, but the men were so eager, and the townspeople so much in need of their help, that he suppressed this feeling,and ordered out all those not absolutely needed at the fort, to accompany the expedition.

Major Sheldon's family, to whom my story belongs, then living in temporary lodgings in the town until their residence at the barracks should be finished, consisted of his wife, a little boy and girl, and an adopted daughter, Letty Mayfield, who might with truth be called the belle of her set, since she was the only young lady in it, though her beauty and vivacity would have given her that position, against many rivals, in almost any town or city to be mentioned. Such at least was the unanimous opinion of the grateful young officers stationed at the fort, who looked upon her appearance there as a special dispensation of Providence in their favor, and thankfully accepted the new and pleasing excitement of the wolves it involved.

The object of these attentions, at first rather dismayed at her banishment to a frontier fort, soon discovered that there was a compensation for her captivity, and a use for her accomplishments, even here. She was just from boarding school, where she had learned music, and could sing to the guitar in a very delightful voice—French, which was of but little use to her with Mrs. Sheldon, who was a Parisienne, and did not understand Letty's "native" accent half as well as her English—all the fashionable "'atics" and "ologies," and to dress, dance, and flirt, in the most bewitching manner. Besides which she was spirited and courageous, and soon learned of her admiring young tutors to ride a prancing young cavalry horse, and fire a pistol without wincing—exploits upon which she prided herself more than upon her progress in Latin or painting. Her education in these latter branches was gradually passing almost exclusively into the hands of one Lieutenant Walter Ashly, who was her "guide, philosopher and friend" when she chose it, but with whom she flirted, as with all her other adorers—kind today and cross tomorrow, greatly to that young gentleman's distress and dismay, which, however, he managed to conceal from the eyes of the pretty coquette, who tried in vain to provoke him to some demonstration. To outward appearance, he preserved a masterly inactivity, while his rivals made sure of winning the prize; but his thoughts were sadly at war. Letty, always too fascinating and lovely, was so much more so when with him—for with a woman's instinct, she knew him to be better worth winning than the rest—so softly charming, so sweetly attractive, that he could not sometimes help expressing his admiration and love, which she, delighted in her coquettish soul, laughingly put aside and ignored. And yet unknown to herself, a deep interest grew in her heart day by day.

But to return to our muttons—I beg pardon—our wolves. The pretty Letty had accompanied her father down to the fort on the morning of the day on which the wolf-hunters went, ostensibly to visit her friends, Mrs. Lindsay and Mrs. Bowles, but really to see the cavalcade start. The two children went with them, Gerard, a handsome boy of six, walking by her side, and the lovely little Rose, carried in her father's arms and caressing his warlike whiskers. In this order, they arrived at the barracks, and Letty was soon seated in Mrs. Lindsay's parlor, receiving the salutations and compliments of the dashing young officers, who defiled before her, "ready for the fray," their martial equipments glittering in the sunlight, and their countenances cheerful with enthusiasm for their first battle—no matter with what—after so long and inglorious a peace. They looked forwards to the prospect of killing Time with quite as much joy as that of killing the wolves, he being the most harassing enemy they had to encounter.

"But where is Lieutenant Ashly?" wondered the lively Mrs. Lindsay, when all the warriors had passed by in martial pomp. The prudent lady had hardly spoken when she disappeared, seeing the spoken-of approaching, and Letty's heart beat high, for she had hoped, without knowing it, that he, as well as her father, was to remain behind and guard the post, instead of joining this really dangerous expedition. But she smothered whatever regret she might have felt, lest its traces should appear in her countenance, and smilingly held out her hand to him as he entered.

He did not smile, or even bow beautifully, as Mr. Gould and Mr. Merivale had done; he did not compliment her like Mr. Day or Mr. Livingston, though she was fresh from her walk, and had never looked prettier; he only took her extended hand, so quietly and calmly, that Letty's coquettish spirit rose up against her heart, and incited it to rebellion and revolt.

"Miss Letty," said he, gravely, "I want to ask a question—did you come alone, and shall you go back the same way?"

She answered no, that her father had brought her.

"But that you intend to return alone?"

She nodded yes. "As all the officers are gone," she archly added.

"Let me beg of you not to do so. Indeed, I do not think it safe. I remained behind to ask your permission to see you safely home before accompanying the rest."

She shook her head; "she was not going just yet."

"Then I will wait till you do, if you will allow me. I am very uneasy—I feel a sort of 'presentiment' of evil. Dear Letty, please be guided by me for once. Go home now, and let me go with you."

"How impolite you are to want to send me home," she answered, laughing, to conceal the uneasiness his earnestness aroused.

"But you consent?" he persisted gently.

"No, I am not so timid as you," she gaily retorted, her pride and self-will coming to the rescue, as she felt her coldness departing. "I am not afraid to walk through a town like this without a military guard. Perhaps, though," she added, in a tone meant to be satirical, "I am depriving you of your last chance of an honorable retirement, by refusing your escort. It *is* rather a dangerous expedition!"

Her heart smote her before she had uttered the last word; she was ashamed of the meanness of her pretended suspicion.

His eyes flashed for an instant; the next, he had conquered the feeling, and answered gravely—

"Promise me, at least," he said, "since you refuse my attendance, that you will ask your father to send two of the men with you when you return?"

This anxious care for her welfare, even after her unjust and insulting speech, touched Letty to the heart. She felt tears rising to her eyes, and to cover her confusion, answered hastily in the affirmative, and with a look and bow he was gone.

She felt tempted to call him back; she was afraid to have him go away among the wolves—she was afraid to go herself, without him; she wished she had accepted his offer—that she had not uttered that cruel, taunting speech, and many, many more of which memory too faithfully reminded her; that she was less unworthy of his unwearied care and kindness, half resolving to follow him and tell him so. While she still meditated and hesitated, she heard his horse's hoofs on the stones beneath, and knew that he was going, disappointed and grieved. It was too late to call him back, but she did what she could; she ran to the window, and put out her lovely face, covered with dimples and blushes, to watch his departure. Some invisible attraction must have drawn his eyes upwards as he passed, for they met hers, and his handsome face, hitherto rather dark and downcast, lighted up in a moment, while Letty thought in herself, with a thrill of pride, that it was not possible to see a more gallant cavalier. He reined in his horse, evidently intending to return, but she felt herself blushing, and was ashamed to relent now, so she only shook her head in answer, and the anxious look returned to his face. She knew that he was disappointed in her, and deeply grieved at the heartlessness, unkindness, and caprice of her conduct, as well as uneasy for her, but she felt powerless to help it, and he waved his hand, took off his military cap, and galloped rapidly away to join his companions, whose departure she had forgotten to witness in the confusion of this interview. When the last sound of his horse's feet had died away, she sank down among the pillows of the sofa, and cried bitterly, the prudent Mrs. Lindsay not appearing for half an hour.

She expressed her determination of going home immediately, but was overruled by the entreaties of her friend, who was lonely, and wanted her lively company. The two ladies spent the morning in various amusements—singing, reading, and chatting together—and after dinner, Letty took her little brother and sister from their playmates, and started homewards. She was so much occupied with them that she forgot her promise till she was bidding her friend good-bye at the very gates of the fort, and then she was really ashamed to go back and ask her father for an escort. In broad daylight, within the very limits of the town, on a frequented high road! the idea seemed so absurd that she did not like to think of it, so laughingly said adieu, and walked on, accommodating her pace to that of the little three-year-old Rose, who held her forefinger tightly in a chubby hand, and chattered all the way.

Thus they had passed several rods beyond the cluster of trees and bushes that served to mark the halfway place between the fort and home, when Letty, hearing some slight noise behind her, turned and saw a sight that froze the blood in her veins, and made her heart stand still. A large wolf, gaunt and famished, but fierce and savage, his tongue lolling out of his open jaws, followed them silently, but with that "swift gallop" which brought him nearer every instant to the defenseless party. The children, following her horror-stricken gaze, uttered a frightened cry, which seemed to stimulate their fierce pursuer, and Letty recovered her self possession in a moment, though her face was deadly pale.

"Run, Gerard!" she said, and the boy darted off like an arrow towards home, while she snatched up the baby Rose, and holding her to her bosom, followed him with flying feet. She could see that he would be saved, light and agile, he went swiftly on, but she, though young and strong, and gifted by terror with almost superhuman strength, was encumbered with the weight of the child, who clung closely around her neck, almost smothering her with her little arms. She could feel, though she dared not look back, that the savage brute was gaining on her, and that death was drawing near; and her thoughts, like those of drowning men, ran back over all her past life, and up to Heaven. She could not speak, but she thought a prayer— not for deliverance—she did not hope it—but for a short and speedy death for herself and her darling Rose, that the agony might be brief, and Heaven receive her soul in mercy. She felt her breath grow feebler, and her footsteps fainter, a confused roaring and rushing was in her ears, through which she only heard the panting of the animal behind her, coming closer and closer. Yes, it drew nearer, her strength was failing, her sight growing dim; she sent up one prayer for her father, and mother, and Walter—for by the revelation of approaching death, she knew that she loved him and was dear to him—she tried with faithful instinct to shelter the child closer in her arms, and closed her eyes. She heard a sharp, quick sound, felt the animal's hot breath upon her cheek, staggered forwards with one last convulsive effort, and fell.

* * *

LETTY RETURNED TO life again, clasped in encircling arms, warmed by tender kisses, recalled by impassioned words. She lay silent for a few moments, still and deathly cold; but a sudden thrill of anguish shot through her as she missed the child from her arms. She remembered nothing of the terrible scene but that she was to hold Rosie tight—not to let her go, and that Rosie was gone. She uttered a sharp cry of pain—

"Rose! oh, where is she?"

"Here I am, Letty, dear!" answered the sweet little voice, and she opened her eyes and saw the beautiful child lying beside her on her own bed at home. But what was that other pale, anxious face that bent above her—whose were those eyes of soft tenderness that met her own—those strong arms that held her so closely in a protecting clasp? As she looked, the past rushed back upon her mind, and she cried—

"Oh, Walter, Walter!—I thought I should never see you again!" put both her cold, white arms about his neck, and lay weeping on his shoulder. She refused to leave him, she clung to him wild and trembling, while he, scarcely less moved, would not have let her go had she willed it. She had always been very dear to him, in the flush of her beauty, in the fulness of her power, but never so dear as now, when all unnerved and shaken she opened the sealed book of her heart, and showed him that his name and his alone was written there. Lying clasped in his protecting arms, she told him in broken words how well she loved him, and how bitterly she remembered in that dying hour that she had left him, wronged and unhappy, never to see him more. She flung conventionalities away; she told him that he had saved her life, and he should have it, worthless as it was; that death would be less bitter now that he loved her and forgave her, and life sweeter than ever before she had dreamed it, if she lived for him; and then she laid down her lovely fainting head upon his breast again, and told him that his place was there forever.

And what did Walter say? Did the Peri speak as at last she entered Paradise?

She was grateful when her mother bent over her and kissed her, weeping tears of joy, and blessing her for saving her children; she was thankful when her father arrived, strong as he was, greatly shaken by the thought of the danger past, and came to her bedside with unusual drops in his proud, dark eyes, unusual tenderness in his deep, faltering voice, to praise her gallant courage with fond caresses, and call her loving names. She was gentle and tender with the children she had saved, but she turned away from all to the unwearied love of her preserver, and it was his presence only that quieted her nervous dread—his look alone that calmed her troubled eyes—his voice that soothed her into sleep upon his breast.

It was many days before Letty was able to hear the particulars of her rescue, even from her rescuer—how he had been haunted by a presentiment of evil to her that nothing could conquer—though, between the double terror of Indians and wolves it was easily to be accounted for—had galloped back in haste when it grew unbearable, and arrived in time to save her by shooting the wolf through the heart just as it touched her, so close that her dress was soaked in its blood; how he had borne her home, the child frightened, but unhurt, so convulsively clasped in her arms that they could hardly separate them, and how they had feared for her life for hours—"for her *reason* not at all," he added, with a mischievous smile, "after she began to speak." "In fact, you appeared far more sensible then than now," continued this excellent nurse to whom Letty had become less demonstrative especially before other people, as she grew better. But even his objections must have been silenced by the fervent and unrestrained caresses she bestowed upon him, as she heard his quiet story, and lived over again the horrors of the scene from which he had rescued her. Later than ever, with the beauty of a soft and sweet tenderness added to her face, she yet betrayed no sign of coquetry or vanity as she returned to health, but clung to the honest avowal she had made in delirium, and to her preserver, so faithfully, that her former admirers, after once testing the strength of her resolution, gave her up, most unwillingly and despairingly, to her determined choice, and remained true to her memory for various periods of time, individually, alternating from six weeks to two months.

She remained so constant to her faith in this case, that when she and Walter Ashly had been married many years, and her saucy niece Nelly, very much like what she herself had been, invited her to tell how and where she fell in love with her handsome uncle, she owned that she did fall in love with him, told this story to explain, and confessed that she was still of the same mind as when she married him for love, "and to keep off the wolves," she added, with a gleam of her former wickedness on her still lovely face, which changed to a blush and a smile as she met his true and affectionate eyes. He has had no need to war with wolves since his marriage, however, for they live in a handsome house in the centre of a city.

I will add, for the benefit of the curious, that the wolves in the neighborhood of L—— were all killed in the famous *battue*, and but one of the hunters injured. No more travellers were eaten, and L—— is a city now.

My Lost Darling

From the *Continental Monthly*

By 1863 the romance of the Civil War had faded, and the casualties it continued daily to claim were becoming a tragic fact of America's national history. In the intimately rendered "My Lost Darling," James reflects something of the tenor of the war-torn times as he gives voice to one among thousands of the conflict's victims—a woman confronting the imminent death of her beloved brother, a Union lieutenant, who has lost two limbs in battle—and makes of an intensely wrought dramatic monologue a singular psychological portrait of Maggie Dunn. Indeed, in the first quarter of the story, the horrors of war are illuminated exclusively in terms of Maggie's personal terror, which consigns her to a shadowy nightmarish reality that her own heated imagination may have created or hallucinated. (James will bring similar ambiguities to narrative perspectives on reality in his later, mature work *The Turn of the Screw*.) Soon enough, though, Maggie finds herself in the military hospital where her brother lies dying. She also finds herself at desperate odds with her brother, and with the God to whom she prays and through whom, in James's religious views at this stage, all worldly things are fulfilled. Not surprisingly, then, it is in Maggie's final vision of "an unseen Hand" that she approaches a resolution to her own inconsolable grief, and in the end is seen to be Swedenborgianly more than seems to be: "a ministering angel . . . in woman's guise."

T HE BOOM OF cannon in the distance, flags floating gaily in the bright morning air, strains of martial music filling it, a waving of caps and handkerchiefs, shouts in the streets below, and the tramp of many feet. A regiment is passing! To a stern fate, that beckons darkly in the distance, these patriots are moving, with firm, determined tread—to long, exhausting marches, and fireless bivouac; to hunger and cold; to sufferings in varied forms; to wounds and imprisonment; *to death!* God knows when and how they are going;—and, amid the doomed throng slowly passing, the bright face of my darling smilingly upturned to mine. I wave my hand and kiss it; my handkerchief is wet through and through.

He came to me but an hour since, decked in his uniform (a lamb decked for the slaughter). 'I'm a lieutenant now,' he said, tapping his shoulder gaily; 'I shall rival Sam Patch at a leap, and jump to the head at once. Three months is enough to make a colonel of me.' And so, with his young heart beating high and warm, upborne by wild hopes like these, he held me to his heart at parting, and went away quite joyously, my poor darling! shedding only a few tears in sympathy with mine. I watch his form until I lose it in the mass before me; then I watch the mass moving slowly, slowly on, bearing him away from me; till the heavy tramp dies out upon the air, and the dark mass, growing less and less, becomes a dim speck in the distance; and the music wanes, and wanes, and dies out also, and in the still air about me only the voice of the wind is heard: coming and going at long, lazy intervals, it speaks to my inner sense with a warning note, a low requiem sound. Why is it that it takes that weird tone always when sorrow is darkly waiting for me in the future? What prophet's voice speaks to me in it? What invisible thing without addresses its wild warning to the invisible within? As I listened, my soul grew chill and dark with the shadow of a coming gloom; my heart grew cold. God help me! How wildly, how almost despairingly I prayed for my darling's life!

Alone in the world, we were all in all to each other. Mine was a wild, exclusive love. Heart and soul were bound up in him. Other girls had their lovers; my fond heart beat for him alone. What tie nearer and dearer than the tie of blood united us? What bond, sacred and invisible, bound our souls together? I know not; I only know that my heart and mind echoed always the thoughts and moods of his; that, no matter what dreary distance lay between us, our souls held communication still; that I rejoiced when he was glad; and wept when I said, 'He is sorrowful today.' He had gone away gay and hopeful, and had left me weeping—oppressed by vague fears and chill forebodings, my heart could not echo *now* the happy mood of his. Wild and weird, all that dreary day, the wind moaned its warning; and the sad echo sounded through other dreary days that followed this; and dreary nights came also, when I prayed and wept, and covered the pictured face with tears and kisses—when I cried, 'God keep my precious one, and bring my darling back to me;' and that was all my prayer;—when I sank to fitful slumbers, and wildly dreamed of shell and cannon ball, and bullets thick as hail, of foes met in deadly fray, of shielding my darling's form with mine—there, where all was smoke and darkness and blood and horror—and dying gladly in his stead. Or the scene changed from horror to desolation, and, with a dreadful sense of isolation on me, alone in the darkness I wandered up and down, blindly searching for him I never found; or finding him, perhaps, covered with ghastly wounds, and dead, quite dead; and then starting broad awake with horror at the sight.

God help us! us women, with our wild, inordinate affections, when Death waits in ambush for our darlings, whom we are powerless to save from the smallest of life's ills and perils! A letter came at last, eight dear pages, with all the margins filled. Long, confidential, loving, with just a thought of sadness in it; a slight, almost imperceptible shadow resting on the glowing hopes with which he left; yet bright withal, bright like himself. The charm of novelty was potent yet. How I read it o'er and o'er, this first dear message from him; how I kissed the senseless thing; how my tears fell upon it; how day and night I wore it on my heart, until another took its place!

They came at stated intervals *now*, and as the time wore on, and their tone changed, little by little, I knew that the hard life he led began to tell upon him—that, petted, fondled, cherished as he had been, unfitted for hardship of any kind, they grew at times almost too great for calm endurance. He never complained, my grand, brave boy; he spoke of them lightly always, sometimes jestingly, but he could not deceive that fine interior sense. I knew there were times when he turned heartsick from the wild life that claimed him; I could see how his noble nature shrank from all that was coarse and revolting in it; how he longed for fireside joys and sweet domestic peace, and pined with dreary homesickness; how his heart cried out for me in the melancholy night. And then even this comfort, that had softened the dull, longing pain within, was denied me—no letters came. Mail after mail went and came, and I grew feverish with suspense. I imagined him beset by ghastly perils, and, with torturing uncertainty wearing my very life away, I watched and waited as women are wont to do. Then dark rumors were afloat of foes making a desperate advance, and of bloody battle pending. One night a horror fell upon my troubled sleep—an appalling gloom, a shuddering, suffocating sense of some impending doom. Battling fiercely and blindly with this dread, invisible something, I awoke in deadly fright, to find the terror no less clear to my perceptions, no less palpable and real, and to wrestle with it still. Some blind instinct in me called aloud for air; with difficulty mastering an almost overpowering impulse to rush out into the night, I flew to the window, raised it, and looked out. A fierce storm was raging—a storm of whose very existence I had until that moment been unconscious. The thunder rolled, and muttered, and broke in wild, fearful crashes. Sheets of lightning every instant lighted up the blackness, and made the sky terrific. Gushes of wind and rain wet and chilled me through and through. Unmindful of it, with that fine interior sense aroused, I listened with all my soul—not to the thunder's fearful voice, to the wild beating of the storm, or to the wind's melancholy moaning, but to *something* on the tempestuous air, and yet a stranger to it.

There came a lull in the storm at last, and then, O God! O God! through the sullen gloom, his voice was calling to me. Now faint and low, as if his life was ebbing; then raised in agony, wild with supplication and sharp with pain. I saw him covered with gaping wounds, on a hideous field, piled with slain and soaked with blood. I went mad, I think: I have a vague remembrance of rushing out into that fearful storm, undressed as I was, with wild resolve to follow the sound of the voice, to reach him somehow, or die in the mad attempt; of being brought back, shut up in my room, and a sort of guard placed over me; of making wild attempts to rush out again, and struggling ineffectually with those that held me back—of raving wildly; then of long and dreamless slumbers, when I had become exhausted, and the sharp agony was past; of rousing myself to go about in a listless, apathetic way, waiting with dulled sense for lists of killed and wounded; of the doctor bringing the paper to me and saying, with his face all light: 'He is not dead; you will find his name among the wounded;' of finding where he was, eluding their vigilance, and travelling night and day until I reached the place. All this seems vague and unreal, as a half-forgotten dream—too dim and lifeless for memory. Entire change of scene, new sights and faces, and, more than all, the conviction that the time had come for action *now*, and that *he* would need me, roused me from this misty state a little. When I landed at the place, I think I recovered the clear consciousness of my surroundings, while standing in the provost-marshal's office (the city was under military rule) waiting my turn to speak.

Then I thought for the first time what a mad thing it was in me to have come at all—at least, to have come in the way I had come; I, so unpractical, so woefully lacking in that sterling common sense, that potent weapon with which women battled successfully with the stern realities of life; and thinking, too, with a dull pain at my heart, that doubtless my darling would suffer by reason of my ignorance and inability. I studied the mass of strange faces about me, thinking to which I would turn for help, if help were needed. After reading them, one after another, and rejecting them, I turned at last to a group in front of me, and singled out one that was addressing the others, a man of consequence among them—at least a certain superiority of air and manner led to that conjecture. He had a fine open face, whose expression changed continually; and the more I studied the face, the more I placed a blind trust and reliance in it. Attracted by the magnetism of a fixed gaze, probably, his eyes wandered from the group about him, after a little while, wandered aimlessly about the room, and then met mine. Seeing that I was watching him, or observing, perhaps, that I was suffering, though, Heaven knows, the sight of misery of all kinds *there* was common enough, he crossed the room and came to me. 'You may be obliged to wait some time longer yet,' he said in a tone of hearty kindness; 'you look ill, madam. You had better sit down.' He found a chair and brought it to me. He was on the point of leaving, but I grasped his arm as he turned to go. 'If you have any influence here,' I said, in a half-distracted way, 'tell the clerk, tell somebody to let my turn come next. My brother is here and wounded; I have travelled night and day to get to him; it's dreadful to be so near, and yet to wait and wait.' He turned in grave surprise, and looked at me narrowly, fancying, from my incoherency, I was taking leave of my senses possibly. 'Your name, young lady?' he said, at last. I gave it, 'Margaret Dunn.' He started at the name, and a heavy shadow came over his face: 'And your brother,' he said, hurriedly, 'is Lieutenant Dunn, of the Fifty-fifth Illinois Volunteers, Company A? I am surgeon of the Fifty-fifth; I know him well. He was a brave fellow, and a fine, manly, and handsome a fellow as one need wish to see.' He ended with a sigh, and mingling with the shadow there came a look of pity in his face. The past tense, which I am sure he used unconsciously; the look of pity; the sigh but half supressed, overpowered me with dread. 'He has not died of his wounds?' I gasped, grasping his arm convulsively, 'O God! he is not dead?' 'He is alive,' said the doctor, gravely. 'Father, I thank Thee, Thou hast heard my prayer!'

The sudden transition from that mortal dread of death to the blessed certainty of life was too much; my joy was too great; forgetful of my surroundings, unmindful of his presence, I wept and sobbed aloud. When I had controlled my emotion in a measure, or at least their stormy outward manifestation, I found the doctor regarding me with the same grave face. 'You should not have come here in your present weak, excited state,' he said, at last, 'or, rather, you should not have come at all. From sights and sounds of a hospital, even strong men turn with a shudder. It's no place for a delicate woman.' 'He is there,' I murmured, tremulously, 'I can suffer anything for those I love.' Regarding me in silence for a moment, he looked as if taking my measure. 'These women that *can* bear,' he said, with a sigh, 'sometimes overrate their powers of endurance.' 'Do you think I shall have to wait much longer? do you think I can go soon now?' I questioned, appealingly, breaking the silence that had fallen between us. 'No, you must wait your turn,' said the doctor, decidedly; 'besides, you are not calm enough yet; the surgeons are at work in the ward where we are going. They are taking off a man's limb— two or three of them, for that matter. I shan't take you there until the operations are finished.' Then first came the horrid thought that *he* might be mutilated in the same way. Vague, indistinct, dreadful visions uprose before me, of all sorts and kinds of horrid disfigurement, and I grew sick and faint. 'Not *his* limb!' I gasped, struggling with a deathly faintness. No, not his, said the doctor, sorrowfully. The same cloud was still there that had settled on his face when he first spoke of him; the same pity for me shining through it. 'There is a room here where the ladies go when they have long to wait. You had better go in there and rest yourself. I will bring you some tea and something light and palatable in the shape of food, and you must eat and drink. Confiscated property, you see,' he said, as he entered; 'a rebel family walked out, and we walked in; comfortable quarters.' I noticed then there was a carpet on the floor, sofa, mirrors, and other comforts. 'Sit down,' said the doctor. He had taken the tone of command with me—a tone I would have resented at any other time; now, nerveless and weak, relying on him solely, I obeyed him like a sick child. He brought the tea, watched me while I drank it, looked on while I choked down tears and food together. He ordered me to go to sleep, and left me. Doubtless even this command had its effect. Things grew dreamy and indistinct after a while; perhaps I slept a little; but the time seemed very, very long. At last his tap at the door roused me from this half-conscious state. 'Ready?' he briefly questioned, as he looked in, a moment after. I said yes, tremulously: now that the time had come, I trembled so I could scarcely keep my feet. He gave me his arm as we went out together. 'It's not far,' he said, encouragingly, just across here. The fresh air did me good. Quite likely, the conversation he perseveringly maintained on indifferent subjects, in spite of my random replies, was also of service to me. I grew calmer as we went along. The distance was but short, and we soon reached the place of our destination—a large hotel, which had been hurriedly converted into a hospital.

'Come,' said the doctor, pausing with his hand upon the door, and turning to me, 'cheer up! There is no misery, after all, but what is in the comparative degree. Things are never so bad but that they may have been worse. I dare say, on occasion you can be a brave little woman.'

'I can,' I returned, eagerly, too grateful for his penetration, or at least his good opinion, and too sad and abstracted altogether, to notice that he was paying me a compliment. 'I can, indeed; indeed you haven't seen the best part of me.'

He smiled just the ghost of a smile in answer, as we went in. He led me through several rooms into what had been a large dining hall—a chill, bare, desolate place. Cots were ranged up and down the room, cots across it, cots filled up the centre, and all, *all* filled with sick and wounded men. I thought if I was once in the room with my brother, some instinct would lead me to him; but I felt no drawing toward any one of those miserable bedsides, and a chill of disappointment fell upon me. 'Take me to the ward where my brother is lying,' I said to the doctor, pleadingly, 'ah, pray do!' 'This *is* the ward, he replied, but he did not take me to him. He stopped at every cot we passed. Of my burning impatience, which he could not choose but see, of the urgent and almost passionate appeals I made to hasten his progress, he took no notice whatever. He stopped almost every moment; he felt the pulse of one patient, questioned another, dealt out medicine here and there—took his own time for everything. We stopped at last where, on the outside of the coverlet, lay a wounded soldier, half-dressed; a poor, mutilated creature; a leg and an arm were gone. The face was turned toward the wall, away from us; not a muscle moved; he was sleeping, probably. 'Take me to my brother,' I piteously moaned, shuddering with horror as I turned from the unaccustomed sight. 'I have waited so long; do take me to my brother.' 'This is somebody's brother!' said the doctor, sharply. Something in the tone, not the sharpness of it—something half-familiar in the broken outline of the form, caused a half-suffocating sense of a vague, unutterable horror. A deathly faintness seized me; I sank into a chair beside the bed. The doctor gave me water to drink—hastily and silently sprinkled some water upon my head and face. There was a movement of the poor maimed form upon the bed—he gave me a warning look—the face turned toward us. It was my darling's! 'My life!' Shivering and shuddering I threw myself upon the narrow bed beside him, clasped my poor darling in my arms, and held his stricken heart to mine. The hard, defiant look upon his features melted into one of tenderness— down the worn face the tears fell slowly. 'I didn't know as you would love me just the same,' he said. It was his right arm that was gone. Calling him by every endearing name with wild expressions of affection, I wiped the tears tenderly away, covering the dear face with kisses, while my own fell fast. The doctor left us together for a little— albeit used to scenes like this, wiping *his* eyes as he went away.

A gust of bitter passion swept over my darling. He started up. 'Rascally rebels!' he cried; 'cursed bullets! Why couldn't they have been aimed at my heart and *killed* me! I was willing to give my life— but to make a wreck, a broken hull of me! Look at me, Maggie, a poor, maimed wretch. What am I fit for? Who will care for me *now*? To be an object of loathing!' he continued, between his set teeth; 'to be a sight of horror; to win, perhaps, after she gets used to the deformity, a little meagre love for charity's sake; to be scorned and loathed and pitied; if I could get only off from the face of the earth—out of the sight of men; if God would let me die!' Wounded sorely as he was, his boyish vanity in his really handsome person, his manly pride in its strength, was more sorely wounded still. Yes, strangers *would* think him a sight to behold: had not even I turned shuddering from that disfigured form, before I knew it was my darling's? He *was* ruined for life, and he was young too—only nineteen. He was very weak, and this passionate outbreak of feeling had exhausted him. It was but a flash of his old fire at best. His head sank back upon my arm again; he lay with his eyes closed, resting for a little; when he spoke again, his voice was low and wavering, tremulous with tears.

'I wouldn't care so much, only—' He paused, hesitated, drew with difficulty a little locket from his bosom, and gazed upon it tearfully. A jealous pain shot through my heart. I had thought until that moment that I was all in all to him, first in his affections, as he was in mine; that no rival shared his heart. *This* was the bitterest pang of all. I looked down at the beautiful face set in the locket, perfect as to form and color, with such a fierce hatred of its original as I hope in God's name I shall never feel again for any mortal breathing.

'It's all over between us,' he sighed; 'even if I were ungenerous enough to ask it, she wouldn't receive me now.' My face spoke my scorn. 'Don't blame her,' he said pathetically; 'it isn't natural she should, poor little thing! This for what she might have been to me.' Then he kissed the pictured face, and sorrowfully laid it back again upon his heart. 'I thought to go back to her a colonel at least—a general perhaps,' he went on, with a piteous smile; 'to be crowned with laurels, loaded with honors, and proudly claim her as my bride: I little thought that this would be the end!' It was a man's grave comment on a boy's wild dream. He had buried his youth in those two weeks of anguish. It was a man's face that looked upon me, and I read in it a man's strong endurance and stern resolve. That, and the smile with which he said it, moved me more than any emotion, however hopeless or despairing, could have done. My grief burst forth anew.

Dearer, a thousand times dearer, now that love had left him, and youthful friends turned coldly away. Ah! thank God! bless God! There are none so dear to each other, so inexpressibly dear, as those whom sorrow joins; no tie that binds so closely as the sacred bond of suffering. I said so brokenly, sobbing out my love and sorrow, as I held him to my heart. His longing for home had been intense; now that he had seen me, it became well nigh insupportable. To go away from this his place of suffering—from the myriad eyes bent upon him here, and creep back broken-hearted to that sacred sheltering haven, and hide his great grief there—this wish absorbed him quite. 'I want to go home, Maggie,' he said, in a brokenhearted whisper, clinging to me the while; 'I want to go home and die.' Die! I wouldn't hear the word; I stopped its half-formed utterance with tears and kisses. The doctor shook his head at the suggestion and counselled delay; but he was burning with impatience, and I was resolute. We started the very next day. We travelled by easy stages, but he grew weaker all the time: toward the last, with his head upon my breast, he would sleep for hours, peacefully as a little child. Reduced to almost infant weakness when we reached our journey's end, they took him in their arms tenderly as they would have taken an infant, and laid him on my bed. There, in that darkened room, I nursed him night and day, striving to win him back to thoughts of life, and love of it. 'Is't too late, Maggie,' he would say, with placid resignation; 'life has nothing for me, dear; I want to go to sleep—to that long, dreamless sleep, where memory never wakes to haunt us!' But I couldn't bear it—I wouldn't have it so. I bade him think of how *my* heart would break if he, too, died and left me. In my earnest love, I called Heaven to witness that I was ready not only to die for him, if need be, but to do a better, nobler thing, God helping me—to live for him; eschewing other ties, to devote my life and heart to this one affection. We had wealth, thank God! (I never thanked God for that before.) We would go to far-off lands as soon as he was able—away from old sights and scenes, where no familiar object would recall the past, and where, cut off from all associations, we could be all and all to each other; and, with ardent hope, I commenced immediate preparations for our voyage. I read him books of travel; showed him the half-finished garments intended for our journey; purchased all things needful, even to the books we would read upon the way—richly paid for toilsome endeavor, for days of patient waiting, if I but roused in him even a passing interest in the subject, won from him but the shadow of a smile. Ah! even those days had their gleams of sunshine. I was his only nurse, his sole dependence, his all; there was exquisite happiness in that! I said to myself, he is mine now, and always will be; and then I thought of the fair face so lovingly resting against the weary heart, and grew exultant, Heaven forgive me! and said, 'Nothing will take him from me now.' One day he rallied very suddenly. A portion of his old vigor seemed to animate his frame; something of the old look was in his face. He took my hand and laid it tenderly against his cheek; he smiled twice during the morning; I kissed him and said, 'We shall be able to start soon now, my darling!' The doctor gravely watched us both, but I would not let his gravity disturb me. He called me to him as he left the room. As I went out, the dear brown eyes were watching me. I turned to nod and smile to him, saying blithely, as I joined the doctor, 'Don't you think we shall be able to start in three weeks, doctor?' 'Shut the door, my dear,' he said; I had left it ajar. The tone startled me. There was compassion in it; and I noticed now that he was walking up and down the room in an agitated way. 'My dear,' he said again, 'you had better take a seat farther from the door.' His voice was hoarse this time—his tone, his air, his unwonted tenderness, were ominous. 'What is the matter?' I said, in sudden fear; 'can't we go as soon as we have intended?'

213

He did not answer me at first; he walked to the window and looked out; he turned to me after a little: 'He is bound on a longer voyage,' he said, with a tremor in his voice; 'he is going to a more distant country.'

I did not start or cry; I did not comprehend the meaning of his words. I sat silent, looking at him. He came to me, took both my hands in his: 'Hush!' he said; 'don't cry aloud—it would disturb him. But I must tell you the truth: he won't live three days.' I understood it all now—took in the *full* meaning of his dreadful words. I did not cry or faint; I did not even weep; I thought my heart was bleeding—that the blood was actually oozing from it drop by drop. I clung to the doctor as I would to the strong arm of an earthly saviour with wild entreaty, with passionate appeal. I prayed him to save my darling, as if he held within his grasp the keys of life and death. I offered all my wealth; I made unheard-of vows—promised impossible things. In the anguish of my supplication, I fell at his very feet. 'My dear,' he said, as he raised me tenderly up again, 'even in this world there is a limit to wealth's potent power; it is always powerless in a time like this.' I had sunk into a chair, exhausted by emotion, and chill with dread, my face buried in my hands despairingly. He laid his hand upon my head in fatherly compassion: 'It's what we've all got to come to, sooner or later,' he went on, tremulously. 'As life goes on, our hopes die out one by one; and, one after another, death claims our treasures. Bow to what is inevitable; pray for resignation.'

I couldn't—I wouldn't. I prayed for *his* life, yet in a hopeless, despairing way. To the All-powerful my soul went out continually in one wild, desperate cry. I battled fiercely with that stern impending fate, yet I felt from the first how vainly. Around my poor, wounded, dying boy, night and day I hovered constantly—I would not leave him for an instant. Every hour was bearing him away from me—drifting him farther and farther out into an unknown sea. I crept to his side when I could do nothing more for him, and laid my head beside his on the pillow. Sometimes I slept there for very sorrow, grasping him instinctively the while, seeking even in sleep, with fierce, rebellious will, to stem the invisible tide of that dark river, and bear him back to life. 'He would not live three days,' the doctor had said: he *did* live just *three days*. It was on the evening of the third, just as the day was fading, that he called me softly to him. I had opened the window and put back the curtain, to admit the air and the waning light.

The wind rose as the twilight deepened, waking at intervals in the gloomy stillness, as if from sleep. It filled the room every now and then with a sad, sighing sound, then died out slowly, again to swell, again to fall, sad as the tolling of a funeral knell. He lay listening to it when I went to him, with parted lips and strange solemnity of face. Too heartbroken for speech, I knelt beside him with a stifled moan. 'Magsie,' (that was his pet name for me,) 'I thought it was your notion, dear, but there is a voice in the wind tonight, and it is calling me.' I made an effort to answer him, to speak; to tell him at the last how precious he had always been to me—how inexpressibly dear; to win from him some parting word of fond endearment that I might remember always; but the words died out in hoarse, inarticulate murmurs. 'Yes, a voice *is* calling to me, and it falls through miles and miles of air; then the wind takes it up and brings it to me. They want me up there, and I am going, Magsie; kiss me, dear.' The one arm stole around my neck; the chilled lips met mine in a lingering farewell pressure. He went on, feebly: 'I have been wild and wayward, Magsie, in the times gone by; I have grieved your great love sometimes, by giving you a cross word or look, not meaning it, dear, never meaning it, but because a perverse mood seized me. Forgive me, dear; don't remember it against me, sister!' Words came at last; they burst forth in a low moan of anguish: 'My darling, my darling, you break my heart!' Then my poor boy crept closer to me, in a last fond effort of endearment, and laid his cold cheek close against my own. The gloom deepened. The form within my clasp grew cold, became a lifeless weight. I knew it, but I could not lay it down. I still chafed the pulseless hand, and kissed it, and still I pressed the poor, maimed, lifeless form closer and closer to my heart, till reason fled, and I remember nothing. They unwound the chilled arm from around my neck; they thought I too was dead. . . . With muffled drumbeat and martial music, with horrid pomp of war, they buried my darling as soldiers are buried that die at home; but on the grave over which was fired the parting volley there fell no kindred's tear: I, the only mourner, lay *raving* in my room.

Wintry winds have piled the dreary snow above that grave; spring has kissed it into bloom and verdure; summer skies have smiled above it; and the maimed form they laid there has melted into nothing *now*! Time has softened the despair of my grief—the worst bitterness is past.

Through the gloomy portals of that dark gate of suffering, an unseen Hand has led me out into a broader and a higher life; and the heart that held my darling *only*, purged from its selfishness by the fierce fire of affliction, beats now for all humanity. Hearts whose love and gratitude God has given me the power to win, say, out of the fullness of their love for me, that a ministering angel is among them in woman's guise; that no hand is half so lavish in its gifts, no heart so full of sympathy, no watcher's form so constant beside the couch of pain. The sick follow me with murmured prayer and blessing; and wounded soldiers turn to kiss my shadow as I pass. Yet ever as the twilight falls I steal away to listen to the night wind's moaning, and ever in the gloom I feel an unseen presence—an arm about my neck—a cheek laid close to mine. Journeying on the lonely, rugged path of duty, 'following meekly where His footsteps lead,' I work and wait, and patiently abide my time—content if, when the welcome summons come, when life's day is fading, I may feel my darling's face pressed close to my own. He may not come to me, but I shall go to him, where he may wear his glorified body forever!

One Evening's Work

From *Peterson's Magazine,* signed "By the author of 'Dora's Cold,'"
who was given as Leslie Walter

In tales as early as "The Village Belle" (1859), James used or alluded to
card games to underscore narrative patterns and highlight thematic
motifs. Although no one is playing poker or patience or whist in Leslie
Walter's "One Evening's Work," the allusively charged language
employed in this story of the stately, queenlike (as we're told three
times) Rebecca Ware is distinctly, forensically (if you're looking for
authorial fingerprints) Jamesian. Rebecca, a queen of hearts, wears no
diamond on her finger at the outset of the tale, but by its end she will
be flashing a solitaire—and games of solitaire and patience may prove
to be her destiny. It is whist, however, that allusively informs the game
played out by Rebecca with James Arnold—in whom she found "her
pride *suited* as well as her *heart*" and with whom she would make "a
good *match*"—and with Henry Thurston, a knavish heir with a history of numerous female alliances. Thurston is also the honoree of the
ball that the bedazzling Rebecca attends, and in games like whist,
honor cards are the higher cards in a suit, especially those able to
trump and score tricks. As Rebecca and Henry, dissemblers both and

both devoted more to self than to another, play out their silent game—in whist all maneuvers must be conducted strictly in silence—three of the game's five basic rules take them to their fate: first, to win tricks by any means; second, to follow suit as best possible; third, to triumph with the highest card at hand. And as the players alternately feel their "triumph," so do they trump, *triumph* being a term in whist for "trump." For Rebecca, the stakes in the game prove to be high, and the outcome is irreversible, as she belatedly realizes: "Staking her happiness with a desperate hand, she had won or lost forever."

A DOOR OPENED and shut in the hall, and a voice called at the foot of the stairs, "Come, my daughter, you will be very late—James has been waiting for you a long time."

Rebecca Ware moved across her chamber, in answer to this summons, and paused a moment at the glass in her old-fashioned bureau, for a last consultation, before she went downstairs. She must have been very vain if the result had failed to please her, for even the little squinting, cross-grained mirror, which grudgingly reflected a tithe of her tall figure, showed her straight as an arrow, slender as Psyche, fair as a marble lily. Too well accustomed to this sight, however, her admiring glances were not dedicated to her own beauty, but to the unusual splendors of her dress, arranged more with reference to her future than to her present position. For the ring which sparkled on her finger—not a diamond, indeed, but bright with stones hardly less costly if more modest—that her lover with better taste had chosen—the flowers which drooped in her hand, the pretty bouquet-holder that confined them; all these expensive accessories, which she now paused to admire, were tokens that she was soon to exchange the plain accessories, provided with difficulty from her father's narrow purse, for the luxuries of another station and life. Too proud to accept more than these trivial tributes from her betrothed husband, her slender means had been taxed to the utmost to properly provide the dresses for the *trousseau,* one of which she was now wearing, half-ashamed to display it so soon, but unable to resist the temptation its silken glories offered by contrast with the older and plainer contents of her wardrobe.

She glanced around the little chamber as she left it, thoughtful of the coming change, and forgetful, I fear, of the happy days she had spent there in spite of its faded carpet—over which she trod like a queen—of its plain, old-fashioned furniture, its dim, small windows, its grudging little glass, which made it more an aggravation than a pleasure to be young, or beautiful, or well-dressed—in the satisfactory vision of the handsome, well-appointed mansion in which she was soon to reign as mistress. It was something to preside over that elegant establishment; to be able to indulge expensive tastes and live amidst pretty surroundings; to move about the spacious rooms and tasteful grounds, and feel herself at home among them all, an ornament in keeping with the rest. In all her affection for James Arnold, truly acknowledged and felt, I think Rebecca must have found her pride suited as well as her heart, and had been half conscious of making what the world calls a "good match."

She glided swiftly and noiselessly down the stairs and entered the dull back parlor, where the family were usually assembled in the evening. Her entrance did not create any very marked sensation; her mother looked up, for an instant, from the great basketful of clothes she was mending for half a dozen noisy boys; her aunt Vavinia shivered and drew closer to the fire as the chill draught from the door reached her; her father had fallen asleep over his paper, and was not awakened by the sound of her light footstep or the rustle of her silk. Only James Arnold arose and came forward from the dim corner in which he had been sitting moodily apart, with a quick, impatient movement that gave him no time to notice her beauty nor her dress. If his glance touched either, it was to bring a look of dark dissatisfaction to his face, and his tone in speaking was abrupt and stern.

"Your shoes will be too thin. You had better change them."

"James thought, my dear," interposed her mother, gently, "that you would like to walk this evening, it is so fine, and you have had no exercise today. I ought to have told you to bring down your thick boots."

Poor Rebecca turned away, vexed and bewildered; the privileges of her belleship were dear to her, she did not like to resign them, and was terrified by this first omission of a usual attention on the part of her lover. Besides, she was really weary with the tiresome duties of the day, and would have enjoyed, as she did all luxuries, the lying back on the comfortable carriage-cushions, and being conveyed without further trouble to herself, or injury to her pretty toilet, across the drear three-quarters of a mile that must be passed to reach Squire Thurston's. She had no fancy for toiling along that bleak, dark road, all the way up hill in the face of a keen March wind, and arriving at her destination disheveled, and disarranged, and unbecomingly flushed, obliged to explain the disgraceful reason to her young companions. It was a crime of *lèse-majesté* in James Arnold, his first, but it was greatly to be feared not his last. It looked like the early throwing off of the mask of courtship, the rude awakening to the commonplace indifference of married life; and Rebecca was too well accustomed to the sweet power of her position as a beauty and a *fiancée*, to be content with this sudden withdrawal of homage, this premature assertion of supremacy. Her vanity was even more cruelly wounded than her love; and she was aware of a strange shock of resentment and repulsion, as she slipped quietly down the stairs, for the second time arrayed for her enforced walk, and took his offered arm, her heart burning hotly with bitterness and rebellion beneath her stately, silent manner.

It was a poor preparation for the brief sentence he launched at her like a deadly missile, without a word of preface, as soon as they had passed the gate.

"Rebecca, I am a ruined man."

She was conscious of starting from him in dismay, of uttering an exclamation of surprise, pity, chagrin; but she did not comprehend how deeply the announcement affected herself, till he went on slowly and laboriously with his explanation.

"It is as sudden to me as to you; the times have long been growing worse, but these rapid fluctuations take everybody by surprise. I knew that my later speculations had not been successful, yet did not fear such disastrous results; but several firms with whom I was connected in business have unexpectedly failed, and their downfall will involve mine. It would be useless to go into details—I shall lose everything—except your love, Rebecca."

His voice slightly trembled in saying this, and his arm pressed more closely the slender hand it supported; but she was busy in calculating the probable results of his information, and hardly heeded this unusual display of emotion, so different from the cold, stern manner in which he had forced himself to speak. What would these losses involve? was the dominant question in her mind; and how far would they affect that near future of her own, which had seemed so bright only this evening? Even in her small experience she had known people to fall, and yet remain surrounded by all the elegancies and comforts they had enjoyed before—but there was a suggestion of dishonesty in connection with this which she believed—and feared— he was too upright to share. Whatever hopes she had dared to entertain were rudely scattered, and many brilliant castles in the air forever dissolved by his next distinct and decisive words.

"Our marriage must be celebrated in the plainest manner. I regret that your preparations have been made on so large a scale. Our wedding trip must be given up, of course; a party is equally out of the question. I told Johnston, today, that I could not take the house; we must go home to my mother."

Now old Mrs. Arnold was the most disagreeable old lady that Rebecca knew, possessing her son's cold, reserved, and distant manner, and somewhat unprepossessing appearance; without the warm heart, the upright soul, the just and liberal mind, the tender and generous impulses that redeemed these qualities in him, and made him noble and loveable. A tacit dislike, which gave promise of ripening into an open enmity, already existed between this severe matron and her intended daughter-in-law; while James, loyal to both, and not given to close scrutiny, had never detected or feared the existence of such a feeling. The elder woman held her son's bride frivolous, mercenary, and vain, exaggerated her love for the luxuries and adornments her beauty deserved, and thought her pretended attachment to the rich merchant a ruse to gain them; the younger, conscious, perhaps, of her own defects, and fully alive to those of her future relative, returned the aversion with secret dislike and silent disdain. No wonder that this proposal following the successive shocks of disappointment—the loss of the fashionable wedding trip which was to make Fairfield stare in respectful astonishment—of the wedding party at which she was to have electrified its society by shining in a wonderful satin dress, at this moment lying in silvery uncut folds in a drawer of the old bureau upstairs; the beautiful house, which she had so long looked upon as hers, and visited, and talked, and dreamed about as such; these were bitter blows and hardly to be borne, but worst of all was this calm conclusion he announced.

"No, no," she cried, interrupting him with passionate refusal, "I will never go there."

"What then can I do?" he sadly said, his voice, for the first time, falling to the low tones of distress and despondency. "Would you have me give you up, Rebecca?"

An impulse of pity overflowed her heart and trembled in some sweet words upon her lips; after all, he was her lover, almost her husband; it was her place to sympathize and advise with, to comfort and console him. If she had been inexperienced and romantic, she would have declared that she did not dread poverty, and was willing to work for and with him; but Rebecca had little romance in her disposition, and much experience of toil and privation in her daily life—she knew what work and poverty meant, for she had felt and suffered both. Not of that lower kind belonging to a class that is not ashamed to demand and receive the alms and assistance it requires, but the more painful ordeal of pinching economy, tastes and feelings cramped perpetually by narrow means, sacrifice and deprivation, in which no aid can be asked, no relief accepted by the proud and poor, who have inherited a position that must be maintained by a daily warfare and constant struggle. In marrying, she had looked forward joyfully to an eternal release from this distasteful life, and to lightening the load for those who remained behind. A sickening sensation of disappointment and despair rushed over her, as she began to realize that it was, instead, to inaugurate a fresh series of trials, in which she was to be principal instead of assistant, and conduct the battle of life at her own proper cost and expense. The soft gush of gentler emotions disappeared, pettish anger took the place of compassion. Was not she more to be pitied who must resign and was expected to endure so much? Was not she, too, to be considered? Were her feelings nothing? The thought of these wrongs gave a shade of resentful fretfulness to her tone in replying, which her lover mistook for sadness.

"We had better postpone it then," said she, sullenly.

Arnold caught at the words with an obvious sense of relief which mortified Rebecca deeply, for her mood was too unreasonable to admit the real cause. "Perhaps it would be better for a little while," he answered at once, "till I can see my way more clearly, find what my liabilities are, and what my means will be. I shall lose a sweet comforter in you, my dearest, but it may be only right that I should give up that hope for the present, until I can save enough to support you, or find something to do."

Something to do! He, the wealthy merchant, the successful man of business, to whom she had so long looked up with veneration and respect that all who knew him shared; feelings whose alloy had so largely mingled with her love that it shivered and tottered from its place in her heart when these firm props were removed. A man whose ventures had never failed, whose fortunes had never faltered, whose ships had always come home full freighted, whose stores had always prospered and increased, till he stood on a safe and secure eminence above the sordid, struggling crowd, who strove and labored for their daily bread, as her father toiled for his poor salary, that this gilded bubble should deceive all eyes for years, and never break till she was involved in its ruin and misery!

James Arnold went calmly on, quite unconscious of the surging rush of emotions his words produced in the mind of his only hearer. He thought her strangely silent, but, in the confusion and hurry of his own thoughts, failed to comprehend and sympathize with hers.

For the past few days this crisis had been gradually drawing nearer, and from long looking forward to it, he had grown accustomed to the prospect, and felt relieved when the painful time of concealment was over. If he missed the clinging pressure of his future wife's light hand from his arm; if he failed to hear her sweet voice respond as cheerfully as he had hoped, the pang that followed was brief, and easily reasoned away. He had been too harsh and hasty in his announcement, the kind fellow thought; she was flurried, frightened, and grieved in her quiet way; he was selfish to tell her all this on the eve of a party of pleasure, to spoil her enjoyment, and burden her already with his cares and troubles before she had vowed to share them as his wife. He watched her stately, graceful figure, as they entered, gliding under the lofty arches of the doors, and sweeping up the broad stairway of Squire Thurston's elegant house like one born to the splendor about her, and, turning away, sighed to think how he had hoped to transplant her to such a house as this, and be repaid in seeing how proudly she would adorn it, and how utterly all such hopes must now be laid aside in the certainty of coming ruin.

In her first sullen pique against her lover in the matter of the carriage, Rebecca had felt a momentary temptation to remain at home, or to exchange her handsome dress for something more suited to the walk. But she rejoiced that neither of these impulses had prevailed as she descended to the drawing room, and noted the festival array of the hall and vestibule in passing through them. Flowers and lights and velvet and satin, and gleaming silks and sparkling stones, were all about her—her own queenlike person reflected in the long mirrors, as she passed before them, like a lovely picture; her own rustling, silken train, and laces and wreaths, were only harmoniously in keeping with the rest, and gave her the confidence and serenity she so much needed and might otherwise have lacked.

A bevy of scandal-loving dowagers, self-constituted a committee of inspection, surveyed her keenly as she passed, and exchanged ominous whispers and meaning looks behind their fans. Rebecca was at no loss to understand why James Arnold had drawn her hand through his arm; he was leading her forward to greet their hosts with his usual grave dignity of manner and unostentatious elegance of dress—her trailing robes and jeweled ornaments shining and glistening in the full blaze of the chandelier. A ruined man, a poverty-stricken woman, who must starve for a year to come to pay for this worthless finery of a postponed marriage, she could feel the sting, and hear the hiss of the gossips' tongues while she strode stately up the long room as if she trampled envy and slander beneath her victorious feet. The momentary conflict of emotions had given to her cheeks a scarlet color, to her eyes a bright light, that enhanced and deepened her beauty. The comfortable elderly couple, the squire and his wife, stood astonished—they hardly knew her; the daughters, finished at a fashionable seminary, seemed dwarfed in manner and stature beside her, and were surprised into deference and politeness. On Mr. Henry Thurston, the newly returned heir, in whose honor the entertainment was given, a more startling effect was produced. Hitherto he had rather languidly received the visitors convoked for his benefit, replying but with indifferent grace to the various welcomes with which they saluted him, and taking refuge as much as practicable behind the smiling civilities of his dressy sisters. Now, however, hastily buttoning a glove with which he had long been toying, and casting a glance downward over the faultless apparel, which a moment before he had not deemed worth a thought, he suddenly rushed forward, forcing himself into a front rank, and monopolizing Rebecca's greeting to her hosts, and somehow succeeded also in appropriating her hand, and, amid a shower of excuses, drew her away to a distant seat.

"Surely these are the last," he exclaimed to his sisters. "Agnes, Caroline—pardon me for a moment while I renew acquaintance with an old friend. Have you forgotten me then, Miss Ware?—Rebecca, may I say? Have a few years of absence effaced all recollections from your mind and parted old playmates and companions?"

His handsome head bent low over hers, his dark eyes looked into her own, longingly, lingeringly. Rebecca was flattered and pleased, but her inward flutter did not extend to the serene beauty of her face, or disturb the sweet and gracious repose of her manner.

Harry Thurston surveyed her, seated before him, with discriminating and undisguised admiration. She was right in assuming that he had forgotten her as a child—so he had. That slender maid, with braids of shining nut-brown hair, complexion of purest Parian, and eyelashes of wonderful length and silky splendor, had disappeared from his memory during his college life and subsequent travels, as utterly as her notes from his memorandum book and her lock of hair from his vest pocket. Their youthful flirtation, carried on under cover of convenient classics at school, and long since superseded by more serious entanglements on the part of both, might have remained comfortably in the background forever, but for Rebecca's transient splendor of array, and flush of bloom and beauty. As she now sat, queenlike, superb and still, the light wind idly lifting her laces, and displaying more fully the rounded contour of the arm and neck they draped. The glare of the lamps reflected on her satin skin, and in her lustrous eyes. Her companion, who fancied himself a connoisseur in such matters, determined, in his own mind, that no more beautiful woman could be found to bear his name, and do his taste credit, in the eyes of what he called "that world."

By various manoeuvers he detained Rebecca in his society for hours; nor was she loth to engross the homage of the hero of the evening, or to enjoy the consequence it gave her among her young companions, who too soon would be able to mortify her by their knowledge of her changed circumstances. Perhaps already the gossips were whispering of her intended husband's ruin, and conjecturing all the consequences that she knew were to follow. Humiliation in the future was inevitable; she determined to forget it in the triumph of the present, and taste the dangerous, delightful pleasure of Harry

Thurston's admiration, so lavishly offered, as a balm for the pangs that pierced her proud heart, with pain most bitter even in the anticipation. Never more beautiful than under the excitement of these goading thoughts, she had the victory she desired, and enjoyed it to the uttermost. She saw the countenance of her handsome young escort flush and kindle with triumphant pride as he bore her away from the circle of her admirers her unusual animation had gathered about her; she saw his eyes return to the fascinating study of her face, and felt the felicity of the conquest his looks and tones assured her she had made. There was a sort of stern satisfaction in so shining among these bright scenes which, perhaps, she might never visit again—like a brilliant rocket, which mounts high through the night, and dazzling all eyes with brief, sudden splendor, sinks down to its original obscurity, and is seen no more. If she was doomed to this fate, she would at least so shine as to be remembered, and thus take a trifling revenge on the man who had made it what it was.

James Arnold, meanwhile, ever kind, thoughtful, and unassuming, had devoted himself, as usual, to the aged and the neglected, leading out forgotten wallflowers, introducing shy young men, and bestowing on awkward Misses all quiet and friendly attentions. He did not follow Rebecca's movements, or give her conduct a thought; his confidence in her was too supreme to be shaken by an hour's frivolity; and if he noticed the feverish vivacity of her manner, or stopped to listen to the frequent music of her laugh, as she swept past him among the whirling crowd with her handsome partner, it was only to regret that she must relinquish hereafter, for his sake, this gay and luxurious life which she so enjoyed, and which she seemed born to adorn. When supper was announced, mindful of his duty, he hastened through the fast-emptying rooms to find her; but she had already joined the moving throng on Harry Thurston's arm, and made no attempt to relinquish it as her own proper escort drew near. Arnold gently explained. "I was detained, Rebecca. Pardon me." She thought he repeated the necessary apology in a mechanical matter-of-fact way, like a husband who knows there is no further need for civility or attention to his married wife. Her lip curled, and her eyes gleamed bright with suspicion. Thank heaven! she was not married yet!—and she moved on steadily without offering to withdraw her hand from the close clasp in which her partner's arm still held it.

"It is of no consequence," she coldly answered, "I am going with Mr. Thurston."

"How? I don't understand."

"I shall go with Mr. Thurston," she repeated, turning her large eyes full of insolent light upon him.

"Rebecca."

Surprise, grief, indignation struggled in his tone; but there was no time for remonstrance or explanation, if either felt disposed to make it. The crowd swept on; James Arnold disappeared; and Rebecca was led by her triumphant escort to the head of a long table, where, under the blaze of the wax lights, and the gaze of the crowd, she must rally her disturbed faculties, and recover her shaken self-possession. Her partner noticed her paleness and abstraction, and tried to dispel them by his attentions; had they lessened her beauty, his interest might have gone with it; but paleness for her was only another form of prettiness, and his sympathies grew warm.

"You are faint," he whispered, "take my arm"—and not waiting for an answer, he artfully insisted on yielding his place to a couple who had been disappointed in obtaining one, and drawing Rebecca after him, plunged into the crowd, from the mazes of which, lost to all observation, they presently emerged on a lonely piazza. The wind was blowing chill and cool, but Thurston had secured a shawl during their hasty flight, which he wrapped about his fair companion with a tender hand.

"I saw you were annoyed," he murmured, "by that fellow's unparalleled rudeness. I wish you would give me leave to stand between you and all further annoyance from him."

Rebecca was silent; how could she reply that the fellow thus censured had almost a husband's right to be as rude to her as he pleased? How explain to one apparently a stranger to the relations between them, the remorse and terror she felt at her temporary revolt? Was it, indeed, only temporary? What punishment would James Arnold inflict? Would he abandon all claim to her, leaving her to the tongues of gossips, rejected and forlorn, or should she be obliged to subdue her pride to the concession of sueing for love and pardon to a man who had ruined all the bright hopes of their joint future by his ill-advised speculations, and then treated her disappointment so coolly. What was she to do? She hardly knew—her brain was in a whirl. The sight of the luxury and beauty, in which she so delighted, which she had so lately thought were now as hers for life, but found forever lost again, half-maddened her; the events of the evening seemed a troubled dream, over which she had no control; and, in a sprit of recklessness, she resolved to let it glide on to what end fate willed, with no further care or effort on her own part. Nothing could be worse than this maze of love, regret, remorse, doubt, fear and hope, irresolution and profound unhappiness, in which she wandered. Welcome the hand that should lead her forth—no matter to what! Mr. Thurston's was promptly extended, as if in answer. By the pale gleam of moon and starlight he had watched her troubled face, and read within it all the conflict that was passing in her heart. None would have fancied, in seeing the almost loverlike devotion of his manner, that he understood perfectly the relations of his fair companion with the person of whom he spoke to her, as, dropping his voice to the lowest and tenderest cadence, he went on,

"Rebecca! you would not have me suppose that this man is anything to you? Surely I have not returned, after so long an absence, to hear such disastrous news; to find you less true to our early dream than I have been, or hoped that you would be? Tell me our weary time of separation has not made you so entirely forget me, or, at least, that it is not love of him or fear of his displeasure, that agitates you, in allowing me to resume my rightful place at your side?"

"No," faltered Rebecca, ashamed of the cowardly denial while she made it, yet unconscious of the further concession it implied, but desperately yielding to every unlucky impulse that prompted her on this fateful evening. She thought of Peter, of Delilah, of Sapphira, of all traitors and false witnesses in sacred history or profane, and despised herself most of all—but the word was said, there was no going back. Her companion bent nearer, his hand clasped closer, his breath came warm on her cheek; most gentle and fond was the tone in which he spoke.

"The annoyance you suffered was my fault; let it be mine to shield you from it henceforth. Will you not trust me, to whom, above all others in the world, your happiness is dear?"

His voice was sweet and thrilling; he raised her hand to his lips; she permitted the salute passively, with a strange confusion of mind, in which misery and flattered vanity strove for preeminence. A distant door opened, she fancied she heard footsteps, and sprang away from him.

"It is cold here," said she, shivering.

"And you are quite faint and exhausted, but the supper room is full, we cannot get in there again for an hour to come; yet you ought to have something. Stay! I know what will do."

He led her to the other end of the long piazza, unlocked a door, and, throwing it open, invited her to enter.

"This is my den," he said, "a place my mother has given me for the storage of the curiosities I picked up abroad. I confess to having occasionally used it also to smoke in; but as it has only lately been set apart for my purposes, the atmosphere is hardly poisonous yet."

The room looked snug and comfortable, and was handsomely fitted up; a bright fire glowed on the hearth, and heavy curtains were dropped before the windows, shutting out the chill and darkness beyond. A lamp burned brilliantly on the reading-table, its glimmer was reflected in the glass doors of a set of carved bookcases, and by a silver tray, with its load of decanters and goblets that stood on the side-board. All the furniture was of polished wood and rich stuffs. The carpet was soft and of gay colors; the walls were hung with a fine French paper, and decorated with choice pictures. Appearances indicated that Mr. Henry Thurston had made himself as comfortable as circumstances permitted, which, with his fortune, he could well afford to do. None of these evidences of wealth and taste were lost on Rebecca—they pierced her foolish heart with a keen pain. Such luxury to her was Paradise lost; through its handsome young owner might Paradise be regained. She felt a longing hope, almost as keen, as she turned her beautiful eyes upon him.

He smiled; his gaze had not been idle either, and in her face he had read the powerful charm these pretty vanities had for her. Nor was this all. He had noted how handsome and elegant she looked among them, how the rich setting of the room enhanced and displayed her beauty; and he determined to win her for his own, the choicest ornament there. One or two well-chosen statues towered cold and fair above a mass of vases, shells, pictures, and antiques, evidently just unpacked, which lay about their feet. Not less fair and stately stood Rebecca on his hearth, her white dress gleaming by fire and by lamplight, which shone so softly on her face in all its pride of loveliness.

The young host touched the bell. "Mrs. Jones," said he to the bewildered housekeeper, who responded to the summons, "this lady and I have been obliged to give up our place at the table, and despair of getting any supper. The room is crowded full. Can't you send us something here?"

"Certainly, sir."

A servant presently brought a tray of delicacies, which Henry Thurston pressed his guest to eat. Much of the strangeness of absence had worn away, and Rebecca felt almost as completely at home with him, as when they used to sit together under the arbor at his sister's juvenile tea parties, or devoured lunch from the same basket at a village picnic. Her natural manner was stately and impressive, and Henry was so easy, so hospitable, so pleasant, that it was impossible to bring any embarrassment to their little *tête-a-tête* feast. She ate the viands, she drank the wine he put before her; the blood sprang back into her cheeks, the light to her eyes, she felt a restless flow of spirits taking the place of the last hour's apathetic misery, and experienced a vivid pleasure in the devoted attentions of her companion, whose look seemed already to claim her as his own.

Sounds were at last heard of the company leaving the supper tables, and the two deserters, winding through half a dozen rooms and passages familiar to both, succeeded in joining the returning procession, unobserved, and proceeding with it back to the flowers and lights of the great hall. Up and down its long extent they promenaded in the stream of moving couples, or whirled through the ball-room, sometimes together, oftener apart, for Rebecca had many other admirers, who, long despondent under James Arnold's superior claims, seeing her now openly free of him, dashing and sparkling alone, needed no encouragement to join the circle about her, and crown her the belle of the Misses Thurston's ball.

"It is too bad, Harry," complained one of these, seeking for consolation from her brother, "for that Miss Ware to make herself so conspicuous! I imagine she doesn't know her place."

"Do *you* know it?" asked Harry, shortly, a red flush mounting to his forehead.

"I know she is a poor girl, a mere adventuress. See her now dancing with Mr. Lenoir?"

"She won't interfere with your designs on him, my dear, for I intend to marry her myself."

"Brother!"

"I intend to make her my wife, so please govern your conduct accordingly." The young heir strode off to join his friends; Agnes followed him with her eyes in weak astonishment. "She is engaged, thank heaven," thought she, "so there is really no danger, after all. I suppose I may as well be polite;" and as the time of departure had now come, she drew near her fair guest and former companion with many gracious speeches. Rebecca was very pale. James Arnold had silently approached and stood waiting. Young Thurston was close at hand, watching her intently, and as she remembered the half-pledge she had tacitly permitted the latter to seal on her hand, she felt there was reason to fear a collision between the two men. Her evening's work was near completion; what she had sowed in sinful folly must soon be reaped in pain. She had delayed, as long as possible, the dreaded moment in conversation with her last partner, who now took leave, and they were left almost alone in the rooms. She rose, trembling, and faltered forth her adieus. Old Mrs. Thurston, struck by her appearance, declared she hardly looked fit to return. They interrogated Mr. Arnold—was his carriage a close one in which she might be sheltered from the wind? His answer was short and stern. He had none, and then came a clamor of voices in dismay and discussion. Mr. Arnold was upbraided for thoughtlessness and want of gallantry; the carriage was offered; she was pressed to remain all night. In the midst of it, a servant came to Harry with a message.

"My light buggy has been made ready," he announced, coming forward, "and I will drive Miss Ware back to the village. For her sake Mr. Arnold will consent to waive privilege, I am sure."

"But it is so late for you to go," objected his mother.

"And Mr. Arnold is her escort," interposed his indignant sister.

Rebecca said nothing. How beautiful she looked, standing there so still, irresolute and pale, more beautiful than any other woman he had ever known, in the flush of joy and gayety; she *must* be his. If he let her go alone with this Arnold there would be a lover's quarrel, a reconciliation, his newly-asserted claims on her would be forgotten, his evening's work in vain—she would be lost to him forever! Surely, the end justified the means! He came forward boldly swallowing a last scruple of honor.

"The young lady has given me the best right to take care of her."

James Arnold heard and a quick change passed over his pale face. Rage, grief, contempt—what was it? Who dared look to see? Rebecca heard, but did not lift her eyes, and the rest were silent.

"Rather sudden, isn't it my boy?" suggested the old gentleman at last.

"Oh, no, sir!" returned Harry, confidently, "an old attachment."

And now Rebecca, compelled by James Arnold's steady gaze, must raise her own to meet it, and shrink and shudder as she might, let him read there confession or denial of the charge that had shaken his faith in her. Yet how should she endure the trial? How could she

look without confessing every fond and tender impulse of her wavering heart, every true thought and generous feeling of her cowardly
soul? How keep from rushing to his feet and falling there, and crying
upon her knees, "Base and unworthy of so great a love, so long a
kindness, spurn me, lest I die." How see in those sad eyes, clear mirrors of the past, sweet memories, precious hopes, gentle emotions so
closely linked together, that to tear them asunder was like a real and
dreadful death? How bear without self-betrayal to both the old love
and the new, this cruel test they offered her, standing in simulated
courtesy and proffering each a hand, which she in taking from either
must forfeit honor and self-respect forevermore.

"Choose, Rebecca," said Arnold.

She knew well he meant "forever," and his cold, clear voice, his
stern manner, swept back in a moment the tide of temptation against
which she had battled all the evening. Weak, vacillating, vain, her
mind unstayed by principle, unprepared by trial, abandoned itself
again to wild revolt in this crisis of her fate. She forgot the sweetness
of the past in the bitterness of the present, long years of loving kindness for a second's stern emotion—ties that had seemed light and
pleasant but so lately, tortured and harassed her now, and held her
back from liberty. An instant before physical weakness alone had
prevented her from making the step forward that would leave her
sobbing on James Arnold's breast; now, in this sudden revulsion of
her wretched weakness, his cold, harsh tone of command seemed that
of a keeper whose chains she would die to break. All the wrongs, trials, humiliations of a life with him crowded before her; the poor,
mean house, the sordid, daily toil, the severe, disagreeable mother-in-
law, poverty, tyranny, drudgery, disgrace, a stern, unloving husband.
Anger, shame, selfishness, revenge, struggled fiercely in her heart
with love, and truth, and duty—struggled and conquered. Reason
was quite obscured, passion reigned in its place, and weakness was
stronger than either. She turned and gave her hand to Harry
Thurston, and fainted at his feet.

The Misses Thurston curled scornful lips at this "romantic scene;"

their mother, with something like motherly tenderness, bent over the fainting girl; the squire was divided between admiration of the "fine woman" who had accepted his son, and regret at her sudden illness; and the son himself, a flush of triumph on his cheek, the light of victory shining in his eyes, lifted his fair burden in his arms, and watched with more than common exultation his rival leave the house.

> "Was ever woman in this humor wooed?
> Was ever woman in this humor won?"

he muttered as he locked himself into the little room her presence had so lately adorned, to dream away the tedious hours till daylight, over the decanter and segars, in waking visions of his future bride.

And Rebecca could not leave the shelter of the manor house that night, though what her rest might be in the costly bed on which they laid her none could know. At her own request she was left alone amid the luxury of the best bedroom, to which she had been taken after her recovery. If thorns pierced her pillow, if regrets tortured her heart in the silence of the state apartment, there were lace, and silk, and damask to bind the wounds, there should have been healing balm in the sight of the pomps and vanities for which she had bartered her truth away. A portrait of her accepted lover hung over the mantle. She looked long into the bright, unthinking eyes, and tried to imagine them fixed on her with the expression she often had seen in those dear ones so lately looked upon for the last time. In vain! A different fate and love must now be hers—staking her happiness with a desperate hand, she had won or lost all forever. Between a true and deep affection that years had tried and tested, and a sudden ephemeral passion that might perish as quickly as it had sprung up, she had made her choice, and must abide by it.

She came down the next morning a cold and silent woman, looking ten years older than the bright girl of the evening before: the family thought it the effect of illness and excitement; her intended husband had his own secret theory which no one shared; but the knowledge he possessed did not materially alter his plans. He drove her home to her mother's house that afternoon, under the black sky and through the tempestuous wind of a wild March day. The carriage whirled along like lightning, the fast trotter did his best over the short mile that lay between the two places; but brief as was the drive, it was sufficiently long to have the wedding day decided. Rebecca showed no desire to postpone it—he might do as he pleased, she said—she even seemed anxious that the time should be short, which she must spend among her present surroundings, full of bitter retrospection, of rebellion how much more dreadfully useless than ever before! She thought her new lover very generous and kind because he did not seek to pry into her disturbed heart; but satisfied himself with giving her assurances of his own love, sweet flatteries that broke upon her dull reflections. These soothed her restless pain, she was glad to be dear to somebody. She felt like the lonely castaway of a wreck—self-made, but all the worse for that—and clung to the one fragment that had risen out of the deep, into which all the rest had gone down with weak, desperate hands.

"Let her only be my wife," thought the handsome Harry, as he drove back again, alone, after a brief undemonstrative parting with his beautiful betrothed, "and she will get over this nonsense immediately and love me dearly. She always did—it is only this fellow's influence over her which makes her restless—and that we'll soon be rid of."

Arrived at home, Rebecca told her family, calmly and quietly, of the great change that had been made in her since she left it, receiving opposition, congratulation, wonder, inquiry, regret, with the same cold serenity of resolve. No one in the household had ever disputed her will—none dared gainsay it now. She received her new lover at the time and place that she had been used to receive the old. She walked and talked, she rode and drove, and danced and sang, as before. James Arnold's gifts were placidly packed up and returned; all trace and token of his presence was removed; in their stead newer tributes came—books, music, jewelry, bouquets—the usual offerings of a lover. I cannot say that these frivolities did not cheer her poor weak heart a little, as old Mrs. Arnold's fierce denunciations eased her conscience. The sparkling *solitaire* upon her hand; the new and rare perfume upon her toilet-table; the daily homage of beauty and luxury, of praise and adulation that surrounded her, served as such dazzling delusions do serve, for a little while, to deceive and comfort the soul that has abandoned for them realities far more precious. But there came a time when these poor follies could baffle pain and cheat remorseful memory no longer. Heartless people can do, and daily do, such things with impunity; but Rebecca was not heartless. Regret and shame, and repressed love, a consciousness of her own cowardice, falsehood, and selfishness, preyed on her mind ceaselessly. While the wedding cakes were being made, the wedding flowers cut, she fell ill of a fever. When she recovered, her lover married her, and took her away. His ephemeral passion was gone—gone with her lovely bloom, with the light of her eyes, the glory of her abundant tresses, the statue-like grace of her figure—but he called himself a man of honor, and would not desert her who had deserted another for his sake. Instead of the bright beauty he had promised to show his friends, he brought with him to the city a pale, faded, sickly invalid, whose only merit was, that she was not peevish or repining; for Rebecca had found help and strength, and courage now, and bore her hard trial uncomplainingly, as the neglected wife of a dissipated, unloving husband. With prayer and patience she won him gently back at last, to love her with a better love, and live a better life than he had known before. They came down to the old home at Fairfield again, he a purer and graver man, she a sweet and noble woman, whose lost beauty none could mourn that felt the gracious charm which had succeeded it, and the pain and sorrow of whose early treachery had died out of the memory of James Arnold, almost an old man now, with a group of rosy children around his knees.

Unto the Least of These

From *Arthur's Home Magazine,* signed "Leslie Walter"

"Unto the Last of These," written under the name of Leslie Walter, returns to a theme long a Jamesian favorite: charity. Tailored to the tastes of the subscribers to *Arthur's Home Magazine* in its wedding of Christian ethics to Dickensian sentiment, it recalls some of the more youthful pieces James published in the *Newport Mercury.* Like "The Rose-Colored Silk" with its allusions to Psalm 27:10, this story, too, originates in a biblical text—Matthew 25:40, which exalts acts of charity on behalf of a needy child ("Inasmuch as ye did it unto the least of these ye did it unto me"). On virtuous impulse, the wealthy Langdon Power responds to a missionary's sermon on this text by adopting an orphaned child. Not unpredictably, his act of charity prompts a common Jamesian crisis, as Langdon is engaged to marry a beautiful but worldly and class-bound coquette who demands that he choose between his concern for the orphan and his love for her. Other choices, however, are not denied Langdon as James, or Leslie Walter, brings his story to a just, if pat, Swedenborgian resolution in the marriage of Langdon's charity to one true woman's intellectual wisdom.

※

THE BEAUTIFUL "CHURCH of the Holy Martyrs," was thrown open for a weekday service, and a sermon in aid of a charity, by an eloquent and distinguished missionary preacher, belonging to another sect from that which worshipped there, but endeared to all by the splendor of his talents, the purity of his self-sacrificing Christian life.

The building was filled to its utmost limit, not only by the fashionable congregation who resorted to it weekly, but with a crowd of strangers, brought hither by the report of Mr.————'s power and eloquence. As usual at such an hour, and on such an occasion, the seats were occupied mostly by ladies, with but a few gentlemen accompanying them, or clustered in the less desirable places near the door.

Far within the interior was one who, attending in his capacity of escort, as in duty bound to his betrothed bride, with the same graceful readiness which he would have exhibited in conducting her to any other place where it pleased her fancy to go, had found himself unexpectedly repaid for his complaisance, by the wonderful power and pathos of the discourse to which he now listened, rapt and absorbed, as one who receives a new revelation.

At first his eyes had fallen admiringly on his fair companion, watching with deeply interested attention, every motion and look of hers; the graceful gesture with which she bent forward in devotion on her entrance, resting a flowery French bonnet against the carved rail of the pew in front—the beautiful droop of her long dark lashes on her waxen cheek, tinged with a rich clear color like the blush of a nectarine—the elegant outlines of her figure in repose—the statuesque symmetry of the little gloved hands lying gently on her lap, her exquisitely tasteful dress; the delicious suspicion of perfume that floated towards him from the folds of her lace handkerchief—and he had followed with pleasure, the sweet, soft murmur of her voice through the responses. But as the sermon proceeded, his interest was

gradually transferred to the speaker, in utter oblivion of the fair creature at his side. In vain she turned upon him the prettiest view of a
remarkably pretty profile—in vain, with as much of petulance and
coquetry as are compatible with the properties of a church, did she
strive to attract and recover his wandering attention; changing and
rechanging her position, allowing her silken robes to brush past and
rustle over him, dropping her tiny handkerchief at his feet, misplac-
ing her footstool, or proffering a surplus prayer book for the support
of his elbow; she could not rouse him from the trance of forgetfulness
towards herself, into which he had fallen. Touched, awakened,
thrilled, he listened with earnest and sincere devotion, to such words
of power as he had never heard before.

The charity in behalf of which the sermon was preached, was an
asylum for orphan children, particularly those of soldiers and sailors,
or others following precarious professions. It was enforced by a text,
common enough, and familiar to the memories of all, yet that fell like
the piercing, penetrating notes of a trumpet—with the divine sweetness and tenderness of a heavenly message, on the thrilling ears, the
melting hearts of that congregation. Under its influence, thoughtless,
fine ladies relented towards the suffering children of poorer mothers,
and gave the price of an expensive toy for their own darlings, to
clothe and nourish these—vain girls relinquished the purchase of
some coveted decoration for the same worthy cause—the miser loos-
ened his purse strings, the Pharisee forgot that he was seen of men,
and left his offering side by side with the publican's—kind fathers felt
pitifully towards the bereaved orphans of other fathers less fortunate,
and showed their sympathy by liberal and large donations—dissipated young men willingly threw down for a good purpose what
they were used to expend so recklessly in a bad one—all yielding to
the overpowering force of the words repeated so earnestly above
them—"Inasmuch as ye have done it unto one of the least of these, ye
have done it unto me."

Langdon Power conducted his fair companion home in silence and
solemnity, quite unusual to him, and quite unbearable to the pretty

coquette, who was accustomed to monopolize his time and thoughts, and felt jealous even of the orphan children and the missionary minister who had momentarily diverted the attention of her handsome lover from herself. All her efforts to rouse him from his reflective mood on the way, proved vain; he was blind to her pouting petulance, deaf to her satirical sallies, and strode silently along by her side, so absorbed in his own meditations as to make her feel for once the diversity of their natures, and that though she had his arm, they might as well be divided by rivers and mountains as by the different thoughts that filled their minds while their feet trod the same pavements and their bodies were hastening to the same elegant abode in "Japonica-dom," where Miss Laura Fleming lived when she was at home.

"You won't come in, I suppose? she said, rather sullenly, as they neared the door.

"Not at present, thank you," he answered, in an absent way. "I will call as usual, if you will allow me, this evening." And lifting his hat, he left her in the custody of the servant who opened the door.

Miss Fleming looked after him as he went, in amazement that contended with pique—he had never so treated her since their engagement, nor, indeed, before it, and she was not used to be eclipsed in the eyes of her admirers by any other interest, past or present. It was very unpleasant and very unflattering, but Langdon Power was a particularly good match, and must be given some little license. It would not do to hold him to so strict an account as the mob of Johns and Georges who are sworn into a belle's service by the dozen, and content to wear her favors and perform her behests, whether they be rue or orange-blossoms, to dance with or to marry her. She had, moreover, other occupations that precluded the possibility of giving much time to this, and had banished her feeling of annoyance at her lover's conduct by the time his retreating figure was out of sight.

Her lover himself, as he walked slowly down the street, was occupied with speculations in which her image had no share, and had, indeed, almost forgotten the fact of her existence. She stood for him as the symbol of worldly happiness and prosperity, and he was thinking of something far more stable, more satisfying, and yet more unsubstantial, than the bright image of those his future wife presented as she bade him adieu—something that he had heard about languidly and indifferently, and believed in vaguely and dimly all his life, but that had never been brought home to his heart, his soul or his intellect, his sympathies, senses and feelings, till he heard these thrilling words to-day—"Inasmuch as ye have done it unto the least of these *my brethren,* ye have done it unto me."

He was wondering if the poor gratuity—the twenty-dollar bill that would have gone for cigars in another hour, and was hardly missed from his well-filled pocketbook—had discharged his obligation, paid his debt in full to Christ's brethren and little protégés—the doing of a good deed to whom was doing it to the Maker of the universe, Lord of heaven and earth. Scattered up and down the world, clustered all about us, guarded by His blessing, protected with a curse the most awful those mild lips ever pronounced against they who wrong by intention—or neglect, it may be—one of His little ones, was there a deeper meaning in the injunction that any hearer in a Christian land, and having a heart or conscience, must be bound to fulfil? In this great city, from within whose crowded streets a score of childish souls went daily up to God, were there none that, with the innocence of their infancy destroyed, the whiteness of their purity soiled and stained, would plead against him in Heaven, and against all those who, hearing and yet unheeding, went their way and left them at the mercy of the world?

Langdon Power was an orphan too, but a very wealthy one. His father had died in his infancy, leaving him heir to a handsome estate; his mother had faded quietly out of life in a lovely Italian villa, where sweet airs and soft skies charmed away half the pain of the hereditary disease that destroyed her. A guardian was easily found for the boyish possessor of so large a property; tutors, governors, companions and friends had been plentiful and kind; they had hardly let him feel the desolation of his lot, the deprivations of his bereaved and orphan life. So had not the same fate fallen on the lonely children he met every day, to whom the loss of parents meant the loss of home, love, protection, any good and kindly influence—meant ignorance of anything virtuous, and knowledge of all vice—meant poverty and pain, hard words and harder blows, and utter alienation from the civilized Christian world that lived and moved all about them, while they suffered and struggled in a darker than heathen gloom.

His steps had involuntarily wandered towards a wretched precinct, which he had often passed in his walks, and stopped a moment to gaze upon before he pursued his way, inwardly wondering if the beings he saw here belonged to the same order of humanity as himself, and had been moulded to their present similitude by the mere accidents of birth and habits, of ignorance, want and poverty. It had been easy for the rich, well-born, and well-bred young man so to wonder and tranquilly pass on, as one who leaves the too close contemplation of a subject in which he can have no possible interest or accountability—but to-day it was not so. The groups of old-faced girls and boys, ragged, neglected, dirty, horribly profane in their language, barbarously rude and wild and uncontrolled in their conduct, who screamed and squabbled and fought like savages in the dingy court, had a horrible fascination for him from which he could not escape. These impish creatures had once been made in the likeness of the Deity they blasphemed—it seemed to him that it was by the fault of such as he that they had sunk so far below it.

He was still sorrowfully looking on—with a new sensation of remorse and responsibility in his reflections—indifferent to the abusive speeches directed to him, and the occasional stones or brickbats flung at the well-dressed stranger, who, to their suspicious minds, was watching their games for no good purpose—when a little girl of two or three years old, issuing from the lowest door of a crazy tenement house, tottered across the street to him and clung crying to his hands, which she could just reach. She was followed and threatened by a slatternly old woman, as intemperate in her language as she evidently was in her habits, who desisted from the pursuit when she saw where the child had taken refuge, and stood at a distance, irresolute.

Yielding to his first kind impulse, the young man lifted the little creature in his arms, and soothed her with a few gentle, caressing words. She was such a poor, sickly, dirty object, that he almost recoiled from her sight and touch, but the silent appeal of those baby fingers twining round his own was not to be resisted. Her eyes were cast down, too weak to bear the light for more than a brief, hurried glance, but on the little face, soft and childish through all its thinness, distress and pallor, there gleamed a momentary smile of happiness and content that came and went like a sunbeam across its wretchedness; and she sat quietly in her place against his shoulder, proudly as on a throne. There was a certain sweetness in this confident dependence upon his protection, and Langdon Power held the child firmly as he addressed the avenging fury who pursued her.

"What has she done?" he rather curtly asked.

"Done, is it? Ah thin, in mischief ivery hour in the day, and the plague iv me life. And what business is it iv yours, me fine gintleman?"

"Only that I don't like to stand by quietly and see the poor baby abused. What were you doing with a big stick to a little thing like this?"

"An' can't I do what I like wid me own?" she whined, "that's sufferin', sure, for the want iv a little correction?"

"Is it your child, then?"

"My child, is it? Divil a bit thin—if she had been I'd a' broke ivery bone in her body before this, when she sarved me like the rest iv thim; but she's a poor little fatherless, motherless thing, so I had mercy on her, the crayther!"

Langdon's lip curled as he glanced from the powerful hand grasping the "big stick" he had commented upon, to the sobbing child on his breast.

"And that is your mercy?" said he, sternly.

"Ah, well," sneered the virago, "if ye wish her betther trated ye can do it yerself hereafter—by that same token I'll have no more trouble wid her, the saints be praised!" and she moved away, leaving her unconscious charge in his keeping.

A strange impulse of pity stirred Langdon's blood. He had no thought of more than a momentary protection when he took the poor child in his arms; but he was ready now to do more—to the utmost, if need be—in his new comprehension of duty.

"Stop," he said to the woman, before you leave this helpless creature on my hands—a trust I will accept and discharge before God to the best of my ability—and tell me if there is no one else who has a claim on her?"

"None, sir, sure," she answered, more conciliatingly, pleased with the prospect of getting rid of her burden. "Her mother was dead, and her father brought her to me to be nursed belike, as if I'd not enough of me own; but he sint the paymint reglar till he wint where they niver pay no more, an left nothing for her. Thin I tried her to the almshouses—I've so many at home—but they were full, and put me off wid one pretince an' another, an' paid me a thrifle weekly that wouldn't keep a cat."

She was going on with the story of her wrongs in a high, loud voice, but he again interrupted her.

"The child's name?" he inquired.

"She niver had one, at all, at all. Only 'a little divil' when she's bad, and something less, perhaps, if she behaves herself."

"Nameless, homeless, fatherless, friendless, poor little waif!" thought Langdon, resolutely lifting his protégé in his arms. "I assume all care of her, then, henceforth," he said, and with no more words turned away, and bent his steps towards the fashionable hotel in which he lived, quite heedless of the curious or amused stare of those he met upon the way. After a brief conference with the landlord, a room not far from his own apartments was placed at her service and that of the nurse he obtained for her; she was bathed, dressed, and provided with all needful comforts, her eyes put under the care of an eminent oculist, and then her protector had leisure to realize all he had undertaken in her behalf. He found his unusual action, natural as he had thought it under the circumstances, attended with a notoriety that he had not expected. People talked about it ill-naturedly and per-severingly; they insisted upon regarding it as a mystery, and striving to explain the same. All sorts of opinions were exchanged, all sorts of stories told; his own simple account was received with demure doubt as he gave it, and utterly repudiated in his absence; and the reason he rendered—the true one—obtained little credence among those who should have known him best, and called themselves his "friends."

"People do not do such Quixotic things nowadays," said Mrs. Grundy—and indeed it is to be feared they do not to any great extent, or we should be more willing to believe in the possibility of deeds of disinterested goodness, and take brighter views of human nature.

"A young man of his fortune and position! Absurd!" And as Mrs. Grundy represents the voice of "society," "absurd" it remained.

Lastly, the news reached Miss Laura Fleming, his betrothed wife, and left her in a state of bewildered indignation, such as seizes minds like hers on hearing of any act of uncommon kindness and benevolence, of pure, unselfish charity like that her future husband was meditating. Working herself up to the proper pitch of injured feeling, by the recapitulation in fancy of all the evils that would follow, to herself, this strange step, she attacked him on the occasion of his next visit.

"I have been hearing a great deal about you today," she said—allowing her hand to rest in his, for coaxing might be necessary—as they sat side by side on the sofa one evening.

"Then I hope it was something pleasant."

"Oh, no! Very unpleasant, I think; all your friends think so—only, of course, we hope it is not true. You don't know how miserable I have been about it," with a slight sob.

"Tell me at least what it is," suggested Langdon, quietly. "Perhaps your dreadful report is one I can conscientiously contradict; if so, I shall be happy to set your mind at rest."

"They say you have been adopting a little girl," murmured Laura, hysterically—"a dirty little creature, nobody knows who, picked up out of some alley—and that you mean to bring her up as your own and leave her all your property. Do say it isn't so, and then I can disappoint so many people who have enjoyed coming here and telling me."

Langdon laughed. "I can't do that, Laura; your friends were quite right in all but the matter of the will; I have not been so thoughtful as they, and had entirely forgotten it; but that shall be set right at once; some provision must be made for her, of course, in case of something suddenly happening to me."

Laura sat watching him with a face of horror.

"Do you mean," she cried, desperately, "that it is all true what they say of you?"

"It is quite true," he answered, smiling, "that I have taken a poor little girl, a mere baby, from a place where she was ill-treated and among evil influences, and that I mean to adopt and educate her, and make her a good and happy woman, God willing. I have no sisters, no family ties of any sort; perhaps this child, who seems gentle and affectionate, may take their place in some degree, and learn to love me as a friend and brother; you as a dear relative. Whether she proves all we could wish or not, my duty to her is plain; under the circumstances in which I found her, she came to me as a sacred trust that I shall strive faithfully to discharge—with your help if you will give it, without it if I must. But surely, dear Laura, you will not object, who are a Christian, religious and charitable by profession, and a communicant of that church in which you heard it said so lately and so earnestly, 'Whosoever doeth it unto the least of these.'"

"I do," she said, violently, "I do object—I don't believe your story; I don't approve your charity; I have no patience with such ridiculous philanthropy. There are plenty of places for a little beggar and outcast like that, where she can be properly provided for, and taken as much care of as you will, without bringing her to your house, giving her your name, making her your heir. Remember, if she comes into your house I will not come to give her an equal right there, to treat her as a companion, to train, and rear, and educate her. Don't expect me to help and countenance you in any such absurd scheme, for I will never do it!"

"Laura!"

"Never!" she repeated decisively. "Choose between us!"

"I can have but one choice," he said, rising. "As a Christian, a gentleman, a man of honor, I will not go back from my word, and break the pledge I have given to that poor unconscious child. It is not merely food, and clothing, and shelter that she needs, or the care and education that charity can give and money pay for, but love, and home, and friends, and kind protection, thought for the welfare of the heart, and soul, and mind, as well as body. These I have engaged to find in her behalf, trusting to you to aid me; and if your womanly sympathies are not joined with mine in this service, I am alone indeed. It is the first time in my experience, I am ashamed to say, that I ever attempted to use my abundant means with an earnest desire to benefit my fellow creatures—that I ever did a wholly unselfish and kindly act. Don't try to make me regret it, Laura, or cease to respect you—don't tell me I am to be punished for the one good deed of my life by the withdrawal of my life's one love. Recall your words, my dearest, while there is yet time, before you send me from you with such as these."

He bent pleadingly towards her and took her hand in his, awaiting her answer. She could not help admiring him as he stood before her, beautiful in his new fervor of emotion, grand in his noble, firm resolve—she felt that she had never understood him, or appreciated the force of the nature within him, in her superficial knowledge of the brilliant, handsome man of society. She respected and admired him in that moment more than she had ever done before; but her temper— a trait the experience of which had hitherto been confined solely to the domestic circle—was now fully roused, and drove her on to say in one instant what she would have given worlds to be able to recall the next.

"I will never live with her," she persisted.

"Then I must live without you," he answered, and was gone. He had never loved his promised wife so well, he had never looked forward to their marriage so expectantly, as since this little foundling came to stir new emotions of affection in his heart. He felt its need, with his own, of the gentle guardianship, the soft, subtle influences wanting in himself. He fancied Laura loving the child for his sake—cherishing and fostering it, lavishing upon it all the tenderness of a sweet womanly nature—they three forming one happy household, and his wife eager to assist and sustain him in his first uncertain attempt at what he held to be right, and Christian duty. She had never been, she would never be, so dear as in her association with this best impulse of his life.

He left her and went home—saddened, wiser, disappointed, but brave, and true, and gallant still—to find what consolation he might in the little waif for whom he had sacrificed all the rest. And his charge gave him much. She was not pretty, but she was growing plump and very fair, and her poor dim eyes were getting brighter. She had learned to come and meet him, and lay her small, dark head against his knee with a quiet, dumb affection like a dog's, and when he kindly took her in his arms she would nestle there silently, as long as he chose to keep her, watching him under her lashes in a rapture of admiring content. As she grew stronger, better, and more playful, he learned to admire her too, and noticed her winning baby ways with great fondness and pride. It was pleasant to receive her greetings when he came home, pleasant to have her childish company in his lonely rooms, pleasant to be so loved and honored, and with such good reason, by the one human creature of whom he had deserved it.

In the first sting of his disappointment in Laura, and of his being misjudged and scandalized by his friends of the gay world, he had withdrawn almost entirely from its society, and rather enjoyed his isolation. It was not easy to come back to his baby charge, who loved him so, and looked forward to his coming, with a clear conscience, from many of the resorts he had been in the habit of frequenting, socially reputable though they might be. The coarse paint of the theater, the idle conversation of the clubroom, the mixed assemblage of the billiard saloon, cards, wine, cigars, races, and betting books, seemed all incompatible with the touch of those chubby fingers twining round his—their atmosphere perfumed and pleasant though it might be, unwholesome beside that in which she drew her innocent breath. His "one good deed" became his best of blessings—in brightening her life he purified his own.

Having patiently braved the gossip and the ridicule of his associates and companions, he removed himself and his charge to a quiet boarding house where she and her old nurse could have pleasanter rooms and larger privileges than in the crowded hotel. Here, being now rather prepossessing in appearance, well dressed and well cared for, the child was allowed to play with others of her own age—to have the freedom of the hall, gallery and stairs. She learned somehow to turn the handle of the great front door, and used to watch for him there, a faithful sentinel—peeping out from her post occasionally—for hours at a time.

One day he was unusually late in returning, and she rushing down the steps to meet him, stumbled in her haste against a lady passing by, and fell. The lady was very gentle and very kind; she put aside her long mourning veil from a lovely face, stooping to lift her, and Langdon Power, who was coming to rescue his adopted daughter, came forward still more rapidly, and eagerly, holding out both hands.

"Charlotte! Charlotte Parks!" he cried, "my dear, where have you been?"

A deep flush rose in her cheeks, and tears ran over lightly from her eyes, as if they were easily used to flow.

"Oh, Langdon," she said, "I have been all round the world since we used to learn our lessons together in papa's study. How could you know me, I have grown so old since, and so sad?"

"How could I forget you? You have grown very lovely and very tall, but you are the same dear girl as ever. Ah! I hope quite the same—you are not married yet?"

"Oh, no—don't speak so. And who is this?"

"That is a very long story," said Langdon, slightly coloring, and lightly laughing; "one of my many eccentricities, Charlotte. I took a fancy to do a good deed, such as perhaps the disciples of old did, in the time when the Gospels were literally interpreted, and not as now, by the "conveniences" of society. I took that baby out of the streets, where she would have grown up a heathen in a Christian land, and engaged to make a human creature of her; and behold I have lost my friends and my love, and forfeited the esteem of Mrs. Grundy. But you won't desert and disbelieve me, Charlotte?"

"No," said Charlotte, unconsciously patting his sleeve with her little hand, in token of approbation, as she had done ten years before, when he was a boy at his tutor's and she his sister-mentor. "You were always good and brave, Langdon, and I don't believe you are anything else now."

"And you were always my faithful little angel guide and guardian; you must be so still. I have been so lonely since, and gone so widely astray. I want you to bring me back. Sweet spirit, did you feel my need of your kind offices, and come to meet me all across the world? But tell me, where are the rest?"

"All gone," said Charlotte, drooping her head. "I came last from Cuba. Papa lies there and I am alone now."

"You have friends here?"

"Only the lawyer who settles his estate, and my dear old Meigs, who takes care of me."

"Poor cross Miss Meigs! How will she receive me, I wonder? Time and trouble should have softened her acerbities, in all these years."

"I think sorrow softens us all," said Charlotte, gently, lifting up her sweet dark eyes.

"You at least had no need of its purifying influences, and have suffered much for one so young. I wish I could have shielded and saved you from these trials; I wish I could help and comfort you now, and be your guard against all further [evils]. We are such old friends!—we were so dear once, and we have been parted so long! I never knew how I missed you till we met again, or, rather, I never knew what I had lost out of my life, that left it so vain and frivolous, so poor and so unworthy. Let me go with you if you are going home—I must not lose sight of you again, and I want to know where you live, that I can come and see you."

And he did come, perseveringly and perpetually, at all times that etiquette permitted, and much oftener than its strictest laws demanded, but Charlotte's duenna, the old governess, who had also had the care of his boisterous boyhood, was not disposed to be critical. Without any knowledge of the "ways of the world" but its rules of grammar and arithmetic, she could not have distinguished a "good match" from a bad one, and had no personal experience of love affairs; but she held a sort of grim fatalistic creed in regard to her pupils—that the gentle sweetness and firm principle of the one which had always been needed to correct the brilliant versatility of the other, during their childish years, would eventually find its mission in modifying the same through life. She was not surprised, therefore, when Langdon installed his adopted daughter in a house of his own, and brought Charlotte there to be its mistress, and her mother, and his own dear wife. The orphan is now the loved and cherished elder sister of Charlotte's children, dear to them for her own sweet sake, and to their mother for her husband's—dearer to her adopted father because through her he found the treasure of his life, and received the richness of the blessing "Inasmuch as ye did it unto the least of these ye did it unto me."

In a Circus

From *Frank Leslie's Lady's Magazine*, signed "Leslie Walter"

Published as a story by Leslie Walter in the February 1868 issue of *Frank Leslie's Lady's Magazine*, "In a Circus" offers a variation on a favorite of James's Swedenborgian themes in its eventual union of the virtuous, purely charitable Leo Gordon with the orphaned and angelic Sophie, whose name signifies her supernal wisdom. The title of the story, obviously referent to its circus setting, may also allude to Swedenborg, who, in concluding his interpretation of the New Testament Book of Revelation, envisions the assemblage of a heavenly "circus" of angels (Swedenborg concordance note R961). There is nothing heavenly, however, about the Evans & Co. Great Combination Circus and Menagerie, which places the ethereally inno-cent Sophie, only eight years old at the beginning of the story, at con-tinuous risk of corruption by its tawdry vulgarity. Shortly after she first appears in the story, Sophie falls asleep in an armchair—no doubt, out of exhaustion, since she is featured as the "Wonder of the World"; but also, Swedenborg notes, "in general the state of Spirits and Angels is a state of sleep, relatively" (A4132). So indeed, for this otherworldly

Wonder of the World, her "very uncomfortable and painful" position in the armchair may have more than an apparent cause. At the center of the story's plot is Sophie's performance of daring and dangerous feats on her pony, which abruptly rebels and refuses to jump the bar at her command. Interestingly, Swedenborg images those "who would afterwards be received into a society of good spirits" as "a youth sitting on a horse," and when it is directed "toward Hell . . . the horse cannot move a step" (A187). In James's story, Sophie's recalcitrant pony sets in motion a sequence of events by which she is borne from the world—and netherworld—of the circus with its grotesque clowns and men "in spangles and pink fleshings" and is delivered into the outstretched arms of her nobly leonine protector, Leo Gordon. Enough do such Swedenborgian allusions, along with themes favored by the young James, appear in this story to connect it to James's earlier, otherwise pseudonymous or unsigned work. The craft it demonstrates shows, too, that Henry James, at the age of twenty-five, like the hero Leo Gordon, has "justified the glorious promise of his youth."

⚜

HALF MY LIFETIME ago—I am thirty—I was schoolboy in the little town of ———, in Pennsylvania, which, as you all know, is four miles from one of its largest cities. Strictly speaking, the establishment I attended was not a school, but a sort of preparatory class for students intending to enter college; and our tutor, Doctor L——, a mild gentlemanly man, full of classical lore, and absurdly innocent of worldly ways, was very little restraint upon us in enjoying to the utmost all the reputable amusements the more important place afforded, whenever our lessons with him permitted.

His almost invariable acquiescence to our applications for leave was accompanied by only one short sentence of advice or exhortation, "Be true to your word, boys," he would say—he had previously put us upon our parole not to be out beyond his closing hour of ten—"and be true to your honor as gentlemen. Don't go anywhere that you would be ashamed all the world should see you. Don't do anything you would be sorry to remember afterward. Don't profane your lips with coarse words, or liquors, or cigars. Don't make any acquaintances you would not be willing to introduce to mine; and don't run in debt. I have always been proud of my pupils, even after they ceased to be such, and I think I have some reason to believe I shall be so still."

And heaven bless the kind old man! his confidence was not misplaced. It would have been as impossible to any of us to deceive, annoy, or pain him by a departure from the spirit of the gentle breeding he inculcated as to rob his orchard, or kill his pet birds, or burn his musty library before his eyes. There was but one black sheep in our flock in my time, and our determined disapproval of the system of deception by which he intended to overreach his amiable teacher ended in the selection of a committee who warned him quietly to withdraw, under penalty of summary ejectment—a hint he took so literally that the worthy doctor was never shocked by hearing of his crimes, nor ever understood the cause of his sudden departure. But I am wandering from my story.

Fifteen years ago the great city itself was not quite so *blasé* and sated as it is now, and turned out a very respectable assemblage to behold the "Great Combination Circus and Menagerie" of Evans & Co., which had been placarded on all the dead walls and roadside taverns for a month, when that magnificent caravan arrived on its annual visit during the season. Of course a large deputation from Doctor L——'s attended, half ashamed of the boyish curiosity, half proud of the manly privilege; and planting ourselves as near as might be to the charmed precincts of the smaller pavilion, from which the various celebrities of the ring made their exits and entrances, enjoyed our position to the uttermost.

I have had frequent occasion since to note the lamentable falling off observable in these exhibitions since my youth; nor is it merely in the disenchantment that follows that delightful season, and the difference in age of the eyes with which we view them, as some would intimate. In those days money was actually spent for something besides the dresses of the performers—talent, such as it was, was liberally paid for; there was a really lavish display of fine horses and carriages; the bands, often of metropolitan reputation, were large, and well worth hearing, and the troupe itself, a small army of men, women and children, swept through the little country villages in a conquering march, and left them quite desolated of food, forage and money, and filled with wonderment.

The canvas was crowded to its utmost limits, and our party occupied only standing room on the strip of turf between the ring and the amphitheatre; the tallest, my friend and roommate, Leo Gordon, and myself, being posted a little behind the others, and looking over their heads. We were also on the very outermost verge of the circle of spectators, and deeply interested in the glimpses of the green room, which we occasionally obtained, as the performers passed to and fro, lifting the loose curtain that hung before the doorway.

Clowns and ponies, zebras, and flying acrobats, jugglers, ropedancers, monkeys, and mountebanks of all descriptions, male and female, in gorgeous raiment glittering with spangles, and with white and red paint thickly plastered on their faded faces, were collected in this retreat; and from the midst of the gaudy group a little girl, in simple dark calico dress and white high apron of checked muslin, slipped quietly beneath the canvas curtain and ensconced herself in a small armchair which some attendant had probably placed for her benefit, just without the line of demarcation, and immediately behind us.

She was a pretty child of seven or eight years old, white and rosy, with plump hands and arms, and dimpled shoulders. Her fair short curls were rolled back from her temples and tied with a silken ribbon, and her chubby feet were dressed in neat black ankle-ties fastened in the same way. She might have been the "mother's darling" of any decent household in that respectable city, but from her air of careless ease and custom, amid her strange surroundings, was evidently the companion of the wandering Bohemians, from whose haunt she had just come, and appeared to be quite a personage among them. A boy of her own age offered her a glass of water; a sallow little girl also belonging to the troupe gazed at her with respectful admiration from afar, and the attendants made way for her as she passed, with deference, which we decided showed her to be the manager's daughter, or connected with some one quite as important and influential in their little world.

Presently the elder of the two clowns, announced on the bills as the celebrated Joe Willis, a lean, nervous-looking, middle-aged man, frightfully painted and dressed according to the traditions of his class, espied her in her corner, with signs of satisfaction visible on his anxious face beneath the leering mask of pigments it wore; and thenceforward his eyes seldom wandered far from her retreat. In the midst of his professional labors he found time to encourage her with looks and gestures, to which she replied with equal pleasure. When he made his time-honored joke about the ladies being always for Union, bless 'em, and the audience laughed as usual, he improved the moment of respite by telegraphic signals to his little friend; and when he propounded his favorite paradox about the wife he some day intended to have, who must for reasons be like a snail, an echo, and a town clock, in order to obtain the honor of his hand; and yet be also unlike the same, or she could never hope to get him, he took one parting look at the armchair to fortify himself before beginning with spirit. But the interval had been rather too long, and as the ringmaster was sonorously demanding, with sufficient appearance of surprise and interest in the subject of his follower's affections, "And yet not like an echo, sir?" the interrogated cast a hasty glance from under his floury eyelashes and discovered that his little favorite had fallen asleep.

Leo Gordon had discovered the same thing some time before, and also that the child's position was very uncomfortable and painful, and he had quietly changed it. Lifting her lightly in his arms, he rested one foot upon her vacated chair, and so supported her on his knee; her pretty head lying against his breast, her silken curls scattered upon his shoulder, her dimpled fingers closed loosely over his, her flaxen eyelashes sweeping the rosebud cheek in sweet unconscious rest. She looked very lovely sleeping so, and her young protector was regarding her with great pride and fondness, but the clown's dismay was absurd to see, and the unstudied contortions of his nervous visage drew shouts of laughter from his admirers, quite ignorant, of course, of the cause. Understanding his gestures at last, Leo put an end to them by gently awakening the little girl, who regained her consciousness as soon as her blue eyes opened, and casting a glance of gratitude upon him, and a look of contrition toward her grotesque friend, slid from his arms at once, and silently disappeared.

The great glory and boast of the caravan was its troop of trained camels, ten in number, who were to perform a sort of Eastern scene or pantomime, which was presently announced by the manager as the occasion of the first appearance of Mademoiselle Sophie, the Little Favorite whose riding, dancing, and singing were the "Wonder of the World in her Grand Scenic Representation" of something or other which has just escaped my memory. The argument was, I think, the capture of a Bayadère or dancing girl by some potent prince of the East, and the display of her accomplishments before him, which ended in his making her his sultana. Accordingly, being prefaced with due flourish of rhetorical trumpets, the band struck up a wild Oriental air, with much clanging of cymbals and banging of bassoons, to which the procession advanced with sufficient majesty, and circled about the arena.

The camels were in tolerably good condition, with handsome housings and trappings, and presented quite an imposing spectacle, to my boyish eyes at least; but the riders were not to be disguised by any tawdry of turbans and trousers beyond recognition as the smooth-haired circus men in spangles and pink fleshings whom we had just seen turning backhanded somersaults and bestriding spotted horses.

Their leader, however, was more in keeping with his character, being no less a personage than the master of the ring himself, a handsome swarthy man of thirty, with a fine beard, a pair of bright dark eyes, and a head of profusely curling hair, on which a gay caftan sat gracefully, while his figure and carriage were too good to be spoiled by the incongruous vestments piled upon him. At his side rode the Little Wonder, the child who had lately left us, a blue gauze scarf, heavily fringed with silver, twisted above her flaxen curls, the end falling below the pink silk waist, which displayed her fair arms and shoulders, and set off her complexion of rose and pearl. Her blue satin drawers, starred with spangles, were fastened at the girdle by a white silk sash, brightly embroidered in colors; and a pair of scarlet Turkish slippers, seamed and sewed with gold, were thrust upon her little feet. The bizarre taste of this dress, which was certainly barbaric if not Oriental, could not impair the natural grace and beauty of the child. She sat her tall dromedary fearlessly, and looked about her with the "baby princess" air we had noted at first.

The scene required that the camels should kneel to let their riders dismount, who gathered round the prince, enthroned upon a stamped leather lounge of faded glory, and presented his chibouque, which he received without any very marked appearance of satisfaction, and smoked as seldom as might be. Then the captive Circassian was introduced, and danced before him, clattering a little pair of castanets, and shaking the tiny bells attached to silver bands about her wrists and ankles, also singing a pretty plaintive song, of which he approved so highly that he set her on the throne beside him, and eventually escorted her away.

She appeared soon afterward in appropriate costume to dance the Highland Fling and the Fisher's Hornpipe, and then dashed in upon the back of her favorite pony, dressed as a little old woman or witch, with a hump and a stick, upon throwing off which disguise she became a radiant fairy with silver wings, who rode as if she was flying. In short, she was the infant prima donna of the troupe—the feature— the star—and justified the puff of the bills, the praises of the manager, the plaudits of the spectators, and the anxious delight that appeared upon the painted features of the clown. In the intervals of her performances she returned quietly to her old place near us, and sat at

Leo's side with the same satisfaction she had seemed to feel on opening her blue eyes to his handsome face bent over her in her slumber.

Many an older girl would have been pleased to excite so vivid an interest in the young student as that he displayed toward his little companion; for he was mature and manly looking beyond his years, and the heir besides of a very fine fortune, left in the care of most indulgent guardians. He had never wanted for anything that money could buy, or position and reputation secure, and perhaps this consciousness had made him somewhat willful and self-reliant, but he showed no other symptoms of being spoiled by prosperity. There was nothing of the pride of birth or wealth about him; he was singularly simple in manners and tastes, and had for the doctor the loving deference of a son.

He used now toward the child his own sweet fascination of manner, so sure to win any heart, and she was evidently charmed and attracted. She refused, however, with smiling scorn, all his offers of toys and sweetmeats from the neighboring stands, and seemed much better pleased when he laid aside this homage to her youth and devoted himself to amuse her with compliments and conversation instead. She let him cut off a little ring of her curling hair, and looked on with great complacency while he stowed it away in a pocketbook, "to keep for ever," as he assured her. There was not a trace of the coarseness and vulgarity of her surroundings in her behavior or speech; she was rather more intelligent and mature than most children of her age, while possessing all their winning and lovable traits of person and character. I could not wonder that my friend was enchanted with the pretty little creature, and wholly shared his admiration.

Just as she left us for the last time, she asked Leo for a little wooden boat he had been unconsciously shaping from a broken bit of cedar as they talked. It was a favorite trick of his; he made them by dozens, in leisure moments, and of beautiful model and symmetry. I had several at home, and so had every one of his acquaintance—children especially. There was quite a fancy fleet, full-rigged and freighted, belonging to the doctor's little daughters, floating on the pond below the parsonage garden. Of course he gave it to her, with many courteous apologies for the smallness of the gift offered, and she received it as if she had been a woman. I did not smile, for there was something sad in the parting of the pretty pair, childish as one was, boyish and untried the other. Leo was an orphan, without brothers or sisters; the little girl was a lonely creature too. I fancied how they might have loved each other, had there been any tie of blood between them; how much the solitary boy might have profited by the secret feminine influence of a younger sister like this—had he been so fortunate as to have one—guarding him against the unusual temptations and perils of his path—how this gracious and innocent child might have been rescued by an older brother from the dangers of her profession before she was old enough to understand them, and placed where her beauty and intelligence might find some nobler mission than amusing a gross populace, careless of her fate.

She was true and artless now, at least, and he impulsive and sincere. He stooped down from his manly height and boldly kissed her fair forehead; unwinding the soft clinging arms from about his neck with a tender hand, regardless of the astonished looks of those near him, and of the signals of departure her grotesque protector was making in the intervals of his jests. She noted them, however, and was quick to comprehend, in the midst of her tearful distress, but her dimpled fingers closed firmly over the keepsake he had given her, and she was apparently much comforted by its possession as she went away to prepare for her last appearance—the performance of several difficult and dangerous feats with her "trained pony" Pizarro.

Pizarro was evidently in a bad humor—the tent was unusually full, and the crowd of people was pressing to the very verge of the rope that enclosed the ring, surrounding him with a sense of whispering and staring that seriously disturbed his equanimity. One old lady, with an enormous umbrella, kept opening and shutting it, in her excitement, directly beneath his sensitive organs, and some mongrel curs, which had surreptitiously obtained admission with their equally disreputable little-boy masters—a class which he utterly detested—snarled and snapped behind his heels to the great derangement of his nerves. It was quite apparent from the glancing of his wicked eyes, the tossing of his head, his swelling nostrils, and the impatient stamping and quivering of his restless feet, that his temper was upset to an extent that might prove dangerous, but his little mistress was perfectly fearless and calm. She maintained her seat with proud indifference through all his swerving and curveting, and put down his attempts at rebellion with careless ease and grace.

Not so tranquil seemed her guardian genius, the clown; his voice actually trembled as he inquired of his master if the young lady's performances were not "lovely indeed" and he strangely forgot to make the stereotyped jokes that should have followed, and set the audience in a roar. His lean brown hand quivered and shook as it caressingly touched her dress in adjusting it, and he gave her a look of warning, as he handed her the whip, that was almost agonized in its earnestness.

This byplay, however, was probably lost on all but those as deeply interested as ourselves; others saw only the pretty little creature in her richly trimmed riding habit of blue and silver, making her look older and more womanly as she flew round the circle like a vision, her fair curls streaming backward, her rosebud lips set in resolute determination, her blue eyes watchful and bright, her dimpled white hands grasping the reins firmly, and holding the whip suspended ready to fall at the least token of insubordination.

She coaxed or coerced her impatient horse through the necessary tricks; he danced an Irish jig with bells on his legs, he climbed stairs, and stood on the top of them with his four hooves drawn close together like a goat's; he marched and countermarched to the sound of music, and waltzed on his hind feet in good time, and reared up prancing and pawing the air, and fell again quietly to the word of command, she sitting like a rock, and casting a saucy smile into our anxious faces as she passed. Lastly they brought in bars and hurdles for the pony to jump, and he, all swelling and quivering, breathing fire and foam, evidently made up his mind that this should be the turning point of his rebellion.

Twice he refused the leap, unmoved by voice or gesture, or even by the stinging eloquence of her keen little whip, and she rode him unconquered away and returned dauntlessly to the charge. Urged beyond endurance, he took it the third time, but in so slovenly a manner that his feet caught the top bar and both rolled on the ground close beside us. Amid the cries and exclamations of the spectators, the screams of women, the groans of men, the pair were disentangled, and the pony helped to his feet, where he stood panting, somewhat subdued, and quite unhurt. His little rider lay motionless like a blanched flower, the breath shocked out of her body by the violence of the concussion; her dimpled hands dropped nerveless, her blue eyes closed, her lips hardly stirring the white feather that floated across them from her cap. Leo and I were bending over her, with many others, but the clown pushed us all away and lifted her in his motley arms, letting all her pretty curls stream over his parti-colored garments.

I felt Leo shudder as he stood, but there was no time to speak, for the life was coming back into the child's face, and she raised herself slowly into a sitting posture on her supporter's knee, shutting her lips firmly as if the effort gave her pain, and refusing all the assistance offered. Her eyes glittered brightly and her cheeks burned red as roses, while she whispered something rapidly in his ear. He shook his head, refusing in a helpless, agitated manner, and holding one of her hands in his, passed his fingers rapidly over her arms and shoulders, to see what injury she had sustained. The brave little creature winced, but made no other sign of suffering, and the hasty examination over, turned to us.

"He will not comprehend," she said impatiently; "I want to be put upon my pony."

While we hesitated she stamped her tiny foot with an imperative gesture, and lifted her earnest face in its flush of feverish beauty imploringly toward us. Without a word Leo took her in his arms and placed her in the saddle. Once there she cast on us all a look of gentle apology.

"You see I must," she explained, in her own clear, childish voice, "or he would never obey me again."

She waved her hand to clear the ring of spectators, and striking him sharply with her whip, wheeled and bounded forward like the wind. The men at the hurdle had just time to get it into place before she shot over it like a flash, and paused quietly beyond. A sickly pallor spread across her face in the very moment of triumph, the rein dropped from her grasp, she reeled in her saddle and fell forward heavily into Leo's outstretched arms.

He had her but a moment, the moment before she sank into total insensibility, while her blue eyes looked gratefully into his, and her tiny fingers twined round his own; then the ring was once more filled with people offering ejaculations and restoratives; one or two physicians tendered their services, and she was transferred to the care of the clown, whose right to her seemed to be universally recognized. I saw Leo's look of shivering repulsion as he gave up his helpless burden and beheld the pure face lying like a blighted lily beneath that hideous painted visage, the fair silken ringlets scattered upon that motley breast, the rosebud lips so close to those ghastly ones; but no one could doubt the distress of the mountebank was real. He watched the grave faces of the surgeons as they examined her with desperate anxiety, and followed every movement with his keen, glittering eyes. I am sure he heard each word of their low consultation afterward, and when they approached him with the result, shrank back a moment painfully, and then turned to bay like a hunted man.

"A very serious case." "Some internal injury." "The best of attendance." "A long and expensive illness"—were all the clauses of the communication that reached us, but we saw the look with which he responded, and felt that they contained a volume to him. Then the ring was again cleared by the bland and smiling manager; the celebrated "Mr. Joe Willis, from Paris and London," bore his crushed burden away, and the equally distinguished Mr. Jim Woods, from

Dresden and St. Petersburgh, delighted the audience; while Signor Marcocelli—known in private life as Mr. Mike Kelly—twirled basins on the points of swords, and tossed balls and knives, with other feats of jugglery too painful to mention.

Escaping from this display, which jarred on us after the scene we had just witnessed, we made our way as quickly as possible to the side of the little procession moving toward a second-class boarding house near at hand. Leo darted on in advance, and beating down all arguments with his purse, secured a quiet, clean room on the first floor, in which the child was laid on her arrival.

"You will allow me to return in an hour or two?" he said, offering his hand to the buffo.

The man took the kind young hand in his with a suppressed exclamation of gratitude, but he had little time to waste in speech. There was the nurse to be obtained, the little girl's wardrobe to be sent for, many small comforts procured, necessary to her situation, through the aid of the landlady, and a painful interview with the physicians at the conclusion of their examination an hour hence, would leave him no time to spare before the evening performance began. Assisting him as far as he would permit in the minor matters to be attended to at once, that he might spend as much time as possible with his charge, and promising to return soon again, we left him.

Leo hardly spoke on the way home, and I did not interrupt his meditations, for, with the quick instinct of friendship, I had nearly divined them. Arrived there, he had a long interview with the doctor, and the two left together for the city on the next train. It was late when they returned, and I was by that time unconscious, and did not wake till my roommate stood over me the next morning with the brightest look I had ever seen his handsome features wear, gayly inviting me to get up and be his companion in a morning call. I had no need to ask where, for I knew that the events of yesterday had taken a firm hold on his tenacious mind, and that his plans, once made, were irrevocable.

We found several persons assembled in the little parlor where the child lay when we entered it, but it was carefully darkened and quiet, and their presence did not seem to disturb her. She was very still, and lay as if sleeping; her pretty face already looked older and drawn with pain, but she stirred and lifted her heavy lids when Leo came in, stretching out her feeble hand with a smile of welcome, to which he responded at once, only stopping to recognize the others. There was no pretense made that his society would excite or disturb her; she had been wearying for him all the morning, and now clung to him with a look of prefect rest and peace that showed how strong, though so new, was the bond already uniting the two.

A man sitting in the shadow at the bedside, with his hat slouched over his eyes, in whom I with difficulty recognized the clown, seemed hurt or troubled by the sight, for he averted his head and pressed his clasped hands tightly upon the knob of a stick he carried. The good old doctor and his wife, from the background beyond, observed him compassionately; the other three present were the surgeons and the circus manager, whose bland manner had altered very little in the atmosphere of the sick room.

"Come, Willis," said he to his employee, whose whole drooping figure was expressive of the distress and agitation he felt, "be a man and look the thing in the face. These gentlemen have told you the child's condition; she is badly off, but it might have been worse, and there is but one thing you can do to help her. You have heard them say it will probably be months before she is well again, and then unfit to resume her profession; in the meantime who is to provide for her unless you return to yours ? for even adding her salary, I think you can't have saved much. With your habits—"

"Spare me, spare me, Mr. Evans," murmured the other, waving his hand, "before *her!*"

"Certainly," returned the brisk manager; "I didn't intend—But the uncommon advantages this young gentleman decidedly offers—"

"I offer nothing," said Leo, firmly, "that may not be accepted without any renunciation or sacrifice on the part of one who has proved himself as faithful a guardian as I could hope to be, and it does not in the least depend upon his deciding to remain. If he accepts my assistance in caring for my charge, I trust she will never be allowed to forget or undervalue his fatherly kindness."

"There, Willis," cried the persevering manager, "you see you would only be standing in your niece's light."

"No, no," cried the badgered man, starting up and wringing Leo's hand; "you are kind, sir, and I thank you, but you are wrong and I am right in this matter. I see it clearer than you. I give you the child, or the little claim on her that years and association have given me, which is less than you think. She is not my niece; there is no tie of blood between us; I found her as you find her now, a little waif, poor and helpless, and so, it seems, I must leave her. I know my life and my companions have not made me a fit guardian for that innocent creature. Yet I took her because I could not do better, because if I left her it would have been to starve. I introduced her to my profession because I had access to no other; no friends, no connections out of it, and because it was necessary she should learn to do something that would support her in case I should die and leave her more desolate than I found her. But do you think my heart didn't bleed when I saw her in that place, so unfit for one so young and innocent as she? Do you think I didn't watch and tremble—yes, and pray, in my way, for the release I couldn't compose for her, even if it should be death; and she, for almost nine years, my idol! Now it has come, don't suppose I would prevent it if it broke my heart. No, sir; and I beg of you to let her forget me, and all her life with me. I wouldn't have her remember it; it will be better for her happiness not. No one must reproach my darling with the circus and the ring, or shame her with the faults of the poor man she called father. Now, young gentleman, let me hear again what you propose to do!"

He spoke quite calmly and distinctly, and seemed to have kept his head clear for this question and Leo's answer.

"I have settled five hundred dollars a year on her for maintenance and education, with my guardian's consent," Leo replied, "and leave ten thousand dollars to her in my will, if I die before her coming of age, otherwise it is hers absolutely, on her majority. I adopt her as my ward, Doctor L—— being joined with me in the guardianship, and she is to reside at his house. My own guardians have been applied to and agree; the papers are signed and ready. I assume all care and expense of her from the present till her nineteenth year, and then if she likes, sir, she may marry me; if not, her fortune is at her own disposal in any case."

The color had mounted and mounted in Leo's fine face, his eyes darkened and sparkled, and he drew his handsome figure up proudly as he spoke. The little girl still lay gazing at him quietly, her hand in his. The clown bent gently over her.

"Did you hear what he said my darling?" he inquired.

"Yes, uncle, I heard it all."

"Do you agree to it?"

"Oh, yes."

A sort of convulsion passed over the man's features, and he dropped his head a little lower.

"Did you hear what I said also?"

"Yes, uncle."

"And will you obey me?"

"I will do whatever you wish."

"I tell you to forget me then, and to love him. He is better worthy, and will do for you what I never could. Your life belongs to him henceforth; try to make it what he would desire; and in order to do so, banish me and my associations out of it. Never think of us, never speak of us; let us pass and be forgotten; do you understand? And now good-bye."

He stooped and kissed her, not on the lips, but on her pearly forehead, and let his hand rest a moment lingeringly upon her hair. There were tears in her eyes, but he pretended not to see them, and turned away with a mute motion of adieu addressed toward the others. Then he walked steadily from the room, followed by the manager, leaving her with her new friends.

This was all I saw of the romantic episode in Leo Gordon's life, which ended in his undertaking so strange a charge. A week later came the midsummer holidays and widely dispersed us; some, among whom were Leo and myself, to return no more. I went abroad at once, and so lost sight of him, remaining away to finish my education and commence professional life.

When I finally returned to the United States so many ties had been broken, so many changes made, that it was useless to attempt to trace most of those whose names my memory still retained.

Last winter, however, being in Leo's native city, I made some inquiries which were easily answered, for he was a prominent person there, and much respected. His large fortune had been well invested and was making him daily richer; he used it in all liberal and elegant ways. He had married, several years before, a lady from the North, whose beauty and grace made her a leader of the society in which they moved, and attracted universal admiration. They had traveled widely abroad, and enjoyed an enviable position at home, and were held by their friends most prosperous and happy people. If youth, and wealth, and station, perfect union of tastes and affections, and every personal and social advantage could make them so, they must have been indeed. My desire to see them was so great, that after finishing my business for the day, I sought Gordon at his office.

I was too late; the place was closed. Proceeding to the handsome residence, in the most desirable part of the town, that had been pointed out to me as his, I renewed my inquiries. The servant regretted to say that his master and mistress had gone to the theatre to witness the performance of a new and celebrated opera troupe just arrived. I had but this one evening, and a moment's reflection decided me to follow and see them myself unknown.

The theatre was not a large one, and the parquette, in which the better class of citizens was seated, correspondingly small. It was but a short time before I recognized my friend. Years had not altered him, except from a handsome boy into a noble-looking and handsome man; the same sweetness of expression lingered about his mouth, the same soft radiance lighted his bright dark eyes. I have always thought him the purest model of manly beauty I ever met. Better and more perfect features, a juster mold of form one sees every day, but of the soul and spirit that animates them, none half so fine. No envious or evil passion had ever marred the outlines of that face, or left their impress in defacing characters upon it; no cold and blighting experiences of adversity had warped or crippled the full development of that kindly nature; supremely fortunate in all we hold most important, he had reached the climax of his worldly prosperity unstained by the vices, unmoved by the temptations surrounding it; and the rich maturity of manhood but justified the glorious promise of his youth.

By his side sat a lady upon whom many eyes in the audience were turned besides mine, so exquisite was the type of her loveliness, so distinguished her air, so elegant in its apparent simplicity her dress; her magnificent masses of fair hair, waved and rolled back in a cloud from her beautiful face, were encircled by a wreath of green leaves, of whose costliness I was not aware, till the sparkling of jewels as she turned her head betrayed their nature. She wore a rich white Irish poplin, with buttons and aigrettes of emerald, a little knot of ribbons at the throat and forehead giving softness to the delicate outline. I could not fail to see, in her ripened bloom and beauty, a likeness that long haunted me to Leo Gordon's childish love; and a little girl in rose and white, sitting between her parents, though younger in years, reflected the same fair image so perfectly that I could not doubt how his romance had ended.

One other person among those present seemed attracted as deeply as myself by her beauty or this resemblance. A small, pale, nervous man in the orchestra had dropped his violin bow by his side and was leaning forward from his place, his dark eyes fixed intently on the pair as if fascinated by the sight they presented, regardless of observation and of the conductor's frenzied gestures with his baton toward him.

When the performance was concluded the Gordon party were very slow in quitting their seats, and stood for some time in the corridor waiting for the crowd to pass out. The little girl was behind. Suddenly I saw her caught up in the arms of a short, dark man, who kissed her passionately on her hands and face—her ringlets of fair curling hair. Before she could speak or move he had replaced her on her feet and disappeared. When we reached the vestibule there was a slight commotion outside; a fiddler from the orchestra had fainted and had been borne into the open air.

A large man, wrapped in a thick greatcoat, in whom I recognized the manager, walked in front of me as I turned into the street, talking earnestly to a companion. A light coupé—the night was fine—had been waiting for Gordon's beautiful wife and child, and received them just as the insensible body of the musician was being borne away somewhat heavily in the arms of four men, attachés of the theatre. The pair immediately before me were discussing the latter incident.

"I knew how it would be," said the elder of the two, "when we first proposed to come to this country, where he had traveled years ago in some disreputable line of business, the circus way, I think, not earning half as much as he did with me, for he turned out a really good musician; but he has been wild ever since we started, restless, excitable, impatient—you saw him tonight, perfectly frenzied; a bad thing for heart disease; the worst in the world. I told him what would happen, but he didn't take my advice, and now—you see!

"Well, what of it? He will be all right tomorrow, I suppose? He has only fainted."

"Fainted? He is dead!"

A Hasty Marriage

From *Peterson's Magazine*, signed "By the author of 'Dora's Cold,'"
who was given as Leslie Walter

By 1869 Henry James had greatly enlarged his narrative skills and his fiction had begun to evidence some of the stylistic flourishes and elegance that would characterize his more mature work. Still, "A Hasty Marriage" bears the imprint of the earlier James in such stories as the 1862 "Breach of Promise of Marriage," which, like this 1869 piece, was published as the work of Leslie Walter in *Peterson's Magazine*. Both stories lodge their drama in legalities regarding marriage, and both feature in their cast lawyers who get enmeshed in romance. However, Sylvia, the heroine and narrator of "A Hasty Marriage," finds herself in a situation more like that of Rebecca Ware in "One Evening's Work" than that of Belle Savage. For Sylvia, like Rebecca, must choose—not between a wealthy knave of clubs and financially ruined king of hearts, but between Mr. Harter, a "common miner," who proves to be not what he seems to be, and her advocate in law and love, Walter Drummond. Unlike both Belle and Rebecca, though, Sylvia is no coquette; and the values she assigns to possessions (for which Harter, surprisingly, wants neither money nor discriminating taste) have little to do with their material worth. For Sylvia, it is love that invests objects and paintings and books and mosaics with great price. It is love, too, that leads her providentially to her choice and by the will of the World's Author (and of the author Leslie Walter, or Henry James) to the opportunity in marriage to realize true conjugal bliss.

✿

I.

A T SEVENTEEN I left school, ignorant and undisciplined, willful, impatient, and reckless. In Madame Dejazet's elegant establishment we were taught many external, but few inward graces; and when she had done all that lay in her art to improve us, some of the hardest lessons of life were yet to learn.

I was to have remained longer, but suddenly my bankers failed, and remittances stopped. Years before, my father, a wealthy sea captain, had died, leaving my fortune invested with his old employers, now no longer shipping merchants only, but bankers also. The letter, announcing the calamity, offered to relieve Madame Dejazet of me. This letter was from my father's half brother, to whom his beautiful villa had been lent at my mother's death, and who now, probably, sought to pay the debt of years by offering me, in my destitution, a home there—a home, alas! how different from the one I so well remembered.

My uncle's wife was a shrewd managing woman, as she had need to be with her small means, and her seven children. No longer the pretty parlors of the pretty house were thrown open for the enjoyment of the dwellers within, but closed and locked against dust and decay, except on grand occasions; while all the other rooms, with their furniture, bore marks of hard usage and careless occupation. The greenhouses were closed, the lawn was turned into a vegetable garden. Ah! Bitter was the change.

As soon as the first heartsick rebellion of feeling had died away, I sought to be useful in my new position. Curbing my impatient disposition, I tried to teach the stupid children, and bore heroically with their blunders and impertinence for a time, till their mother's eager jealousy, and my own superficially concealed ignorance, released me from the distasteful task.

Then came domestic drudgery, harder to execute, not less hard to endure. Last of all were wild revolt and utter rebellion against destiny, and it was in this mood that Mrs. Samuel Morris bade me leave her house forever, and I obeyed her.

I had stayed there six long months, and was worn-out body and mind. The manifold insults and annoyances of an ill-bred and ill-governed woman would have been of themselves enough; but when to these was added the constant and urgent struggle of my own undisciplined nature, and my haughty temper and strong will, what wonder that life grew unendurable!

I had begun, too, by this time to find contrasts to my own fate in the children of my father's old neighbors—my own former playmates and companions, who had found me out and flocked about me with welcomes, attentions, and invitations. Glad to escape from the tedious miseries of home, I left it frequently to accept these kindnesses, and found my vanity soothed, and my heart comforted by these warm and faithful friends. I plunged into the gayeties they offered me with reckless and thoughtless eagerness, mindful only of the enjoyment of the present, and the pleasure of being again beloved and admired. Of these attentions, and of my wardrobe, which was still handsome and complete, Mrs. Morris had long been jealous. Her wrath at last reached its climax. A sleighing party was projected, or rather a series of sleighing parties, that would lead the gay revelers, who joined it, visiting from house to house for a week or more. Walter Drummond and his sisters were to come for me! Walter Drummond was my knight, my champion, my rescuer on a hundred such occasions—-so kind, so handsome, so good to me, that I almost loved him. I had dressed in the gayest spirits, and in my prettiest ornaments and garments suitable to the occasion. Mrs. Morris came in while I was placing others, for all emergencies, in a trunk, which a man below, provided by Walter, was waiting to remove. Sternly she bade me pack all I owned, and if I insulted her by leaving her house at all with people who were not her associates, to leave it forever. I answered hotly. My blood was boiling, and my nerves were tingling with bitterness and anger. Pride, self-will, haughty recklessness and temper would not let me yield. "You shall be obeyed," I said, and packed two trunks instead of one. My anger and determination did not leave me till I had left her house forever, till I had told Walter and the girls, till I had heard their pitying sympathy and warm assurances that their home should be mine.

Then, indeed, I realized what I had done. But it was too late. The woman I had left was inexorable as death; she would never receive me back. Meantime, the Drummonds were not rich, and I felt bitterly what an additional burden I would be in their house. I shrank, too, instinctively from compromising myself with Walter by accepting such a favor at his hands. It was impossible—I did not love him enough to wish to owe so rash a debt to him. But what then could I do? I could not teach—I had been too indolently bred, and my education was too superficial for that, nor labor with my needle; nor did I know any other useful branch of work—yet something I must do. My brain was in a whirl that left me time to see or hear nothing through all our rapid, exciting drive; I was hardly conscious of Walter's tender kindness, or his sisters' endearing sympathy and caresses.

A very gay party was assembled at the house where we stopped. But only a few persons, mostly gentlemen, old friends of my father's and of mine, were in the library, whither Mrs. McDonald, my hostess, conducted me. She and the Drummonds gathered about me, exclaiming at my pallor and nervousness, as they began to remove my wrappings of velvet and fur. I did not like this being made a heroine of, however. I blushed and declined assistance, beginning with trembling fingers to unfasten the white furs from my throat and shoulders. As I did this, my little muff slid from my lap, and rolled across the hearth to the feet of a tall, bronzed, black-bearded man, who stood there intently regarding me.

Hitherto, I had known him by sight only. He was a Mr. Harter, a stranger, who had just bought a beautiful villa in the neighborhood, and was fitting it up with great taste and liberality. Report said that he had been merely a common miner, who had made a fortune in Australia. He picked up my muff and brought it to me with a low bow. Seen nearer, he looked even less prepossessing. His jet-black hair was cropped close to the head, like a private soldier's. A heavy beard and whiskers concealed the lower part of his face; the upper was embrowned and reddened with long exposure to the sun and wind; only a pair of bright, dark eyes, and teeth white and beautiful as pearls, visible when he spoke or smiled, redeemed the rugged features from positive plainness. His clothes were quiet enough in cut and material, yet he did not seem at home in them: and his hands—how dark and long the fingers looked, grasping the silvery ermine and little blue tassels of my muff! He appeared, in short, just as I had fancied him, a large, almost coarse-featured man of forty, bearing marks of all the exposures, hardships and vicissitudes he had seen; a self-made millionaire, a *nouveau riche*, whom once, from my patrician height, I should have despised; but whom I now felt only humiliated before, as I marked the contrast of his unpretending plainness with my deceptive magnificence.

For by this time my wraps had been removed, and the mirror over the mantlepiece reflected clearly my dazzling white poplin, whose thick, shimmering folds hung long and doubled, as they lay upon the floor, in a train that followed like a snowy wake as I moved. It was cut square in the neck *à la Pompadour*, and trimmed with a treasure of rich French lace; the sleeves were scarcely more than beribboned puffs, and arms, and throat, and ears were enriched with beautiful shining sapphires, glittering and blue as dew might look on a flax flower. Only a little while ago—but how long it seemed—I had been vain of these sparkling drops, had matched them against my eyes, and held them near my fair flaxen hair, as Margaret might have done with her jewels, delighted at the envy and admiration they provoked; but now I could scarcely bear the sight of the slender, elegantly-dressed figure, so delicate and so adorned, reflected in the mirror before me.

"Another day shall not see me," I vowed, "masquerading in this pauper splendor, and eating the bread of dependence—sparkling and smiling abroad, and devouring insults and tears at home. Home! I have no home! Shelterless, helpless, friendless, I am cast upon the world to-night as poor, but for these baubles, as the night when I was born. They will support me till I can show that I can work. But what shall I do—where shall I go?"

I could have wrung my hands in idle anguish; but this was no time for tears and heroics. The "little sleighing party" had become a ball. Already the band had struck up a spirit-stirring waltz. Partners pressed round me; invitations, introductions followed; I could no longer delay to join them. My blood rose warmly through my veins as I listened; the lamps seemed to burn more brilliantly, the flowers to smell more sweetly; above all I heard pealing the wild, intoxicating notes of the music in the hall, entreating, defying, alluring. At the familiar sound, doubt, fear, and sorrow fled away; I was myself again, gay, reckless, seventeen; and in an instant my feet were skimming the ballroom floor, and I was laughing lightly in Walter Drummond's grave face.

That was a triumphant night—my last though it might be; nay, for that reason I would not be robbed of a second. The music had never seemed so sweet and so intoxicating, the guests so happy, the rooms so bright and festal before; and, alas! never had I so prized the delightful enjoyments they offered as now that I must relinquish them. How would it seem to be poor, and leave all these splendors behind? to sink into the ranks of the workers and toilers who uphold this gay society; to be forgotten by these refined and educated women, and these well-bred men? What would life be worth, to the quick-beating blood of youth, divested of this flush of splendor and of joy?

I could not live without it, I felt each moment more truly, as I breathed that enchanting atmosphere of praise and flattery; and yet, it seemed, I must. At every interval in dancing, at every pause in the music, the black shadow of tomorrow haunted me like a ghost at the banquet, and whispered dolefully in my ears.

But pride compelled me to hide my wound, and with the very effort my spirits rose higher. I would not bow to the tempest of trouble whirling over me; I would not see the glances of pity and sympathy cast upon me; I would not understand the compassionate sentences addressed to me—indeed, I hardly heard them. The few hours that still intervened between me and banishment were my own—I chose to enjoy them to the utmost, to reign in them like a queen, and use them royally.

Supper went off gayly. Walter Drummond was my escort, almost loverlike in his attentions, as usual; and Mr. Harter, the self-made millionaire, my neighbor on the other side. He, too, was very kind in his way. He talked to me. I was surprised at his sweet voice and correct intonation. He sent away my champagne, ordering some still, iced-wine of his own servant. I was sure he was right, for he looked at me with a sort of pitying intentness of interest that won me to obedience—and I felt my head already dizzy between triumph and pain.

Other heads, less racked than mine, were dizzied, too, by Mr. McDonald's generous vintages. When we returned to the dancing room the band was set aside; a series of Christmas games began, impromptu tableaux followed—statues, charades. In the last they wanted a marriage scene—a runaway couple before a village magistrate, or something of that sort.

A fat neighbor of Mr. McDonald's, snoring comfortably before the library fire, answered to the character of the magistrate, and messengers were dispatched to request him to serve. Meanwhile public opinion ran high on the question of the bride—the honor being contested between a dozen young ladies in white. All unconcerned, I was talking in a windowseat to my companions at supper. Suddenly I found my place surrounded.

"Sylvia, you must come—you are in white; it will be just the thing—and Mr. Harter."

"But I am not—"

"Oh! yes you are—the very person! It is the elder of her two lovers she runs away with, you know."

They put a cloak on his arm, and a sword in his hand, and placed my unresisting fingers in his. The squire marshaled us solemnly before him, and the curtain was about to ascend, when some slight altercation arose between the lady managers, and the scene was suspended for a moment. Walter Drummond took advantage of the interval to come to my side.

"Sylvia," he whispered, pressing my arm earnestly, "this thing is very real. The squire is a legal magistrate, and has had too much wine. What will you do if he marries you in earnest, for no license is required in this State?"

But Mr. Harter had heard him and turned. Clasping my hand more closely in his, he looked into my eyes with a sudden sparkle in his own.

"And if he did—what then? Could you take me, Sylvia?"

"Don't jest," cried Walter, impatiently; but his voice faltered.

"It is no jest," said Mr. Harter, quietly, my hand still locked in his. "Sylvia, you hear me? The question is between us. I have heard your story; I think he is right, and I ask you to risk it, knowingly, with me?"

I heard, but could not answer, nor move while he held me so firmly; but I looked at him an instant, half in fear, half in surprise. He had never seemed so nearly being handsome as at that moment. A warm flush covered his dark cheek; his black eyes bent eagerly and anxiously on me, were softened by a pitying and kind, almost a fond expression; his voice was very sweet and low as he spoke. In that light, and in that picturesque attitude and costume, his tall, broad figure showed graceful and commanding. I had not time to reflect calmly. I only thought that here was a shield offered against the dread future. The hand so firmly holding mine could pluck me back from the gulf that yawned before me tomorrow.

That moment of indecision was final and fatal, for the curtain was rising, and Walter was no longer beside me. We stood alone before the squire, who stretched his fat figure to its utmost height, and pompously began, with what formula I do not know. Mr. Harter, after one glance at my face, stood in his place immovable, and answered whatever fell to his share; I suppose I did the same, mechanically. The bystanders listened and looked, some in delight, some in wonder, the rest simply in horror. I heard low-toned exclamations mingling, "What a dear!" "How sweet she is!" "Just like a bride, with that wreath of roses in her hair!" from a few of the very youngest and silliest. But, "How pale!" "How very natural!" "It seems almost too true!" from the older ladies; and downright murmurs and imprecations among the gentlemen. A dozen sprang forward to interrupt, but Mr. Harter sternly waved them back. When it was over, he strode up to the complacent squire,

"You have made me the happiest man in the world, Mr. Bannister," he said.

Then it rushed over me like a whirlwind what I had done. Was I mad, or dreaming? Were the deeds of this night a real horror? Was this man truly my husband? I had disengaged my hand, and stood alone. It was the cue for the Drummond girls and others, to rush up to me and cry over me, to declare that they never could have believed it, and ask me how long I had been engaged.

II.

THEY MIGHT AS well have talked to a statue, for I was in a still frenzy of trouble, and could not heed them—and chilled by my cold, unresponsive manner, they all withdrew. It was time to go home, and we hooded and cloaked, in mysterious silence, in our dressing room; I, with my trembling fingers and nervous haste, the last to leave it. When I came down, all were in the sleighs. Only one tall, dark figure waited in the hall for me, beside Mrs. McDonald. The icy wind from the avenue sweeping up, flared the lamplight in his face; it was not Walter Drummond, but Mr. Harter. Could it be true, then? Was he really my husband?

Good Mrs. McDonald took me in her motherly arms, as she bade me good-bye, and kissed and blessed me. She was the first who had thought of doing that, and I could have burst into a tempest of tears on her kind breast, but I dared not yield to the impulse. My strength was already fast giving way, and only pride kept me from fainting and failing at sight of that dark, sentinel figure.

In silence he offered his arm. I took it—there was no help. Walter Drummond sat in his place before his sisters, the seat beside him vacant. He had chosen to desert me, I said to myself, in this trial hour. We advanced toward it, though Mr. Harter's own beautiful little sleigh was drawn up on the opposite side, his man holding the pawing horse, who neighed and shook his bells impatiently.

I trembled on his arm—was there to be a collision between the two men? We halted before the double sleigh; but Walter never moved, while my escort lifted me gently into my old place, only kissing the hand he released. Raising his hat, he stood bareheaded in the starlight till we drove off; and then we heard his horse's feet and bells hurrying away in the direction of his own house.

Some tender, gentle impulse of my heart seemed to go with them; and a thrill of pity, in the midst of my own trouble, followed that lonely flight; for there was something knightly, almost, and grand, in the rude miner's chivalry. More than this, I was deeply grateful to him for the act of renunciation.

I was free, it was evident. Periled by my own fault, how sweet seemed liberty now, even the poorest, liberty to toil! Now that I had felt, for one moment, what bonds might be, I willingly accepted the pains and penalties of freedom, and was ready to find them light. And yet—and yet—he had been kind, and he seemed to pity me; the touch of his kiss was still soft upon my hand. Had he been younger and more graceful, I might, perhaps, even have loved him in my friendless and helpless state, my utter isolation from others.

As it was, I could only rejoice, silently, it is true, for nothing was said during our short drive. Our destination was soon reached. The handsome house was blazing with lights from roof to basement; and late as the hour was, the great doors were thrown wide open, and the servants, with the master and mistress at their head, ranged along the broadhall on either side. Here our large company was to be entertained for the night; was to spend the next day, and be present at a great dinner party that would call all the county together.

I was assigned a room to myself, and hastened to its shelter as soon as politeness permitted; neglectful of the mulled wine and other refreshments, in which some of the ladies, and all the gentlemen, were indulging, for I feared to encounter any of the mirth or jesting that would be sure to follow; to hear, perhaps, some playful allusions to my mimic marriage, and be toasted as "the bride." I slept brokenly, and woke with a wracking headache, feverish and faint, and absolutely unable to stir. My kind hostess came and took charge of me; all day she held me in the pleasant captivity of the quiet, perfumed chamber, keeping intruders away; and not until dusk did she pronounce me convalescent, or fit to appear at her dinner party.

I would gladly have evaded this ordeal; but I was really well enough now, and her kindness was not to be resisted. With all her other cares she lent her own assistance to her maid's in arranging my toilet, and took as deep an interest in the result as if I had been her daughter. I selected a rich black dress covered with violet ribbons, and with many pleasantries about my sober taste, she led me downstairs.

"You have been missed among us, I assure you," she whispered, as she paused a moment in the anteroom to shake out her lace flounces. "I have had a thousand questions to answer in your behalf, and Mr. Harter has been waiting impatiently to lead you down."

We were in the room before I could reply, or control the hurried beating of my heart. What could she mean? The floor seemed to whirl beneath my feet as Mr. Harter took my hand, and at the signal for dinner, transferred it to his arm.

I suppose I answered when addressed, and otherwise sustained my part—for the habit of society teaches us so far to control our emotions; but the grand dinner was a Barmecide feast to me, and less. Mr. Harter sat beside me—silent, except for the ordinary courtesiesof the table; but by his very presence, manner, and attentions, seeming to establish a claim upon me that I felt unable to comprehend or resist.

He was to be, it appeared, the hero of the evening; for he invited all those present to spend it at his house, and go from Mrs. Martyn's delightful hospitality to his own. "All," he repeated, with a wistful, deprecatory glance at me, "if no one objects."

No one objected; but, on the contrary, his proposal was received with acclamations, and coffee was served earlier to facilitate our departure. As we left the room, Mr. Harter spoke, for the first time, directly addressing me.

"Sylvia," he whispered, "would it be too much if I asked you to change that sober dress for something gayer and lighter, more like yourself, to do honor to my *fete*?"

His tone and manner were constrained, but there was an indefinable something in both—an assertion of interest in, and responsibility for me—that made my heart stand still at first, then throb more quickly. An instinct of rebellion urged me to refuse to oblige him; to reply that I should not join the party, and was going elsewhere—but this was quite impossible. Mrs. Martyn had accepted the invitation for all her guests. I could not remain behind, and at this hour—what could I do, where should I go? For this one day fate and fortune had, somehow, prevailed against me—my destiny seemed in the hands of others, and I no longer my own mistress; but the next, I averred to myself, both should be conquered, and I be free as air.

While I hesitated, some one spoke behind us—it was Mrs. Martyn, exhorting such as desired to make any change in their dress, to do so at once, while the sleighs were getting ready.

I went upstairs mechanically. Like one in a dream I put on a gay blue silk, the handsomest I had; a white cloak with a tasseled hood; pearls on my neck and arms, and in my ears. When I returned, Mr. Harter stepped forward; everybody seemed already paired off. Could my old intimates leave me so readily to a stranger? A certain hard, defiant feeling came to me with the pain of this conviction, and taking my escort's offered arm, I walked on proudly.

Mr. Harter's sleigh was again waiting, but this time it was an elegant little affair, drawn by a pair of spirited black ponies, that tossed their pretty heads and champed upon their silver bits with pretty impatience. As soon as they were set free they darted off, leading the way lightly, and with a motion so swift and straight that the shell, with its trailing robes, must have seemed to those behind to be shooting like a bird onward, and imitating its arrowy flight.

It was a lovely moonlight night, very mild and fair, and the mellow rays shone full on white roads and whiter fields. The task of guiding the fairy vehicle seemed so easy and delightful, that I broke the awkward silence by expressing my admiration of the ponies, and requesting to be allowed to drive them for a moment. The fresh air and the rapid motion had so far revived my spirits; but they sank again as my companion relinquished the reins, with the single simple answer,

"Certainly—they are yours."

I would have drawn back, but dared not, and, cowardlike, dreaded more than anything else, question or explanation. I drove on desperately in utter silence for miles; Mr. Harter sitting by my side, motionless and speechless, like an Indian. Something in his mute patience touched my heart, and I was mistress enough of myself to smile, and say a few words of thanks and kindness as I gave up my charge.

The great gates were open for us to drive through, and the dark fir avenue leading to the house was hung with colored lamps that cast rainbow reflections on the snow. The house itself was ablaze with light, and festal with music. It looked like a fairy palace, with its quaint, beautiful windows crowded with plants and flowers, the glass glittering like diamonds, the birds and blossoms behind them shining in the brilliant glare like colored jewels all along the picturesque, wide front. I thought I was dreaming still as we alighted and ascended the marble steps. In the vestibule Mr. Harter turned, and with unusual softness in his black eyes, took my hand, and welcomed me to "Paradise."

"Paradise," for so public opinion in the neighborhood had named it—and Paradise, indeed, it was, as lady guests, now fast arriving, declared, as they wandered from one to another of the gemlike rooms. I followed, too, on the arm of my escort, secretly reluctant, but reassured by his silence, and the presence of the others. Close beside me, like my shadow, moved Walter Drummond, neither speaking to, nor looking at me, but keeping over all my motions an incessant surveillance, that made me doubly uncomfortable.

We visited the basements, with their wide and convenient offices, the garrets, the chambers, beautifully furnished and appointed; the very roof, battlemented and smooth as a floor. Everywhere were evidences not only of mere wealth and opulence, or large expenditure, but of the taste that knows how to use, and the tact that rightly applies it. There was a harmony and fitness in the whole, not wholly the work of upholsterer or architect. Evidently a skilled hand had guided, an artist eye overlooked their labors—the rough miner dwelt in a house in which not merely a prince, but a poet, might have found himself at home.

We came back to the parlors after a lengthened survey, and dispersed about them, examining the beautiful things they contained. Without any appearance of ostentation or overcrowding, there was a real wealth of objects, famous from association, or rare in art. Mr. Harter kept near me, looking quietly pleased at my pleasure; on the other side Walter Drummond stood speechlessly, with a gloomy frown on his forehead. When I explored with others the treasures of the library shelves, and found there all my old favorite books, and many more that I had long desired to see, his face was darkened with an unsympathetic sneer; and when I paused before some exquisite pictures and mosaics from Italy, such as my dear father used to bring back from his voyages, to ornament our pretty home, he resented the tears that filled my eyes, and the loving delight with which I bent over them.

"I see, Sylvia, you are like all your sex," he said, "and gradate your admiration by the price of the object to be admired. A cheaper article would have moved you less."

His tone stung me, and I was roused to retort.

"They are rare and precious," I returned, "but they have another value in my eyes. I have seen such only once before, Mr. Drummond, and it is no wonder the sight disturbed me, for they remind the homeless of home."

I said it recklessly, angry at his notice of my weakness, and looked up quickly, in time to see his baffled look, and meet Mr. Harter's eyes. Were there actually tears in them? At any rate, his countenance was strangely softened and beautified by the momentary expression it wore. A little while before, I could have wondered how this common, self-made man had possessed himself of such treasures of art, as not merely wealth alone, but time, and taste, and training, sensitive perceptions and delicate instincts, were needed to buy; yet since seeing him, for the first time in his own home, where he was at ease and unconstrained, and now moved by another's grief to gentle sympathy and pity, I began to understand how this dark, impassive mask might conceal much that we had never fancied he could feel. He had looked both genial and good while receiving his guests with noble hospitality; and as the duties of a host obliged him to lay aside much of his ordinary reserve, there was a refinement of kindness in his manner, to which even Walter Drummond's sneers could not blind me.

He regarded me now a moment in silence, and turned to speak to Mrs. McDonald, who with her husband drew near, I fancied, at a sign from him. The group we formed was somewhat apart from the others, who were intently examining the various curious and beautiful objects the room contained; and I understood that we were going to see something not yet exhibited, as I put my hand reluctantly in Walter's extended arm.

III.

OUR CONDUCTOR PAUSED before a little white door, at the end of a suite of rooms we had lately examined, opened it, and disclosed a beautiful "boudoir," or parlor—I prefer theEnglish word—furnished entirely in white and blue. A white carpet covered with wreaths of light blue violets and forget-me-nots; window draperies of lace lined with silk, and furniture of damask and satinwood: all blue and white, like the dress I wore, were reflected in the mirror above the marble mantle. There were books, and birds, and flowers, pictures, and music, and a sparkling fire lighted in the grate; but the room had no occupant till the others stood aside to let me pass.

I put my hand in my kind old friend's, and we went in together. A little sofa was rolled before the fire, and she drew me upon it, with her arm about my waist. Walter Drummond stood beside us like a sullen guardian; and opposite, Mr. Harter leaned his elbow on the mantle, and looked at the group we made. I trembled when his eyes met mine, for I somehow knew that the beautiful room had been furnished for me that day, and that he was going to ask me to occupy it as its mistress. Yet when he spoke, it was something very different that he said.

Addressing me directly, as if there had been no other person present, in a hurried but most straightforward manner, he gave me the plainest history of himself, concealing nothing, and excusing nothing that it was needful we should hear. Perhaps few lives could have borne the test of so close a chronicle—no word was said in his own praise or favor, no effort made to gain sympathy or win credit; I never listened to such a frank confession."You and your friends should know," he said, "what the man is who is about to ask so much of you. To report alone you cannot trust, as I will prove to you; nor solely to the opinions gathered from testimony like this," for he had offered a pile of letters and documents to Mr. McDonald and Walter Drummond, which the young lawyer was examining with keen, inimical eyes, the elder with anxious and cautious observation through his spectacles. These, it would seem, were satisfactory, for the careful scrutiny ended in their being tendered back with many assurances to Mr. Harter, who received them with a smile.

"After all, these papers," he said, "tell you less of my life and character than I will tell you, or than common rumor had already told, and told mostly wrong. It is said that I am a man of low birth and no education, whose fortune has been gained by a lucky accident, and who is not wholly worthy of all he aspires to possess. The last is the only truth.

"If my education has been neglected, it was my fault alone, and not that of my father, an accomplished surgeon, spending always more than his large income in gratifying elegant and artistic tastes. From my birth I lived among luxuries, never, I fear, entirely paid for, and fancies gratified at an extraordinary sacrifice. My time, and that of my brother and sister, was spent at the best schools and academies. In my first college year, my father died, leaving two motherless children, a rough, healthy, active boy, and a delicate little girl.

"His library, horses, carriages, and house were swallowed up by his debts; the beautiful pictures and statues were sold; the scientific, literary, and artistic treasures he had so carefully collected, were widely scattered, and after their sacrifice, much was still left unpaid. I saw the very end of the ruin and destruction, put my sister in the only place where I hoped she would be kindly cared for, and went to sea before the mast, to support her.

"The schedule of my father's debts in my pocket, and the memory of the little life dependent upon mine, urged me to energy and industry. I was away for years, following fortune wherever others had seemed to find it—in India, Japan, and China, on the Pacific Coast, in the Black Sea. At first I heard often from home—during the latter part of the time, not at all; but I was neither stimulated by tidings, nor unnerved by their absence—the stake was too great for that. I continued steadily to forward letters and remittances, and at last was able to come home. Neither letters nor remittances had been touched—my sister was lying near her father and her brother; and her grave, thick-grown with grass and daisies, looked as old as theirs.

"I spent the sum that was to have brought us together, and given us again a happy home, in paying the last remaining debts of my father. Then again, poor, homeless, friendless, and forlorn, I went away to seek relief in the ceaseless struggle of existence at the very ends of the earth.

"The gold fields of Australia had just been discovered, and I repaired there with thousands of others. Alone, motiveless, with nothing to lose, and comparatively indifferent to gain, fortune singularly favored me. From a mere miner I became a proprietor, a merchant, a millionaire—and here only report will not have belied me, while it says all my earnings were honest ones. Weary of the rough colonial life, and of an existence devoted to selfish gain and accumulation, I remembered the education of my boyhood; and now that I was able to gratify those dormant tastes and tendencies, I traveled widely, collecting curiosities of art and beauty, that would have delighted my father's heart, but gave hardly a throb of pleasure to my own; for to what end should I gather treasures or riches? No one on earth sympathized with my success, or shared my happiness.

"Tired of drifting about the world, I came back at last to my native country, with the purpose of establishing for myself a place to which I might return from time to time, and, perhaps, rest wholly in at last. My bankers sent me here: and I have found much occupation and healthful pleasure in arranging and founding it. Yet, now that it is finished, I am more than ever conscious of the want in it, and in myself—the void that money cannot fill, or art supply, and which alone can make it what it is not, but should be, yet what others, with far less pains and toil, have been so blest to win—a home.

"I have seen," he went on, his hand trembling a little in its rest upon the marble, his dark eyes still lifted, "in Arabian deserts, tents of poorest structure, in western prairies rude huts of log and clay, that were happier houses than mine, for the voices of children, the laughter of women, the busy life of household cares and household joys and sorrows, filled them all day long. There were united affections, undivided interests, hearts that beat and brains that planned to the same good and cheerful end; there was poverty lightly borne for the sake of the love that sprung from it—and there would riches have given tenfold the pleasure they can ever give to me, because they would have gladdened many lives in blessing one.

"In my home," he said, "which they ignorantly call 'Paradise,' birds sing and fountains rustle; but there is silence, for no voice I care to hear can speak to me. The flowers grow with none to pluck them; the rooms are empty and dull; the beauty and the luxury you so admire, to me are but fairy illusions, for my eyes see them as the worthless dross they are. Poor in the midst of riches, I want something better than they can offer, better than my life has hitherto known, without which it is useless, insensate, dead. I want to give my future an aim, my heart a new existence of hope and joy, my house a mistress. Sylvia, will you come?"

He moved nearer, and looked and spoke as if unconscious of any presence but my own.

"When first I saw you I admired, as all must do, but never thought of loving the sparkling ballroom beauty, with whom I, a dull, plain, middle-aged man, could have nothing in common. Then, with others, I heard the story of your sad losses, your domestic trials; finally, of the crisis which left you as utterly homeless and forlorn as I had been at your age. Too well I remembered my own efforts and sufferings, yet I had been a vigorous boy, you were but a delicate and helpless girl. I resolved to be your defense against ill fortune. How, I did not yet perceive, but I hoped to discover a way. Last night, all through the gay festivities, I watched your face, and read in it all the tortures of anxiety, regret, and fear you suffered. While I pondered, vexed and bewildered by my own helplessness, distressed by the sight of your repressed anguish, a sudden chance threw in my way an opportunity to accomplish all I had desired in your behalf, and more. Temptation took a form so fair and dazzling, that if I was selfish in yielding to its dictates, believe me, Sylvia, I did not know it till too late! I swear to you that, until I held your innocent hand in mine, until I heard your voice pronounce the words that pledged you, unconscious, to so much, I never thought at what a cost to you my resolution of saving you must be fulfilled.

"Your hesitation, your half-consent in the face of urgent warning; the look with which you seemed at once to doubt, and fear, and trust; your continued presence at my side, and the touch of your passive fingers, emboldened me to a step which all my life I must regret or bless. Forgive me if I knew, even as I challenged it, the fearful risk incurred. With the beating of your pulse on mine, I recognized the mysterious tie between us. I felt the tempest that shook your soul, and I realized more fully than you could do all that must follow, yet I was selfish enough to permit the ceremony to go on, for in that moment pity and admiration disappeared; a love was born in my heart, so deep and fond, that I fancied it could avert all, atone to you for all.

"And, Sylvia, I am selfish still, for I love you, and I wish for you still—I want you for my wife. I would bring your beauty to bless my ugliness, your brightness to cheer my gloom, your blooming youth to adorn my stern, middle age. I can give you little in return for so much; but all I have and am is yours, and there shall be no bound to my affection or my care for you.

"On the other hand, if the sacrifice is too great, the thought of all it involves too painful and irksome; remember that my wealth, value-less but for this, shall break the nominal tie between us with a breath, while in its name I shall bestow on you what will keep the woman I love forever safe from poverty and dependence. Choose then freely, for in either case your future is assured and clear, and by my hurried yielding to a moment's impulse I shall have done you no wrong. If you justly refuse to regard its consequences as binding, the old friend at your side, to whose kindness I owe this interview, will take you to her house, which will be yours until a happier one shall open to receive you, and your girlish heart be given to a better mate than mine. Choose then, Sylvia, unencumbered by thoughts of the past, or fears for the future in this crisis of your fate. Pray heaven to guide you, and decide the happiness or the misery of your life."

Walter Drummond came to my side as Mr. Harter ceased—his faced was flushed, his manner excited and eager. He, too, spoke with an absolute oblivion of the presence of others, but how differently!

"Accept his offer, Sylvia," he urged. "Take the reparation he tenders, and which he owes you, for thus, in your ignorance and helplessness, linking your name with his; repudiate that hasty action—let him repay you and release you."

I saw Mr. Harter's lip curl. But he listened patiently.

"It was wholly my fault," I said, "and I will take nothing."

"You will take my advice," he insisted, "for I love you, Sylvia, and I know that you love me—our interests are one. The claims of our long friendship, and our constant associations—often sought by you—our community of tastes, feelings, and sympathies; our congeniality in youth, even in personal attributes, prove it impossible that you should submit willingly to the fate that threatens you. Had I feared such weakness on your part, such daring on that of others, I would have spoken before and set your heart at rest. Come with me, then, and trust your case in my hands; a little time and patience will set you free, and you shall be my wife, the daughter of my parents!"

Strangely enough, this bright prospect could not move me; I was growing cold and dull, and his sharp sentences fell faintly on my ears. Torn and weakened by long excitement; always unequal to the crisis through which I had to pass; swayed by many conflicting emotions, and hardly understanding the wish of my own heart, which Mr. Harter had generously besought me to follow, much less the arguments by which Walter Drummond appealed to my reason, I was incapable of answering either. I only knew that the younger man had been my friend, possibly my lover; but that I could never wish him to be dearer or more near—his friendship sufficed me, perhaps, even less—for since he claimed me so boldly, I shrank from him with an invincible repugnance. His rapacity and want of delicacy, albeit for my sake, disgusted and mortified me deeply; his reading of my thoughtless encouragement in times past was humiliating to hear; his judgment of his rival's forbearance and generosity, of his noble motives and deeds—both narrow and mean. Although I could not have put my hurried thoughts, my confused sensations into words, I felt an instinct of aversion so strong, that if my choice must lie between the two men, I knew now that he, at least, could never be my husband.

"Do you consent, Sylvia?" he impatiently demanded, annoyed, I suppose, at my silence and stolidity. "Will you do as I have said?"

"I cannot," I faltered.

"Ah!" he sneered, "then wealth and luxury are, indeed, as powerful with you as I had thought them. I know the temptation is strong; with a million of money, what a setting might not your beauty receive! Truly, it would be pleasant to reign like a queen in this charming little palace, and to find every whim gratified as soon as formed, like the Beast's fair bride in the fairy tale. Better, no doubt, to you than to be the wife of a poor professional man, absorbed in the struggle of the world. Forgive the error, but I thought your nature impassioned, not frivolous, and fancied love might be something to you!"

I could have answered his sarcasm with tears; his anger with passionate avowal: my heart ached with such an empty, longing pain under his words. "It is much," I could have said; "it should be all, if you but offered anything so sweet and so divine. But this that you bring me is not love; pique or admiration it may be, vanity and self-interest it surely is. No pure or gentle feeling so dictated softens your hard glance, or speaks in the milder modulation of your tones. Even your friendship, once so prized, I doubt, if it wears this form and-holds this language. True love is modest, generous, and gentle; I have seen it tonight for the first time, and recognized it by those attributes in the man you so despise. If it is this you would have me seek, how can I turn from him and follow you?"

I could have said all this, I mean, could I have had strength to pronounce it, or even to arrange my thoughts in collected form—but the words remained unspoken, the meaning unexplained, for, in truth, I was fast sinking into insensibility. I heard Walter's voice impetuously, almost angrily, urging me to answer, and Mr. Harter, in a tone that thrilled me even then, proving how severely, by that long suspense, his partial endurance had been tried, repeat once more, entreatingly, its formula, "Sylvia, choose!" and then I heard no more. My heavy head sunk lower and lower to Mrs. McDonald's lap, and all worldly trouble swept by me like a wave.

When next I raised it, two faces only were bending over me—two faces that had nothing in common but a look of anxiety and dismay. One was young, smooth, refined, even passably handsome; once it had been pleasant and welcome to me in its kindness; but under this new phase of vision, it seemed hard, and eager, and cold. The other, with rougher lineaments, but softened and warmed by a feeling almost divine, bent above me with pity and tenderness like an angel's. Love alone, most gentle, most compassionate, purest, and least selfish of earthly passions, had etherialized that older and more rugged face, till it wore a beauty the youthful one never knew. I could not reason, nor think, nor weigh and ponder, had I felt disposed; for a time sense and memory were in abeyance, and I realized only that a shadowy trouble overhung me, from which I sought protection. By a blessed impulse of instinct, I stretched out my hands, not to the wealth with which Mr. Harter might fill them; not to the husband I had wedded in haste by a contract which pride compelled me to ratify; but to the love in that kind face and noble heart, that has been my rock of refuge ever since.

Afterword

I N 1865, THE year that Henry James began to sign his stories
and in effect distinguish between those published under his name
and those under his nom de plume, it is still less readily possible to
tell the difference between the two when closely comparing their
content, especially that of an improbable kind. Even in a literary age
when borrowing was common and allusion to certain topics, ideas,
and procedures was general in practice, the occasion of finding two
or more stories outfitted with the same details, the same highly
improbable mention of rarely occurring symbolic motifs, allusion to
exactly the same Swedenborgian concordance footnotes, and mathe-
matically astonishing repetitions of cognate words from the same
Greek root strains the laws of probability. What such similitude more
soundly indicates is that the work of two supposedly different
authors in fact can be traced back to one, as is evidenced, for instance,
by the consistent appearance—both in stories signed by James and in
those by Leslie Walter, his most commonly repeated nom de plume—

of the very same assortment of coquettes, thirty-year-old qualified bachelors, wounded heroes, loving heroines ready to nurse them back to life, and yet many more of the themes and story details that James chose and treated for years. Far from supposing such unlikely coincidence difficult to discover and evidence, the number of actual, unrelentingly same coincidences is unbelievably high. Indeed, statistical study of particular recurring words, just one of the many variables employed to determine Jamesian authorship, reveals that the calculated chance against the likelihood of such a similitude between James and the author known as Leslie Walter runs to a number with sixty or more zeroes after it. Such evidence is context-free.

Selective Bibliography

Benham, W. Gurney, *Playing Cards.* London: Spring Books, 1957.

Brown, J. Allston, *History of the New York Stage*, vols. 1–3. New York: Benjamin Blom, 1964.

Burton, Robert, *Anatomy of Melancholy,* London: New York Empire State, 1924.

Cousin, Victor, *The True, the Beautiful, and the Good,* trans. O. Wight. New York: Appleton, 1858.

Dictionary of the Bible, vols. 1–5, ed. James Hastings. 1898. Reprint, Peabody, Mass.: Hendrickson, 1988.

Dictionary of Greek and Roman Antiquities, ed. William Smith, Walton and Maburly. Boston: Little, Brown & Co., 1859.

Dictionary of Greek and Roman Biography and Mythology, vols. 1 & 2, ed. William Smith. Boston: C.C. Little and J. Brown, 1849.

Dunlap, S. F., *Spirit History of Man.* New York: D. Appleton, 1858.

Edel, Leon, *Henry James*, vols. 1–5. London: Rupert Hart-Davis, 1963.

Frank, Adolphe, *Kabbalah.* New York: Bell Publishing Company, 1940.

Gensenius, H. W. F. , *Hebrew Chaldee Lexicon to the Old Testament,* trans. Samuel Tregelles. Baker Book House, 1979.

Hoyle's Book of Games. Philadelphia: Crawford and Company.

James, Henry, *The American Scene.* New York and London: Harper Brothers, 1907.

—*New York Edition*, vols. 1–26. New York: Charles Scribners, 1908.

—*A Small Boy and Others.* New York: Charles Scribners, 1913.

—*Notes of a Son and Brother.* New York: Charles Scribners, 1915.

—*Complete Tales of . . .* vols. 1–12, ed. Leon Edel. London: Rupert Hart-Davis, 1964.

Kucera, H. and Francis W., Nelson, *Computational Analysis of Present-Day American English.* Providence: Brown University Press, 1967.

Lamb, Charles, *Essays of Elia.* Boston: Thomas Crowell and Company.

Leland, Charles Godfrey, *Memoirs.* New York: D. Appleton, 1893.

Mott, Frank Luther: *A History of American Magazines,* vols. 1–4. Cambridge: Belknap Press, 1957.

Muller, Max, *Lectures on the Science of Language.* London: Longman, Green, and Longman, 1862.

Oxford Essays, London: Parker and Son, 1856.

Perry, Ralph B., *Thought and Character of William James.* New York: Little Brown and Company, 1935.

Sperling and Simon, *The Zohar,* vols. 1–5. London, New York: Sonano Press, 1984.

Strong's Exhaustive Concordance of the Bible. 1890. Reprint, with keyword comparison, Nashville, Tenn.: Abingdon, 1980.

Swedenborg Concordance, vols. 1–5, comp. John Potts. London: Swedenborg Society, 1978.

Swedenborg, E., *Arcana Coelestia,* vols. I–XII, trans. John Potts New York: Swedenborg Foundation, 1978.

—*Heaven and Hell, Divine Love and Wisdom.* New York: 1875.

—*Conjugial Love,* trans. Samuel Warren. New York: Swedenborg Foundation, 1954.

Wilson, H. H., *Religion of the Hindus,* vols. I–II, ed. Reinhold Rost. London: Trubner, 1862.

The Computer and the Search for Henry James

(1) An Overall View and Explanation of How and Where the Computer Serves This Search

THE COMPUTER ANALYSIS of probable HJ fiction text was formulated to help distinguish differences between HJ's story texts and those of any other author who was writing during the same general period and was thus quite possibly concerned with the same general subjects, since writers in the same age often share the same tastes. Broadly, the theory behind the program is that a style strikingly similar to that of HJ's fiction most probably can be expected to be HJ's own: In this respect, probabilities reckon importantly in the calculations that the analysis commits to. Implicit in this theory is the assumption that usually strong linguistic factors distinguish one author's style from another. But, in the event that comparison of two stories results in a dead heat, other factors may well decide the issue, such as HJ's known characteristic use of a word whose frequency of occurrence in the English language of the time is so low (less than one occurrence per million) that two occurrences in a test story of 2,400 words would weigh the scales in favor of it representing HJ's style. And should a combination of several different stylistic characteristics be involved, as happened on occasion, then the probability would favor HJ by a factor of one in several trillion possibilities. Though not the most exact science of determination—most sciences are not geared to perfection—calculated possibility counts decidedly in such a final estimate of attributed authorship.

In this way, using a known base of HJ contemporaneous stories and letters (and perhaps essays), most stories chosen to be tested for HJ's stylistic fingerprint yield a quick electronic estimate, probably a nod, whereas in ordinary reading the mind would find it quite difficult to keep track of the many characteristic words. Computer analysis, then, is intended as a polished substitution for the human mind, which can be easily waylaid by linguistic distractions in its search for evidence to support corroboration. Importantly, the process involved in such an analysis can be said to be context-free, in the sense that it does not depend upon the meaning of the word text in any ordinary direct manner. Coincidence of occurring in the text at large—what is called "matching" between the word elements of the textual databases—is alone what counts in measuring the statistics of probability in the comparison.

Other ways of attributing authorship have been tried. One such, perhaps theoretically best, had had long-standing practice though virtually no partial success. Adapted to computer search was the thought that if a significant match could be detected between a known author's text and a test text, it would be a common-sense conclusion that they both represented work by the same author. Dismissing the most common frequencies and lengthening the sequence of words—the "string"—involved, the computer was programmed to search out concatenations of five, six, or seven words, which, if found, should have been dilly. But the probability of such five- or seven-word string occurrences ran into two disturbing problems. Even with super-fast machines, the chances of such matches were beyond astronomical; and though such a common-sense test result has long existed as the criterion for academic plagiarism, an author him/herself, however repetitious, considerably less than seldom could be expected to repeat such a chain of words, and if it should happen but once, it would little serve as conclusive evidence.

Thus, the computer analysis devised for author attribution here was accordingly adjusted. Instead of an analysis based on six- or seven-word strings, all matches of two words of any frequency were recorded and then compared to what became a growing base of all match words in all the stories attributed to HJ. If, for instance, early in the matching the verb *is* was regularly matched, and the continuing program of matches showed ten or fifteen HJ stories further showing the same proportional match profile, the statistics compiled on that base showed little deviation from a norm distribution of occurrence on the verb *is* in the English language usage of nineteenth-century English writers. But if the matching word, for example, was *knuckle* or *flogged* or *stranding*—whose frequency of usage was one in a million words—then, if the same word occurred as a match in five, seven, or occasionally ten of the stories provisionally attributed to HJ, the chances of such a combined event was one millionth x one millionth x one millionth x one millionth x one millionth x one millionth (and on, let's say, to ten multiplicands), which arithmetic result would test a mathematician's patience in recording it. And importantly, if the word total in the sum of all ten stories equaled but 38,000 words and not a million, the arithmetic result would be even higher.

The results of our computer analysis for HJ-tested stories quite often showed that a very low frequency match word recurred from five to eleven or thirteen HJ-attributed stories, while virtually none of any of the match words appeared in more than three of the control stories by authors contemporaneous to HJ. In itself, the probability factor of a recurrence in even three stories by a given author can seem very daunting when looking at the improbability of the word recurrence itself, but the fallout of words in any text in a language needs study to determine what norms, if any, are being considered.

To advocate that an anonymous or even signed text (by a nom de plume) is really by a given known author admits of many ins and outs. In that sense, the use of the computer to aid a decision is just that, an aid, even when intended as the first stage in the process of attribution. Other, more regularly fruitful ways of garnering evidence are certainly in order. Here, for instance, HJ's subtle and thorough understanding of the Bible text ranked high as a factor, with his specialized attention to Swedenborgian doctrine providing a defining distinction.

(2) The Computer Procedure, Specifically

THE FIRST PHASE of the search program was to build a database. Since our intention was principally to cover HJ's literary activity commencing in 1858 and continuing through 1871, and since HJ had no writing history prior to 1858, the database comprised his letters through 1864 and his earliest known story, "A Tragedy of Error," published in 1864. Had more extensive HJ literary materials been available, a typically prudent procedure would have been to divide his works for comparison into three- or four-year parcels and thus account for the linguistic changes representative of each parcel, mainly the acquisition of vocabulary. Still, a total of 20,783 words yielded a quite decent basis for comparison. Against this word base was begun the task of comparing possible HJ fictions, starting with what at that time appeared to be HJ's first story publication in the *Newport Mercury* in 1858.

The procedure included for comparison to the HJ database ten known stories by known authors other than HJ. Thus, the program calculated how many times in at least ten passes—usually called "runs"—each and every word in non-HJ stories matched one of the words in the HJ database. Common high frequency words in the English language could be expected to regularly appear, of course, while other match words had but a few repeats over the course of ten passes. In effect, the results recorded a profile of correspondence between the HJ database and a random non-HJ set of ten stories, including in that process a calculation of probability according to how many times in ten passes a given match word had occurred. The choice of having ten such stories was quite arbitrary; any other number could have provided a reasonable sample. The testing goal of this particular analysis was to compare the profile it built of the ten unsigned and possible HJ stories against the ten known-author control stories.

Ten stories from each category made up a viable sample and afforded the possibility of arithmetically tracking all word matches up through ten. Thus, ten chances existed for a given word to match. For instance, if a given word match possible in the HJ stories occurred in six of the test stories—which normally was high—and the frequency of that particular word was (let us say) thirteen in a million, then, calculated at 6.2748517e-35 to 1, the probability of such a recurrence would be extremely low; and if by chance that same word match recurred in all ten stories, then the improbability would be 1.792160394037e-54 to 1, wherein "e" expresses exponentiation and "54" denotes the trailing number of zeros—an imposing number better relegated to intention than to chance. Actually, as the procedure presented itself, any recurrence over three word matches was deemed to demonstrate a departure from blind chance and to constitute a consistent element of style.

In order to view and interpret these data most easily, the HJ database and data in all twenty of the stories under consideration were merged and alphabetized, with the source of every word (the name of the story or file) attached and retained. In this way a printout of all the combined data would graphically reveal every word that had at least one match, and could in fact extend to the most rare possibility that a given word match recurred in all ten of the control non-HJ stories as well as in the full range of test-for-HJ-authorship stories in the HJ database.

Analysis could be further conducted according to the following directive: If any of the word matches included words from both non-HJ and from test-for-HJ stories, those matches were to be disregarded. This left distinctly separate clusters of matches in either non-HJ or test-for-HJ stories. A printout readily illustrated how often the recurrence of a match evidenced itself, and the program also provided calculations of probability for each cluster.

(3) Results of the Test That Determined HJ Authorship, Authenticated by Probabilities of Unchance

THE FOLLOWING ACTUAL examples are usually of a lesser length than a complete story, whether the test was to determine that a possible HJ story was indeed by HJ or to determine that the non-HJ control story being analyzed was in fact just that—a story by a known author other than James. The procedure of comparing words beginning with several successive letters of the alphabet—say, *d* through *h*, or *a* through *c*—though in one sense quite arbitrary, in its fuller perspective quite readily defined the different profiles associated with known or anonymous HJ stories as opposed to known or anonymous non-HJ control stories. In the non-HJ control stories, over a given number of (let us say) forty-six stories, matches of two, three, and occasionally four out of the analyzed total of computer runs was usual. In the HJ-attributed computer runs over that same analyzed total, however, the usual profile looked like about twice or three times as many occurrences of two- three- and four-word matches, as well as occurrences of five- through as many as eleven- twelve- or thirteen-word matches. The calculated odds against the recurrence of (say) one occasion of four-word matches in a non-HJ control story, while it appears large—1 in 7.07281e-15—hardly compares with the recurrence of two occasions of a nine-word match in an HJ-attributed story. But the computer runs yielded even more dramatic results. A documented few follow.

Searching through words beginning with the letters *d* through *h* and comparing "A Tragedy of Error," a known HJ story, against a base of forty-six intermixed HJ-attributed stories and known non-HJ control stories, the profile of match word recurrences included only four occasions of a two-word match for known non-HJ control stories, but for the HJ-attributed stories there were twenty-one occasions of a two-word match, six occasions of a three-word match, eight occasions of a four-word match, four occasions of a five-word match, one occasion of a six-word match, one occasion of a seven-word match, one occasion of an eight-word match, and one occasion of a nine-word match. The calculated odds associated with these occasions were individually determined depending upon the frequency per million of which word came into analytic focus.

Searching through words beginning with the letters *d* through *h* and comparing "Jessica's Lesson," a known non-HJ control story (by Frank Lee Benedict), against a base of forty-six intermixed HJ-attributed stories and non-HJ control stories, the profile of matchword recurrences included not even one occasion of any word match for the HJ-attributed stories, while there were five occasions of a two-word match, three occasions of a three-word match, and two occasions of a four-word match for the known non-HJ story.

(4) A Miscellany of Comments Concerning Aspects of the Analytic Procedure as Run by Computer

ONCE A MEANINGFUL basis for testing comparisons between HJ stories and stories by other authors during the years 1858–64 had been built, decisions could methodically be made as to which was which and the stories could be grouped either as HJ-attributed stories or as non-HJ control stories. This gradually resulted in the numerical growth of each list until forty-six intermixed stories were queried as the basis for an analytic test run to differentiate between the HJ-attributed and the non-HJ groups. Theoretically, each group would grow larger with the addition of further test items, and since the base of pieces attributed to HJ then grew, only reasons of testing convenience would limit the total number of items concerned, although some reservation might warrant an attempt to keep the HJ-attributed stories to certain two- or four-year limitations. This rigorous restriction was not introduced, but the choice of prospects for analysis rather closely followed a chronological advance of publishing dates. The procedural plan of the general computer analysis was to maximize the size of the database being tested because an ever-expanding database naturally enhanced a simulation of probabilities inherent in the resultant occurrence of matches. On the other hand, the chances of finding styles like HJ's (slowly but naturally changing) authorial style increased. The program incorporated the risk of assuming that no very significant change of style had taken place in HJ's writing over the course of the few years between 1858 and 1864, although further unreported tests of comparison between the pseudonymous Leslie Walter's style and HJ's quite broadly affirmed the same profile of probability.

Concerning Leslie Walter's openly attributed stories, the following three examples are typical of all:

First, Leslie Walter's "A New Story of Cinderella" (January 1862), which was originally published under the name of Fannie Caprice, was analyzed against the non-HJ control group and resulted in a profile similar to that of the HJ-attributed stories. Specifically, there were twenty-three occasions of two-word matches, seven of three-word matches, five of four-word matches, two of five-word matches, six of six-word matches, one of seven-word matches, one of eight-word matches, and one of nine-word matches, while the non-HJ control group showed only five occasions of two-word matches, and nothing more.

Second, Leslie Walter's story "The Sprite Transformed" (February 1863) was analyzed against the non-HJ control group, and again the profile resembled the previously HJ-attributed stories, with thirty instances of two-word matches, twelve of three-word matches, ten of four-word matches, two of five-word matches, two of six-word matches, one of seven-word matches, and one of nine-word matches.

The non-HJ control group showed only six cases of two-word matches and but three of three-word matches. The ratio of words in the "Cinderella" and "Sprite" stories is as 5601 is to 7155, roughly 5.5 to 7, which ratio roughly translates into the number of matches found across the match groups in these stories; where the odds against a probable match were very high, as in match groups of seven and higher, only one such match might occur.

Finally, Leslie Walter's February 1865 story, "One Evening's Work," was compared to HJ's March 1865 first signed story, "The Story of a Year." In this test it was assumed, first, that both of these stories were by HJ and would therefore show the same general profile further than a three-word match and, second, that the non-HJ control group would show few if any cases beyond a match of three words. The results bore out both assumptions: For words beginning with the letters *d* through *h*, "One Evening's Work" showed twenty-five instances of a two-word match, sixteen of a three-word match, eleven of a four-word match, thirteen of a five-word match, five of a six-word match, two of a seven-word match, one of an eight-word match, and three of a nine-word match. Likewise, "The Story of a Year" (a considerably longer story) showed forty-eight occasions of a two-word match, twenty-eight of a three-word match, twelve of a four-word match, twelve of a five-word match, eleven of a six-word match, five of a seven-word match, three of an eight-word match, three of a ten-word match, and one of an eleven-word match. By contrast, in neither case of comparison with the non-HJ control group did that control group exceed three-word matches.

Allusion as Proof in the Search for Henry James

IN THE COURSE of two decades of research, the more I investigated Henry James's long-hidden literary past, the more I recognized that the evidence of his youthful authorship in numerous unsigned works for magazines like the *National* and the *Newport Mercury* lay not only in particular characteristics of literary style but also in a universe of allusions: allusions to biblical wisdom and to often obscure biblical verse; allusions to words and rules in *Anthon's Latin Primer and Reader;* allusions to plays Henry as a child had seen at Barnum's Museum Theatre in New York City on Saturday afternoons; allusions to the plots of dramatic productions the young Henry saw downtown; allusions to eclectic items he gleaned in his formative years from his reading in history, art, philosophy, and law.

Quite naturally the question arose: Where had HJ found these source materials, if they indeed showed HJ at work? A likely bet, I thought, was that they were to be found in his father's home library, a sizable trove, and one from which snippets in later signed HJ work also seemed to have come—beginning with HJ's first signed story,

"The Story of a Year" (*Atlantic Monthly*, March 1865), in which references to an 1864 Government Printing Office pamphlet, Goethe's *Faust,* and a German lexicon appear, and continuing into the last phase of his mature fiction.

So it was that in the library of Henry James Sr. in the 1850s—a substantial portion of which I was able to document through the generosity of the James family—I found the first substantial evidence to link the airy stuff of theory to matters of fact. An iconoclast of no uncertain bent, an early humanist, and an ardent student of the nearly inscrutable doctrine of the Swedish mystic Emanuel Swedenborg, the senior James's library reflected his eclectic interests and erudition (he read in Latin, weak Greek, German, and French). His books included sets of the English classics, philosophic treatises in German, the rendering in French of the philosopher Victor Cousin's popular lectures at the Sorbonne, the voluminous output of Swedenborg's occult biblical wisdom (in Latin and English), and such miscellaneous items as *Smith's Dictionary of Greek and Roman Antiquities, Liddell and Scott's Greek Lexicon,* and Berenger's illustrated poetic works.

Once I had thoroughly perused the texts of these works and again scoured the texts of the unsigned stories I had identified as the work of the young HJ, I found it reasonable to conclude that the library of Henry James Sr. was the source from which the junior James had borrowed in his early fiction. The abundant allusions in the stories to elements in the wide range of volumes in James Sr.'s library thus helped me to establish the fact of HJ's earliest work as well as to assess the exceptional talent that has made imaginative use of them.

What follows is a protracted example of the kind of analysis I applied to the stories that I strongly believed to be the work of HJ. It is the story that marks the modest start of HJ's literary career—modest but also remarkably promising.

HJ's first opus, "The Pair of Slippers," published in the August 1852 *National Magazine,* imitates the mode of the Arabian Nights adventures and appears to be a slight tale about an overly acquisitive Near Eastern merchant. Mistakenly taken before the corrupt Cadi (governor) as thief, in his excess this merchant foolishly unable to escape official punishment until he came to the realization that his avaricious inclinations were no substitute for humane brotherly concerns: his selfish attitude then changed from heathen to Christian in a flicker. Given its dense construction of borrowings, "The Pair of Slippers" can be described as an inventive nesting of allusions, and the main literary sources borrowed from were to be found in James Sr.'s home library.

The first five of these sources were (1) Edward Lane's three-volume set of *The Arabian Nights' Entertainments* (1839–41), enhanced by extensive notes to each volume; (2) Lane's *Modern Egyptians* (3) *Smith's Dictionary of Greek and Roman Antiquities,* second edition (1842); (4) *Liddell and Scott's Greek Lexicon,* second edition (1846); (5) *Anthon's Latin Primer and Reader,* then held by HJ for working through the exercises of his Latin class; and (6) a copy of the 1850 King James Oxford Bible, with cross-referenced notes showing the main constructions that have parallels in "The Pair of Slippers." Except for Lane, HJ later reused all these sources, Liddell and Scott as late as 1908.

Reading "The Pair of Slippers" against these sources shows the following borrowings:

1 and 2: Material borrowed from the two Lane sources included the near Eastern setting of the story, the corrupt character of the Cadi, who meted out punishment motivated by his own private interest in the case, and the characterization of the recalcitrant Casem, the fumbling victim of the tale. Also included from those Lane sources was HJ's information on Near Eastern policy regarding theft, fines for personal injury, and the jurisdiction of the Cadi; the idea that the governors and judges were generally corrupt; details of the public baths, slaves, turbans, slippers, flat roofs; and even the patronymic that changed to Casem from "Abu-Kasim," found in the original. Three of the four misfortunes that befell Casem were gleaned from Lane's notes to Chapter V.

3: Borrowings from *Smith's Dictionary of Greek and Roman Antiquities* were legion during HJ's long career, from 1852 up through 1916; elements of diverse articles and interestingly explained definitions in the book's 1,293 pages of small print catered to his appetite for eclectic information. One article in particular immediately attracted him, allying two of the main interests he already held; his enthusiasm for the imaginative mystery of the stage and his acolyte conviction that Christian providence determined all, and for the good. By 1852, the themes in the dramas of Charles Dickens, whose work we know from HJ's autobiography, *A Small Boy and Others,* profundly impressed him, already had served as a model of how the grim became the happy. A denouement of Christian goodness flavored the morality of Dickens's well-known novels. Now with an insight that marked his precocious talent, HJ used his father's home library effectively to make out his own system for the construction of imaginative moral tales.

It was this: Robert Whiston, M.A, Fellow of Trinity College, Cambridge, had taken on the Smith assignment of explaining the Greek and Roman ideas about, dramatic practices in, and key terms of classical tragedy in a long article entitled "Tragoedia." In exercising that task Whiston centered a good deal of his discussion upon Aristotle's formal definition of stage tragedy, quite precisely listing its key terms in Greek though the article itself was written in English. Aristotle listed six categories that explained the elements he felt all tragedies should have: *story, manners, expression, sentiment, decoration, music.* Since HJ would have been taught to use the Greek alphabet printed in *Anthon's Latin Primer and Reader,* he would have been able to make out these terms, as well as a few others that Whiston treated specially.

Whistion paid particular attention to Aristotle's concern with tragicomedy, which form Euripides rather realistically had developed. It was a form that first seemed to be hurrying its hero into a surely styled grim tragedy, but, by last minute discovery and revelation, by special favor of the gods or the like, it returned the hero to a socially stable, healthy, and happy situation. In a flash of his imaginative intellect HJ may have recognized the potential of such a tragicomic form in the construction of his own quite morally didactic works. Didactically placed Christian revelation as the turnabout point—a moment of biblical wisdom or fulfilled prophecy—and the concept of a saving grace, Providence enacted—would save the day and change grim to happy. It may be that as soon as he conceived this idea, HJ adapted this blessed envisionment of a godsend into the form of his first storytelling. Casem, who had been painfully dragged by circumstances of his own making into the ever deeper mire of tragic despair, suddenly discovered Christian reason to reform—compassion and pity for his fellow humans. As mechanically as that, HJ caused Casem to voice a slightly veiled biblical allusion just then in the text: "I will endure and pay all . . ." The underlined words were from the fabled account of Jesus's compassion and pity in Matthew 18:23–35. The words affirmed God's efficacious power to secretly direct all that transpired.

5. In *Liddell and Scott's Greek Lexicon,* which translated Greek words into English, the words that would have been of most interest to HJ were Aristotle's terms defining the key aspects of tragedy, and more especially of tragicomedy. Liddell and Scott listed each word's cognates quite fully. To illustrate how it appears HJ used Liddell and Scott in writing "The Pair of Slippers" we can look at the Greek word *Lexis,* Aristotle's name for one of his six categories, which meant *speech, diction, glossary, text,* and had some fifteen or so first-cousin implications that included *telling, retelling, choosing for one-self, gathering, point,* and *purpose.* HJ (as storyteller) might allusively comment about the tragic trend in his story-*telling* by using any of these word-ideas. And the same of course for any other of the key Greek terms of categorization, according to the aspect of the story's meaning that HJ sought to obliquely qualify. Since Aristotle had listed six categories that defined the stages of tragedy, and the names of each of these categories had roughly twenty cognate distinctions of definition, HJ could employ roughly 120 code words in his secret commentary on how the story text allusively followed the form of tragedy or tragicomedy. As in "The Pair of Slippers," so in later stories HJ was

to use this particular code quite often, fondly so because he so often chose the tenets of Christianized tragicomedy as the main structural mode of his stories. At the outset of this 1852 first tale, in the act of assuming the right to take slippers not his own, Casem positively seemed to have "hasted" toward his apparently fated tragic end: *haste* is a cognate of Aristotle's seminal term for the important start of tragic action, *spoudaias*.

6. The material borrowed from *Anthon's Latin Primer and Reader* in one sense is the most interesting and significant of all the borrowings here reviewed for HJ's "The Pair of Slippers." Traditional *Anthon's*, while popular with the tutors, was the bane of the schoolboy's daily existence according to HJ's passing autobiographic mention of the book along with Anthon himself, whom the family knew. *Anthon's Grammar* came in two parts, "First Latin Lessons" and "Latin Prose Composition"; an eighty-seven-page dictionary appended to Part I served both parts. A young schoolboy such as HJ might readily have encountered *Anthon's* in successive years. In the 1854–55 school year, HJ was relieved to at least exchange it for the more imaginative format of Andrew and Stoddard's Latin textbook. However in 1852 and 1853 he apparently made use of *Anthon's* in very diverting ways. The stories written for the Reverend Abel Stevens's *National Magazine* were a testing ground for HJ's Latin lessons. Whole paragraphs and columns of his fiction reflected the Latin construction being undertaken in school with *Anthon's*: exercises on comparison, interrogative pronouns, the rule for the genitive, later the subjunctive mood, still later the supine. Sometimes, the example given by *Anthon's* in Latin was translated and incorporated whole into the fiction text. Then, for instance, it might be very difficult to discern HJ from Virgil.

HJ played his *Anthon's* game as a composition exercise not unknown to the more imaginative students of Latin. Once having begun his story with translated key Aristotelian, biblical, or other terms of his thematic intention pretty well in mind, he would look up one and another of them in the *Anthon's* glossary.

Illustration of *Anthon's* Dictionary Page

297:A		297:B
Crassus, a, um (adj.). *Thick*	!	*Crus, cruris* (neut. 3 decl.). *The leg.*
Crastinus, a, um (adj. fr. Cras).	!	Crux, Crucis (fem. 3 decl.). *A*
Of or belonging to tomorrow, to-	!	*cross.*
morrow's.	!	Crystallum, I (neut), & Crystal-
Creator, oris (masc. 3 decl.). *A*	!	lus, I (fem. & masc. 2 decl.). *Crys-*
creator, a master.		*tal.*
Creber, crebra, crebrum (adj.).	!	
Frequent, repeated, thick, close.	!	Cubiculum, I (neut. 2 decl. Fr.
		cubo).
Crebro (adv. fr. creber). *Fre-*	!	*A bedchamber.*
quently, often.	!	Cubile, is (neut. 3 decl. Fr. cuno).
		A couch.
Credo, credere, credidi, credi-	!	Cubitus, I (masc. 2 decl. Fr. cubo).
tum (a. v. 3 conj.). *To credit, to*		*The arm below the elbow, the elbow, a*
believe, to trust, to confide.	!	*cubit.*
	!	Cubitus, us (masc. 4 decl. Fr. cubo).
Credulus, a, um (adj. fr. credo).	!	*A lying down.*
Credulous, easy of belief, simple.	!	Cubo, cubare, cubui, cubitum
Cremo, are, avi, atum (a. v. 1	!	(neut. 1 conj.). *To lie down.*
Conj.). *To burn, to reduce to*	!	Cubus, I (masc. 2 decl.). *A cube.*
ashes, to burn up.	!	Cucumis, eris (masc. 3 decl.). *A*
Creo, are, avi, atum (a. v. 1 conj.)	!	*cucumber.*
To create, to make.	!	Cujas, atis (adj. pron. Fr. quis).
Crepida, ae (fem. 1 decl.). *A*	!	*Of what country, belonging to whom.*
slipper, a sandal.	!	Cujus, a, um (adj. pron. Fr. quis).
Crepusculum, I (neut. 2 decl.).	!	*Of whom, whose.*
Twilight.	!	Culeus, I (masc. 2 decl.). *A leathern*
Cresco, crescere, crevi, cretum	!	*sack or bag.*
(neut. V. 3 conj.). *To increase,*	!	Culina, ae (fem. 1 decl.). *A kitchen.*
to grow.	!	Culmen, Inis (neut. 3 decl.). *1. The*
Creta, ae (fem. 1 decl.). *Chalk.*	!	*thatched roof of a house. 2. The top of*
Creta, ae (prop. N. fem. 1 decl.).	!	*a house, the summit of a*

Crete, a Grecian island.			*building.*
	!		*The top or summit of anything.*
Crimen, Ines (neut. 3 decl.). 1. A	!		**Culpa, ae (fem. 1 decl.).** *A fault, failure,*
charge, an accusation. 2. A	!		*blame, guilt.*
crime.	!		**Culpo, are, avi, arum (a. v. 1 conj. Fr.**
Crinis, is (neut. 3 decl.). *The hair*	!		**culpa).** *To blame, find fault*
of the head.			*with, censure, to reprove.*
Crocodilus, I, (masc. 2 decl.). *A*	!		**Culter, tri (masc. 2 decl.). 1. A**
crocodile.			*knife. 2. The coulter of a plow.*
Croesus, I, (prop. N. 2 decl. Masc)	!		**Cultor, oris (masc. 3 decl. Fr. colo).**
Croesus, an ancient king of Lydia.			*A cultivator, tiller, husbandman, farmer.*
Crucio, are, ivi, atum (a. v. 1 conj.	!		**Cultura, ae (fem. 1 decl. Fr. colo).**
fr. crux). *To torture, to torment, to*			*Cultivation, culture, tillage, husbandry.*
rack, to agonize, to distress.	!		**Cultus, a, um (part. Fr. colo).**
Crudelis, is, e (adj.). *Cruel.*	!		*Cultivated, tilled.*
Crudus, a, um (adj.). *Crude, raw . . .*	!		**Cultus, us (masc. 4 decl. Fr.**
297a			297b

Extending not more than a couple of pages backward or forward from a target word, say *Crepida* (slipper, page 297:A column), he systematically would learn Latin vocabulary and, as best he could, work into the fiction text their English meanings. If no long run of esoteric Greek or Latin names intervened, those three or four pages of Latin yielded about five hundred English words from which to choose—considering an average of three English definitions per Latin item. These chosen words became HJ's story text. The tight rules of this little inventive game challenged him to be flexible in forming the concepts of the fiction out of any word cluster, specially nesting meanings that served several levels of the story at once. Thus it was allowed, when *cremo* (burn) was found in page 297:A column along with the original target word *Crepida*, that Casem be made to extemporaneously decide to burn the slippers after first drying them on the roof (*culmen*, 297:B column). As well, these English words were the adjectives, nouns, and verbs that could be fitted between what

315

already had been borrowed and determined as the main structural lines of the put-together story. Underscored here in one of the story's six key thematic passages are the *Anthon's* items, in bold type the key Aristotelian and biblical backbone of the passage:

> . . . , for his **innocent** slippers (CREPIDA, 297:A) had nearly killed one of his **fellow-creatures** (CREATOR, 297:A). "Just **Judge**," (DECERNO, 299:A) said Casem, with (CUM, 298:A) an **earnestness** (CUPIDO, 298:A) which **made** (CREO, 297:A) even the Cadi **smile**, "**I will** (CUPIDO, 298:A) **endure** and **pay all** (CUNCTUS, 298:A) to which you have **condemned** (DAMNO, 298:B) me, only I ask your protection (CUSTODIO, 298:B) against (CONTRA, 296:A) those implacable enemies, which have been the agents of all (CUNC-TUS, 298:A) my trouble (CURA, 298:A) and distress (CRU-CIO, 297:A) to this hour (CUNCATOR, 298:A)—I mean those miserable slippers (CREPIDA, 297:A)."

The rules of this form of dictionary game were compatible with a principle of logical nesting: with no other logics preferred at a given place in the developing text, then the inclusion of words from *Anthon's* or, later in HJ's writing career, some other glossary, might determine how the adjectival structure or the plot itself might be formed there. On the other hand, at this hypothetical given place in the text, there were all sorts of logics that HJ might not care to dissipate. It would not do to break the continuity of a biblical allusion being used without quotation marks. It would not do to break the Arabian Nights tone of a story when HJ already had gone to the trouble of gleaning words and passages from the translator's imitative style. The tone of the texture of an HJ story consequently had very special reasons for being what it was. Well into the era of signed materials, 1865 and on, this continued to be so—not always to the benefit of a product he would finish with grace.

At this 1852 starting point, then, such an *Anthon's* vocabulary game had relatively low priority in reshaping the tragicomic form of the story HJ had determined to tell, in which, as in Dickens, Christian good cheer eventually triumphed. Quite naturally by the formula of having the drama take a Christian turn into happy experience, random chance by no means exercised itself, even though it had been made to appear as though it had. What had really taken place was that, by clever manipulation of the words, HJ had devised one string of cognates to give the appearance of life's misery and bleakness, even while a cousin string of cognates subtly foreshadowed Christian-style glories to come. The only thing in doubt in the whole literary business of it was, which of the key Aristotelian words had cognates that, when put to use, would offer the illusion that a war of opposing human values played itself out as the action of tragicomedy prior to the conflict's reversal. Those inclined like the young HJ had an option to interpret the art of such mechanical foreshadowing as a mark of their supreme trust in God, as the evidence of biblical prophecy fulfilled, as a show of the Lord's most subtle operation of Providence. But really not all that was necessary.

As long as supposedly opposing aspects of the story could be traced to the same key Aristotelian word, all should be well. An example from the excerpt just shown, is the word *earnestness*. First, it suited the rules of random selection for the *Anthon's* game (<u>CUPIDO</u>, 298:A). Second, it directly was named the cause of the Cadi's "smile," which signaled the change from impending tragedy to redemptive comedy. Third, it played out that change by fulfilling the meaning of one of Aristotle's key terms explaining what spurs the action of drama: *Spoudaias* (important; also both hasty and earnest). For long years after, HJ began the representation of tragedy with the hero's "hasty" action (in "The Pair of Slippers" it is Casem's spur-of-the-moment decision to appropriate someone else's slippers at the baths), and later, at the climax, prepared to change to the comic by having the hero act in "earnest" (recall that Casem addressed the judge "with an earnestness . . .").

Rooted in this way upon Whiston's pithy description of tragicomedy and its relationship to the key cognate word structure that described Aristotle's ideas of formal tragedy in general—and, of course, tickled by the fun of playing his devised *Anthon's* game—still other variations of how HJ employed his source borrowing developed. It quite seemed he had a natural inclination to concatenate, that is to say, to integrate, the eclectic elements of his wide-ranged reading. He coursed through many of the definitional articles of *Smith's Dictionary of Greek and Roman Antiquities*, Victor Cousin's spirited perspective of principal philosophic ideas that had shaped and moved world cultures, and Emanuel Swedenborg's unrelenting notes intended to reveal the secrets hidden in Christian scripture.

In what he read and what he wrote, my search revealed now, HJ the son closely emulated the themes of his father, whose published work reflected some of the same sources (held in the home library) and whose home teaching often voiced the same messages and oft repeated images. Many of the elder James's noblest ideas were clichés of the home.

To an outsider denied entrance to this intellectual trove shelved as the home library, to its qualifications in the margins in Latin, Greek, French, and German, HJ's young progress in fiction should seem hardly believable. But warmed by strong native talent, and stimulated in such an environment, the universe of its meanings had quite realistic boundaries. Still later, the sources the nineteen-year-old college-bound HJ employed to create his multilevel fictions extended to Adolf Franck's *Kabbala* (in imitation of the elder James's attraction to this work) and Max Muller's impressive publications on East Indian culture. Harvard College has saved the record of HJ's 1862–63 library borrowing, included in which is Muller's famous treatise on the development of multidimensional myth from language, "Comparative Mythology." Also in the early 1860s, what might have been HJ's personal satisfaction with Robert Burton's *Anatomy of Melancholy* further seemed to be reflected in his story-making: he employed it as a homey guide to lay psychology.

What becomes clear in the study of HJ's secretly and imaginatively crafted early fiction is that HJ did not simply create a texture of allusions from all his various sources, no matter that it lent his literary style its particular Jamesian élan. Rather more decidedly he used these now discovered and discoverable sources to continually widen the structural base of the ideas he was tirelessly reinterpreting and reshaping in his work, so that his work as a whole reveals an ever-expanding sphere of interconnected reference. In his signed 1908 short story "The Jolly Corner," the sixth from the last of those in his canon, for instance, HJ again utilizes *Liddell and Scott's Greek Lexicon* and in the highly nuanced verbal play of the story proceeds from the key Greek word *eidola*, for "image," to its listed cognates for the related concepts of "seeing," "idea," and "fantasy." The 1908 story not only returns to a favorite source and favorite game of the much younger James; it also offers a psychological variant on the longtime favorite Jamesian theme of acquisition and possession—a theme that HJ introduced as a ten-year-old in "The Pair of Slippers" and that, in 1908 as in 1852, draws upon Victor Cousin's Sorbonne lecture on Greek psychology of perception and cognition. Such thematic parallels and allusive connections abound between the signally inventive unsigned fiction of the young HJ and the mature work of the great American master. The standard Jamesian canon and the anonymously or pseudonymously published stories that textual evidence convinces me can be attributed to HJ together constitute a solid whole that discloses a certain geometry of aesthetics—that reveals a "figure in the carpet," so to speak.